CRANK

The Kensington Killers
(Book Two)

MIRA GIBSON

Prologue

HE HATED THESE kinds of places. The projects. Slum apartments where rough-looking children cut their eyes at him.

Courtyards made of concrete, surrounded by dying grass, connected one brick building to the next.

Pitbulls snarled at him through open, first floor windows, as he crossed through the public housing complex.

The sun never seemed to shine in these neighborhoods. Like today. An overcast sky, fat with the threat of rain, pressed down on him, reminding him there was no way out.

What was known could not be unknown.

What he had seen could not be forgotten.

Much less forgiven.

He wasn't blending in with the residents, he realized. He had worn the wrong outfit. He hadn't meant to, but he was dressed like money. It would've been better if he looked like he was slumming it. But he was wearing a pair of G-Star metallic jeans and a leather jacket, its collar flared, its front undone and flapping in the wind. He looked like he owned the city, and not like someone who lived in one of the apartments.

He veered over dying grass to avoid a pitbull that was yanking its owner along, a tired-looking woman who was focused on lighting her cigarette. When her dog lunged at him and barked, the woman swore and gave her dog's tight rear a thwack.

Feeling eyes on him, he glanced across the courtyard and saw a cluster of teenagers—hood rats—staring at him.

It occurred to him this mission would've been better executed at night.

Flashy as he might have appeared, he reminded himself that thanks to his nondescript face, physical build, and ethnicity, he should be able to pass for someone who belonged here in the seedier side of Kensington.

"Yo' girl, hold the door!" he called out when he saw a skinny, twelve-year old coming out of Building 7.

He jogged, as she held the steel door for him.

The girl was swimming in a bulky winter coat and holding a crumpled paper bag in her hand. Her lunch, he hoped, and not crank.

Methamphetamines had flooded the projects, replacing crack and smack. Since the early 2000s, the statistics had worsened, and he had every intention of using this to his favor.

As he entered the building, the girl squinted up at him through the overcast glare. She screwed her face up, as if she had learned long ago that when it came to this particular block, doing what she was told was required. And yet, she would be damned if she did, and damned if she didn't. She had that look about her—furious and resigned.

He wanted to hold her. Hold her until the protective warmth of his body convinced her that there were places in this world where she wouldn't have to be alert, on guard, and expecting the worst.

No child should have to be meek and deflecting, yet hypervigilant and distrusting.

These kids weren't kids. Perhaps they never had been.

It killed him.

"Be fierce, lil' mama," he told her, and she met him with a toothy grin that finally revealed her young age.

As she padded quickly down the cracked concrete path, she kept her head down, ignoring leering junkies and barking pitbulls alike.

He figured she was on her way to the bus stop or subway, whichever would take her to elementary school, a place that was just as dangerous as the projects.

Kids and guns.

It twisted his heart.

He hadn't had a childhood either.

In Building 7, the lobby smelled of stale piss and moth balls.

Dingy.

He took the elevator, and after a shaky climb, he stepped onto the ninth floor.

The overhead lights flickered, as he walked down the corridor.

An ironic grin tugged at the corner of his wide mouth when he came to the apartment and saw the number on the door—911.

Like a bad omen no one saw coming.

Or could she sense it?

Was she on the other side of this door?

Had she woken up this morning with a dull, nagging feeling that something wasn't right? Had the bad feeling stayed with her?

Could she feel unshakable dread rotting her insides?

He doubted it.

He rolled his shoulders back, getting into character. He cracked his neck, then, ignoring the buzzer, he pounded on the door. Hard.

If the courtyard outside had been filled with prying eyes, the general rule of thumb for the residents *inside* the buildings was to mind your own goddamn business, or else.

Knocking as loudly as he could told every resident that was tucked inside their apartment to stay there.

The door of apartment 911 opened, drawing inward.

A bohemian beauty with dark circles under her eyes filled the open doorway.

Her frail figure was draped in shawls and a long skirt dripped off her pointy hips.

Her milk-chocolate complexion was scarred with pocks and welts.

She looked doped up and relieved to see him until it dawned on her that the man who had knocked wasn't her usual dealer.

"Chill," he warned her, as he noticed another junkie seated on a couch, deeper in the apartment.

The junkie, a man, was shirtless. The couch, a sunken heap of trash, seemed to match the rest of the filthy decor.

The scent of patchouli and dog feces wafted out of the apartment, and he tried not to cringe.

"Raffi sent me. It's all good."

Skeptical, the bohemian beauty sobered from her drug-haze and yelled over her shoulder to the junkie.

"Call Raffi!"

The wiry, amped up junkie had been more concerned with packing marijuana into a glass pipe than with the unexpected visitor.

"Call Raffi?" the junkie questioned, barely invested.

"Raffi's supposed to be here, not some stranger. Call him. I don't like surprises, and I'm not about to take this guy's word for it."

When she returned her dull brown eyes to him, having watched the junkie dig his cell phone out of his jeans, the fiend in her pushed skepticism aside.

"What did you bring? The usual crank? Quantity, quality, all that?"

He had been calm and silent until now, grounding his energy, channeling his intention, and patiently waiting for her to open herself up to him.

She was realizing now that she needed him. She needed what he was there to sell… to *provide*.

He had her.

"Of course," he promised, as he offered her a thin smile. "Plus, I have a freebie for you."

"Freebie of what?" she asked, interested.

He let his eyelids go slack, matching her vibe, and forced a devilish grin to spread across his face, mimicking her whet appetite for these kinds of adult candies.

It was a tactic.

Mirroring.

In general, it had never failed him, but this time he knew that this woman would be especially malleable.

"A freebie of nothing you've ever done before," he told her, reeling her in, his tone so deep and soft that without realizing it, she was already drifting towards him just to hear more. "Better than anything you've ever experienced."

"Better than crank?" she questioned, but she had already abandoned all skepticism. Her voice was full of intrigue.

Good.

From the sunken couch, the junkie complained, "Raffi ain't pickin' up," as a cloud of pot smoke billowed around him.

The junkie didn't have to tell her to let the strange man in. She already was.

On the other side of Brooklyn, at one of the waste management plants, Raffi's dead body was lying on a mountain of trash, waiting to be crushed and transported on a barge out into the middle of the ocean, and dumped.

Where Raffi belonged…

Stepping inside apartment 911, he closed the steel door behind him.

Neither the bohemian beauty nor the junkie thought about Raffi again. They were too interested in the freebies that he had brought to entertain them.

He felt that much *closer*.

Patience, he told himself.

Soon.

He waded into the apartment, entering the living room.

As the junkie on the couch asked a bunch of half-hearted questions about the price, and the bohemian perched on a chair, he took a slow lap around the cramped room, getting a feel for the place.

Without letting him answer those questions, the junkie rambled on with anecdotes that seemed to go nowhere.

But then the junkie alluded to the dark arrangement that he had with their drug dealer, Raffi—*cash wasn't the only form of payment that Raffi accepted… He also liked 'trades'… Are you interested in cutting the same deal?*

No.

No he wasn't, was his resounding reply that came only in his mind.

The bohemian woman rose from the chair and oozed beside her man on the couch.

There was a plastic coffee table in front of them, cluttered with smoking apparatuses, loose marijuana dregs, the white coarse residue of crushed prescription pills, and a saucer of what appeared to be sweaty cheese. The knife beside the cheese wasn't a regular serving knife. It looked like a fillet knife, the kind used to gut a fish.

The knife was perfect.

"So, you up for the same trade?" the junkie pressed. "Kayla's down like that."

Beside him, the woman concurred with a lazy, hazy nod that did little to convince him that she actually enjoyed turning tricks in exchange for crank.

Disgusting.

He had been watching them for weeks. He had heard the word on the street and around the projects.

It wasn't Kayla who had been trading her body to get them high.

These two junkies were far more evil than that.

"Raffi's got me under strict orders," he declined.

The junkie squeezed Kayla's thigh, and a nasty grin spread across his face.

"Raffi don't like to share, eh?"

Kayla recoiled, but she kept the plastered smile on her face.

Remorse, this late in the game, will get you nowhere, he thought, as he produced a fat ball of meth rocks from his inside pocket. The meth was encased in a tiny plastic bag. He dropped the drugs on the coffee table.

Frowning, the junkie checked out the goods while Kayla groaned, fished some cash out of her bra, and smacked the bills onto his palm, annoyed to be paying in full.

"You said you have freebies, so where are they?" she reminded him.

Her junkie boyfriend's interest was highly piqued.

Before answering the junkies, he crossed to the naked windows like he owned the place, peered down at the dismal courtyard where skinny slits of rain had begun to tick over concrete, and yanked the cord to the blinds.

He didn't want any witnesses.

The blinds fell with a rattle, and as he turned to face his victims, he suggested, "You're going to want to be listening to music when you get high on the freebies I have."

Nodding in full agreement, the junkie slid off the couch and crouched in front of their stereo system, while his girl gnawed her thumb and watched him. He pushed a few buttons, cursed under his breath, and then shoved their stereo to life.

A heavy bassline began vibrating through the speakers as a loud reggae tune played.

It wasn't quite loud enough to muffle their screams, he thought. But he reasoned that he could adjust the volume once his 'freebie' had worked its way through their veins and had rendered both of them highly, highly suggestible.

"It'll smoke just as smooth, just as easy," he mentioned, as he pulled the freebie from his metallic jeans along with a squeaky-clean pipe he had bought at the one smoke shop in Brooklyn that wasn't crawling with video surveillance cameras.

Better safe than sorry.

He couldn't allow the drug to touch his skin, so he handed both the baggie and pipe to the junkie who had returned to his girl on the couch.

He instructed, "Pack it hard and hit it heavy. You'll thank me."

As the junkie went ahead, Kayla salivating beside him, he asked, "What's the cost of this drug if we like it?"

The junkie hit the pipe, pulling in a huge lungful of smoke.

He waited and watched the junkie, but didn't answer.

Waiting for the silky smoke to fill the junkie's lungs and seep into his bloodstream, patiently—*patiently*—waiting for the 'look' to come over him, the one that indicated the dark side of heaven had washed over him, waiting, waiting…

…and *there* it was.

Kayla stole the pipe the second her man's grip loosened and he slumped. He leaned his head back against the sunken couch.

She sucked hard on the pipe. She heaved her chest and held the smoke in her lungs.

Soon her eyes were lolling, her limbs turned heavy and watery.

He let them enjoy it for a long moment as melodic reggae wailed through the speakers.

Then he began testing.

"Kayla," he cooed.

"Hmm?"

She met his gaze. Doped up yet attentive. The drug was working. She was as vulnerable as a rabbit now.

"You like that knife, don't you?" he suggested in a flat voice, no intonation to imply he had meant it to be anything other than a statement for her to confirm.

"Yes," she said. No questioning. No slang. She had slipped into the land of 'yes' where her greatest pleasure would be pleasing him.

"Have you ever felt the tip of a knife graze across your skin?"

A confused look clouded her expression. Answering 'no' would be difficult for her, so he moved on.

"How would you like to feel that?"

"I would like that," she went along.

As did her man, the junkie.

Towering over them, he verbalized the first suggestion.

"Pick up the knife."

Without hesitation, the junkie obeyed. He picked up the fillet knife from the coffee table.

At his next suggestion, the junkie didn't hesitate. He did exactly what he was told. He was a zombie. This was easy.

"You want to cut her cheek."

He grazed the sharp tip down Kayla's cheek. He trailed the knife further, listening, obeying, grazing the tip down her neck and chest, the thin material of her shawl absorbed her blood.

Kayla couldn't feel a thing.

They were under the full effects of his drug now.

Pleasing.

Malleable.

Ready to play the game.

Chapter One

THE KENSINGTON projects were the last place anyone wanted to be in the dead of night. But Detective Carter Dobbs didn't share the sentiment.

A murder was a murder, and Carter was always ready to investigate no matter where the crime had occurred.

The wind howled, as he drove at a crawl through the housing projects. Rain streaked the windshield of his sedan, and the wipers fought to keep the glass clear.

Carter hadn't grown up in the projects. He felt no sense of personal connection to the place, its culture, or its people.

He wasn't intimidated by the types of characters that lived here—the tough dealers, the strung-out working girls, the teenagers who at times seemed to run things. More than anything, Carter was eager to help make this public housing block a safer place.

The kid in him was envious of these people.

When he had been a child, he would've killed to live in the projects. If he had, he could've gotten his hands on a gun, demanded respect, and claimed authority or died trying.

But Carter hadn't had the chance.

He had grown up in a wealthy, suburban household with a white picket fence, and no one passing by the quaint house had ever guessed that Carter had been tortured there, kept under lock and key, and caged like an animal.

Building 7 would've been too hard to find if a police cruiser hadn't parked at an angle in front of the rear entrance door. A cherry light, flashing red and white, sat atop the cruiser.

Two officers cloaked in rain gear stood beside the vehicle. Their job was to limit who came in and out of the building. But the place was a virtual ghost town.

He pulled up behind the parked cruiser, killed the engine, and climbed out into the rain.

Standing 6' tall with the musculature of a linebacker and skin so black he could disappear in shadows, all but for the whites of his eyes, Carter had used his looks to his advantage when he had worked undercover in the Vice Enforcement Division of Sex Trafficking for upwards of ten years.

That was before he had transferred into the Special Victims Unit in Kensington, his wife having finally had enough of his long, undercover assignments and the emotional toll it was taking on each of them, straining the marriage and saddening their kids.

Earlier in the month, he had worked his first SVU case with his new partner, Detective Danielle Foster.

The case had hardly been straightforward, and he had learned one very important lesson. Working a single case at SVU was distinctly harder than ten years at Vice combined.

It was the nature of the crimes, he determined. Special victims were generally women and children. The crimes were usually sexual in nature and almost always ended in murder, or so he had been told.

Working one-on-one with a victim—a woman or child who had been attacked in the worst possible way—as she struggled to restore her life, wrestle with anger, and cooperate throughout a lengthy investigation, was no easy feat.

Yet for all its difficulty, the satisfaction he had felt when—after following a twisted trail of smoke and mirrors—he had solved his prior case with Danny, was unparalleled. Maybe even a little addictive.

Which was why he hadn't hesitated to answer his lieutenant's phone call at two o'clock in the morning despite his wife's sleepy objections.

Carter flashed his badge at the police officers, but didn't wait to get their approval before entering Building 7.

He yanked the steel door open and found his way to the 9th floor where, according to Lieutenant Martin Franco, a crime like 'he had never seen' had occurred—*bring something to cover your mouth and nose, the dust masks aren't enough, but the barf bags have proved helpful.*

Another two uniformed officers stood guard outside of the crime scene apartment, the door of which was ajar.

In the corridor just beyond them forensic techs were organizing their equipment. Carter could only assume the apartment unit was cramped if forensics was stationed in the hallway.

Carter slid his large hand over his shaved head, wiping away raindrops, as he neared the police officers. After a curt greeting, he motioned to slip past, angling his broad frame in-between them and through the doorway.

The smell hit him first. The scent of iron. Spilt blood. Something rotten like sour apples commingling. The distinct scent of feces competing.

It filled his mouth no matter how shallowly he breathed and, recalling Franco's advice, he brought his silk tie to his face and pressed it hard against his nose to ward off waves of nausea that were threatening to make him sick.

Then he saw his partner choking down the same urge.

Detective Danielle Foster held her long fingers across her mouth, pressing the length of her index finger to her nose for a long beat. Those big, sad eyes of hers widened.

As Carter reached her, she met his gaze and immediately pulled it together to say:

"Vic's name is Kayla Samuels. She's the leaseholder. We're working on identifying the man."

"Two victims?"

She affirmed with a grim nod, running all ten fingers through her short mop of brown hair. She wiped her nose again, and the asymmetrical slant of her mouth accidentally looked like a wicked smirk as always. She had one of those faces. Bold. Challenging. Like she was ready for anything—*just try me.*

"I've got five officers canvassing the building and projects," she told him before glancing over her shoulder at the bloodbath.

Reading her pessimistic tone, he agreed, "No one's going to talk."

"No one's going to answer their door." She sucked in a fortifying breath, gave him the once over, and seeing his loafers, she pointed out, "Booties are with forensics in the hallway, gloves too."

It was then that Carter noticed Danny had covered her sneakers with white, disposable shoe covers.

He wasted no time gearing up in the corridor and was sure to sling a dust mask over his face, not that it would be more effective than his tie at blocking the stench.

He returned to Danny who was now in the living room.

She was standing on what forensics loosely referred to as an evidence preservation stone—a brick of plastic meant to prevent investigators' shoes from contaminating crime scenes.

In this case, stepping only on the plastic bricks would prevent anyone from wading through congealed blood.

Carter stepped carefully across the bricks, marginally aware that the medical examiner, Jill Andover, was crouched and inspecting the dirt under the female Vic's fingernails, Kayla Samuels.

The Vic lay sprawled across a deflated-looking couch.

Naked.

She had been skinned where her face and breasts should have been. Her arms and thighs were a grid of cuts. Some deep. Others, superficial.

It was harrowing.

The unidentified male Vic was lying face up in a pool of his own blood. His throat had been slashed on one side across the carotid artery. This fatal wound looked like a mangled gash at best.

He was completely covered in dark, gooey blood, an indication that after his throat had been slit, he had dropped to his knees and fallen face forward onto the ground where he had bled out.

Forensics must have turned him on his back to examine him further after thoroughly documenting the position he had been found in.

"Who called it in?" Carter asked as he tugged off his face mask. It wasn't doing a damn thing, and he was getting used to the stench.

"The building manager," said Danny. "He could smell it from the hallway when he did his routine mopping. He took his damn time checking it out, though. It wasn't until after midnight that he circled back and knocked on the door, but he got no response. Hours later, he keyed in and discovered the bodies."

"Where's he now?"

"At the hospital. Weak heart," she said with a shrug.

Jill piped up from the sidelines:

"They've been like this for at least two days."

She straightened to her feet, coming into all five feet, four inches of her plucky height.

Jill was young considering her position—Chief Medical Examiner for Kings County. But youthful playfulness didn't show on her face or in her personality until she was off duty.

If Carter was being honest with himself, Jill was playful enough. She had definitely flashed him a flirtatious smile once or twice, hoping to garner his attraction. The wedding band on his finger hadn't deterred her, but apparently that was just how Jill was. Carter figured she would eventually move on to the next handsome, new face in the department as soon as there was one.

"I'll have a precise time of death for you once I'm back at the lab," she added before wading her way over the trail of preservation stones that led towards the corridor where her pared-down team was organizing the digital photographs and video they had taken.

He didn't want to have to say it out loud, but he had gotten a firm read on Danny over the weeks and sensed she might be thinking the same thing.

"The Vics are 'special victims'?" he questioned.

She nodded, pressing her slanted mouth into a hard, disturbed line.

"How exactly?"

"We won't know the specifics until Jill examines the Vics at the lab, but I'll tell you one thing, if Kayla hadn't been naked, never mind skinned alive, SVU wouldn't have been called in."

He agreed.

But Carter was glad they had been. Danny was the smartest, most cunning investigator he had ever worked with. If this was the work of one extremely demented individual, he knew that Danny's natural tenacity would ferret the killer out. And Carter would be right there beside Danny, under her wing and investigating with the utmost respect for the deceased.

"Jill's gonna run some tests," she went on, "let us know if they were high, and if so, on what drugs. We already bagged and tagged a knife that I'm certain was used to murder our male Vic. Jill said the blade could also be a match for the cuts on our female. Worst part?"

Carter met her gaze, giving his full attention.

"The building manager had to *key* in," she stated.

It had already been on his mind—if the killer had locked up on his way out, then he had the key, but why? Because he knew the Vics? Or…

"Were the windows locked as well?" he asked, considering that the guy could've left down the fire escape, but Carter didn't give her much of a chance to answer. "The killer could've taken the Vic's keys and locked up on his way out."

It was a matter of questioning whether the killer had known the victims or not. Was this personal or random?

"It's possible," she agreed dubiously. "We'll see. This case might be more open and shut than we think."

He read her implication loud and clear, but it didn't sit right.

"You seriously think two tweakers could've done this to themselves?" he questioned, skeptical as hell.

She considered his point, weighing it against some nagging thoughts of her own.

"Have a look around," she suggested. "Bedroom's in the back."

Rather than question her further, he stepped carefully over plastic bricks until he reached the unstained floor and veered into Kayla Samuels' bedroom, as Danny made her own way out of the apartment to join Jill in the corridor.

He vaguely overheard Jill gushing to Danny about the 'hot date' she had been torn away from—well, that explained Jill's slightly better behavior around Carter—but he quickly tuned her out and focused on Kayla's bedroom.

The room immediately stirred questions in his fast-working mind.

There was an overwhelming quantity of mannequins around her bedroom. The displayed mannequins wore feather headdresses, sequined bikinis, beaded tribal bras, coin belts, and gypsy skirts. To Carter's untrained eye, the outfits looked like dance performance costumes.

It gave Carter a slightly creeped out feeling. He had nothing against professional dancers, but the vacant stares of so many dead-eyed mannequins that weren't real witnesses seemed to mock the crime.

The walls and windows, he soon realized, were covered in a massive collage of photos.

All of the photos featured Kayla, wearing the dance performance costumes.

But she wasn't dancing.

As Carter neared the closest wall, having taken the room in as a whole—pink comforter disheveled on a full-sized bed, nightstand lamps on either side, and the wooden floor strewn with dirty clothes—he was struck by the dark nature of each photograph.

Kayla the dancer was posed in sexualized positions. She had a glazed-over look in her eye. In many photos, she wore a dog collar tightly wrapped around her throat.

BDSM.

She didn't look happy.

So, why had she plastered these images on all four walls of her bedroom?

He did a slow lap around the room, pondering what he saw.

The nightstand drawer was ajar, drug paraphernalia within. The dresser drawers were no better, there were more pipes and bongs than clothing.

The room seemed to tell a story that tugged hard on his heartstrings.

Kayla had been a woman who'd had a dream, but the ghetto had forced her to sexualize her dance skills for quick cash.

Had drugs softened that sting?

Why had she covered these walls with photographs that depicted the services she had provided in order perhaps to make ends meet? Had she surrounded herself with these images in some kind of effort to embrace who she had become?

Or had she taped the photos to the walls to benefit the Johns that came here? Did the photos create atmosphere and aid in their arousal?

Carter was speculating, of course. There wasn't a single man in any of the photos, but that didn't mean there weren't plenty behind the camera.

Nevertheless, Danny's point was well taken.

Until they learned who this woman was, her habits and lifestyle, the characters she had crossed paths with, especially the male Vic out there, they wouldn't be able to rule out the possibility that the cause of death had been the result of a sex game gone wrong.

A drug induced murder-suicide.

Unless, of course, Jill uncovered hard evidence to the contrary.

He turned and noticed a closet door was ajar.

The closet was located at an odd angle behind the open bedroom door, a design flaw perhaps.

With a gloved hand, he opened the door, pulled a dangling overhead chain so that the naked bulb would shed light in the closet, and was met with more evidence of the same bizarre clash—dreams of performing as a professional dancer juxtaposed with a BDSM secret.

He crouched, eyeing the mess on the floor, and came face-to-face with a dog crate—54 inches tall, durable wire, and large enough for a pitbull, maybe even a taller breed.

The dog crate was empty except for a dog bowl. The door was unlatched.

He expected to find dog food in the bowl, but instead he saw Cheerios.

Glancing around for a leash, dog toys, anything, he found nothing and called out:

"Hey, yo' Danny! Does our Vic own a dog?"

"Why?" she hollered back as she trailed her way into the bedroom.

Carter straightened up and showed her the crate that he had discovered.

"You think it's significant?" she asked, coming up beside him to stare down at it.

"I think it's weird."

Danny jabbed him with her elbow, showing a lighter side, and said, "Of all the evidence in this place that's weird enough to keep me up at night, I'm not sure I'll lose sleep over a dog crate…"

Implying that he shouldn't get hung up on the crate, she left the bedroom.

Carter had to admit, this was the projects and it seemed dangerous dog breeds were a commodity of sorts. Why wouldn't Kayla have owned a dog at some point?

But something felt off.

Carter crouched once again, stared at the dregs of Cheerios in the bowl, and felt his stomach tighten.

It was a very long moment before he tore himself away.

Chapter Two

"YOU WERE OUT all night?" Kathy asked groggily, her mussed blonde hair spilling over her shoulders as well as the loosely draping sweater she had thrown on.

She was hunched over a steaming mug of coffee on the kitchen islet.

Her ordinarily big, blue eyes were tight and a bit puffy. Her creamy porcelain skin glowed in the low morning light.

Kathy held Carter's gaze, as pancake batter sizzled softly on the stove behind him.

She meant everything to Carter. Always had. Always would. But there had been bumps along the way. Serious, axle cracking, hubcap popping, tire-blow-out bumps in the road. The vehicle of their marriage was technically still in the shop.

"It's time to flip those," she said.

Carter turned to the stove where thin tendrils of gray smoke had begun twirling up from five pancakes.

He ran his big hand over his abdomen, smoothing his apron down away from the burner to get close. The apron was a frilly thing with little cherries that barely covered the broad wall of his chest, but served its purpose in terms of protecting his button-down shirt, tie, and slacks from pancake splatter.

He tended to breakfast, flipping each pancake and discovering, much to his satisfaction, that each was a perfect golden brown color.

The way his wife, Kathy, had commented about him being 'out all night' felt like bait. An accusation.

Old fears from his days undercover in Vice surfacing in her chest, days when she'd had no control over when or how she would see him, days when she had assumed the worst, not out of concern for his safety, but for their marriage.

She hadn't trusted him with other women.

She still didn't.

He wasn't up for an argument, so he didn't point out that working a crime scene in the middle of the night didn't exactly constitute being 'out all night.' It wasn't as though he had tied one on with the guys and lost track of time.

Instead of taking the bait, he plucked the coffee pot from the counter, refilled his wife's mug, and addressed the question he knew she was honing in on.

"The lieutenant gave us a few hours to catch some Zs before going back out there."

He offered her an adoring smile, but Kathy was too busy doing the math on when she would lose her husband again… Would it be this morning, or in general, was anyone's guess?

"But you know me."

Falling asleep did not come naturally for Carter. If anything, in the quiet dark of night his internal alarm system went on high alert, every cell in his body poised for danger. It was one of many lingering reminders that he was damaged. Some wounds weren't designed to heal, and Kathy knew it.

"You would never fall asleep," she agreed, finally softening with appreciation, and returning a little smile. She drank her coffee in silence for a moment, then asked, "Was it a bad one?"

Again, history told him she would rather hear about how demanding this new case was going to be, instead of how bad the actual scene had been.

"It could go either way," he answered truthfully. "It might have been a murder-suicide, in which case all we would have to do is file some paperwork."

"But there will always be the next case and the next," she reminded him, instigating the same fight that had been circling the drain of their marriage, but refused to go down.

Carter had given up an undercover career that had made him feel like he was doing some serious good in the world. It had fulfilled him. But it hadn't meant more to him than the wife he had cherished since the day he had set eyes on her.

He had transferred out of Vice for Kathy, because she had needed him to, because he hadn't been able to stomach her long face and disappointed eyes, and he hadn't been able to stand what he had been doing to her.

But he wasn't about to retire from the force altogether.

And he wasn't about to spoil what little time he had this morning with her and the kids, should they ever roll out of bed, by responding to her comment.

He poked the pancakes, turning his back and gingerly scooping each one off the griddle.

"Carter?"

"I thought the smell of these things would get the kids sprinting down the stairs."

With an air of authority, Kathy stepped off her stool and planted her fist on the inviting curve of her wide hip.

"You've made a commitment to go to marriage counseling," she reminded him, the implication of which could directly affect his case—he would have to show up to couples' therapy *no matter what*. "I'll get the kids."

As she started off for the stairs, he dared to watch her. She had always had a dangerous hold on him. If only she knew that some broken things could not be fixed.

He arranged the pancakes on a plate, set the kitchen table with maple syrup, butter, and plates all around, and returned Kathy's apron where it belonged.

Their nine-year-old son, Matty, was the first to trample down the stairs and race into the kitchen, the grin on his face so big you would think it was Christmas.

"I want that one!" he said, pointing to the fluffiest pancake on the plate. "And can I have that one, too?" he asked, as Carter, having been ready on the quick with a spatula in hand, served him the first and second pancake.

"Sure can, little man."

"And that one?"

"Let's leave a few for Amanda and Christopher," he suggested, hearing the soft padding of his teenage daughter trailing sleepily down the stairs followed by the unmistakable thuds of his oldest son, a twelve-year old duplication of Carter himself.

A few more years and Matty would look the same. He would shoot up like a beanstalk and suddenly bulk out of his skinny limbs just like Chris had, just like Carter had all those years ago. Must run in the family, not that he had ever known those people.

"What about some milk?"

As Matty drowned his pancakes in syrup, and his pajama-clad siblings, Amanda and Christopher, joined him at the table, excited about the unexpected treat and fighting over the serving spatula, Carter fetched milk and orange juice from the fridge and felt his heart swell in his chest with love.

Somehow, despite his flaws, he had managed to give them what he had never had growing up. Stability. Protection. The right to feel safe and happy.

The limited time he had with his family flew by that morning, but it was enough to recalibrate and center himself.

By the time he met Danny at the 66th Precinct where the building manager had agreed to be interviewed, Carter had gotten a second-wind, and didn't feel like he hadn't slept for thirty hours.

Danny was already seated at her desk on the Special Victims Unit floor, her computer humming, a mug of coffee steaming beside her, and the early morning light cutting into her eyes, when Carter arrived.

Their desks faced one another, forming a station of sorts, and as he rounded to his chair, he spied the crime scene photos she was clicking through.

The medical examiner, Jill Andover, was nothing if not prompt in her ability to email all she had as soon as she had it.

"Did you sleep at all?" she asked without lifting her eyes from her computer screen.

"Spent the hours with the wife and kids," he said, as he hung his suit jacket on the back of his chair and booted up his computer.

He had made a concerted effort not to share too much about his home life with his partner.

Danny had been reserved as well, and though he ultimately wouldn't mind having her ear from time to time on a more personal level, they just weren't there yet.

She had gone through some heavy personal trials before returning to the SVU, which she had opened up about. Danny had lost her infant son to SIDS. Discovering that Carter had been assigned as her new partner hadn't helped matters once she had returned from the maternity leave she didn't need anymore. Carter didn't know how to mention his own kids to Danny without feeling a stab of empathy for her loss. That's why he avoided depth and details. It was working.

Danny glanced at him through her side-swept bangs and teased, "There's coffee in the breakroom. If you didn't catch at least an hour's sleep, you're going to need caffeine."

"You can do that?"

"What?"

"Your head hits the pillow and you're out like a light?"

"Jealous?" she asked, flashing him a grin.

Danny was a jeans and sweaters woman. Tall and lean. She kept her hair short and intentionally boyish, never dyed it, didn't wear a stitch of makeup as far as Carter had observed.

He respected her.

Everything about Danielle Foster, from her appearance to her attitude, seemed designed for the sole purpose of being the best SVU detective she could, not that adding a feminine flare was hindering the other investigators in their department. But Danny had this undeniable edge about her that went beyond gender.

Half the time, Carter didn't even see her as female. It made Kathy's perpetual concern all the more intolerable. There just wasn't a damn thing to worry about, and it was getting more and more exhausting trying to convince Kathy of that.

After heeding Danny's suggestion, Carter returned to his desk with a steamy mug of coffee and began pouring over the crime scene photos that Jill had sent, following his partner's lead.

Unsurprisingly, the high-def shots were even more gruesome than the real thing, and it called to mind that Carter hadn't fully absorbed the magnitude of the horrific slaughter when he had stood over the bodies in apartment 911.

"This is hard to look at," Danny commented, pushing back from her computer and getting to her feet to stretch. "We've got Lamar DeRozan in ten."

"Got it," he said, as she turned for the break room with her empty coffee mug in hand.

He returned his attention to his computer where a photo of Kayla Samuels' bedroom filled the screen. Carter spotted, beyond the open closet door in the left quadrant of the image, the dog crate.

Under his breath he said, "Thank you, Jill."

Leaning in, he clicked to the next photo and felt a grin tug at the corners of his thick mouth. She had gotten her team to get full coverage of the dog crate, its bowl, and the dregs of Cheerios.

He hadn't noticed it when he had been there in person, but bunched up at the back of the dog crate was what appeared to be a tee shirt of some kind—thin, moth-eaten cotton, light pink, a ratty unraveling hem.

He clamped his desk phone between his ear and shoulder and pressed one of the speed-dial options he had programmed into the console weeks prior.

"Why, hello there," was Jill's breathy greeting, having recognized Carter's number, he presumed.

"'Morning, Jill," he replied curtly. He had never given her the wrong idea, but that was thanks in large part to his hypervigilance. "There was some kind of tee shirt or pink material in the dog crate?"

"If you say so," she said breezily, letting out a long yawn. Carter felt his jaw clench. "You're at the precinct already?"

"Could you run DNA on it?"

"Oh, Carter, Carter, Carter," she teased in a sultry manner. "Need you even ask?"

"You're way ahead of me," he realized out loud.

"And we're running prints on the dog bowl," she explained before he could ask about it. "Not that we'll get lucky in that department."

"So, you found it odd as well?"

"Honey, I found you staring at it every time I peeked into that bedroom," she told him frankly. "I aim to please."

He *was* pleased. He would give her that.

He thanked her, and after she mentioned the importance of her beauty sleep, he let her go.

There was something about that dog crate that kept nagging at him. Something was off about it. Kayla had worn a dog collar in most of those photos. In others, her arms or thighs had been wrapped tightly with a chain-link leash. But he couldn't see her in that crate. Something about that scenario didn't feel right to him, and the hunch that had been gnawing at him was also pushing another thought—dark and unshakable—through his fast-working mind…

…one that cut too close to home and was so tangled up in his past that to even consider it caused his stomach to burn like acid.

"DeRozan's here," said Danny. He hadn't even heard her return. "I've got him in Three."

Interview Room Three was the smallest one available. It had no windows. And it could make just about any suspect claustrophobic enough to slip up, which meant that Danny wanted to approach this thing accordingly.

It wouldn't be an interview. It would be an interrogation. And neither of them had had a second to do their homework on the guy.

"How long do you want him to wait in there?" asked Carter, as he clicked his screensaver open to conceal the crime scene photos.

As he got to his feet, the screensaver filled the monitor—a family portrait of Kathy and him hugging their youngest son, Matty, who proudly held a baseball trophy in his hands, his older siblings looking on with smiles on their faces.

Danny suggested, "Let's head in. With any luck, we'll actually have something to tell Franco by the time we're done with DeRozan."

Carter cut his eyes to the lieutenant's office door, which showed no signs that Franco had drifted in yet this morning.

Lamar DeRozan was a shriveled shell of what Carter could easily see had once been a tall, lean, and perhaps even proud man. An African-American with frazzled, wiry hair, sunken cheeks, and wide, worried eyes, Lamar locked his attention onto Carter, as the detectives entered the room, and a glimmer of hope came over him that 'anotha brotha' might go easy on him.

DeRozan shifted uncomfortably in his chair. His green, custodial overalls seemed to bother him. He pushed his sleeves up nervously, as Carter and Danny sat on the seats across from him, without saying a word.

Anxious, he rolled his sleeves down again, wondering which detective was going to start. When neither did, DeRozan began stammering, since all eyes were on him.

"Like I said to the police officer," he began in a scratchy voice, his thick Brooklyn accent hollowing out each vowel that refused to leave his dry mouth. "There was a smell, and I kept telling myself, you know, if that smell don't go away… because you got to understand, I don't want to be knocking on the tenants' doors, you know? But then, midnight came around and I was about to go to bed, but I thought, I gotta check on that smell."

He was shaking his head now, and a frown formed on his face, in grim recollection.

"So, I keyed in."

Carter held his tongue, knowing Danny would lead.

"Did you know Kayla Samuels?" she asked unemotionally.

"I don't know nobody," he was quick to assure them. "I mind my own, keep the halls clean, take the rent checks out of the drop box. If a tenant is late with rent, I don't go knocking on their door. We do everything by mail, certified."

"You went above and beyond for Kayla when you keyed in, then?" Danny supplied, cornering the guy who probably hadn't meant to contradict himself.

"I didn't know Kayla," he insisted. "You got the wrong idea and—" he was speaking only to Carter now. Pleading. "I'm just here to help. I want to help. The sight of them... I mean, I had to go to the hospital, you know what I'm saying?"

Danny wasn't about to let up. "I know it's convenient to get the hell out of dodge—"

"There was no 'getting out of dodge'," he promised, a bit desperately as far as Carter was concerned. "You want to see my medical records?"

Carter, for one, didn't, and the pressure his partner was applying was obviously working against them.

"Do you know if Kayla had a dog?" he asked and immediately felt Danny's questioning eyes on him.

"I don't know nothing," he declared, having shut down. He folded his arms and leaned back in his chair, denying both of them eye contact.

"Do you also live in the building?" Carter prodded, asking an easy question that wouldn't be risky for DeRozan to answer.

"Yeah, I live on the ground floor," he told them.

"Facing the street? Or the courtyard?"

"The courtyard," he answered, catching on.

He wasn't a suspect anymore. He was a potential witness, or so Carter wanted him to believe. It would get him talking freely at least.

"I might've seen something," he offered, leaning forward, eager to help if it meant that Danny would stop suspecting him. "I sweep outside, too. I know the usual faces. Might be able to recall a non-resident if I thought about it."

"What about the man who was in Kayla's apartment?" he asked. "Was he a 'usual face'?"

"That piece of garbage?" DeRozan responded as if haunted. "Everybody knows Andre Durant. They know to keep away, keep to themselves when he comes through. Fourth floor. Apartment 407," he informed them, shaking his head as if he wished he didn't know even that much about the guy. "I don't mop that corridor no more."

They had their male Vic's identity now, so that was progress.

Carter shot Danny a guarded smile of accomplishment, and her eyes were all praise.

It felt good.

As though he had never been more sure of anything in his life, DeRozen told them, "If anyone had it coming to 'em like that, it was Andre Durant."

Carter touched eyes with Danny once again then said, "Tell me about it."

LIEUTENANT MARTIN Franco had an intimidating presence. It didn't matter who you were, if he was angling his dark, Cuban-American eyes at you, your voice wasn't going to come out quite as steady…

…which was Carter's problem, as he briefed Franco on the ground they had covered with DeRozan.

Carter was still the 'new guy,' still in the throes of proving himself, proving that he was a fine detective and not a hot-headed, loose cannon. Unfortunately, he had come across like the latter in their last investigation.

"Possible revenge murder," Franco surmised, as he mulled the information over.

Franco's jet-black hair and prominent bone structure defied his sixty years.

"Kayla Samuels gets the worst of it, why?" asked Franco.

Carter wasn't about to speculate, though images of BDSM and the secrets they implied came to mind. Judging the woman's physicality and, he could only assume, willingness, she certainly had the means to bait any enemy of Durant's into compromising positions. If she had done this, it could have invited revenge onto her head. Likewise, if the junkies had taken photos and blackmailed a John…

It wasn't lost on Carter that his theories weren't provable, not yet.

"That's what we hope to find out," Danny answered, gripping the back of one of the chairs across from their lieutenant. "According to DeRozan—"

"Who we cleared," Carter interjected, having anticipated the question that Franco liked to ask whenever they had finished an interview. "Surveillance video shows him up and down corridors, and out in the courtyard, he wouldn't have had time to do the kind of damage we found at the crime scene."

"That was fast," Franco commented, as if thoroughly skeptical that a government employee working for the Housing Department would've turned over footage the same day it was requested.

It had been fast, but Carter had worked fast. He had used every break from questioning DeRozan to call his contacts at the Housing Department, the people who had the authority to obtain the surveillance footage.

Beyond Franco's office window, the hazy May sun had sunk behind the concrete cityscape, casting the room in an orange glow.

The lieutenant remained skeptical of his newest detective.

"I called in a favor," Carter explained, "got the tapes, some of the ladies in the Computer Crime Unit had down time."

Danny rolled her eyes and pointed out, "His pretty face comes in handy from time to time."

Franco had no sense of humor.

Getting back on track, Danny barreled ahead with the briefing.

"DeRozan told us our male Vic was generally feared. A junky not a dealer. He had tweaked in the courtyard on more than one occasion but nobody called it in. Surprisingly, he has no record."

"That *is* surprising," Franco agreed.

Carter said, "No one wanted to get into it with the guy. Tweaking out, Durant assaulted DeRozan one time, and left him with a split lip and bruises. This was according to DeRozan, but he said calling the cops didn't even cross his mind. He still had to live in the building with the guy. It wouldn't have gone well for him if he had reported it."

"What was the beating for?" Franco asked, trying to get a feel for the types of things that would set Andre Durant off, what his threshold was.

Straightening up from her grip on the chair, Danny told him, "DeRozan was guilty of mopping right outside of Durant's door."

"The guy was doing his job, cleaning?" asked Franco. "That's why Durant beat him up?"

"Yes. A paranoid overreaction, we're thinking," said Carter, as he touched eyes with Danny.

He silently suggested to Danny that she should clue the lieutenant in, since she was the senior detective of the two of them.

"We're not angling to victim-blame," she started, "but Kayla was into some kinky sex-play if the photos plastering her bedroom walls are any indication, and that's what she allowed in plain view. Now that we know Durant's identity and address, we can get into his apartment with your help, see if they were involved in some kind of lifestyle that ultimately got them killed."

"A lifestyle that got them *skinned alive*," Franco corrected, and the implication was crystal clear.

If the victims, Samuels and Durant, had brought that on themselves, they would've had to have been tangled up in some serious evil.

"If that's *not* the case," Carter allowed, "and our Vics are innocent outside of smoking crank, then we would be looking at a killer who skins junkies alive for fun."

The conjecture hung heavily in the airless room. No one wanted to address it. But all of them knew anything was possible.

"Let's get you into Durant's apartment," he told them, as he took hold of his desk phone to make the call. "I'll let you know when we have the all-clear."

"Thanks, Lieutenant," said Danny before starting out of the office with Carter at her heels.

When they reached their conjoined desks, she commiserated with Carter, "Looks like we'll break our record for sleepless nights."

"You have any personal stuff you need to handle before that call comes through?" he asked her.

She sank into her wobbly desk chair and a knowing grin came over her face. "No, but you do."

"My son's baseball game," he admitted, and immediately Danny's big, brown eyes turned pained.

She did a soldierly job of clearing her throat and shaking off whatever memories of her deceased infant son had surged to mind.

"I don't need to stay the whole game," he explained. "Just need to make an appearance."

"Of course," she said in a small voice. "Take all the time you want."

Whipping his suit jacket off the back of his chair and throwing it on, he promised, "Text me as soon as the warrant on Durant's apartment comes through, and I'll meet you there."

The Glock in his shoulder holster needed some adjusting, but he took care of that on his way out.

"Have fun!" she called out just as Carter began crossing the bullpen, heading for the exit.

Prospect Park wasn't far from the 66th, but traffic would've been unforgiving if he hadn't popped the cherry siren on top of the Crown Victoria he had essentially adopted from the precinct without permission.

He hadn't made it to any of Christopher's basketball games nor Amanda's play performances last month due to the demands of his transfer and the Bauer case.

His kids had stoically accepted his absence, filled him in on the blow-by-blows of their victories when he had gotten home, and hadn't meant to make him feel guilty. His guilt was all his own. But this evening, he actually had a shot at making it to Matty's game on time.

Cars pulled over and yielded for him, as he muscled the boxy vehicle up avenues and across side streets, weaving his way to Brooklyn's largest park.

When he reached the Northwestern side, parking proved no easy task, and he had no more police tricks up his sleeves, so he nosed the Crown Vic at an awkward angle in front of a fire hydrant, told himself it should be fine there for a few minutes, and hustled into the park along a path that would take him to the baseball fields.

Matty and his team were just finishing their warm up, as Carter reached the bleachers where Kathy had set up camp. She was bundled in a sweater to ward off the biting night air, and there was a cooler with every snack imaginable—including wine coolers for the other Moms—tucked near her feet.

She beamed a great big smile at Carter, those big blue eyes of hers hooded under a baseball cap. The ballcap was their son's team, and Kathy wore it to show her support.

"Super dad!" She sprang up and planted a kiss on Carter then shouted, "Matty, your father's here!"

The skinniest kid in maroon turned, lit up like a Christmas tree at the sight of Carter waving from the stands, dropped his bat, and ran over.

That's my son, thought Carter, who met him on the grass and dropped to his knee to give him a giant hug.

"You made it!"

"I wouldn't miss it for the world."

Chapter Three

ANDRE DURANT'S apartment on the fourth floor of Building 7 was every bit the slum that Danny had expected, but it wasn't cluttered. Quite the contrary. There was virtually nothing to hunt through.

As Danny took another slow lap through the five-hundred square feet that comprised the tightest studio apartment she had ever set foot in, she noted a cracked, brown couch and a full sized bed complete with box spring and headboard—not your typical grimy mattress on the floor—though the sheets were soiled, the bed unmade.

The windows were covered with cardboard that was held in place with duct tape, blocking out all light.

The overhead bulb barely lit up the room.

There were no other pieces of furniture. Nothing on the walls except cobwebs and fly stains.

The kitchen was just as bare unless she counted the roaches that skittered away when she opened the cabinets above the sink—also bare—and cupboards below.

The refrigerator proved equally fruitless, but there was a nice stash of marijuana in the freezer.

She'd had no reason to call in Jill and the forensic team.

Carter, herself, and the two uniformed police officers that had accompanied them would be more than enough.

Danny had half a mind to excuse the officers since they had been waiting in the corridor anyway and their presence would likely intimidate any neighbors from coming forward. Not that Carter and Danny would have better luck, but at least they were dressed in street clothes.

"Remind me again what we're looking for," Carter said from where he was crouched in front of the brown leather couch.

He had set the cracked seat cushions on the floor with gloved hands and was feeling his way along the seam between the back of the couch, the armrests, and the seat.

"I have no idea," she admitted. "But I'll know it when I see it."

"I thought we would find a photo of Kayla at least," he complained, straightening up to his feet and giving his neck a little sideways stretch.

"She might not have been very important to him," Danny allowed, then quickly doubled down. "Or he was smart enough to keep their recreational activities, and all evidence of it, in *her* apartment and not his."

She felt his tight, brown eyes on her, as she slipped a frozen brick of Durant's marijuana into an evidence bag. Once she closed the freezer door, she gave him her full attention.

But he didn't say anything.

"What?"

He ran his large hand over his shaved head thoughtfully, then planted both fists on his hips.

Carter had no idea how massive he was. He was a thick wall of a man, and when he postured like that, brooding with his shoulders squared and elbows out, his presence was downright threatening.

That's what Danny liked about him.

That, and the fact that the initial arrogance he had shown her last month when she had returned to the force had quickly melted.

He had wanted to get along, work well together, and even learn from her. Carter had shown her that he could be a team player, have her back, and put their partnership above all else, and even be vulnerable and take the kinds of risks that great investigators often do.

But he had also been hot-headed. Emotional. Fast with his fists.

She was still getting used to his moods, still trying to master the art of determining which side of the professionalism line he was functioning from. Sometimes it was hard to tell if Carter was in control of himself, or about to catapult off half-cocked and ready to cross that line.

"This place is bugging me," he finally said, looking around. "No computer, no laptop, no cell phone charger, no TV, no nothing."

It didn't seem right, she agreed.

"He assaulted DeRozan for mopping outside his door…"

"Like he's hiding something illegal in here," Carter supplied.

"But there's nothing in here."

"Could he have moved it?" he suggested, thinking out loud. "He anticipates the killer will want it or take it so he moves it—whatever 'it' is. The killer finds him at Kayla's, has to torture the woman to get Durant talking…"

"But he refuses to talk, so the killer slits his throat?" she asked. "I don't like any of that," she told him honestly, which prompted Carter to go off pacing again.

This time, both of his hands raked over his shaved head.

She knew that behavior. He didn't like it either, and his prior suggestion, as grim as it had been, came to mind.

"There has to be a motive, Carter. Whoever did this, didn't do it just for fun."

He was staring at the bed now.

She had already done a cursory sweep of the dusty floor beneath the bed, but didn't object when he told her, "Grab that side, would you?"

Her lower back wasn't quite what it had been before she had worked through a nine-month pregnancy, before she had delivered her son, and before she had lost him, but she still did what she could to move the bed.

"Martinez! Wong!" she called out, summoning the two uniformed officers now that she had something for them to do. "Give us a hand?"

The police officers came in from the corridor and helped the detectives move the bed. They each lifted a corner of the wrought-iron bed frame and shuffled it as far to the side as it would fit.

The headboard, which they realized hadn't been attached properly to the frame if at all, slammed against the wooden floor. And the footboard—a miniature version of the headboard—nearly fell off as well, but with one bolt in place, held its own.

With the headboard face down on the floor, Danny saw it immediately—an orange GLYPH hard drive, no bigger than a paperback novel.

It was taped to the backside of the headboard.

Similarly, on the wall that was now exposed since the headboard had fallen, there was a web of duct tape in the shape of a rectangle. The duct tape seemed to be holding a device to the wall.

Unless Danny was mistaken, the device appeared to be the approximate size of a laptop computer.

Huffing to catch her breath, she touched eyes with Carter and breathed, "Nice work," as she began stripping tape off the hard drive. Wong hovered over her, ready with an evidence bag.

Pleased, Carter's jaw clenched with a satisfied yet reserved grin, and he started the careful work of freeing the laptop from the wall. It was a 15.5" Apple MacBook Pro laptop computer. Top of the line. Two years old. A big-ticket item for a junky on welfare who lived in the projects.

"You might have just cracked this thing wide open," she told him after they had scoured the rest of the apartment in search of other hidden devices.

There weren't any, but as far as Danny was concerned, between the external hard drive and the laptop, she felt confident whatever contents they found would sufficiently supply them with both evidence and motive.

Her money was on them being one in the same.

Danny directed the officers to deliver both items, bagged and tagged, to the precinct and excused them from the corridor where Carter was pulling his latex gloves off.

"Why don't you head home to the kids?" she offered, checking the time on her cell phone before shoving it into the back pocket of her jeans. "Catch them before bed."

A rumbling chuckle spilled out of him.

"My kids were in bed hours ago, but thanks."

"How'd the game go?"

"Great," he said, as he put on his suit jacket. "Matty didn't exactly hit a home run, and his team lost by a landslide, but they're only nine years old. They're in it for the ice cream."

Danny felt a tug of remorse for her infant son who hadn't made it past a few months. Would Gregory have liked baseball? Or would he have turned out more bookish than athletic? How would her mothering have shaped him? Influenced his personality? How much would he have ended up looking like her, would he have a slanted mouth, the same wicked smirk? Or would he have been the spitting image of his father? Would Tommy have seen so much of himself in his son that he would've never stopped loving Danny?

Not that Tommy, the father, hadn't told her that he had stopped loving her. Despite learning that their infant son had in fact died—a walloping blow that there had been no getting around—Tommy had told her that he loved her, that he had loved her the whole time, that their estrangement had done nothing to diminish his feelings, that it had made his feelings for her stronger if anything…

Her heart tangled with warring emotions she hoped hadn't reached her face, and as she forced those hard emotions down into the pit of her stomach and locked Durant's apartment, she kept her tone steady and said, "I'm glad it worked out for you being there."

The tears were coming now, blurring her vision and threatening to spill down her cheeks, so she kept her head down, finding something complicated about the deadbolt lock even though it was as straightforward as they came, and again told him, "You go on ahead."

It took Danny longer than expected to collect herself after Carter had disappeared down the corridor, after the faint din of the elevator had reached him beyond her sightlines, after she had allowed more than enough time to lapse, giving herself clearance that she wouldn't accidentally catch up with him in the dingy lobby.

When she stepped out into the withering courtyard, a chilling wind bit at her sideways, but it wasn't so cold as to deter her from walking home.

It might not have been the best side of town to hoof it all the way back to her one-bedroom apartment on Ocean Parkway, but Danny trusted the *don't-mess-with-me* vibe that she naturally gave off.

As she made her brisk way back under a starless Brooklyn sky, passing dime-store bodegas among other low-rent conveniences, her *don't-mess-with-me* attitude held up.

No one bothered her. There were no leering drunks or aggressive junkies watching her.

Soon the stiff breeze didn't seem so biting, the crisp May chill having softened in the heat of her racing thoughts.

She wished it was the case distracting her. She was ordinarily as focused as a razor's edge.

But it wasn't.

She was harboring a dark secret from the one man who mattered more to her than anything in this world. A secret she had no choice but to keep from him. If Tommy found out, she would lose him all over again. Danny would do anything to prevent that from happening.

Anything.

But it was eating her alive.

Her mother, Nora, had killed the baby.

And Tommy didn't know.

As she rounded onto Ocean Parkway, having woven her clouded way across Kensington, she came to the corner of Caton Avenue where Tommy's bar, O'Toole's, sat like a glowing beacon at the end of a long line of closed shops.

The grand picture windows weren't so steamed up that she couldn't tell who was working behind the bar, serving the loyal patrons. Cops and firefighters frequented O'Toole's and treated this watering hole like a second home.

She felt her mouth curl into a nostalgic smile, and was even happier to discover that one of Tommy's new hires was pouring pints behind the bar.

It meant she would find the love of her life inside her apartment...

Danny entered the musty lobby of her building where the super, Camil Usov—a grouchy Russian who had grown strangely friendly with her over the years—grumbled as he changed a fluorescent light bulb that had blown.

When she keyed into her apartment, having taken the stairwell stairs two at a time, she found Tommy inside just as she had thought.

"Hey," she breathed, raking her long fingers through her side swept bangs.

Tommy never ceased to give her a thrilled twinge of self-consciousness.

She neared the kitchen islet where Tommy, on the other side, was setting two longneck bottles of beer on the counter. He must have heard her key in, and she had to admit, she liked how he was in the habit of offering her a beer and a sexy smile whenever she got home.

A retired firefighter in his 40s with salt-and-pepper hair and the muscular build of a lightweight boxer, Tommy was a man of few words.

But the scars on his body told stories.

Some she had listened to intently, lying with him in his cramped apartment above O'Toole's. Others hinted at tales too dark to share. He was mysterious in some ways. A stranger. In other ways, however, she felt like she knew him so intimately, she didn't know where she left off and he began.

"You took another night off?" she asked.

"The new guys know what they're doing," he said, his steel-gray eyes searching hers.

They had gotten into a somewhat reliable routine, and yet they still stood on shaky ground, the subtext of their every exchange riddled with doubts—were they crazy to try to make this work? Could they get past the death of their son? If they did, would their contentment be ruined by guilt?

His questioning eyes seemed to always ask it all, and it was becoming harder and harder to hold his gaze.

After cracking the beers open and handing her one across the islet, he asked, "You too beat to watch something?"

He jangled the TV remote control.

Her eyebrows shot up to her hairline and an excited smile came over her face.

"It came?"

Tommy produced the Netflix DVD she had been waiting for, a documentary about an FBI investigation gone wrong in the late 80s.

She practically squealed her way to the couch. She plopped down with the beers in hand, while Tommy popped the documentary into her archaic DVD player, flipped on the TV, and got the thing playing after a few minor adjustments.

As they settled in for the night, sipping IPAs and watching the pioneering female detectives that had ultimately botched the case of the century—Tommy's muscular arm wrapped around her and Danny's head nuzzled into the crook of his warm neck—she thought to herself, this was what they could handle.

No conversations.

No discussions.

Their history and past, unacknowledged.

Just two warm bodies, lonely minds, heavy hearts, enjoying the feel of one another with the television's glow on their faces.

Their connection was purely physical.

Innocent at first.

Then hungry.

Dire.

Hours later, their beers had spilled and their clothing had been discarded, as the credits of Disc One rolled down the television screen.

From the couch to the bedroom and until the break of dawn, everything about their need for one another fell just short of feeling secure and lasting.

The next morning, her alarm clock sounded too soon.

Having shoved her Glock into the holster of her hip, she pulled a black blazer on, while drinking in the sight of Tommy's nude body bundled in a comforter that couldn't contain him.

Danny left Tommy asleep in her bed and got out of the apartment miraculously on time.

Not twenty minutes later, Danny stood waiting for Carter outside of the Kings County Hospital with two to-go cups of coffee in her hands.

Carter walked up Winthrop Avenue towards the entrance and greeted her.

The coffee dispensing vending machines inside the hospital brewed notoriously weak cups if they were working at all, and Carter had gotten her enough times that she felt she owed him one, or a dozen, which was why she had also shown up with a bag full of doughnut holes.

She was in the best mood ever…thanks to Tommy…

"You read my mind," he said, carefully popping the plastic lid off his coffee and giving it a blow.

"Eat up," she told him, passing the doughnut bag as soon as he had taken a few sizable gulps. "Something tells me Jill's about to kill our appetite."

Taking turns, they each shoved doughnut holes in their mouths, making slow, salivating, eye-fluttering work of devouring every last one. Then they washed down the sugary breakfast with the rest of their coffee as the brightening sun warmed them.

Inside the Kings County Hospital, they trailed through the corridors and came to the morgue where Jill had laid the bodies of Kayla Samuels and Andre Durant face up on two stainless steel tables.

This would not be pretty.

Jill, on the other hand, was.

Her ordinarily ponytailed hair had been curled and was styled in impressive tendrils. Her washed-out complexion was made up with pink lipstick and blush. And she had darkened her eyes with liner and mascara.

Though she wore her standard white lab coat, the hem of what appeared to be a red dress poked out, and her feet beneath were pointed in stunning black heels.

Danny was so thrown that she blurted out, "You look amazing."

"Hot date," said Jill, beaming.

It would have to be, because unlike every other time Jill had been within spitting distance of Carter, she had laid her flirtatious interest on pretty thick. This time she hadn't even glanced in his direction.

"Tonight might be *the night*," she gushed.

It was definitely too much information, but Danny wouldn't begrudge the woman for letting her thrilled anticipation spill out of her. Tommy had the same effect on Danny, and she was sure Carter's wife could inspire the same glee in him, as well. They were human. They were alive. They might as well enjoy it.

Jill sobered up from whatever fantasy had momentarily washed over her and invited them to the tables where their Vics lay as two massacred reminders never to take a single breath for granted.

"I've got some good news for you," she announced. "The fillet knife found at the scene was in fact responsible for skinning Samuels and also for killing Durant."

Danny figured as much.

"I took the Vics' prints," she went on, "and lifted only one set of prints from the handle of the knife."

"Lay that good news on us, Jill," said Danny.

"They belong to Durant."

For a rattled moment, it didn't compute how this was good news for the investigation until it dawned on her that there wouldn't be one.

"Murder-suicide?" she questioned, sliding her skeptical gaze from Jill to her partner and back again.

Carter looked a disturbed mix of frustrated and relieved.

"All evidence points to Durant," said Jill, but her confirmation still felt...

Strange.

Off.

Deceptive.

"You don't look happy."

Danny thumbed a pocket-sized moleskine that she was in the habit of jotting observations inside of, unsure of how to respond.

"Hey, I can keep digging," she offered. "I'm still waiting on the blood panels. I've got a couple techs combing over that dog crate, but in terms of finding evidence of who killed Samuels and Durant, I found it. It's Durant."

"Ok," Danny breathed, then she cut her eyes to Carter. "We've got some paperwork to file."

"Just like that?" he questioned.

She didn't know what to tell him. If it was a murder-suicide, then the case was open and shut.

"The possibility crossed our minds," she reminded him.

She thanked Jill on their way out, and Carter chimed in with a curt, "Good work," then they returned to the 66th to handle the paperwork.

When all was said and done, Danny having used painstaking scrutiny to type up each form before Carter and her submitted the documents to Franco for approval, their meeting with the lieutenant was brief if not anticlimactic.

Even though the Cyber Crimes Unit would run with anything they found on Durant's hard drives, the case, for all intents and purposes, as far as the SVU detectives should be concerned, was closed.

At the end of the dragging day, Danny clocked out at six, wondered about the next case she might catch—nothing had rolled in for them that afternoon—and parted ways with her partner who seemed stuck lingering at his computer where a crime scene photo of Kayla's dog crate filled the screen.

If she'd had it in her to ask, she would have.

But Danny felt suddenly consumed with a far more personal matter that had been slowly strangling her, an ice-cold secret around her throat.

Her son, Gregory hadn't died from Sudden Infant Death Syndrome in his crib that night when Danny had stepped out to get some air, leaving her mother, Nora, to babysit.

He had died at the hand of her delusional mother.

Smothered.

And once Danny had found out, once the horrifying truth had surfaced between mother and daughter, an even more horrifying result had followed.

Danny hadn't been able to bring herself to turn Nora Foster in.

She hadn't had the strength to have the older woman arrested.

She had sought no justice for her son.

Coming home to Tommy O'Toole night after night was a constant reminder of just how dark and damaged and sick and broken Danny had become.

She might have kicked Nora out of her life, but it had amounted to a small, sad measure that had accomplished nothing except calling to mind one dangerous possibility:

Danny couldn't bring her mother to justice…

…it was easier to keep Tommy in the dark, to go on lying, and to go on protecting her mother, than it was for Danny to tell the man she loved the truth.

Nora had twisted her hooks into Danny far too deep.

Chapter Four

CARTER COULDN'T let it go.

It wasn't the dog crate that was bothering him.

It was the Cheerios.

They hadn't been lapped up or slobbered.

They had been picked at. Broken. Crushed.

It was familiar. It touched some deep, faraway nerve, a festering wound that had been buried long ago and mostly forgotten, but one that had never healed.

Dressed in gray sweats and sneakers, having seen the kids off to school and checked in with Kathy about her day, Carter set off jogging into the misty morning, his shaved head covered with a hoodie in case rain decided to tick down.

He felt light on his feet despite the kettlebell weights in his hands. Together, they were 50 lbs, but that was nothing compared to the heavy ball in his stomach.

An image filled his mind for a flashing moment—a child's little fingers, the distinct lack of dexterity used to pick up a single Cheerio.

The memory, the image of those little, brown fingers could've been his son, Christopher's when he had been five or six, or his daughter, Amanda's. Matty's as well.

The images unfolded in his mind's eye.

Carter fought it all the while, doing everything he could to focus on his breathing, his sneakers striking pavement with every stride, and the dreary Brooklyn scenery around him.

But he knew that those small fingers he was remembering were his own, and the child they belonged to was himself.

He didn't want to remember—that hell he had lived in, on his knees, crouched down, those metal rungs digging into his shins, never eating, only picking at Cheerios, in a cold basement, too dark to see, the crate too small...

Carter shook the memories out of his head and turned a corner where a huddled cluster of homeless men passed a cigarette around and waited for a soup kitchen to open.

He had been avoiding couples' counseling for this very reason. Whenever he actually went with Kathy, he kept his mouth shut, knowing that if he opened up at all, an entire Pandora's box of nightmares would spring out.

Kathy had found a smart, knowledgeable, and surprisingly well-educated female therapist to help Carter, as well as their marriage, survive the decades-long aftermath of his unfathomably difficult—and highly abusive—upbringing.

The therapist also had a compassionate knack for helping Kathy work through her jealousy issues, and she always advocated that authentic trust would strengthen their at-times tenuous relationship. The woman was good. But the sessions had been weakening him.

It didn't help him to be reminded.

The image of Cheerios in that dog bowl refused to let up.

Carter realized he had been sprinting. Prospect Park came into view just across the street, and the Kensington projects where Kayla and her seedy boyfriend had engaged in some kind of drug-addled death pact was only a handful of blocks south.

What the hell had happened between those two junkies, the 66th Precinct might never understand.

He had every intention of darting straight into the park, hooking onto one of the jogging trails that looped through woodsy terrain, and getting lost in the rhythm of his excursion to clear his mind, and hopefully shed the dark knowing that had been pressing down on him unforgivingly.

But the traffic light changed.

Carter stopped abruptly, as a long line of vehicles accelerated through the intersection. He jogged in place. It would be a long time if he decided to wait for the light. There was no chance to jog between cars to speed things up. Lacking patience and perhaps without thinking, he gave up and started jogging south.

It wasn't until he reached the projects that he admitted to himself this might have been his destination all along.

A belly dancer. A BDSM slave. A junky. Ultimately, Kayla had been a woman tortured to death.

Her case had been opened and shut in the blink of an eye.

The fast closure of the case hadn't even given Danny and him time to notify Kayla Samuels' family, an often uncomfortable if not heartrending step in the investigative protocol.

Danny was handling that now, while Carter took a day, then he would return the favor tomorrow.

She didn't shirk the hard stuff, he would give her that.

But Carter had been a bit thrown that Danny hadn't fought a little harder to keep investigating. Instead, when Franco had deemed their case over and done with, she hadn't batted an eye.

Carter was alone on this one. It wasn't lost on him this might be crazy, which was why he had no intention of cluing his partner in on his nagging hunch, much less the lieutenant or anyone at the 66th.

When he came to the entrance of the courtyard, Building 7 looming across the way, he slowed to a huffing walk and planted his large fists on his hips.

Though there were a few residents outside, the courtyard wasn't exactly the bustling picture it would've been on a sunny day.

Teenagers were gathered under the brick overhangs of most of the buildings. Carter could guess what the teens were up to. They were ready to sell drugs in quantities so small you could pass them with a simple handshake. Their pockets were probably stuffed with crank, their shifty eyes gave them away.

Here and there, residents who had to get to a legitimate job, as evidenced by their factory-outlet pants or skirt suits, trailed through with their umbrellas low against their heads, not that the rain ticks warranted it.

The occasional pitbull barked from either an open apartment window or between a teenager's legs, but for the most part the projects were subdued on this dreary day.

Having caught his breath while pacing along the sidewalk at the courtyard entrance, scoping out those teenagers all the while, Carter pulled his hoodie as low as it would go down his face, hunched his shoulders, and made his unarmed way to Kayla and Andre's building.

It wasn't hard to slip inside Building 7.

Carter jogged up to the fourth floor where Andre Durant had terrorized what few residents had dared to venture down his slick stretch of corridor.

His apartment wasn't blocked off with crime scene tape, but the warrant notice was still sealed in a transparent pocket and taped to the door.

Carter didn't need to go inside, that wasn't his objective.

The police officers' effort to canvas for witnesses had been lax at best. The uniformed officers had gotten nowhere, and the case had moved too quickly for Danny and Carter to go out knocking on doors themselves.

Carter lingered outside the apartment, he listened for sounds. He took a slow, heavy-footed lap farther down the corridor then looped back.

If there were any residents sitting in their apartments and listening to Carter stalking the hallways, they might assume that the Black man walking the fourth floor was interested in talking to Andre Durant. If they did, it meant that they hadn't heard about the murder-suicide.

Maybe someone would come out and talk...

That was Carter's half-baked plan, anyhow. He was obviously working off the cuff. He was all impulse, and little forethought. Images of dog crates and broken Cheerios motivated him to see this thing through, if it even went anywhere.

It worked.

Just as Carter was turning on his heel to double back for the sixth time, he heard the distinct scraping sound of a deadbolt lock sliding loose.

The door across from Durant's apartment unit cracked open.

Carter wasted no time approaching the door, but whoever was inside pulled the door shut, too cautious to proceed.

A long moment passed.

Then the door creaked open again.

Carter felt eyes on him and glanced over his shoulder at Durant's door, but there was no one else in the hallway.

Behind him, the door creaked open yet again.

Carter turned with his fists on his hips, agitated, and found a willowy Latino man in the doorway of the apartment across from Durant's. His hazy eyes peered out.

"Are you looking for Raffi?" the man asked.

After taking in a fast impression of the guy—late 20s, heavily tattooed arms, an ash-streaked wife-beater tank hanging loosely down his sunken chest—Carter played along, "Have you seen him?"

The man snickered. "I wish. The whole building is *dry*. Are you selling?"

So, whoever 'Raffi' was, he dealt drugs, and has been gone long enough for residents of the entire building to deplete their drug supplies.

"You out?" Carter asked.

"Yeah, I finished my stash a day ago. Man, today's gonna be rough as hell if we don't get some flow going. Where is Raffi? It makes no sense."

"You think he's holding out?" asked Carter, anxious to find out from the guy what Raffi's exact relationship with Andre Durant had been.

"I doubt it, I think something's wrong," he said. He was scratching his neck now, dirty nails leaving raised, red marks as if the very notion of embarking on withdrawal had initiated the process. "Yo', so are you selling, or what?"

"Selling? Nah. Durant owes me," he said, casting a wide net.

The guy's eyes brightened with a strange glint, as he said, "What's he owe you?"

It definitely occurred to Carter this could backfire, but he forced a sleazy grin and told him, "Kayla."

"Damn," he snickered, two fists to his mouth now as if he had once been on the receiving end of that debt. Then his glee clouded over, and he began shaking his head. "You outta luck on both fronts, man, cuz them two got offed."

Forcing an edge of shock into his tone, he replied with, "They were *offed?*"

"Crazy as hell, man, I'm telling you. Kayla's dead. Andre's dead. Ain't nobody seen Raffi. Whole building is about to be jonesing."

"Raffi was tight with Andre?"

"Eh, you know Andre," he said with a shrug. "Always jamming himself into some other brotha's deal. Raffi was hookin' Kayla up, had this whole arrangement going with her. Then Andre's in the mix. That's how I heard about it, Andre's big mouth."

"That's my beef with him," Carter chimed in.

"Man, everybody's got beef with Andre the way he shoots his mouth off like that, but no one's gonna have it out with him 'cuz he's crazy as hell," he commiserated, going off on a brief tangent before adding, "I don't go for that *kinda deal*, though, all that whips and chains stuff. I seen it once when Andre owed me and I was like, nah, I'll take her regular, know what I'm saying?"

Carter offered his fist in solidarity with the sentiment and the guy fist-bumped him and slid his swimming gaze up and down the corridor just to check if anyone was coming.

"Hey, look man," said Carter. "I can't start no turf war, but I might have the hookup—"

"Yeah?"

"You got Raffi's number?" Even before Carter could finish his point, the guy fished his cell phone out of his pocket. "I'll make sure I ain't pissing on his corner, and if all's good, I'll be back."

"No doubt," he said as he angled his cell screen at Carter, presenting Raffi's number. Carter used his own cell to snap a photo of the contact then shoved his phone back into his sweats. "Good lookin' out, man."

They fist-bumped again, and Carter told him, "Keep it real, 408," as if the Latino's apartment number was his name.

Carter started down the corridor for the stairwell.

When he reached the courtyard outside, he had an intense urge to dial the number and see if Raffi answered. What if Carter could lure Raffi to meet in person?

But if Carter called from his own cell, then Raffi would have Carter's phone number.

Carter needed to play this thing smart.

Instead, he placed a quick call into the 66th and asked one of the officers to run Raffi's cell phone number. It would take at least a few hours, no more than a day, to hear back with any information on this Raffi character that might be in the system. Worst case scenario, if Raffi didn't have a record, Carter would at least learn about the cell phone account and the associated home address.

"If there's GPS tracking on the cell," he said lastly before letting the officer go, "I would love the current location."

"Need a warrant for that."

Carter was all too aware but that didn't stop him from saying, "You've never used a little muscle with a cell phone company? Come on," he joshed, stirring the officer's competitive streak—they all had one. "What ever happened to going 'above and beyond'?"

"It's 'serve and protect,' but I'll see what I can do, Detective."

After thanking him and ducking his way across the drizzling courtyard, he wondered what the Cyber Crimes Unit might have discovered on Durant's hard drives.

He checked his cell phone for the time. He could get away with a call or two, but would have to jog back to the house soon. Kathy had yoga for another hour or so, but even factoring in her walk home, Carter couldn't get away with being out for much longer.

If he wasn't home and showered before she got back, he could expect a cold shoulder and the same old jealous fight they always seemed to be tangled in, as if his every jog was an elaborate front to hide an affair.

He wasn't that guy.

Not anymore.

It had only happened once during a long undercover stint years ago. And worse than the adultery itself had been the fact that he had confessed it to Kathy. They had never been the same since. Regret was too small a word and didn't even begin to capture how he felt about what he had done to her the second he had selfishly needed to get the infidelity off his chest.

Some secrets, if exposed, were far more damaging than the lie of omission that had once defined them.

He started off walking in a direction that would afford him a wide loop home, his sneakers tapping pavement. He avoided the shallow puddles that were accumulating on the sidewalk.

It crossed his mind to check in with Danny, but he quickly ruled out sharing his interest in following up with Cyber Crimes. He called her desk phone instead of her cell, left a brief and vague message to cover his bases, then as his stomach churned for breakfast, he pushed a call through to Vince Tenenbaum, his ruddy-faced, bleary-eyed contact in Cyber Crimes who had worked the Agatha Bauer case with them last month.

"Dobbs?" he greeted in a pinched, nasal tone that sounded more knowing than questioning.

"Vince, my man," he shot back with the aim of buttering the guy up. "You're not going to make me explain why I'm calling, are you?"

Teasing right back, the techie supplied, "The Durant hard drives. I should've expected your call except, like a fool, I believed the captain when he told me the case belonged to my department."

"Like a fool," he agreed.

Franco had tossed the case file up the chain of command, getting the captain's approval before the case dropped into the department Franco had recommended—Cyber Crimes.

Carter knew the drill. He also knew that Vince would have no vested interest in withholding any details that he might've uncovered.

"Any reason the case might bounce back to SVU?" he asked Vince.

The pause that followed was not promising.

"I've got a lot of adult sex play going on, photos and videos," he allowed. "It's kinky, but none of it looks criminal. Consenting adults, as far as I can tell."

Damn.

"I'll let you know if anything violent comes up, anything involving a minor, but—"

Carter didn't need to hear Vince's prediction that such incriminating photos would not likely be found, so he interrupted, "Did you notice any dog crates in any of the photos and videos?"

"Dog crates?"

"Something's not sitting right with me."

"Well, that I gleaned," said Vince with a little chortle. "You wouldn't be calling otherwise. I haven't been looking for dog crates—you mean like what you would put a dog in to travel?"

"No, like a small, metal pen meant to contain a puppy so it won't tear through the house and eat and poop on everything."

"And that's why I'm not a dog person…"

"How's the whole 'nine cats, no sex life' workin' out for ya?"

"Ha, ha," said Vince before promising, "I'll comb back through the images and let you know if I find anything."

"Thanks, man," and with that Carter ended the call just in time to slip into the Kings County Hospital where Jill Andover, the medical examiner who had been getting herself dolled up more and more with each passing day, was definitely not expecting him.

Jill lifted her glittery, made-up eyes and pulled off the white, examination mask from her face, having perhaps sensed more than seen Carter slipping into her morgue.

A look of sudden surprised recognition came over her and her red lips spread into a smile. She stepped away from the cadaver she had been working on in favor of getting a good look at Carter.

"Are you feeling okay? You aren't wearing a suit!" she laughed.

She had never seen him off duty, and unlike the majority of detectives at the 66th who got away with dressing casually, Carter had had enough of that working Vice undercover for ten years. He was a suit and tie man now so long as he was on duty. But if he was off duty, he dressed in tracksuits and sweats.

"For what do I owe the pleasure of this unannounced visit?"

"I was jogging through the 'hood," he said, beaming a sparkly grin at her. "Thought I would see if you had anything for me."

"Right!" she said as she clicked her high-heeled way over to her computer. It took her a second to get her bearings, as she pulled up a few reports to refresh her memory, presumably. "The dog bowl and pink tee shirt… I have some info…"

He waited patiently, as she scanned her computer screen. When her delicately arched brows knit together with either confusion or concern, he was a breath away from asking but held his tongue

Jill mumbled, "Oh," as if making sense of whatever had troubled her. "Danny didn't call."

The comment implied that Jill wasn't aware the case had been closed, a potentially related element—those hard drives—having been bounced to a different department.

But rather than leveling with Jill and asking her not to mention any of this to his partner, Carter opted to change the conversation instead.

"You've been looking nice."

"Ha!" She flashed him a sultry smile meant as a joke. "Things are getting hot and heavy with my sexy accountant."

"I doubt I've ever heard those two words in the same sentence."

"Sexy and accountant? Or hot and heavy? Because, Carter, I gotta tell you, if you've reached your forties and have never had a little 'hot and heavy'—"

"Sexy and accountant, Jill," he clarified dryly.

"First time for everything, right?" she said, giving her mouse a few more clicks and then doing a bit of a double-take at Carter. "Come to think of it. He's like the horn-rimmed glasses version of you."

That would explain why Jill seemed satisfied and hadn't been hitting on him, he thought to himself both arrogantly and humorously. Not that he was God's gift to women, but women didn't seem to know that. Jill herself had swooned at him time and again. But that was before she had done a 180, running awkwardly hot then cold. If she had met the accountant version of Carter, well, that put things into perspective. Women *might* be crazy, but they were nothing if not *consistent.*

"He sounds extremely, extremely attractive," he teased.

"Someone's hungry for a compliment."

Hungry in general better described Carter's current state.

"Okay, I did lift prints from the dog bowl."

"You did?" he asked eagerly, immediately straining to see her computer screen, not that he would be able to make sense of it.

Obligingly, she angled the screen at him then said, "One set belonged to your Vic, Kayla Samuels, and the other was only a partial." The partial print was what filled the screen. "There's no sense in running it," she informed him. "It's not enough."

Unwilling to dwell on setbacks, he asked, "The tee shirt, any DNA?"

"That hasn't come back yet," she told him, cautiously optimistic that it would lift his fallen mood. He hadn't meant to sink, but Carter had never been great with masking his emotions. "I'll let you know what the lab techs come back with."

"You have my cell?"

"Why, Mr. Dobbs, I memorized your number long ago."

"Hey now, don't make four-eyes jealous," he warned.

Jill let out a telling, little feminine sigh and complained, "I wish I could."

Before she could launch into a series of dating-Mr.-doppelganger anecdotes meant to solicit Carter's masculine take on what he could only imagine was her somewhat disappointing sex life with the accountant, he gave her the one piece of advice he was certain was true:

"Jealousy is rarely a good thing."

"You think?"

"Don't push a man's jealous side, and don't get jealous yourself, trust me."

Jill twisted her mouth to the side and showed no signs of pulling out of her sudden and deep contemplation.

So, he thanked her, slowly backed away, and told her to call as soon as she had something.

He had to get back to his jealous wife…

…who he planned on having 'hot and heavy' sex with for as long as the kids were in school.

Chapter Five

HE STILL FELT the need to wash blood off of himself even though not a single drop had touched him.

It had been days, but the feeling had persisted.

Their blood had been black, tarnished, *diseased*.

Despicable. The essence of who they were.

He couldn't get the shower hot enough. He adjusted the dial once again, steam like thick clouds billowed up all around him, opening his pores, but still he felt unclean.

Taking the same bar of soap that he had just scrubbed every inch of himself with, he began the meticulous routine all over again, as scalding hot water pounded on his chest.

The dark Brooklyn night beyond the narrow bathroom window reminded him there wasn't much time.

He had never orchestrated and executed such a masterpiece—a double murder.

He had experimented with the drug, of course, tested it on seedy characters and good Samaritan-types alike, exploring their willingness, their reluctances, and how to bridge the gap to his advantage.

But those little tests had been benign. Why *wouldn't* a person buy him a pack of cigarettes? So simple. No moral complications.

Over the months, his little mind-control experiments had gotten bigger—could he succeed at suggesting that he and his victim take a nice walk to the ATM? *Let's withdraw $500, that's good. Now, hand it to me, you've done very well…*

Like an eager child, each of his victims had aimed to please, and most of them, once the effects of the drug had worn off, hadn't remembered a thing.

As he had executed more and more tests, building his confidence in both the reliability of the drug and his own talents for using kindness, praise, and assertion to shepherd his victims into doing exactly what he wanted, he had also done his homework on Andre Durant.

Men like Andre had to be exterminated.

What he hadn't foreseen when he had picked Andre Durant was the man's involvement with Kayla.

At first, he had researched Andre. He had stalked him, learning all he could. During this investigation of Andre, he had determined, beyond a shadow of a doubt, that the world would be a better place without Andre Durant. With Andre dead, balance would be restored to the earth.

But again, he hadn't foreseen the Kayla aspect.

From what he had learned about her, the woman was even worse than Andre.

It was one thing to sell your own body to get high, to get your drug-addled boyfriend floating off into the same dark dream with you.

It was quite another to sell the innocent flesh of a child.

Evil.

He felt his jaw clench. His breathing had turned rapid and shallow. He swallowed hard, turned off the water, and stepped out of the shower, allowing the chilly air against his hot skin to anchor him back to the present.

Away from the perfect murder.

Away from the innocent child he had saved, the one he had done it all for, the one who's soulful eyes had, in their misery, in their silent strength, begged him to make the world a safe place.

Away from his own dark past and torturous memories that the girl in the dog crate whom he had rescued a day ago—those sad Cheerios she had been pushing around—had reminded him of.

Of *him*.

The pocket watch.

Its slow turning crank.

Don't keep him waiting.

The decades-old memories refused to die, and these constant reminders, these children all around Brooklyn with their pleading eyes and haunting secrets…

Maybe if he saved enough of them…

Killing the junkies had given him a taste. Incredible power. He couldn't wait to find the next one.

But for now, it was time to toy with his little pet.

He dressed in tailored wool slacks, having retired the metallic G-Star Raw jeans until his next foray into the projects.

Instead of putting on a button-down shirt that would make him feel like he was going to the office, he pulled on a gray knit sweater then slipped his feet into a pair of loafers.

The bedroom blinds were drawn so he corrected the error and returned to the full-length mirror. The dresser beside it was where he had left his glasses so, giving himself the once-over from where he stood at the foot of a contemporary, queen-sized bed—the bedroom itself was furnished with a modern, minimalist style—he placed his glasses on his face.

Horn-rimmed.

He was still getting used to them.

But the plucky, blonde woman he had begun dating seemed to like them.

With her in mind, he opened the bottom dresser drawer and eyed his stash.

Scopolamine.

The drug didn't always have to be smoked. As a liquid, it could be dropped into a cocktail, and at a small enough quantity, Jill *would* remember, which was how he wanted it.

Leaving her with a huge hole in her memory would backfire terribly.

But that didn't mean he wouldn't be able to get her to play one of his games.

He loved games.

He truly was a kid at heart.

Chapter Six

IT WAS BOUND to happen sooner or later.

The pessimist in her had been warning her.

Ever since she had threatened her mother to stay out of her life for good, Danny had feared her mother would test the boundary.

As Danny walked along Ocean Parkway, a bag of warm bagels in one hand and a tray of coffee in the other, she squinted through the morning glare and saw her mother.

There was Nora, on the stoop of her own brownstone, which was exactly one door down from Danny's.

Nora seemed to be sweeping the stoop, not that it was her job, and futzing around the potted plants.

If her mother was good for anything, it was pushing her luck, and Danny could only assume this wasn't a coincidence.

Nora could've easily spied her daughter on the street from her bedroom window when Danny had started off down the sidewalk, having left Tommy in her bed in favor of grabbing breakfast. It was Danny's day off from the 66th after all.

As Danny rounded towards her own building, she kept her eyes down to avoid her mother. She hated that she could feel her own face growing long and her mouth tightening, every part of her shutting down as if that alone would ward off her unwelcomed mother.

She had been naïve to think so.

Feeling eyes on her and only having a split second to decide between engaging in a confrontation or attempting to ignore the older woman, she went with the former and barked, "You're pushing it."

"I'm just tidying up out here," said Nora defensively, dressed in her signature cardigan and khaki pants, her hair styled sensibly, her nails short and manicured, nothing flashy about the seemingly sweet old woman.

Nora lifted the broom in her hand as proof of her innocence.

Danny couldn't believe the woman compensated her social security checks by *babysitting*.

Underneath it all, she was a monster.

So, then why was Danny lingering, risking the coffee getting cold?

Stammering for some kind of concluding retort was why she had stopped just shy of her building's entrance, Nora's sad, expectant eyes still in view. But was that the real reason?

Pleadingly, Nora clutched her broom against her heart and said, "I miss you, Danny. I never meant for—"

"Don't."

Biting her tongue didn't last. "You're my whole world, Danielle, I can't—"

"Ma, don't!"

Emotion had edged too strongly into her tone, and she didn't want to get trapped in the realization that she missed Nora as well. It was as though her heart and mind had somehow completely divorced from each other.

Compartmentalized in her broken heart was the tight-knit, intimate history she had with her mother—the aspects she missed, the ones that had left a hole in her life. But her mind was poisoned with the fact that Nora had tried to sabotage Danny's relationship with Tommy and taken Gregory's life.

All the while, Nora had played the role of the compassionate, supportive mother.

It had been sick, and yet in her weaker moments, like this one, the horror of it all seemed to slip through her fingers.

She could barely grasp it.

All she could think and feel was *loss...* but for who?

For which one?

Her son or her mother who had killed him?

It was all too dark and confusing to reconcile.

"I think we can get past this," Nora said softly, having wedged herself between a potted plant and the railing to keep Danny in her sightlines.

Fortifying herself, she said, "Nothing has changed. Stay away from me."

She hadn't been able to look her mother in the eye, but her tone had been firm, and with that she shouldered her way into her building where the super, Camil, was working on another fluorescent bulb.

He grunted a greeting, but she wasn't paying attention.

It was supposed to be her day off, but the second she got back to Tommy, who was sitting up in bed, groggily checking the time and yawning, she felt the chest-tightening clamp of knowing she couldn't face him. Not hot on the heels of having spoken with Nora.

"I thought you ditched me for the precinct," he said intuitively through a crooked grin, his tone deep and raspy with sleep.

"Bagels and coffee," she said, deflecting.

As she set both on the nightstand nearest him and wriggled out of her jacket, he must have noticed her off-balance mood, or maybe it was the holstered gun at her hip, because his easy grin dropped and he asked, "You're not thinking of going in on your day off, are you?"

"Would you hate me?"

"I could never hate you," he promised.

If only that were true.

Showing him that she wasn't in any kind of big rush—at the very least she needed to give Nora time to tuck herself back into that cluttered, hoarder's apartment she called a home so that there would be no danger of encountering her a second time—she handed him one of the coffees and began drinking her own.

She hadn't caught a case yesterday, which meant the likelihood of one rolling in today would only increase, but that wasn't the main reason she was leaning towards making an excuse of 'the Nora ambush' to get to the 66th.

She felt most like herself at SVU even if there was a lag between cases and her day amounted to filing paperwork and commiserating over the lack of vending machine options. It was where she recalibrated and rejuvenated herself.

Why couldn't she do that with the dreamy man who was drinking coffee, bedraggled and sexy as sin, in her bed?

Guilt.

Merciless, gnawing guilt.

She ate quickly, told him she wouldn't be long though in the back of her mind she was already doing the math on when he would have to leave for the bar. If she got back an hour prior, there would be just enough time to do the one thing she constantly craved—spreading her legs for him—with no added room for conversation.

So, preparing to head out, she invited him to stay as long as he liked, threw their empty cups and bagel wrappers in the trash, and left him in favor of walking to the 66th.

When she reached her desk, it was a little before 8:00am, which explained why Carter had yet to arrive. In-between cases, detectives could easily roll in at nine or sometimes as late as ten if they kept their pagers close and their cell phones closer.

The floor was quiet as she booted up her computer and checked her voicemail messages. There was nothing pressing, so she erased the messages and opened up her email.

The lieutenant had yet to arrive as well, which she felt a momentary twinge of relief over. Ever since she had lost the baby because of what Franco and the rest of SVU had believed had been SIDS, he had more or less given her a hard time about working unnecessarily long hours, coming in on her days off, and otherwise refusing to relax in favor of letting her partner handle things solo for once.

There was one email of interest. It jumped right out at her. It was from Vince Tenenbaum in the Cyber Crimes Unit—subject line: Durant Hard Drives.

When she opened the email, which came with a zipped file attached, she noticed right away that she had only been CC'ed on it. It was addressed to Carter.

"Productive day off?" she murmured to herself, leaning in to read Vince's note in the body of the email.

Since Vince's department was now handling any criminal activity that might be discovered on Durant's hard drives, should it incriminate any of the guy's living associates, Danny knew there was no way Vince had sent these files over in some kind of administrative error.

The body of the email simply read—*Gonna let me know why you requested these? Vince.*

"Gonna let your *partner* know?" she tacked on, under her breath, as she double-clicked the zipped file to open it. "I should've guessed."

Filling her computer screen was a blown-up photo of Kayla Samuels, strung up in the usual BDSM fair. She appeared fuzzy in the foreground, courtesy of Vince, who had zoomed in and cropped the image to maximize the background. Specifically, the dog crate.

Danny took a moment to scrutinize the photo and determined it had been taken in Kayla's bedroom. The dog crate shadowed in the closet behind her was definitely the same one they had found at the scene.

Rather than right Carter off as preoccupied with some baseless obsession, she studied the photo then opened the next. The same dog crate. She zoomed in on the dog bowl inside. The bowl was filled to the brim with what appeared to be Cheerios. The crate itself, empty of any inhabitants.

That didn't soften the unsettling feeling that had begun churning in her stomach.

"Damn," she breathed, putting two and two together. "Cheerios? Where's the kid?"

She startled at the loud sound of Carter's desk phone ringing.

As it continued to ring, she clicked through more photos—Vince had sent a total of six. She fell into deep contemplation.

Was it possible?

Did Kayla have a kid they didn't know about? It hadn't come up when they ran a background check, but that didn't mean she hadn't taken on raising someone else's child. Or worse. Could she have abducted someone? Could Andre have?

Going from Cheerios in a dog bowl to presuming a child had been abducted was one hell of a stretch, even for Danny who had never shied away from working every theory, no matter how outlandish, through to its furthest conclusion, if only in her head.

Carter's phone began ringing again, startling her just the same.

Had he set the volume to max or something?

On her feet, she leaned over his desk to see about lowering the ring volume, and that's when she caught sight of the caller's number. It was coming from upstairs.

He already had at least one voice message as indicated by the flashing red light and, moments after the caller gave up, the number of messages on the console increased from two to three.

Danny hadn't asked for anything upstairs, and if memory served her, neither had Carter when they had worked together last…

What have you been up to, Detective Dobbs? she wondered, adjusting the ring volume down then settling into her chair to resume pouring over the dog crate photos.

She had barely gotten situated when his phone began blaring all over again. Someone from upstairs was trying to get through.

She answered her partner's desk phone impulsively and barked at whoever was being so persistent, "He has a cell phone, you know."

"He wasn't picking that one up either," said Cruz, one of the uniformed officers from the second floor. "Detective Foster?"

"That's who you're speaking to," she confirmed. "What's up?"

"Carter asked me to run a cell phone number. I've got the info."

Just then, Franco breezed onto the floor and started through the bullpen.

It wasn't until Danny found herself hunching in response that she realized she was probably doing something wrong.

A creature of habit, Franco took a detour into the break room to fix himself a cup of coffee, giving her just enough time to tell Officer Cruz that she would be up in one second.

After hanging up and putting her computer to sleep, her eyes cutting time and again to the break room in anticipation of Franco catching her here on her day off, she padded swiftly and soundlessly to the stairwell stairs, and found Officer Cruz on the second floor behind the front counter with sheets of what she could only assume were cell phone records in his hands.

"Carter's not in?" Cruz asked apprehensively.

The guy was no shrinking violet and apprehension wasn't in his DNA. But the last time he had stood in Carter's way—through no fault of his own—the detective had nearly reached across the counter and throttled him.

"Not yet," she told him before promising, "I'll get everything to him the second he's in."

"Because I know he's going to want to see this first hand," he hesitated.

Bulldozing right through his concern, she asked, "What have you got for me? Hustle up."

Cruz froze, hesitated, then decided Danielle Foster was just as formidable.

"It's the 347 number, who Detective Dobbs referred to as 'Raffi' when he called to check in."

"Raffi?" she asked, making sure she had that right, as she found her pocket-sized notebook and jotted the street name down.

"The cell phone account is held by one—" He paused to read the sheet, then recited, "Raffael Sanzio."

Danny jotted this down, taking hold of the paper, which was not the man's cell phone records but merely a one-sheet on the guy, then confirmed what she had just noticed, "Home address, employment history, it's all there?"

Cruz shot her an affirmative nod. "I did manage to get the GPS tracking on it and have an exact location for—"

"You forgot to invite me?"

Carter's voice boomed as he came up behind her, and Cruz turned white as a ghost.

She turned to face her clearly annoyed partner, who was doing a soldierly job of trying not to seem that way—Carter didn't do 'jovial' except for poorly.

Danny immediately began defending the officer.

"He tried to get ahold of you."

"Yeah," said Carter, indicating his cell phone. "I got the message."

"I did, too," she winced, as she confessed, "your desk phone rang and…" Shrugging, she tried to change the subject by asking, "Who's Raffi?"

"That's what I'd like to know," he said, his tight brown eyes staring daggers at Cruz who had smartly shied away. "Aren't you supposed to be taking the day off?"

"I had some personal stuff," she replied as vaguely as humanly possible.

Carter's accusatory mood shifted and a wry smile threatened to soften his hardened expression.

"When I have personal stuff, I take a day or afternoon off. When you have personal stuff, you come in and hunt down someone else's lead?"

"I'm a complicated person." She held his gaze, Officer Cruz waiting in the wings, then mentioned, "Tenenbaum sent an interesting email."

"You did not seriously go through my emails. Answering my phone, reading my mail—"

"Relax, he sent it to both of us," she interrupted even though he had only been teasing.

"I suppose you want me to fill you in."

"It would be nice. Let's start with why you requested GPS tracking on Raffael Sanzio."

"That's his name?" Carter asked, finally pulling Officer Cruz back into the conversation. "Is he in the Kensington Projects? That's where he lives?"

Cruz handed over the sheet, and as Carter skimmed it, he explained, "The GPS location has been stationary for days."

"Yeah?" said Carter with interest. "Where?"

Cruz slid his worried eyes from one detective to the other and said, "The Waste Management Recycling plant in the Gowanus."

The Gowanus was a thin, mangy strip of Brooklyn, significantly west of Kensington. Its streets were a complicated and often truncated grid of side roads thanks to the many canals that cut through that section. The area had been turning over as the years had gone by, from industrial to slightly residential, but on the East River side where waste management was located the streets were primarily warehouses and recycling plants.

"Days?" Danny questioned. No one stayed put in one place for days. "Please tell me he works there."

Carter shifted his attention from the one-sheet on Raffael Sanzio to Danny and answered on Cruz's behalf. "He doesn't. Something tells me we're not going to find the guy alive."

"Carter," she said, speaking low and turning her shoulder to exclude Cruz. "How are we supposed to justify an excursion to the Gowanus to the lieutenant? We're supposed to be sitting tight and waiting for our next case."

"This could be it."

She shook her head, "Unless we find Raffi sexually assaulted—"

"Well, here's hoping."

"Carter," she warned.

"*We* don't have to justify anything," he told her, placing the one-sheet with the GPS location and all of Sanzio's information in her hand. "I'm on duty, you're not." As he started off for the stairs, he said over his shoulder, "Let me know what you find."

"So, your rogue investigation is now *my* rogue investigation, is that it?"

He didn't respond, but Danny didn't need him to. The thrilled grin tugging at the corner of her slanted mouth told her that she had absolutely no qualms about checking waste management out.

Anything to get Nora, Tommy, and her deceased infant son off her mind.

Chapter Seven

"SORRY, I FEEL a little out of it," said Jill as she sipped piping hot coffee that by all appearances had been doctored with generous amounts of cream and sugar. Her hair had leftover curls, but she clearly hadn't run a comb through it. Nor had she bothered with lipstick, eyeshadow, or any of the usual fare that she had recently adopted since meeting her 'sexy accountant.' "I didn't think I drank that much last night."

By Carter's estimation, she must have.

She had the distinct look—bags under the eyes, slumping shoulders, and an overall air of exhaustion—of someone who'd had a great time then suddenly realized the wine bottle was empty.

It had happened to his wife, Kathy, once or twice. No shame in it, except he was eager to get through Jill's autopsy report on Raffael "Raffi" Sanzio, who was lying under the white sheet that they were all standing around.

"Happens to the best of us," said Danny, eager as well.

A faraway look of confusion came over Jill, and she absentmindedly began buttoning her lab coat when it was clear she had meant to skim the contents of her findings.

"Maybe," she agreed in a small voice.

Danny's excursion to the Waste Management Recycling plant in the Gowanus to locate Raffi's cell phone had been fruitful—she had found one very dead Raffael Sanzio attached. But the excursion hadn't necessarily been helpful, not yet.

Danny had called it in, as the recycling employees had looked on in abject horror at the dead, crumpled body that had been brutally compressed in a massive brick of recycled plastic. Over the phone, she had reluctantly admitted to Franco that at first blush, *no this was not a sex crime,* and Franco had had no choice but to kick the case up the chain of command where the captain assigned it to Homicide.

It was possible that Raffi's murder had nothing to do with Kayla and Andre's.

Possible.

But in Carter's mind, it was unlikely.

To him, it was obvious that all three murders were connected, which meant that Kayla and Andre might *not* have been a murder-suicide.

Jill knew it wasn't their case, and though she really wasn't supposed to walk them through every detail of her autopsy findings, Danny had convinced her to take the risk. She had agreed, but on the condition that the detectives swing by first thing in the morning and well in advance of the homicide detectives who she was scheduled to meet with at nine.

But now Jill was moving as slow as molasses, willing her tired eyes to see properly, her every movement a sign of lost dexterity.

"I am *not* myself today," she commented as if shocked before making a concerted effort to choke down the rest of her coffee. She widened her eyes a few times, took a deep and—from where Carter was standing—fortifying breath, then with gloved hands began rolling the white sheet back.

"He might not be easy to look at," she warned. "He was crushed pretty badly."

Danny shot Carter a *you-better-believe-it* glance, as if she too was still haunted by the image of how she had found the dead man at the dump.

What Carter noticed first when Raffi's entire body was exposed, was that he no longer looked human.

A lump of pulverized flesh.

"Damn."

A grim look came over Jill, her dainty eyebrows drifting up to her blonde, mussed hairline, as she told him, "Yeah."

Danny had a cursory understanding that Raffi was Kayla and Andre's drug dealer, but Carter hadn't yet gone over his working theory with her, that there was a killer out there who had taken pleasure in orchestrating the horrific murders of the junky couple, who he wouldn't have necessarily had access to, had he not taken Raffi out first.

"Any signs of… anything? Any clue as to who might have done this?" asked Danny, who was trying to wrap her head around how Raffi had met his fate.

"Give me a break, Danny, he's a friggin casserole," said Jill, as she made her way to her computer. The detectives trailed along. "I *am* a genius, however, so I did find a possible link between the two cases."

Carter felt his pulse rate starting to pound hard—the two cases they had been robbed of, the ones he knew in his gut were connected, not just by a killer's madness, but also involving a child.

A child so like Carter had once been that it made his teeth ache knowing he couldn't yet prove that this woven tapestry of murder centered on a 'special victim'—a little boy or girl.

"The bloodwork on Samuels and Durant came back," she went on, clicking into select files on her desktop. "They were methamphetamine addicts," she explained, not that this was new information to Carter.

He could've guessed as much judging the vast quantities of pipes and drug paraphernalia they had come across in Kayla's apartment.

"But…"

She trailed off from her point, taking a wobbly breath and again widening her eyes as if some kind of dizzy spell had threatened to come over her.

"You okay?" asked Danny.

"Yeah," she said confusedly. "I was out with Damian again and after a glass of wine, I decided to try a drink I've never had before. My electrolytes are probably off."

"Which means coffee isn't helping," Danny pointed out kindly.

"Right." Jill took another moment to fish through her purse, which she kept tucked in the bottom drawer of one of the stainless-steel tables that wrapped the perimeter of the morgue.

She found a bottle of water.

After downing as much water as her unsettled stomach would allow and apologizing profusely, she returned to her computer and picked up where she had left off.

"Because of the nature of the murder-suicide, the fact that Samuels was topless, the upper portion of her chest skinned along with her face…"

The reminder caused Carter's stomach to lurch.

"I did a general five-panel test on Samuels for your basic, run of the mill, date rape drugs," she told them.

Carter's interest was fully piqued.

"That panel came back clean, but," she paused, meeting each detective's gaze, "the basic five-panel is somewhat antiquated. New drugs are cropping up all the time, so I tested for one that hasn't been added to the panel even though it's been surfacing in certain cities over the course of the last four or five years."

She shifted her computer screen so they could see the single panel she was referring to. It was kind of her, but honest to God it might as well have been a Rorschach test as far as Carter was concerned. He could make just about as much sense out of it.

"Scopolamine," she informed them. "Both Samuels and Durant tested positive, and though I'm still learning about this drug, and I don't often see it in autopsies, they each had what I would call the maximum dose. Of course," she quickly revised her point, "that is my estimation *after metabolism*."

The gears in Danny's fast-working mind started to turn, and she held Carter's gaze, thinking. He was pondering as well, trying to mentally fit pieces together that might not necessarily go.

"They were dabbling in some brand-new date rape drug and…?" said Danny, prodding the medical examiner to give them a reason this wasn't a cut-and-dry, albeit disturbing, murder-suicide.

"I can't speculate on their motives," Jill reminded her. "I can only tell you that they both had high levels of the drug in their systems. Ordinarily," she went on and again reminded them that her speculations should not be taken as fact, "the drug is used to make the victim highly suggestible. That's what it's known for."

For the second time that day, Carter's heart lurched up his throat, punching hard with a sudden surge of adrenaline.

"In the US, the drug is actually prescribed for motion sickness, but the street date rape drug I'm referring to comes from Colombia in its purest form, derived directly from any tree in the Solanaceae family."

Whenever Jill got too technical or scientific, Danny reeled her back to the investigation at hand. "What's the appeal?"

"Volition," said Jill. "It's known as 'the zombie drug.' It removes the victim's free will. It's odorless, tasteless, and its effects kick in almost immediately whether it's drunk, smoked, or the powder is blown into the victim's face. Within seconds they're highly suggestable, almost forgetting who they are, and will do just about anything. Or, in Samuel and Durant's case…"

"They did do just about anything," Carter supplied.

"It appeals to a certain type of rapist," Jill concluded. "One who has delusions of consent. But in Bogota, the drug has been used to get people to empty their bank accounts, hand over the keys to their cars, and agree to all kinds of criminal activity they would never otherwise commit if they had remained in their right minds," she explained. "And often the victims have no memory of the entire ordeal, so the cases are very hard to prosecute."

"The zombie drug," Danny ruminated.

"Devil's Breath," Jill corrected. "That's its street name as far as New York City is concerned."

"And this links to Raffi, how?" asked Carter, needing to hear the medical examiner say it.

"I found high traces in his blood work, as well."

"So, someone drugs Raffi and gets him to leap head-first into a trash compactor?" Danny theorized. She cut her eyes to Carter. "How'd the killer get into the waste management plant, get out, go through with it if he didn't work there?"

Carter's knee-jerk response was that they would have to carefully comb through the surveillance footage as soon as the warrant they would obviously request came through, but just as he was about to tell her as much, he remembered the case wasn't theirs.

"If you're asking how predators generally coax their victims into doing whatever they want," Jill began, answering the detective's mostly rhetorical question, "there usually has to be a constant feeding of instructions since the actual memory and mental capacity of a victim high on scopolamine is extremely limited."

Danny had shifted into theorizing mode, and Carter was there as well, so in an effort to wrap up the meeting, he asked, "Anything else come up?"

"You betcha," she said, a mischievous grin spreading sideways across her face. She was perking up from whatever debauchery she had indulged in last night. "I found trace amounts of DNA on the pink tee shirt from the dog crate…"

Now Danny's interest was piqued, just as badly as Carter's had been, to hear how the mysterious dog crate might tie into all of this.

"I don't know who it belongs to, but it's definitely a familial match to Kayla Samuels."

Carter could've punched his fist victoriously into the air, he felt so validated. Instead, he thanked Jill with such emphasis that she let out a bubbly laugh and promised she would email over her findings—confidentially since the cases weren't theirs.

"Working theory?" Carter asked his partner ten minutes after leaving Kings County Hospital.

They had grabbed 'street meat' at a Greek Gyro truck stationed at the southern edge of Prospect Park. Danny was munching a falafel wrap and Carter ate a straight-up slab of beef that he had dipped in tzatziki sauce.

They were seated at one of the many picnic tables that lined this stretch of the park.

Danny wasn't prepared to answer him with a mouth full of falafel, and it wasn't until Carter had worked through a thick chunk of meat, barely chewing and choking it down whole, that he launched into the supposition he had been privately building.

"This is a child abduction case," he stated bluntly, which caused his partner's eyes to widen with intrigue and a gleam of apprehension.

"That's quite a leap."

"It's a working theory," he reminded her. "The killer, somehow—I don't know how—knows about some kid being kept in a dog crate."

He had to swallow hard to fight down a sudden swell of rage at how that kid had been treated. No one puts a child in a dog crate unless they completely devalue them. Pedophiles came to mind, and his jaw tightened even harder.

It wasn't until he told himself that similarities in this case to his own childhood did not automatically mean the purportedly missing child had been or was now suffering the same fate that he had growing up.

Danny was patient with him, perhaps sensing how this case had struck a nerve.

"So, he wants to take the kid," he went on. "Don't know for what reason, whether it's genuine concern for the child's welfare or nefarious, but he knows he can't get into that apartment. Which means—"

"The killer didn't know Kayla and Andre personally," she supplied. "So, how did he even know there was a kid in a dog crate?"

Carter sawed off another hunk of meat, not that he had the appetite for it.

"Rumors float through those corridors," he postulated. "Kayla had been developing a reputation for quite some time. It wasn't hard for *me* to get one of Andre's neighbors talking, and he had a lot to say about Kayla, I might add. Point being," he went on, pushing his plate of saucy meat aside and wiping his fingers with a napkin, not that he had made much of a mess. The plastic fork and knife had saved him in that department. "The killer decides he has to kill

Raffi in order to get into the apartment, and that he has to kill Kayla and Andre in order to take the kid."

"If there is a kid, Carter."

He knew exactly where she was going with this, but she was dead wrong.

"Of course, there's a kid. There's a familial DNA match on that ratty tee shirt."

"You know what Franco's going to say?"

"Yeah, I do," he shot back. "And I also know Kayla had no siblings, no kids, and I don't know what to say except that… hell, she could've had a bathroom labor, never went to the hospital because she's a crank-head, kept the kid off the record in that respect. DNA doesn't lie."

"I'll give you that," she agreed, as she consolidated their plates and trash. "And I don't want to begin to imagine why a kid or anyone would be kept in a dog crate."

Carter leaned in, searching Danny's big brown eyes, as a crisp breeze rustled through the park.

"What's happening to that kid right now? There's a kid, Danny," he insisted when once again her expression had shifted from empathetic to doubtful.

"It's not our case, Carter."

"We have to relay all of this to Franco," he pushed. "We're no longer dealing with a murder-suicide, that closed case just got opened, and someone's got to tell Homicide that their Sanzio case is linked to another. It might not get us the triple-homicide case, but we can't keep this to ourselves."

"The presence of Devil's Breath in all three Vics could be coincidental. It doesn't mean the same killer did all three."

"Stop lying to yourself."

She sucked in a deep breath and stared out across the park. The look of tired dread that came over her was confirmation enough that she agreed. Then her expression shifted abruptly again, her brown eyes narrowing into a squint of recognition at someone in the distance, as a quirky smile crept onto her face.

"Is that Kathy?" she asked.

Glancing over his shoulder, vaguely aware it was a little after three in the afternoon, he saw his wife with their two boys, Christopher—nearly towering over his mother, wearing a football uniform, tight and shiny—and little Matty, dressed in his practice outfit, baseball mitt in hand, out of breath as ever, as they approached.

Kathy gave a wave meant to stop Carter from taking off with his partner, not that he would do such a thing after spotting his wife. He was already on his feet.

"I'm going to say 'hi' to these guys," he told Danny, who was also on her feet, ready to dispose of the trash she had consolidated. "You haven't met my kids, have you?"

"Nope," she said with a smile, tossing the trash into a nearby waste bin before joining him. "Is this the whole 'fam'?"

As they started off across the grass, his gaze locked with Kathy's, it wasn't lost on him that his wife's easy expression was quickly hardening at the sight of Danny by his side.

"My oldest, Amanda, must be at her dance class. Kathy usually drops her off then takes the boys to their respective practices."

Last month, Kathy had had her suspicions about Danny and her motives for working long hours with Carter. Those suspicions had been easily dispelled, but there was some lingering resentment there, jealousy. If Kathy had her way, Carter would not have been assigned to work with a female partner.

"God, he looks exactly like you," she commented good-naturedly, referring to his older son, as they approached his blonde bombshell of a wife.

Carter boomed out a laugh. "Somehow Matty got the 'White' gene, but we don't hold it against him," he joshed, trying to see his sons through Danny's eyes—Christopher's dark complexion versus Matty's remarkably lighter shade.

"Hi kids," said Danny, beaming a smile down at each of them though Christopher was almost her height. She said to Kathy warmly, "It's nice seeing you."

"Likewise," Kathy said coolly before glaring at Carter.

He wondered what he had done this time, and how long he would have to pin her between the sheets before she would forgive him.

Without letting any lulls pass, Carter introduced Danny to Christopher, who promptly shook her hand, and Matty, whose reaction was the opposite. He seemed to shrink in the presence of strangers and had difficulty making eye contact.

"This is my partner, Detective Danielle Foster, but it's not a *crime* to call her 'Danny'."

"God, Dad," Christopher rolled his eyes at his father's corny sense of humor.

"Matty's got another game coming up," Carter mentioned conversationally.

"Saturday!" his son enthused, punching his flimsy fist into his baseball mitt.

Carter laughed and rubbed his son's ballcapped head, as Danny made small talk with him about how she used to be bad at T-ball growing up. As a kid, she never went on to play softball.

Though the conversation was one-sided, Matty shyly smiled up at her when he wasn't glancing at his mom for encouragement to interact. Danny faithfully kept the conversational ball in the air, so-to-speak, and included Christopher when she could. But none of this endeared Kathy to her.

"Hey," he turned to Danny, "could you give us a minute?"

"Sure," she said easily. "Nice meeting you guys. Nice seeing you, Kathy."

"Hmph," was his wife's tight-lipped reply.

"Have fun at your game on Saturday," she told Matty before starting off for their Crown Vic that was parked along the sidewalk where the Greek Gyro truck continued to serve greasy, late lunch to a long line of customers.

Stepping in, Carter gave his wife a kiss on the cheek, and Christopher screwed his face up and diverted his eyes, the very concept of his parents' affection thoroughly offensive. Matty was unfazed.

The sparkle returned to Kathy's blue eyes. "It was fun running into you here."

"Yeah?"

"Do you guys have lunch together often?"

Here it came.

"Only when we're on the go," he assured her before quickly changing the subject and addressing the kids. "Hey, I was thinking about taking you guys to the Cheesecake Factory tonight."

Matty cheered, and his older son, Christopher was thrilled, "Yeah, that would be the best!"

Their excitement was short-lived thanks to Kathy. She shot him a pinched frown and reminded him, "We have that *appointment…* remember?"

"Appointment?"

The kids started chanting, "Burgers and milkshakes and chee-eese cake!" oblivious to the silent tension rising between their parents.

Kathy widened her eyes as though pantomiming would jar his memory. "The *appointment* we go to every week, together…" she hinted.

Oh, therapy…

"Right," he said, catching on. "Well, couldn't we all go after?"

"Then the kids will get to bed too late," she countered. "How about another night?"

Matty did not like the sound of that and knowing his mother, he tried to nail her down by asking, "What night? Tomorrow night? When?"

Kathy's sharp, parental response was, "We'll discuss it later. Come on, you've both got homework, and I don't want to keep Amanda waiting at that musty, old dance studio. I'm convinced it's making her asthma worse."

"Bye, Dad!" Matty sang, throwing his arms around Carter.

He squeezed him tightly in response, while Christopher groaned about what a girl his younger brother was, an insult that prompted Matty to take a swing at him.

"Boys!" Kathy barked when it seemed an all-out brawl might ensue, for which Matty—as always—would come out on the losing end.

"Later kids!" he called out, as they jogged off towards the trail that would spit them out on the right side of the park to get home. When he turned to Kathy, she was stepping in close and the critical glint in her eye had been replaced with gleaming affection.

"I'm wound up a little tight, if you couldn't tell," she breathed into his ear, sending a lightning bolt of arousal through him.

"Yoga didn't do it for ya?" he played along.

Her expression was kittenish as she searched his eyes and shook her head, 'nope.'

"We could always skip therapy?" he proposed.

"We could always pay the babysitter to take the kids out for an extra hour when we get back...?" she countered.

Ordinarily, the idea of romancing his wife after he had dredged up disturbing childhood issues for their therapist to analyze sounded awful. But lately Kathy had been running so hot and cold with him that the only way to get her into a good mood was to make love to her pretty much whenever she hinted or, as the case currently was, boldly demanded it.

"Sounds like a plan," he growled in her ear, having pulled her close. He tipped her chin up and gave her a soft kiss. He had never gotten sick of the way Kathy melted into him like this. He didn't want to have to let her go. It was a very long moment before he released her and said, "I'll see you tonight."

"Be safe."

"I couldn't be further from harm's way if I tried," he assured her then after one more affectionate peck he started off for the Crown Vic where Danny had been leaning and enjoying the clear skies and warm day.

The short afternoon hours had a way of disappearing into biting darkness without warning.

"Ready?" she asked as soon as he returned.

She tossed him the car keys and eight minutes later they were back at the 66th, trapped under the weight of making their case to Lieutenant Franco in his airless office, while the lieutenant ruthlessly combatted their theory at every turn.

When Danny had played devil's advocate in the park, Carter should've heeded it as a warning and stepped up his argumentative game to practice.

This was no trial run, and Franco had his fists planted on his hips as he paced the narrow space behind his desk, not liking what he was hearing—*a triple homicide? a child neither detective could prove was out there? a calculated killer using mind-control drugs?* Franco had a logical explanation for every one of Carter's 'outlandish' suppositions.

This was brutal.

"Talk to the M.E.!" Carter insisted, raising his voice from where he sat beside Danny on the chairs across from Franco's cluttered desk. "Jill Andover can confirm that Durant did not kill Samuels of his own volition!"

"No, she can't," he shot back, his dark eyes fiery. "She can only confirm the presence of what you've been calling 'Devil's Breath'—"

"Scopolamine," he corrected.

"—in both the Vics' systems," Franco said, plowing right through Carter's objection. "That doesn't rule out murder-suicide, which Andover herself confirmed with hard evidence. Only Durant's prints were on the knife that first skinned Samuels. And then he slit his own throat."

"Because of the—"

"Mind control drug?" Franco snorted. "It can't be proven. Jill's team found no evidence that anyone else was even there."

"She found DNA on the tee shirt in the dog crate," Carter reminded him like a horse that had already been beaten within an inch of its life but stubbornly refused to die. "A familial match."

"You want to circle the drain and talk to the parents again?" the lieutenant challenged. "You want to ask them point blank if there was a grandkid they didn't know about? Think about what those people have been through."

Danny piped up with the voice of reason, but from where Carter was sitting, it sounded an awful lot like betrayal.

"The Lieutenant's right. We got nothing."

"And," Franco added, "Homicide is on the one active case that exists—Raffael Sanzio."

"I'm not wrong about this," he warned.

Franco held his gaze, the older man's eyes were no longer fiery but filled with compassion, which was how Carter knew the lieutenant's hands were tied.

Carter knew it and accepted it, but didn't like it.

He didn't wait to be excused, either.

Danny followed him back to their desks. The concept of sitting in front of his computer for another two hours and waiting for a fresh case felt all kinds of wrong, but begrudgingly he did just that.

As the hours wore on, the detectives shared silent moments of exasperation at times. Carter brooded, and Danny shook her head, a helpless glint filling her naturally sad-looking eyes.

Later, when Danny was somewhere in the break room, bonding with another SVU detective, Carter collected his suit jacket from the back of his chair, ready to clock out for the evening.

As he walked across the bullpen to leave, he dreaded the marriage counseling appointment he had agreed to, yet looked forward to spending time with Kathy afterwards.

Deep in thought, he didn't notice Officer Cruz approaching him until Cruz thrust a glossy 5"x8" photograph into his face.

"Caught you a fresh one," said Cruz. "This just came in, sent anonymously."

Carter froze, staring at the photo.

That wasn't a 'fresh one.'

Carter studied the photograph of a scared-looking Black girl. She was maybe five or six years old. She reminded Carter of a porcelain doll the way she was posed, but she wasn't wearing the usual pink taffeta that dolls do.

When he understood what the little girl was wearing, he immediately realized the significance.

One of the mannequins that he had seen in Kayla Samuels' bedroom instantly sprang to mind.

The girl in the photo was dressed up to look exactly like a professional dancer turned BDSM slave. Just like Kayla Samuels had in all those photos on her bedroom walls.

A shimmering coin halter-top was strung tightly around the little girl's flat chest, she wore a headdress to match, golden jewelry and bangles adorning her skinny limbs. Long chiffon skirt, a royal blue color, hanging to her ankles, as she cowered in the bright and unforgiving camera flash.

Carter could feel in his bones that this was the child who had been kept in a dog crate for reasons only God knew.

And if Carter's gut wasn't dead-on, the collaged caption pasted across the back of the photo was proof positive:

"The sins of the fathers shall be visited upon the sons."

Chapter Eight

DAMIAN WAS IMBUED with a sense of God-like power. He felt electric on a cellular level, his clarity of mind razor sharp, the blood in his veins zinging with life. Every breath, each punch of glorious oxygen in his lungs, brought him higher and higher—naturally so—as he absorbed the rich magnitude of his infallible influence.

He wasn't *like* God.

He *was* God.

And just as God could be found in all living things, so too could Damian be found in Jill Andover. Her mind was no longer her own, and her body belonged to him as well.

She swayed beside him with the rhythm of the taxi cab, happily staring out the window, as their driver navigated swiftly over the Brooklyn Bridge.

The night vista was classic. The bridge twinkled with lights. Manhattan was a glittering glow on the other side of the river, the dark dome sky overhead, black as hell, but oh so beautiful.

He had wine-and-dined her at one of Manhattan's finest steakhouses. When she had excused herself to the ladies room after dinner, he had ordered another round of Merlot, doused it with a pinch of Devil's Breath, and felt an indescribable sense of glee when she returned.

She had *thanked* him—*of all things!*—for having ordered another round. She had brought the red wine to her lips and had savored each lusty gulp, falling easily into the same spell he had been casting over her, to a stronger and stronger degree, all week.

The porcelain complexion of her thigh was momentarily illuminated by a flash of lamplight, as their driver maneuvered the taxi off the bridge and came to a brief stop.

Her purple dress had slipped up more and more with every bump and bend in their journey, unbeknownst to Jill, who was floating somewhere beyond her body, feeling elated, and most importantly, feeling *willing* now that she was free from her own free will.

The paradox aroused him.

He couldn't help himself. He had to wrap his large hand around that thigh of hers and feel her firm flesh.

She responded not at all to his squeeze.

Perfect.

"You like it when I touch you like this, don't you?" he coaxed.

"Yes," she said without hesitation or personality, the smile on her face the sole indication that on some level she *was* enjoying herself.

This time he had given her enough of a dose that she wouldn't remember what would soon transpire. He could easily mask it by offering her more wine at his place, so that her last memories would be of drinking past her limit. Her mind, and logic itself, would provide all the explanations she would need tomorrow when the mystery of the blackout would finally begin to dawn on her. She would be bewildered and perhaps self-blaming.

Imagining her scratching her head tomorrow and promising herself never to drink so much again in the future made Damian stiffen hard in his slacks.

Women were so silly, so useless.

But men were worse, like monsters, the wolves of our society in sheep's clothing. Why did innocence evaporate with age? Why couldn't we all remain children forever?

Damian couldn't figure it out, all he knew was that it wasn't fair.

And for those, like him, who had grown up trapped in a loveless hell and raised by parasites who fed off of that innocence until there was nothing left… Well, the apple never fell far from the tree…

Could anyone blame Damian for having turned into a monster?

A devilish grin tugged at the corner of his mouth as he thought about what awaited him at his condo. The games he could play. The ways in which the puppet pet beside him might play along, too.

"You're coming home with me," he informed her, as he felt the dwindling drug in the inside pocket of his suit jacket. It was wrapped in plastic. He was running dangerously low, but estimated it would be enough to get Jill through the night. "Are you glad?"

"Yes," she repeated.

It was the only word she was capable of saying, *'yes,'* and it was beautiful.

He felt eyes on him and glanced at the rearview mirror to find their driver, an Indian man in a turban with black eyebrows, staring at him and Jill, perhaps finding something off about her robotic agreeability.

Mitigating the driver's budding suspicion, Damian adjusted his horn-rimmed glasses and said companionably, "I can always tell my girlfriend's had way too much to drink when her vocabulary is reduced to one word."

"Huh," the man grunted, not nearly as friendly as Damian would've expected.

He felt the blood harden in his veins and a sudden fantasy swept through him of drugging the Indian driver and suggesting that he skin his own face off...

But the Devil's Breath in his pocket was running far too low to waste on petty revenge.

He decided to let it slide, broke eye contact, and realized they were coming to his high-rise condo that sat on the western side of Prospect Park where views of both the park and surrounding city were worth every penny.

"It's up ahead on the left," he told the driver then he nudged Jill. She surfaced from her zombie-ecstasy and fought hard to pay attention. "Wouldn't you like to pay the taxi driver?"

"Yes," she breathed and fished her wallet out of her little, black purse with heavy hands.

He helped her with the cash then returned her wallet. It's not that he couldn't afford cab rides or steak dinners—which Jill had also been paying for—he just enjoyed commanding her to do whatever he desired.

After paying the taxi driver and helping Jill out of the cab, Damian cradled her with mock affection as they made their way into the handsome lobby of his luxury building. The doorman greeted them with polished smiles, and soon the scent of roses filled the air.

"Where am I?" asked Jill, as he helped her into his leather-furnished living room.

It wasn't a good sign. She shouldn't be asking anything. It meant she was lifting out of the heavy fog.

"My apartment," he said, remaining calm. "Remember, you asked to see it?"

Before she could answer, he scooped her tightly against the firm length of his body and pressed his lips roughly to hers. He could feel her melt into him, which was to be expected. She was attracted to him, after all. Had been from day one when they had met at that little coffee shop in-between the Kings County Hospital where she worked and his accounting firm where his staff of thirty accountants and bookkeepers continued to make him rich while they struggled with low-end wages.

"Wine?" he asked, as he held her close and searched her glazed-over blue eyes that were brightening with life by the second.

He hadn't bothered to clean up or hide his little scopolamine operation, and Lord knew he had a little girl in his office. The last thing he needed was for his pretty little date to sober up and discover either.

"Oh, I don't know," she declined.

"Jill!" he barked, using a domineering tone.

It snapped her into wide-eyed obedience.

"You *would* like another glass of wine."

She said nothing. No agreement. No objection.

He tested her, "Why don't you get the bottle? There's any number to choose from. There's a wine rack in my kitchen."

"I've—"

An objection?

"Ut-ut-uh," he warned.

It infuriated him, and it took every shred of patience he had not to show it.

Again, he pressed his lips to hers, and in a fit of mock-passion, he pulled her into the kitchen, kissing her all the while.

He left her with puffy lips and mussed hair—*wanting*—so that he could open a bottle of Shiraz and pour a single glass.

As he proceeded to do just that, she questioned whether this was a good idea.

"Hand me another glass," he ordered in a firm tone.

When Jill turned around to find a second glass, obeying him, he flicked the remaining white powder into her wine, shoved the plastic back into his suit pocket, and swirled the glass. It was then that it occurred to him that he had mixed in way too much.

To appease her, he poured himself a modest three ounces with the glass she had just provided, and without further ado, he proposed a toast right then and there in the kitchen.

"To the greatest adventure of all…" he said, lifting his glass to hers and watching her big blue eyes light up in anticipation of how he might finish his toast. "Love!"

"To love at first sight," she agreed, thrilled that they were falling in love.

His stomach turned at the possibility.

She drank three great big gulps, then leaned in and gave him a kiss.

Time for round two, he thought.

Her eyes were glazed over and her expression was vacant by the time he urged her back from their kiss.

Now *that*, he thought, drinking in the sight of her zombie stare, was arousing.

After testing her willingness to obey his every command with little requests, they made their way through the living room and into his bedroom.

Damian was confident she was ready to start playing his game, and that she would have no memory of it, or of *anything*.

"Do you like playing dress up?" he prodded.

Her answer was what he expected, *'yes,'* so he threw the doors of his walk-in closet open.

A set of mannequins stood inside, each donning a traditional Samba costume or belly dancer's ensemble that he had seen Kayla Samuels performing in, countless times. He had replicated them carefully before he had taken painstaking measures to sew miniature versions for the girl who should've never been kept in a dog crate.

The sins of the fathers shall be visited upon the sons…

Indeed…

Children paid for their parents' sins, he had accepted this long ago. It had been the only explanation for why God would've allowed him to suffer the horrors he had as a child. His parents—who he had never known—must have been truly atrocious. But once Damian had suffered those punishments, clearing the sins of his father and his mother, he had been blessed with fortune—with power—as unstoppable as it was glorious.

He had saved the little girl called Nahla, but the sins of her horrendous so-called mother had yet to be fully cleansed from her soul. Once they were, Nahla would be just as free as Damian.

This was his mission, his duty, and it wasn't meant to be orchestrated in a vacuum. It was meant to be played boldly upon the world's stage, for all sinners' eyes to see, so that no father would ever again sin without the fate of his son first crossing his mind.

Having instructed Jill to put on a traditional Samba outfit—a shockingly bright yellow headdress of wild feathers, a feather and beaded bikini to match, yellow fishnet stockings, and dangerously high-heels of the same canary-yellow color—he took leave of his bedroom and entered his office where sweet Nahla had been entertaining herself with cartoons and coloring books.

The little girl was seated on a fluffy, pink bed, his office having been transformed into a princess's playland.

In hindsight, and considering Jill was Caucasian and not Black like Nahla, maybe he shouldn't have slaughtered the junky…

But, he reasoned, he could still get the point across if he lit the photographs just so…

Unlike any given adult, Nahla and children in general never required the influence of drugs to demonstrate their willingness to please.

That's how Damian knew they were eager to clear their fathers' sins. No child wanted that weight on their head forever.

Nahla's smile went slack when she realized Damian had filled the doorway.

"It's time to play," he informed her, as a grin spread across his face.

She had been apprehensive about his games, but in the end, Nahla had always come around. Any game of his was better than eating broken Cheerios on her knees while locked in a dog crate.

It took some coaxing, but soon she cooperated, allowing him to dress her in a miniature replica of the Samba costume he had instructed Jill to put on. He was tempted to caress her, hold her close, and stroke her smooth young skin, absorb the vibration of her innocence, which would ultimately carry them both into a nude, lustful embrace—the only kind of lovemaking he was truly interested in.

Pure.

Sinless.

Perfect.

Women were so dirty, but children…

Oh, children were the light of God, *His* very essence embodied. Damian was ever thirsty to drink from that heavenly well, and with Nahla here, he could…

Every night.

He only had to remind her of the dog crate, the former cruel treatment, how he could return her there if that's what she really wanted, and any recoiling defiance was quickly replaced with hollow willingness.

He deserved it.

It was his reward for helping her clear those sins that Kayla had selfishly placed onto Nahla's head.

But before bonding with her in that special way, before orchestrating Jill's involvement in what would surely become a very eventful night in Damian's bedroom, he first had a wealth of photos he wanted to take.

So, he guided little Nahla, fully dressed in her Samba costume, into his bedroom where Jill had been waiting in a drug-haze.

Taking each of their hands, he brought them into a guest bedroom that he had transformed into a photography studio, having blacked the bay windows out. A white ream of paper hung from the ceiling to the floor like the professionals used.

As the night unfolded, Damian posing his beautiful pets in symbolic stances, ones that would become iconic, he hoped, he thought about the inner workings of Phase Two of his mastermind plan.

Teaching the world the Biblical lessons he had learned firsthand. He would continue to slip photographs to the police, each with their own message.

Soon those images would appear in the news, the media would sink their greedy teeth in, and Damian's method of cleansing children of their parents' sins would take the world by shocking storm.

"Hands on your hips, Jill."

She obeyed.

"Nahla, would you smile?"

The little girl certainly tried.

Very deep down, where he could barely feel it, Damian knew he was deranged.

Chapter Nine

"BUT YOU SAID *Andre Durant* killed my baby girl!" yelled Karen Samuels, who was the late Kayla Samuels' mother.

Karen was known as 'Queenie' to her friends and family.

Heartbroken and furious with Detective Danielle Foster, Queenie kept yelling and cursing, her tight dreadlocks swinging out from under a flamboyant Dhuku headscarf.

Her husband, Raja, captured Queenie and pulled her back down onto the African bench in their living room.

The African bench matched the rest of the decor, which contained a museums'-worth of traditional African art and artifacts.

Queenie and Raja directed almost none of their horror at Detective Carter Dobbs, but they didn't exactly consider him a hero.

Danny wondered if 'Raja' was the man's legal name since it meant 'king' and seemed awfully fitting considering the woman he had married.

"*Now* you come into my home where my husband and I are struggling to find peace, as we try to figure out how to go on living when we know our baby girl has been killed, and you tell us Andre *didn't* do it?" Queenie raged on, irate. "You're telling us that Kayla's murderer, that *devil*, is still out there, and you don't know who he is?"

Queenie's piercing green eyes felt like they were penetrating all the way through Danny, down to her soul, demanding answers that the detectives simply didn't have.

But Danny and Carter weren't here to answer questions. They were here to gather information, and had more than a few questions of their own.

Not that Danny hadn't anticipated this particular brand of resistance from the Samuels. She had met both Queenie and Raja days ago when she had delivered the tragic news of what she had thought at the time was a murder-suicide.

In a lot of ways, Queenie's current reaction was a toned-down version of the wailing, chest beating, drop-to-her-knees response she'd had that day.

"We need your help finding whoever did this," Danny explained with genuine compassion, as she made a point to hold each grieving parent's gaze, though it was significantly easier to hold Raja's.

Raja struck her as a quiet, contemplative man. He was proud of his African heritage and dressed traditionally. His outwardly unemotional reaction to all of this gave Danny hope that he would be willing to tell her everything she and her partner came here to find out.

"We gave our daughter everything," Raja told Carter, who was seated uncomfortably between Danny and what appeared to be a wooden fertility-God statue that seemed to loom conspicuously over the entire conversation. Carter gave the older man his full and undivided attention. "From the time Kayla was a little girl, she knew she wanted to be a dancer—"

"We begged her," Queenie angrily interjected, "to learn San Dancing of Botswana, learn the Pat Pat of Senegal, the Aduma of Kenya, learn the art of your heritage, even the popular West African styles! You must understand, we begged her! But did she?

Oh, no!" she complained with disdain. "She didn't want to be *that* kind of African. She didn't want to be the dignified daughter of two professors—"

Queenie gripped Raja's hand, the glint of determination in her penetrating green eyes was enough to send chills of empathy down Danny's back.

"Not *that* kind of African. No, no," she went on, filled with strength. "Instead, she used her 'blackness' to live, low-rent in the projects. She restricted her beautiful African figure, and tried to squeeze herself into those belly dancing costumes like an Egyptian! She tried to pass for a *Brazilian* Samba performer! Was she ashamed to be *African*? Hmm? It seemed Kayla was willing to dance *any* style so long as it had nothing to do with her *real* heritage! Then, she *perverted* her dancing even further!"

Queenie frowned with disgust, and Raja immediately comforted her.

Interest fully piqued, Danny asked, "You knew about her… sexual proclivities?"

"She threw it in our faces," hissed Queenie. "Said she could make money however she liked. We knew by that point that she was on drugs. She didn't want to live the life of a dignified African queen! She wanted to live out the humiliating stereotype of a hoodrat! As if *that's* what it means to be *Black* in America! She even started speaking *Spanish*!"

Queenie looked like she might faint.

Raja told the detectives, "We begged her to come home."

They hadn't mentioned any of this to Danny when she had first come to their handsome though modestly sized apartment on the north end of the Prospect Park. Their home was in the general vicinity of Brooklyn College where both Queenie and Raja taught.

Danny asked, "According to what we know about Kayla, she didn't have a daughter… Or did she?"

Carter and Danny had agreed not to mention the photograph that had been mailed anonymously to the 66th Precinct. The envelope had not been addressed to anyone in particular.

They had to play this one close to the vest.

Franco had graciously allowed them to pay the Samuels a visit today, but it was a fishing expedition. Identifying the little Black girl in the photo, who had been dressed up as a belly dancer, was the goal.

"Kayla couldn't conceive," Raja told them grimly, as he glanced up at the looming fertility God.

"A blessing after all," Queenie practically spat. "But for a time, we prayed Kayla could." She shook her head. "This was before she got hooked on the drugs, before she met Andre, and moved into that filthy building… We had always hoped she would meet a distinguished African-American man—like yourself, Detective," she told Carter, as a hint of a smile curled her wide mouth. "We hoped she would come into her true nature and eventually give us grandchildren."

Raja finished the point. "But she never met Mr. Right."

"Never met Mr. *Black*," Queenie echoed.

"And the next thing we knew, Kayla had turned into a junkie, selling her body, and using *Spanish* words."

"Using the *N-word* frequently," Queenie added, shaking her head.

Danny recognized immediately that the woman was about to launch into another anecdote, so without mentioning the possibility of abuse or abduction, she asked, "Was Kayla taking care of a little girl?"

Raja's eyes widened tremendously and he breathed, "Nahla?"

"Who's Nahla?" asked Carter. "Her daughter, niece?"

"Nahla is Kayla's cousin's daughter," Queenie explained, having grounded herself once again.

"Oh, that bastard," Raja seethed, and again Queenie gripped his hand in hers.

He was shaking his head now, too angered to say more. It was the first flare of emotion Danny had seen as if the older man had more love for the little girl than he did for his own murdered daughter.

"Kayla's cousin, my brother's daughter that is, Sapphire… Nahla is her daughter. Sapphire was killed by a stray bullet years ago—"

"Four years ago," Queenie supplied before snorting, "stray bullet."

"It was some kind of shootout, Sapphire was killed, Nahla's father, Khan was arrested. Kayla, being Nahla's godmother, took Nahla in."

"But when Khan got released last year, he took Nahla back," Queenie told them. "*We* wanted Nahla. We knew Kayla couldn't care for her, and an ex-con would be no better, but it was Khan's right."

"What's his last name?" Danny asked, her pen poised to her notebook.

"Rashad," said Raja, and Danny jotted it down. "Why are you asking about Nahla?"

Suddenly terrified, Queenie broke out into another riot of emotions, "She wasn't…? Was she…? Did they kill that sweet innocent child, too?"

"No," Carter was quick to put her fears at rest.

"How can we get in touch with Khan Rashad?" Danny asked.

"Why are you asking about Nahla?" Queenie demanded, the strength having returned to her voice.

Danny and Carter exchanged a grave look, each detective knowing full well that disclosing the truth to Queenie and Raja would only hurt their investigation.

Being a hard-ass and pushing for answers while ignoring a witness's concern never went over well, but Danny had no choice, so she again said, "We need any and all contact information you have for Khan Rashad. Phone numbers. Addresses. Anything."

"We don't associate with that man," Queenie said, thoroughly offended. "He's in the system. Call his parole officer. For all we know, he could be dead or back in prison."

That would certainly explain why a child like Nahla could go completely unnoticed and unaccounted for, for years. No school enrollment. Nothing. Locked in a dog crate and fed Cheerios in the dark.

It was heartbreaking.

The sins of the father…

Kayla was certainly guilty, not that any sin warranted being skinned alive, but the killer's logic wasn't insane or incomprehensible. It made some degree of sense… as sickening as it was.

But to presume that those sins should land squarely on an innocent child's head…

In Danny's opinion, if anyone could misconstrue the Bible that badly, then the Bible had to be wrong. In so many ways, it invited perverted interpretations. It didn't have to inspire hate. But that was often the heartrending result.

The sins of the fathers shall be visited upon the sons.

Upon Nahla…

A six-year old girl.

Her kidnapper—a deranged killer—had taken it upon himself to deliver a punishment that the child had done nothing to deserve… a punishment, one could argue, her godmother had already suffered, having been skinned alive at the hand of her drugged boyfriend, Devil's Breath twisting through both their veins.

The photo they had received—scared Nahla dressed up like the woman she had never asked to take care of her—was the beginning of a dark story that Danny didn't want to hear the rest of. A belly dancer's dream—Kayla's dream. What would the next stage of the story be? What images would come next? Those of drugs? Would the detectives receive another photo depicting Kayla's downfall?

If they didn't find the killer in time, would a photo of the child skinned alive arrive as the final, haunting image of this horrendous display?

Danny would be damned if she let that happen.

"Photos of Nahla," she demanded. "We need them. Now. And all contact information you have for Khan Rashad no matter how outdated."

If they had to comb back through a ten-year history of his every associate in order to pinpoint who the killer-kidnapper was, so be it.

Raja quickly accommodated the detectives, this time without glancing at his wife for approval.

After gathering three framed photos of Nahla and taking the glossy prints out of each African frame, Raja combed through an old rolodex and jotted down Rashad's information, everything they had. The contact information amounted to an address in the Kensington Projects—of all places—as well as a yahoo email address.

Raja handed it all over to Danny, who was waiting with Carter in the zebra-print anteroom of the professors' home.

"You find that girl," Queenie begged, looking up at Danny, her piercing eyes now round and full of worry. "You find Nahla and bring her back to us."

Raja wrapped his arm around his wife, as Danny fought the urge to promise the couple that she would.

Instead, she offered them her business card and said, "You're welcome to check-in. We'll tell you what we can, and we'll inform you of what we are at liberty to share."

"I'll find her," Carter said with chilling conviction, promising exactly what both detectives had been trained to avoid at all costs.

Danny couldn't blame him, but she did shoot him a warning look.

If he felt her sharp eyes on him, it wasn't enough to stop him from adding, "I have kids. I will hunt down whoever took Nahla with the same tenacity I would use if he had taken one of my own children."

Raja breathed, "Thank you, my brother," and Queenie resonated the sentiment with a grateful, teary-eyed smile.

"You shouldn't have done that," Danny told him when they reached the street, the afternoon sun causing a wicked glare, as they made their way to their parked Crown Victoria.

Without looking at her, Carter said, "I do a lot of things I shouldn't. Get used to it."

Her eyebrows shot up to her hairline and she stared, somewhat stunned, at Carter, as he slid in behind the steering wheel, completely unapologetic.

Well, damn, she thought, collecting herself enough to settle onto the passenger seat.

It was a very quiet ride back to the station but when they reached the bullpen, making a beeline for Franco's office where they were due to report back, Carter finally justified his conviction, "I don't make promises I can't keep."

"It's a risky one—"

"I said," he barked, "I don't make promises I can't keep."

He stared her down, both detectives at a standstill just shy of the lieutenant's open office door.

"I hope you're right," she told him honestly.

She had always sensed from Carter that somewhere deep inside of him was a wound that just wouldn't heal. It was never lost on her when she had accidentally struck that nerve, or when a case had.

Sometimes it was the glimmer of hope in a witness's eyes that yanked on Carter's heartstrings. Heartstrings, which were somehow connected to a wealth of hurt that ebbed and flowed, never resting, in Carter's soul.

…or so it seemed to Danny.

It wasn't until Franco teased, "Stop flirting and get your asses in here!" that the detectives broke their fused eye contact and wasted no time claiming the chairs across from the lieutenant's cluttered desk.

Carter launched into briefing Franco on all they had learned from the Samuels. He mentioned the three photos of Nahla that they had obtained. The photos were now logged into Evidence. He went on to explain how they had a few potentially outdated addresses to locate Khan Rashad, which of course would come second to contacting his parole officer.

Franco praised their work then took a long moment to silently mull the fragments over, while Danny and Carter exchanged a quick glance meant to decide which of them should propose the next stage of their investigative plan.

Something told her to defer to her partner.

"Someone had to have seen the killer go into Kayla's apartment."

He had made that argument before, so Danny attempted to appeal to Franco from a different angle.

"I say, I take the lead on looking into Rashad and his associates, and we get Carter into Building 7 undercover."

When Franco opened his mouth to object, presumably, she reminded him, "Carter has ten years of experience working undercover. We never would've found Raffi or even known about him if Carter hadn't gone into Building 7 on his day off to gather intel."

"True," Franco agreed, considering her proposition.

"Last I heard, the building's 'dry'," Carter mentioned, easing into his idea. "If I could get some crank from evidence—"

"Jesus," Franco breathed, and a laugh rumbled out of him.

Unfazed, Carter went on, "If I have something to deal, some good drugs, there won't be a single door that doesn't open for me."

"I'll give you that," Franco laughed.

"Between the two of us," Carter pressed, "we're going to get leads. We're going to find this girl."

The lieutenant drew in a deep breath, studying his newest detective, as he leaned back in his creaking chair.

A decisive moment later, Franco had his desk phone to his ear and informed the clerk in Evidence to release—"How much crank do you need?"

"At least twelve eight-balls to get the operation flowing," Carter told him.

The way Franco shook his head, a wry grin tugging at the corner of his mouth, had 'strangely proud' written all over it, and he relayed the order to the clerk on the other end of the call.

After dropping the phone into its cradle, he informed them, "I'll alert Narcotics so no one busts you," then Franco excused the detectives to dive into their organized plan.

"You think it'll work?" Danny asked him when they reached their conjoined desks.

"I think Kathy's going to rip me a new one, that's what I think."

"So, that's a 'yes'?"

Danny found herself letting out a muffled laugh at how right he was, and as Carter grabbed the keys to his own car from his desk drawer, readying to head out so he could get home, changed, and into the projects, he told her, "What we really need to find out is who deals Devil's Breath in Kensington and how our killer-kidnapper got his hands on it."

"One mountain at a time, Carter," she said encouragingly. "Stay safe."

Danny didn't make a tremendous amount of progress as the late afternoon turned to night. By seven o'clock, she had contacted Khan Rashad's parole officer, but was only able to leave a voice message. In the message, she requested the ex-con's current address. After that, she decided that was as much progress as she was going to make. She might as well head out.

She threw her arms into her jacket and raked her fingers through her mop of hair, sweeping her bangs to the side.

She found Franco in the break room where he was doctoring a steaming cup of coffee with a steady stream of sugar, his usual burning-the-midnight-oil routine. Paperwork was a bitch. She peeked her head in and bid Franco goodnight.

There was a deep chill in the air when she came upon Tommy's bar, the wooden sign for O'Toole's swaying in the sharp gusts that cut up the avenue.

She thrust the heavy door aside and entered to find Tommy behind the counter. He was wearing his signature gray tee shirt and worn-out jeans. Tommy was in the throes of what appeared to be a hilarious conversation with one of his bar's long-standing patrons, a fellow retired firefighter.

Tommy had one hell of a smile. His deep laugh. That beautiful sound. It was what had drawn her to him years ago when she had first started coming to the bar, because it was a few doors down from her apartment building. The local watering hole for cops and firefighters alike—New York's finest.

Call it love at first sight or *lust*, it had been his crooked smile, those deep-set eyes of his and devastatingly good-looks that had stolen her breath away, kept her ordering, drinking, tipping far too generously until the night had ended with just the two of them in the empty, darkened pub, Tommy's apartment just up the stairs in the back.

It had started with an unspoken, electric need and had ended with a pregnancy, one which Tommy hadn't even known about until after his infant son had died…

…at the hand of…

Danny winced, forcing the very concept of her mother's twisted attempt at protecting Danny from her mind.

But what had Nora been protecting Danny from…*what?*

A burden?

From anything that might have diverted Danny's attention away from her mother who seemed to suck her every ounce of energy in order to go on functioning, like some kind of parasite…

Nevertheless, Danny forced it all from her mind, hating that the very sight of Tommy had a way of reminding her of this tremendous secret.

He met her gaze, those warm, kind eyes of his drinking in the sight of her approaching his bar, as if she was the most beautiful woman he had ever seen.

"There's my girl," he said, as she returned a smile, resting her elbows on the bar. Tommy waved over one of his new hires who was wiping down a recently vacated table then asked her, "How 'bout a cold one?"

"Sure," she said.

After pouring two mugs of ice cold beer and giving his new guy a chance to get situated behind the bar counter, Tommy led her to her favorite table in front of the large picture windows that faced the street.

"Rough day?" he asked, giving her shoulder the kind of squeeze that promised a serious massage to come.

"I might have to let you think that," she flirted.

He stole a quick gulp of his beer, set the mug down, and worked both of her shoulders from across the shallow table. Danny hadn't a prayer of muffling the relieved groan that spilled out of her. He laughed, and as she opened her eyes, his large hands having stroked down her arms and returned to his mug, she felt eyes on her that weren't his.

Standing across the street, fat grocery bags in each hand, and staring straight at her was Nora.

She looked crushed.

Danny couldn't take her eyes away, and soon Tommy saw what had stolen her attention.

"You don't have to cut her out forever," he told her.

He had no idea how in the dark he was.

"Yes, she lied to me time and again," he acknowledged, summarizing only what he knew of the situation. "She did everything in her power to keep me away from you, but we're together now. She can't rip us apart. Maybe her heart was in the right place?" he suggested.

She wasn't sure her mother had one.

"I know how close you two are, and if you still want a relationship with her…" he offered but soon trailed off, understanding that for Danny, or at least according to the pained expression on her face, it wouldn't be that easy.

And the last thing she needed was Tommy's encouragement. She was already dangerously close to bridging the gap with Nora. The last thing she needed was encouragement. As it stood, she was nearly half way to finding some kind of insane justification to live with the fact that she craved restoring that relationship. What in God's name was wrong with her? How could she genuinely miss that woman?

"Danny?" he said, calling her back to him.

"If she tries to talk to you for any reason," she warned. "If Nora approaches you, I don't care for what reason," she stared dead at him. "You ignore her. You shut her down. Don't listen to a word she has to say. And get the hell away from her. Promise me?"

His brow furrowed, as he fully registered her desperation, unsure of how to respond.

"Tommy," she demanded with marked terror in her wavering tone. "Promise me."

Chapter Ten

THE KIDS HAD snagged a round booth at The Cheesecake Factory, a diner-esque commercialized joint boasting reasons to eat pie at every turn. The lights were bright, the wait staff flashy, and the hum of reverberating voices in the air never ceased to surprise Carter. It was loud.

Matty was sucking on a chocolate milkshake, his bony hands between his knotty knees beneath the table, his cleated feet swinging.

Beside him on either side were his brother and sister. Christopher was working on his bun-less burger since he had read about the ills of grain based carbohydrates on an athlete's performance. His new motto was 'beef for breakfast!' even though Kathy hadn't actually allowed such a thing to occur.

If Christopher's dietary restrictions were radical for a growing twelve-year old boy, Amanda's were even more concerning.

At fourteen, she had long since discovered fashion magazines and the unrealistic ideals of Caucasian beauty. It probably didn't help that her mother was one of the most gorgeous women Carter had ever seen—blonde hair, blue eyes, complexion creamy as milk.

No matter what Kathy ate, her curves remained perfectly proportioned. Amanda's DNA drew heavily from the Dobbs genepool instead—dense bones, muscular limbs, thick thighs and lips. She probably knew she couldn't diet genetics away, but she pushed her mashed potatoes around her plate with a spoon anyway, having slowly eaten the green beans and ignored the ribeye steak that Chris had convinced her to order since it was 'all protein and good fat.' When it had come, she didn't trust it.

"Amanda, hun," said Kathy from where she sat curled under Carter's arm. "Do you want that wrapped up to go?"

Even though their daughter scrunched her nose up at the very concept of having to look at the same deflated hunk of meat and potatoes ever again, Kathy talked it up.

"They can keep it warm for you."

"Or I can eat it," Christopher offered, his tight brown eyes widening as it dawned on him, "beef for breakfast! Finally!"

"You are not having beef for breakfast," Kathy reminded him, exasperated.

"It has Vitamin C," he countered, which might or might not be true.

Carter had no idea and as far as Kathy was concerned, she didn't need to research the validity to know no child of hers would ever rush out the door without having eaten eggs, orange juice, bacon, and two slices of toast, and she declared as much to all her children, as Carter sat in silent, head-nodding support.

"How do you not have any fat on you?" Amanda accused.

Christopher was quick to explain, "I'm telling you: meat, eggs, water. I've looked into this."

"But," Amanda objected, wrinkling her nose at her brother who would probably always disgust her to some degree, "you slather everything in butter."

"Exactly," said Chris. "It's ketogenic."

"Keto-what-ic?" she glared.

Matty had been looking from Chris to Amanda and back again as if his siblings were a whiplash tennis match. His straw had migrated to the corner of his mouth and he happily sucked on his milkshake until it made the gravelly, telltale sounds that he had fully devoured it.

As Kathy went on to remind their daughter that there was nothing wrong with eating fat or having body fat—Amanda was a developing young woman after all! *Ew! Mom, never say 'developing'! Ugh!*—Carter sat back and a warm feeling swept over him.

This was what it was all about. His family. Kathy and him had done alright, he thought, looking at each of their children.

For all the friction that had risen between them behind closed doors, and as smart, sensitive, and intuitive as his kids were, Carter felt certain that Christopher, Amanda, and Matty hadn't been negatively affected. They were happy, healthy kids focused on themselves as they should be.

Their waitress came around and Carter released Kathy in favor of leaning across the rounded booth to beam the biggest grin at his kids. "Who wants cheesecake?"

Amanda groaned and Christopher pinched his athletic face, both declining—damn they were growing up too fast—but Matty lit up like a Christmas tree, started hopping and bopping in his seat, and actually went so far as to raise his hand as if his dad might not have seen him. "Ooh, ooh, me, me! I do!"

"That's like, literally a hundred grams of fat," Amanda warned her youngest brother.

Christopher, again, was quick to correct her, "Fat is *good*. Seriously, though, Matty, the refined sugar is gonna give you diabetes. I wouldn't eat the cheesecake."

"But this is the *Cheesecake* Factory," Matty argued with flawless nine-year old logic.

The waitress, who had been patiently waiting through the banter, let out a little chuckle, and Carter told her, "Let's get a full cheesecake."

"Twelve inches, or fifteen?"

Kathy's eyes widened, but she was being modest. The two of them had polished off a 23" cheesecake once. It wasn't pretty, but it was possible.

As their plates were cleared and they waited for their humongous cheesecake to arrive, which Carter didn't need a crystal ball to know they would end up taking the majority of home, he adjusted his dark hoodie so it wouldn't come between his shoulders and the back of the booth, then slipped his hands into the front pouch where a sick number of eight-balls sat in plastic, courtesy of Evidence at the 66th.

He had never been one to feel eager to part ways from his kids, but the fact that Nahla Rashad was somewhere out there, alone, scared, and being posed to look like her godmother by some kind of lunatic or maniac or plain old crank-head, had been gnawing at Carter's insides. He wanted to get out there, get inside the projects, and find someone—anyone—who might've seen the sick son of a bitch, track him down, and rescue that little girl.

It wasn't only the dog crate that had been so familiar to Carter, that had cut right down to his very core. The slavery of it all, being passed and traded, a child being taken against their will, and photographed... *Familiar* was too small a word.

Carter knew he had lived it.

He hadn't recovered every last memory, or even half of them. No matter how many years passed, no matter that he was in his mid-forties and far from being a terrified little boy, his psyche was still protecting him from remembering grim, soul-murdering acts of abuse he had survived.

Again, his mind—as if a separate entity from his own personality—circumnavigated his ruminations back towards Nahla and the case at hand.

Who was behind this? A common junky? Someone who belonged in Kayla and Andre and Raffi's world? Someone who would've had knowledge of Nahla's ill treatment since his ear was to the ground in that particular stretch of depravity—Building 7 of the Kensington Projects?

Or was the killer-kidnapper an outsider? A mastermind perhaps?

Without warning, Carter saw the golden sheen of an antique pocket watch flash through his mind's eye.

Taken aback, he tried to tune in to his family's conversation—Christopher was laughing and Amanda was recoiling with sisterly affection—but his mind wouldn't latch on.

The pocket watch surged to the forefront of his mind.

Click, click, click filled his ears, his family's laughter muffled in the distance.

Click.

The pocket watch—those *hands*—consumed him.

Winding the pocket watch—*click, click, click.*
Cranking the pocket watch—*click, click, click.*
Don't keep him waiting.

Those large, manicured hands that had sickened Carter… they would hold the polished pocket watch, they would crank it. That faceless monster who had liked to time the torture, make meticulous notes of how long each boy lasted.

Bent over. Exposed. Violated.

And then Carter had been returned to his cold dog crate in the musty basement… hidden in plain sight.

Carter jerked out of the vision without realizing he had muttered, "No."

"Hun?" asked Kathy, doing a bit of a double take, then taking in the sight of his long face, sweaty brow, and stiff shoulders. "Carter, are you okay?"

He told her he was.

But nothing could've been further from the truth.

✵

CARTER DIDN'T KEEP his head down, but walked with swagger like a boss as he made his way through the darkened courtyard heading straight for Building 7.

The residents that were out took notice. Even their pitbulls stared.

He felt eyes on him from above, ghetto grannies frowning down at him from their open windows.

Good.

Word would travel fast and that's what he wanted.

The steel door to Building 7 sat flush in its frame, locked.

Recalling Andre Durant's sleazy neighbor whose eyes had refused to hold still, Carter punched the Latino's apartment number into the buzzer pad.

Gruff and distorted with static, the guy said through the speaker box, "Yo', who dat?"

"Your hookup," Carter said boldly. "Ain't no one around to let me in down here."

There was a pause, then, "I know you?"

"Yo', Raffi's out. I'm in, buzz me up."

With recollection, the guy exclaimed, "Dark ass brotha!"

Carter rolled his eyes. "Call me 'C'."

The door buzzed and he slipped inside, took the stairwell stairs two at a time to the fourth floor, and found the jonesing Latino man lurking in the cracked doorway of his smokey apartment.

"C, my man," the guy welcomed him, slapping his clammy hand against Carter's before inviting him inside what turned out to be, unsurprisingly, a real dump.

Practically giddy with anticipation, the guy introduced himself as 'Slim' and lingered without sitting on his sunken couch, as Carter took in the place, shoulders back and sucking his teeth.

"Raffi's out?"

"Tell me what you know about it," Carter domineered.

Not wanting to anger the man who held his happiness in the pouch of his hoodie—Slim's eyes had been glued to the bulky pouch ever since Carter had stuffed his hands inside—he said, "Just that he hasn't been around, man."

"You didn't hear, then," he said, drawing him in.

"Hear what? Nah, man, I didn't hear nothing. What are you selling?" he was on the couch now, pulling cash from his wallet, counting it out, and checking his front pockets and back for more bills.

"Slow your roll, kid," Carter warned. "Raffi got taken out."

"What?"

Carter nodded and let the fact sink into Slim's soggy mind. "I got buyers, I got crank," he highlighted to get the Latino to cooperate. "I can take over this territory, no problem, y'all will never go dry again."

Slim was grinning now, and if Carter wasn't mistaken, a trickle of drool glistened down his dehydrated lip.

"But I need to know who took out Raffi. Was it one of his own?"

"Can't be," Slim guessed, anything to help. "This place wouldn't have gone dry."

"That's what I think, too. So, some dealer wants this territory and takes him out?"

"Why'd we go dry, then?"

For a complete disaster of a human being, Slim was remarkably smart when it came to figuring out the logic behind why he had been deprived of methamphetamine for nearly a week.

"Help me out, Slim. I need to track this guy down. He must have known Raffi. He must have known Kayla and Andre upstairs."

Slim really put on his thinking cap, his scabby face scrunching up, his chin resting on his fist.

"Someone who'd want Kayla's *kid*," he prodded.

Slim glanced up at him with curious eyes.

"You didn't know she had a little girl?" Carter questioned.

"Did the killer take that little girl?" he asked right back, clearly knowing full well about Nahla—too bad he hadn't mentioned it their first encounter. When Carter confirmed as much with a nod, Slim commented, "Kid's better off. Yo' maybe you'll end up liking this killer?"

"How's that?"

"Raffi was a shit and we both know Andre had it coming. Kayla, fun as she was… man, the stuff she allowed happen to that little girl… that ain't right."

"You agree with homeboy's justice?"

"He ain't *my* 'homeboy', but maybe," Slim said thoughtfully. "Depends on what he's doing with that little girl."

A sudden sense of urgency surged through Carter's veins. "So, help me out, man. Someone must have seen something. I can't deal my drugs, free flowing', unless I track that killer down, you know this. You know how it works."

Slim agreed he did, but all he had to say was, "Maybe someone across from Kayla's door saw the guy, I don't know man. Whenever Andre was upstairs, things were quiet down here, and if Homeboy went into Kayla's apartment… what the hell would I have seen?"

It was a good point, but left Carter in no better a position than he had been when he'd first set foot in the projects.

Nevertheless, he sold crank to Slim, who, in a somewhat lonely manner, invited him to stay and get high.

Carter declined, but told him to spread the word. It was a bold strategy, but the undercover detective wanted to have an immediate presence in this particular building if not all of them.

If he was viewed as their supplier, their protector, their *king*, then ultimately whatever they knew, he would know, so long as he asked the right person the right question.

On the ninth floor, which Carter rode the rickety elevator to get to, he swaggered towards apartment 911, which already had new tenants, disturbingly.

He could hear their TV blaring through the closed door, their kids playfully arguing, and their dog getting in on the action with a bark or two.

Carter wondered if management had cleaned the bloodstains or simply laid down the cheapest wall-to-wall carpet they could find.

He proceeded with the same approach as he had originally employed on Andre's floor during his day off.

He slowly stalked the hallway. Lingered. Stalked back, confident that any hardworking, sober residents would stay tucked in their apartments, while the junkies—jonesing—would be too curious not to peek out.

Carter prayed that the apartment door directly across the hallway from 911 would open. Their peephole would have had the best vantage point to see strange characters coming and, more importantly, going.

But that wasn't the apartment door that popped open.

"Hey, handsome," came a woman's slippery voice.

Carter turned to find a tall, lean African-American woman in her late thirties draping herself against the doorframe of her apartment unit and making no apologies for drinking in the sight of the attractive stranger who had graced her quiet corner of the corridors.

She didn't look like a scabby junky, but sober eyes were more valuable in court.

This could be good…

Playing along, he checked her out—she was in tight yoga pants and a skimpy tank that showed off her toned stomach and boobs—then swaggered on over with a pimpin' limp and a growing grin on his face. Because he was in character. He loved his wife. And Kathy would definitely kill him if she found out about this…

"Hey, Ma."

"You don't live here," she pointed out in a flirtatious tone.

"I could…" he suggested, "for a night if a fine ass bitch like you let me in."

"Ha!" she laughed, throwing her head back. "What's your game, honey?"

"Call me 'C'," he told her. "I got business in the building."

"Business?"

"Like I said," he grinned, "could be *pleasure*. Up to you, Ma."

"Stop playin', Playah," she lightly warned, drinking in the sight of him once again.

"You always interrogate strangers in the hall?"

"Not always," she conceded.

"But you take notice?" he asked as if it was a compliment. It was so much more valuable than that.

Her thin, black eyebrows drifted up, as she agreed, "Mm-hmm."

"Then maybe you can help me out."

"Maybe…" she smiled, and every instinct in his body told him that this woman only needed the thinnest excuse to pounce and pull him inside.

"You hear about Kayla and Andre?"

All flirtation vanished and a grave look came over her pretty face. "Please don't kill my vibe."

"Did you see a new face, someone who doesn't belong, go in? This would be a few days back, May 12th."

"What's your hustle?" she asked, her brow now furrowed as she stared dead at him. "Only stranger I saw go in there was you."

He stared at her for a long, confused moment, which gave the woman pause, her conviction wavering.

"He looked like you," she said. "Didn't wear no sweats, though. Fubu and G-Star Raw, and lookin' tight, with his chains an' all. He looked like money."

Carter felt his heart punch hard in his chest cavity. She had just supplied a solid description of their killer.

He held her gaze then asked, "What's your name?"

❄

WHEN CARTER got home that night, it was late.

Amanda was up listening to Nicki Minaj and flipping fashion magazines.

Carter looked in on her and smiled before checking in on Christopher who was already deep asleep in his dark room, an athlete who knew the importance of a good night's rest.

He found Matty tossing and turning, the nine-year old's comforter a bunched heap at the foot of the bed, his jammies scrunched up his skinny legs as if he had been much too hot to fall asleep.

"Hey, Kiddo," he said, nearing the bed.

"I can't sleep," he complained.

Carter plucked one of Matty's <u>Goosebumps</u> books from the bookshelf, one they'd been working on whenever Carter had been home early enough to tuck him in.

"This should do the trick," he offered, settling down on the bed beside his son, who nuzzled sweetly against him.

He began reading out loud and was sure to do all the 'voices,' but soon Matty took over, his little finger trailing under each sentence as he slowly read.

The sound of the door creaking stole his attention and he found Kathy looking in affectionately.

She mouthed asking him if he would like a slice of cheesecake.

He smiled at her to say 'just a little' then returned his attention to the paperback in his hands just as Matty turned the page.

When Carter had been Matty's age, he didn't have books and hugs and cheesecake waiting for him in the fridge.

He'd had a musty basement, a dog crate, and fear so dark and cold that it seemed to split tendons from bones, rumbling deep inside of him.

He had lived by the rules of the pocket watch.

It's cranking.

Click, click, click.

And the man who had kept the time.

The man none of them had ever dared keep waiting.

Chapter Eleven

"LET'S PLAY THIS one close to the vest."

"Carter," she warned, keeping her voice just as low as his.

It was way too early in the morning to be scheming, thought Danny. Withholding evidence from the department that, at least for the time being, was still working the Raffael Sanzio homicide would not be a good idea.

Danny peered through the narrow window of the door that separated Carter and her from two old-school Homicide detectives who were speaking privately in one another's ear.

One had a droopy, bulldog face, and the younger, a wiry man with razor thin lips and a crisp shave, was actually wearing suspenders. There was a soft-pack of cigarettes in the breast pocket of his button down.

Christ, it was a real boys club up here on the Homicide floor.

They were supposed to play together and play nice until they uncovered ironclad evidence that proved one killer had orchestrated both Raffi's murder and Kayla and Andre's deaths, and also took Nahla Rashad.

The presence of scopolamine, or Devil's Breath, in the junkies' systems wasn't enough according to Franco to *prove* they had been killed by anyone other than each other.

Homicide was working the Sanzio murder.

The 'murder-suicide' conclusion had been wiped and so the Samuels-Durant case was reopened, and with it, of course, was the task of finding Nahla's kidnapper, both of which had landed squarely on the SVU detectives' shoulders.

Everyone was supposed to get along.

Carter and Danny hadn't had so much as a minute to brief one another on where they had each gotten, working their respective angles of the investigation. He had only told her he had gotten something 'big' and though her own effort hadn't been even remotely groundbreaking, oftentimes ruling out a suspect was equally productive.

"Look at them," he rhetorically suggested—she had been. "Can you see those two canvassing in the projects? Can you see them getting in on the handshake-drug-trade in order to gain insight into who might've taken their Vic out?"

"Could you see *me* doing that, Carter?" she countered. "Just because they can't do what you can is no reason to write them off, and you know it. Let's see what they have for us," she proposed, pressing her palm against the door, "and give them what we know."

He was having trouble swallowing the last part—he hadn't even given *her* what he knew; what he had found out last night working undercover in Building 7.

"Come on," she prodded and finally swung the door open and entered the no-frills conference room.

The SVU floor had been designed, in part, to make child victims feel comfortable. Its conference room had a play area, vending machines, cozy rugs and couches, comforting pillows, and consoling blankets—an overall atmosphere that implied all who entered were safe.

Homicide was the dismal opposite.

"Detectives," said the bulldog, who was obviously the senior of the two if for no other reason than age alone. Extending his hand to Carter even though Danny had neared him first, the hardened investigator said, "I'm Detective Crouse," and shook her partner's hand. "And this is Toliver."

Toliver boldly shook Carter's hand, having intentionally bypassed Danny with, "Excuse me, sweetheart."

She was getting the distinct impression she was invisible.

It hadn't escaped Carter's attention either so he forced the introduction before the boys from Homicide could give their drink orders to Danny and slap her ass—not that they would dare, but hey, crazier things had happened.

"Working under Detective Foster's tutelage," Carter went on companionably, "has been invaluable. It can be rough being the new guy."

"You wanted that department?" Toliver questioned as if Carter had somehow been slighted when he was assigned to the Special Victims Unit. "With the rapes, questionable victims, all the 'he said, she said' spats?" He shot Crouse a chuckle.

Danny was about ready to drive her fist through the guy's ugly face, which would be a real role reversal, especially considering Carter seemed to be holding his own—calm, cool, and collected. He was ordinarily the hot-headed of the two.

But before she could put the insensitive moron in his place, Carter dropped the bomb of all bombshells, stating matter-of-factly something Danny herself had never known.

"I used to get raped a lot growing up," he said easily. It was haunting. "There wasn't much evidence when all was said and done. There were a lot of 'he said, she said' spats, you could say, my teenaged-word against an adult's," he said sarcastically. "The prosecution was good at their job and didn't mind that I was a 'questionable' victim." His tone was twisting now, a bitter edge cutting through. "We don't call them 'victims,' by the way, unless they're in a body bag. We call them *survivors* because that's what they are."

Crouse and Toliver had fallen deathly silent, neither able to look at Carter, at a loss for how to move forward from his harrowing admission to the meeting at hand.

Danny wanted to break out in applause, but instead she pointed to the TV monitor setup on the far end of the conference table and said, "You got something for us? We don't have a lot of time and it could really help our investigation to learn whatever you have on Raffael Sanzio's murder."

"Ah…" Crouse cleared the frog from his throat then ordered his partner to, "Start up the footage."

As Toliver neared the DVD player beneath the monitor, turning everything on and cueing up the surveillance footage, Crouse mentioned to Danny, "The M.E., Andover… the autopsy," he stammered, his brash personality having collapsed in the wake of Carter's comeback. "We're still separating wheat from chaff, seeing how to lock this Devil's Breath aspect into our killer's motive and method."

"Proving cause and effect," Toliver chimed in, "is going to be one hell of a challenge."

Carter and Danny were up against the same hurdle, obviously, but she wasn't about to commiserate with them.

Instead, she got situated on one of the stiff chairs next to Carter and leaned in, her big brown eyes narrowing as the footage skipped and started to life on the TV monitor.

The black-and-white static-shot opened on a nearly aerial view of the East River side of the Waste Management Recycling Plant in the Gowanus where Danny had found Raffi's crumpled body.

There was a parked set of recycling trucks filling up the left side of the screen.

The footage was grainy, obviously nighttime. Only a few lampposts illuminated patches of the ground.

The right side of the screen, nearly off camera, was the open mouth of what appeared to be a trash compactor.

"Is it playing?" Carter questioned when the screen remained static for what felt like a long time.

Toliver nodded with an affirmative grunt from where he stood to the side of the TV, watching grimly.

A shadow appeared first, indicating movement near the trash compactor.

"There," said Toliver.

"The Vic?" asked Carter, and the wiry detective only nodded his head as if to say, *the killer.*

"That's all we have of him," Crouse explained as one very heavy-footed Raffael "Raffi" Sanzio began zombie-walking into frame from where whoever the shadow belonged to was standing. "That shadowy shape of a man is all we have to *make the case* that

Sanzio didn't pop the wrong pill and kill himself. It's hardly proof."

Danny gritted her teeth, watching as Raffi staggered this way and that, zigzagging his way to the open mouth of the trash compactor.

On the flickering, grainy screen, Raffi hesitated at the maw.

He didn't want to do it, she thought. The drug might have trapped him deep inside his own mind, but Raffi had still been in there. Cognizant. Understanding what a madman was commanding him to do, and *hesitating*.

Danny felt her stomach clench at what it must have been like obeying. Not wanting to do it, and knowing it meant death, but ultimately having no control.

Bile stung the back of her throat, as she watched Raffi divert his gaze from the off-camera man who was controlling him.

Suddenly, Raffi threw himself head first into the trash compactor, the metal anvils clamping down the second the machine sensed new weight.

The most disturbing aspect was that, if Carter and her theory was correct, the killer-kidnapper had only taken Raffi out to get inside Kayla's apartment, likely posing as her dealer. Which meant that Raffi didn't have to die. The killer could've found another way.

But he hadn't.

He had taken pleasure in exercising power over this man, so much power that he had compelled Raffi to kill himself.

It was almost unfathomable.

"We're no date rape drug experts," Crouse began, "that's your department, and I'm sure we would have a lot to learn. But we're on board with the M.E.'s assessment, that Sanzio was mind controlled into leaping head first to his death like that. Anderson told us—"

"Andover," Toliver corrected.

"Right," Crouse allowed, but only marginally, as if the actual surnames of female coworkers were of no real consequence to him. "She mentioned your Vics Samuels and Durant also had scopolamine in their system, so we're on board that this is likely a triple homicide and we want to work together."

Carter and Danny exchanged a skeptical glance.

"Toliver," said Crouse, giving his partner the floor.

The wiry detective pursed his razor-thin lips for a thoughtful beat, collecting himself.

"Our first consideration was that the killer perhaps worked at Waste Management or knew someone who did. No such luck so far. We're still working on discovering how he had access."

If the man was as calculating as he seemed, thought Danny, he might have drugged and controlled person after person along the way, like human stepping stones, to get inside the plant, but she didn't interrupt the detective to say as much.

"We've spoken with Sanzio's family and friends," Toliver went on. "The guy wasn't especially well liked, had a lot of enemies, and we're still hacking through our interviews, coming up with a suspect list—"

"Who's on it?" Carter asked eagerly then interjected before Toliver could answer, "Do you have photos we could look through?"

"You got a potential ID on the guy?" Crouse cut in, having immediately read between the lines.

Danny was just as surprised and stared at her partner who seemed guardedly remorseful that he had let it slip.

"I've got a description," Carter admitted, "of a man who went into Samuel's apartment. Could be the killer."

"An eye-witness?" Crouse asked aggressively.

"Connected to the *Samuels-Durant* murder," Carter reminded them, his way of denying them the physical description or giving up his witness.

"Look, buddy," said Crouse, "we're all in agreement here that the same guy murdered all three Vics."

"We're going to need to talk to your witness," Toliver insisted, backing his bulldog of a partner up. "Do a full interview, maybe a lineup if we can make headway on our list."

It was becoming painfully clear that 'working together' was not going to play out as smoothly as Franco had expected.

"I was undercover when I ferreted her out," Carter explained. "She doesn't even know she gave a cop a description of a possible killer. You aren't going to show up in the projects and get any kind of cooperation from her."

"We have our ways," said Crouse in such a way that Danny could smell the racist threats those so-called 'ways' likely included—yanking away Section 8 housing privileges, food stamps, contacting her employer, and otherwise squeezing her life dry.

Voices were raised. An argument ensued. Danny made several attempts to shout over the men, inserting a shred of reason and compromise, but they were deaf to it.

Soon there came a knock on the door and the receptionist reminded them their booked time in the conference room was up and another party needed the space.

By the time Danny and Carter reached the elevator, a flimsy compromise had been agreed upon, one which Danny wasn't confident would come to fruition.

Toliver would email them his list of working suspects, people from Raffi's life who might have had reason to take him out. And Carter would send the homicide detectives a written description of what his witness had detailed for him.

"You didn't tell me you got a description," she said quietly to Carter, as the elevator doors dinged open and they stepped inside.

"I got a hell of a lot more than that," he told her.

"Yeah?"

"What did you get on Khan Rashad?" he asked, shifting gears as they rode down to the SVU floor.

"After leaving word with his parole officer, the guy called me back and actually alibied Rashad himself for May 12th," she explained. "Not that I talked face-to-face with Rashad yet, but I have to tell you, my instinct is that the ex-con doesn't give a crap about his daughter. Since getting released, he's had to tell his P.O. everywhere he's planning on going and for how long. There were no trips to see Kayla and Nahla. Period."

"A dead end," Carter surmised as if it made perfect sense. "The description I got," he said, but immediately paused when the elevator doors chimed open.

It wasn't until they returned to their desks that he leaned towards her, framed photos of his family spread aside, and said, "The guy looks like me."

"What?" she whispered, thrown.

He nodded and let the possibility really settle into both of their fast-working minds.

"She wasn't kidding around with me, either. Lacy Marcel, the neighbor witness. Said she only saw the guy come and go once—May 12th. He had dark black skin, my shade," Carter explained, keeping his tone hushed. "Short hair, not shaved like mine, but the same build, same height. If I wasn't posing undercover, I would've asked her to sit down with a sketch artist. I mean, she *saw* this guy."

"Face-to-face?"

"Face-to-face and she would be dead," he leveled with her. "It was through her peephole."

"Did she have a plausible reason for looking out?" asked Danny, anticipating what the District Attorney, Sarah Hovey, would need to know if this case moved forward and they ended up using Lacy Marcel as a witness in court.

"Plausible enough," he told her. "She's no junky, either. Teaches yoga. She's clean, likable. Has a bit of a mouth on her, though."

"Good," said Danny, thinking. "Not a lot of guys look like you."

Carter leaned back in his seat, his brows drifting up his forehead in agreement. "Why do you think I want Homicide's list so bad?"

"Two reasons," she said. "One, just because your look-alike went into Kayla's apartment, doesn't mean—"

"Yeah, yeah," he allowed sarcastically before supplying, "doesn't *prove* my look-alike killed them."

"Don't 'yeah yeah' me. You know Franco's going to go there. He might not be our killer. Second," she said, back on point, "we both know Homicide is spinning their stupid wheels. That list…" she was shaking her head now. "I doubt it'll include our guy."

"Process of elimination," he told her.

She was in agreement, and after they silently mulled over the ground they had covered, she kept coming up against Carter's shocking admission.

He had never so much as hinted he had been sexually abused as a boy and yet he had so easily slammed two old-school detectives with the information just to make a point.

Having done so didn't mean Carter would be open to her questions, and yet he *had* opened himself up to the possibility that she *would* have questions…

"Carter… did they get put away?" she asked, sticking to the one thing she truly wanted to know. "Whoever abused you like that growing up… were they caught?"

He stared dead at her for a long beat.

There wasn't hurt behind his dark eyes, only the whispering tendrils of lingering vengeance.

Vengeance he might never get to execute.

"Yes," he said finally. "I was told he went to prison. I don't remember much, not even testifying."

She nodded understandingly and breathed, "Good."

They stared at each other for another long, intimate beat, which ended only because Danny's cell phone began vibrating in the front pocket of her jeans.

"It's Jill," she said, reading the M.E.'s name and number on the screen. Accepting the call and placing her cell to her ear, she said, "I'm at my desk, what's up?"

She was met with a stuttering sigh then Jill said, "I would've called your desk phone if this wasn't personal."

Danny frowned, touched eyes with Carter, and then sprang up from her chair and made her way into the break room where one of the detectives was blowing on a steaming cup of joe and turning to make his way back into the bullpen.

It was as much privacy as she was going to get, so she said, "I'm listening."

"I don't even know how to say this," Jill tried to begin, her tone flat with either concern or trepidation, it was hard to tell.

Sensing the potential seriousness—Danny was an SVU detective after all, and even though it might not be a 'work call' for Jill, it could very well be one for Danny—she gently coaxed, "There's nothing I haven't heard, and I have all the time in the world, okay?"

"Okay," Jill breathed, after which Danny heard the sound of a door closing come through the

M.E.'s end of the line. "Well, I've been dating this guy. His name is Damian Payne."

"Okay," she said, tenderly demonstrating she was all ears and no judgment.

"And… God, this is so weird…"

Silence ensued as Jill breathed and collected herself. She didn't sound emotional, only confused.

"Things were going good. I was seeing him regularly. Then… God, I don't know if I'm crazy or jumping to conclusions or—"

"You aren't," Danny told her with conviction in her firm voice.

It didn't matter that she didn't know what Jill was about to say exactly. She knew exactly where this conversation was going and could already feel the rage boiling in her veins because of it.

Jill had been attacked.

And like way too many women, she hadn't yet brought herself to believe it.

"Well," she began again. "I had a blackout episode. But the thing that doesn't make sense is that I'm so certain I only had three or four glasses of wine. I know that sounds like a lot…"

"It doesn't sound like a lot," Danny assured her. "And it can't be used against you."

"Christ," Jill said. "I know that logically, but I've never been on this side of it. I don't even know for sure that I *am* on this side of it, Danny. And, I must be insane, I've continued to see him. It's been like three dates now where the next day I swear to God I don't remember anything that's happened once we got back to his place."

"'Damian Payne' you said?" she asked, wanting to be sure she had that right. She spelled the surname out loud, and once Jill had confirmed she was correct, Danny asked, "Where does he work?"

"Oh, God, Danny, I don't even think—"

"I'm not going to do anything," she promised. "I'm just going to get a feel for the guy. I won't stop in as an SVU detective."

"You know what," Jill cut in, her voice fully shaking now. "I shouldn't have called. I shouldn't have said anything. Just forget it."

"Jill—"

"Just forget the whole thing."

She hung up.

Forget the whole thing?

She stared at her cell phone for a beat as another detective drifted into the break room.

Not a chance.

Carter rapped his knuckles on the break room door frame.

"Franco's office. The D.A. is here."

Her head was spinning for the second time today, but she reeled it in as best she could and followed Carter into Franco's office that had never felt so tight thanks to the District Attorney's hard-nosed and surprisingly domineering presence.

Sarah Hovey kept a sleek, manicured appearance for someone on government wages, though the creases in her otherwise youthful face indicated many a long and stressed night stealing smoke breaks in the stairwell and parking lot as a means to collect her thoughts and keep her energy up.

Her coarse, brown hair was secured in a slicked back bun and the mauve lipstick she had applied had faded all but for a dark line around her mouth.

She was standing poised as if she were in court, holding the disturbing, belly dancer photo of Nahla in her hands.

She used a reserved, unhappy smile to greet them.

"Detective Foster, good to see you," she said in a deep and grounded tone that made everything sound grave, a genetic quirk that suited her line of work perfectly.

"Please, call me Danny," she reminded the younger woman, as she briefly shook her hand. "Have you met Carter Dobbs?"

Like most women, Sarah's flat, derisive eyes brightened at the sight of the tall, very dark, and very, *very* handsome man extending his hand to her.

Her tight smile spread wide as she said, "Detective," and it wasn't until she had released his warm grip that she seemed to recall the reason she had stopped in today.

Touching eyes with Franco who was standing behind his behemoth desk, fists on his pointy hips as always, brow furrowed with the seriousness of the situation, Sarah began, "It's to everyone's benefit that we keep this case out of the press for as long as we can get away with it."

Carter eased the door closed with respect to her point then came up beside Danny forming the same uniformed front they tended to use whenever confronting Franco and extensions of his adversary.

"I don't foresee," she went on, "that we'll be able to get away with it for very long. Have you put out an AMBER alert on Nahla Rashad?"

"I delayed it intentionally," Franco admitted. "She wasn't snatched off the street, and she isn't with a relative who thinks she's better off with them. Alerting the general public would only hurt the case for the same reasons you're explaining."

"Agreed," Sarah said curtly before cutting her eyes to Danny and Carter.

Preemptively, Danny offered, "Other than Nahla's maternal grandmother—"

"Once removed," Carter corrected, doing the math on the fact that Nahla wasn't Kayla's daughter, but her cousin's.

"They're aware, the Samuels," she went on. "Homicide is in the loop, but they're much more concerned with their Vic and suspects than the missing girl."

Danny could go on, but Sarah stopped her.

"I'm no fortune teller, but the fact that the kidnapper mailed this photo to the precinct tells me that he might want this whole thing to go public, turn it into something high profile. He might force the case in that direction. The fact that he hasn't yet…"

She paused, perhaps for effect but certainly to hold each detectives' gaze before turning her point to Franco.

"It means that we have a critical window of time—we have no way of knowing how long—to find him and rescue this girl."

As Sarah let that hang, she read the determined expressions on everyone's faces.

"Are the crime scene photos secured?" she asked as a means to troubleshoot those images—Kayla skinned from the chest up and Andre's slit throat—from getting leaked to the press.

Franco assured her, "No one in this precinct would dare."

Sarah lifted her brows as if to say *that's debatable*.

"Depending on the news outlet, one could earn a pretty penny."

Stepping forward, as strategies occurred to her on the fly, Danny questioned, "Why not use the press, control the story, maybe even get it wrong on purpose?"

The D.A. met her suggestion with a frown, but Franco sharply asked, "What would that do?"

"I'm no profiler," she allowed, "but I honestly think the guy believes he's righting a wrong. The '*sins of the fathers*' quote."

Danny indicated the back of the photo Sarah was holding and though the D.A. had likely read it over and over again, she gave it another pass.

"He's conducting some form of justice, punishing Nahla for Kayla's sins, but also, and I hate to put it like this, but also saving her in his own way."

"Let's hope 'saving her' doesn't mean taking her life," Carter interjected grimly.

"There's that," Danny admitted. "My point is that he has a message and he probably thinks he's smart and superior. Could we flush him out of hiding if we went on the news and got it so, so very wrong on purpose?"

"He would feel compelled to correct us," Carter agreed, latching hold of her plan and liking it.

Sarah, on the other hand, didn't.

"We don't want to force his hand, because like you said, his version of saving Nahla could very well mean killing her. I want to keep this out of the press," she reiterated. "And I would like an ear to the ground for any more missing children, because whether or not it's crossed your mind, that's where I fear this case is going."

"You think he'll abduct more kids?" Franco questioned.

"Unless he personally knew Samuels and Durant, and wanted to correct one very specific sin of one very specific, so-called 'father,' which I doubt because both your effort to probe into the Vics' friends and families as well as Homicide's for Sanzio hasn't turned up anything useful, then I think we have to acknowledge that we may have a crusader on our hands."

"I don't disagree," said Franco, mulling over the dueling strategies—Sarah's versus Danny's. "Attempting to control the story in the press, even inaccurately to provoke him, comes with risks."

"Thank you," said Sarah.

"But like you said," he went on, staring hard at the D.A., "he could be angling to get his message to hit the press in one way or another anyway. If that happens, how is that going to play out for us?"

"Like I said, I'm not a fortune teller."

Tension rose between the lieutenant and the district attorney, causing the airless room to feel downright suffocating.

The bottom line was that Franco's detectives might build the case, but Sarah was the one who had to argue it and win in court.

As cases built, she looked for crucial elements, she conveyed needs, she not only worked closely with cops, but also doled out her directives.

She wasn't Franco's equal.

She was his superior. Hence their longstanding history of butting heads and flying into flares of heated arguments.

To mitigate the tension, Danny broke the silence, backing down. "Just tell us what you need from us, Sarah. We want this bastard put away for life when we find him. If forcing this thing in a high-profile direction isn't the way to go, then—"

"It's not," she snapped. "But it *is* inevitable…"

Was she wavering?

Carter stepped forward and proposed, "We're working with a description—"

Franco huffed in exasperation and said, "You could've led with that!"

"It's decent, not great. Let me and Foster see how far we can get with it. Homicide should be shooting over a list of their suspects any second now. If our description matches a real face, then this thing will move fast and end well."

Sarah's sharp gaze softened with thoughtful consideration as she finished his point.

"And if it gets you nowhere, you want to go ahead with Danny's limelight strategy?"

"No, let's sit on our hands and let that sicko keep wielding his deranged plan," said Carter, his angered tone so thick with sarcasm that Franco barked his name, silencing him.

"Alright, fine," said Sarah, proving she could play ball. "But we meet *immediately after* you hunt for the guy based on this description you have, and *before* you contact the major news outlets."

"Of course," Danny assured her.

"Hopefully the latter won't have to happen," she concluded, her gaze falling to the image of Nahla in her hands.

Sarah's eyes rounded with emotion that Danny had never before seen in the D.A.

"I can't stand it when it's kids," she confessed in a tight, hiccupping sigh.

"We have every reason to believe she's still alive," said Danny tenderly.

The fire returned to Sarah's eyes as she cut her gaze to the detective and shot back, "And that's better?"

Than being dead? she thought... When it came to child abductors, pedophiles, monsters hiding among them that could rival the devil himself...?

Danny wasn't sure.

"We're going to find her," Carter promised. "And we're going to get you every piece of evidence you need to prove the twisted extent of every crime he's committed to get as far as he has."

Would they, though?

The greatest trick the devil ever pulled was convincing the world he didn't exist...

That's what scopolamine was.

Devil's Breath.

The method that enabled their killer to go on without 'existing.'

FOR A BROOKLYNITE who lived and worked in the gritty neighborhood of Kensington, Manhattan could feel awfully far away.

Danny rarely made the trip in, and if recollection served her, she hadn't been to Manhattan since last month when the Bauer investigation had brought her and Carter into the dark underbelly of NYC's modeling world.

Standing on West 40th Street where traffic inched its honking way towards an intersection and pedestrians hustled in both directions, Danny scanned the buildings through a grid of scaffolding that spanned the block, trying to find the right address.

It didn't help that the scaffolding casted eerie shadows, shielding light from the various street lamps along the block.

When she finally found the number '213' etched in the corroding stone face of a pre-war building, she wasted no time yanking the glass entrance door open and skimming the directory of businesses and their respective floors on the marquee in the bare and bleach-scented lobby.

It really wasn't the nicest building, that was for damn sure, but Colton, Payne, & Diedrich CPA located on the top floor was as elegant as any corporate stronghold this side of the river.

"I'm here to see Damian Payne," she informed the doe-eyed receptionist who had greeted her with a perky smile from where she sat behind a shiny desk. "*Detective* Foster."

Scanning her computer screen, she politely began informing Danny, "I don't believe—"

"He's not expecting me," she told the young woman who had probably graduated college yesterday if at all.

"The partners don't generally—"

"He'll make an exception," she said firmly, and when the implication didn't properly sink into the girl's brain, Danny mentioned, "I'm not looking for tax advice and the only courtesy I can extend to Mr. Payne is that I speak with him *privately*, so why don't you announce me, hmm?"

The receptionist's glossy mouth hung open and she fought intrigue long enough to dial the accountant.

"I have a 'Detective Foster' here for you, Sir," she said, her heart rate so elevated that her voice had come out clipped and breathy.

When she returned the phone to its cradle, she asked in a hushed, curious way, "What did he do?"

Interest piqued, Danny countered, "What makes you think Payne did something?"

The receptionist frowned, hesitant, mum, as she scanned the cubicles of bookkeepers, checking for eavesdroppers and prying eyes.

But she didn't get a chance to respond.

A towering black man dressed in a crisp suit that flattered his muscular build was approaching.

The man exuded confidence, class, and a hint of swagger, the horn-rimmed glasses he wore adding a bookish look to his otherwise *007* appearance.

Damian Payne had obviously done well for himself partnering with two other accountants to run his own firm.

And he had drugged and raped Jill Andover in his spare time.

Danny felt her jaw tighten and made a concerted effort to smooth out the sneer that was threatening to come over her face.

"Detective?" he asked, understandably a bit thrown, as he extended his hand and forced a friendly smile that to Danny looked nervous.

"I'm Damian Payne, one of the partners."

He flashed her another smile, this time showing no sign of paranoia or worry, as he invited her to come to his office.

"You would be my first cop, but I have several clients who are government employees," he explained good-naturedly, as he escorted her into a handsome corner office with stunning views of Bryant Park.

"Please," he said, rounding to the business side of his grand, mahogany desk, "have a seat."

"I'm not here to hire you," she glared without sitting.

"Oh?" Keeping up appearances that came across like bad acting, he innocently asked, "Then what can I do for you?"

"I work with a woman named Jill Andover."

It only lasted a fraction of a second—if Danny had blinked, she would've missed it—but Damian's pleasant expression hardened, and his dark eyes turned cold and flat.

In the next breath, he grinned at her as if they were destined to become great friends and boomed, "Jill's an amazing woman. It's so wonderful to meet a friend of hers. Wow, she told you about me?"

Danny stared daggers at him, unrelenting in her seething expression.

"I know what you did," she said to rattle him.

That polished grin of his, the one that indicated his parents had sent him to finishing school and might have even beaten him into perfection, faltered, but again it was nearly imperceptible.

"What did I do? Wined and dined her? Confessed my growing affection?" he challenged, his cordial tone deepening before he corrected the error and repeated, "She's an amazing woman."

"You think she isn't going to run a blood panel on herself to find out what you slipped her?"

The mask came off, and the man who had once looked like he had just walked out of a Cohen's Fashion Optical ad now appeared dangerously soulless.

"I have no idea what you're referring to."

"Of course you do," she shot back.

Cocking his head almost performatively, Damian asked, rhetoric thick in his deep voice, "You're misinformed, Detective. Jill just sent me this text."

He read from his cell phone, "*We on for tonight?*"

He returned his cell to his desk and seethed, "What you're implying is highly offensive."

"She wasn't supposed to remember a thing, was she?" she pressed. "She was never supposed to even suspect it."

His plastered smile was back, and as Danny glared at him, closing in on him and coming right up against the client-side of his desk, she realized she wasn't dealing with a recreational rapist who would scare easily.

The man was cool, calm, and collected.

Calculating.

Was he enjoying this?

It gave her the creeps.

"Stay away from her."

"Or what?"

Chapter Twelve

"WHEN THEY SAID 'list'," Danny's tired voice blared through his cell phone, "I foolishly assumed they had narrowed it down to *less* than every adult male in Kensington."

"That bad, huh?" asked Carter in a low tone, his shoulders hunched secretively where he stood, angling into a corner of Dr. Ling's anteroom so that his wife and the other patients couldn't hear.

Most of them were too busy wiping away tears or having revelations to notice the towering black man with a Glock in his shoulder holster and badge clipped to his belt.

The receptionist had, but she seemed more intrigued than alarmed.

Carter was used to the evening girl. He didn't ordinarily come on his lunch break because he rarely had any in the traditional sense.

"I'm looking at over thirty pages," she complained, and he could faintly hear her clicking her mouse. "And this is literally a list of names. They're hyperlinked, but I have to click each one and check the person out."

She sighed then sucked in a fortifying breath.

"I can do it. It'll just take time."

"Skip everyone that isn't dark skinned black," he suggested. "I would like to bring all the African-Americans to Lacy—"

Kathy's ears pricked up at the woman's name, and though she tried to keep her interest discreet and her attention focused on the entertainment magazine in her lap, Carter could tell alarm bells were going off inside her head.

"To the eye-witness," he corrected for his wife's benefit.

"You're going to have a heap," she warned. "Most of these guys are black and of the right age range. Looks like Raffi was a popular guy."

"Maybe," he said doubtfully. "Or maybe Homicide wants to slow us down."

"You give them too much credit," she balked. "Terrible as it's going to sound, I think they would be coming at this with some real urgency if their Vic was a white family man with a respectable job. They want this thing to go away."

Carter didn't have time to argue that if the D.A. had paid them a visit, she had certainly had the same discussion with Crouse and Toliver. If it hadn't occurred to the homicide detectives that the triple murder could hit the press any second, they were well aware of it now.

Some cops lived for the spotlight, mainly because it wasn't an everyday occurrence.

"Get me what you can," he concluded. "I'll swing by the precinct in about an hour before I head to the projects."

"I'm on it," she said, and after hearing the light click of her disengaging the call, he returned his cell phone to his pocket and joined Kathy in one of the waiting room chairs.

Her attempt to sound casual was a disaster as she asked, "Who's Lacy?"

At least they were at their therapist's office if she launched into the usual argument that had been plaguing their marriage for the past year.

Ninety percent of every fiber in his being wanted to dismiss the ludicrous question with a curt 'she's no one,' but that response had waged wars between them in the past.

So, instead he opened his mouth to remind her that he couldn't discuss the details of the case.

But then he quickly remembered that he had been sharing tidbits all along. He had even asked Kathy to pack his flashiest sweat pants and a few thick, gold chains to save him time.

The duffel bag was resting between her feet.

He leaned into her ear and explained, "She's a potential witness."

"Who saw that little girl get taken?"

"Shh," he warned, looking around at the other patients. They were all too wrapped up in their own emotional diarrhea to care.

"She didn't see that, but she saw something, the perpetrator we're hoping."

Kathy seemed to appreciate being included. The accusatory glint in her narrowed eyes had melted away, and a look of compassion came over her angelic features.

She took hold of his hand, gave him a squeeze, and with a fine mist of tears clouding the blue of her eyes, she whispered, "I'm really glad you're here."

He knew what those tears were about.

He had opened up to her a while back when he had confessed the regretful mistake of his one-night affair with another woman—a mistake that had hit him hard emotionally but had propelled the case he was working forward, cracking it wide open and ultimately leading to a massive take-down of one of the worst sex trafficking rings in the northeast.

It had been a tangled logic. He had known it at the time.

He had attempted to excuse his transgression by blaming it on just how bad things had been for him. In the basement. As a boy. How surviving that kind of abuse had left a fault line running straight through his mind and soul. One that could erupt at any time, splitting his seemingly normal, functioning personality in two. An earthquake of destruction manifesting in the form of self-sabotaging and escapist behavior.

Kathy had wanted to understand him, wanted to buy his explanation, wanted to forgive and forget.

But the longer she had stared at him in their darkened bedroom after he had told her everything he could and fallen silent, her eyes had turned cold and she had looked at him as though he were a weak man, an adulterer, someone she should've never married.

It had been a very long road back into her bed.

But he knew there was quite a ways to go before he would be back in her heart, never again at risk for her looking at him like that.

The receptionist flashed him a smile, staring at him expectantly.

"Hmm?" he asked, catching on that both Kathy and him hadn't heard her announce that Dr. Ling would see them now. "We can go in?"

Duffel bag in hand, Kathy followed Carter down the familiar little hallway, passing other therapists' closed office doors on the right and left until they came to Dr. Ling's open one.

The office was all bamboo and bubbling water fountains. Tranquil, Asian-sounding, New Age music played faintly.

The blinds spanning two large bay windows were drawn just so, helping the warm afternoon light bathe the room without blinding it.

Dr. Ling was already seated on her armchair, comfortably across from the matching couch where Kathy and Carter were trained to go.

She scrawled a few final thoughts from her last session, but welcomed them in without lifting her angled, black eyes.

Carter offered Kathy an *I'm present and cooperative* smile that felt just as heavy as the trepidation in his gut.

If he could corral the conversation away from his childhood and towards the concept of building trust with his wife, he might be able to walk out of this office an hour later unscathed.

But as he had been learning, one had everything to do with the other.

He gave his attention to Ling, wondering why she intimidated him so badly when she was as petite and thin-boned as a bird.

His heart rate was elevating by the second, and as she met his gaze, tucking her pin-straight black bob behind her ears then folding her toothpick fingers on her open notebook, he hoped like hell she wouldn't 'call on him' first.

Luckily, Kathy had her own agenda.

But unluckily, it placed Carter right back on the hook he had been trying to wriggle his way off of.

"I know this is usually my one-on-one hour, but I felt it was so important to include Carter today because of the case he's taken on… It's triggering and I don't want him to relapse."

Carter gritted his teeth.

Politely, and without a shred of judgment in her tone, Ling asked, "Is that true, Carter?"

"What am I supposed to say? That it's *not* true, which would imply my wife is lying? That'll go great," he snorted sarcastically. "I didn't tell her my case was triggering. I don't have a problem with my case, and I didn't 'take it on.' It was assigned to me. I'm in no danger of 'relapsing,' if what Kathy means by that is I'll have another one-night affair—"

"I overheard him mention a woman named Lacy," she told Dr. Ling then pressed her mouth into a thin, worried line. "Just now as we were waiting."

Here we go.

"I hear a lot of assumptions, Kathy," said the therapist, looking kindly at her. "I see someone who's afraid her assumptions are right. I don't see Carter making assumptions. I *do* see him responding *defensively*—"

"Thank you!" Kathy blurted.

"When someone assumes wrongly about me," said Ling, "I take offense, I take insult, I respond defensively, because in order to correct their error, their mistaken impression of me, I must literally defend myself."

Kathy sank back onto her seat, realizing her own error. She folded her arms, and soon the weight of silence in the room brought tears to her eyes.

"Well, if I can't say how I feel!"

"You can say how you feel," Ling invited. "So, go ahead."

Kathy cut her eyes to Carter and said, "I *feel* like Carter hasn't properly dealt with his past, and until he does we're just going to have the same problems rear their ugly heads up in our marriage."

He loved this woman. But sometimes he didn't recognize her. Sometimes her self-righteous narrow-mindedness, her stubborn argumentative style caused her features to distort her face. She looked like a stranger.

"What if Carter doesn't need to be changed or fixed?" Ling proposed. "What if his past, as painful as it may have been, doesn't need reconciliation? What if the so-called damage it did, didn't flaw him, but strengthened him? And what if the problem you're anticipating and fearing has nothing to do with the man you married."

"We *were* fine. He had an *affair*. Now we're *not* fine," she insisted.

"You forgave him. Said you would move forward. And now you're not," she countered in an identical, staccato manner.

"*I* didn't have an affair!" she blurted out, exasperated. "I'm not going to let him dictate to me that we're 'fine'! If I ask 'who's Lacy?' I want the whole truth and nothing but the truth!"

Carter was smart enough not to fuel this fire with any kind of audible response.

"I think you want a 'slave' to your 'master'," Ling boldly countered, taking Kathy aback.

Even Carter's jaw dropped.

"I'm talking about you, as a White woman of privilege, choosing a Black man with a so-called damaged past—a past of actual enslavement—as your partner. Carter?"

Oh, God.

"When you first met Kathy and began dating her," she went on. "How did you treat her?"

"Like a goddess," he said without thinking.

"We had a very *equal* relationship," Kathy angrily maintained.

But Carter quickly corrected his wife, saying, "I worshiped you. You know that. I still do."

"If you would like to spend this session talking about 'the past,' let's get down to what's really there. Carter was kept as a slave," she said grimly. "He was held against his will. He served. He was treated inhumanely, worse than an animal. And it shaped him. But not necessarily for the worst. In his adulthood, he found a woman to be his master. Someone he could serve. He hasn't broken free of the same role."

Damn, Carter hoped that wasn't true.

"Him cherishing me isn't the problem," Kathy disagreed.

"Not to you, it's not," Ling allowed. "Because your past taught you to be the master, the one who demands to be cherished. It would be inconceivable to you *not* to be worshiped and cherished. You're both perfect for each other in this sense. But there's virtually no equality, which is why when Carter shows strength in his profession, you become afraid. And it's also why," she cut her discerning eyes to Carter, "when Carter senses you growing lax, loosening your controlling grip, and no longer lording over him, he goes out and does something so egregious that you have no choice but to tighten the reins, throw him in the 'doghouse,' and whip him back into shape."

It was haunting how much sense she was making.

"He didn't have to tell you about that woman," she reminded Kathy. "And he didn't tell you out of the goodness of his heart or because his conscience was too pure to let it stand. Carter needs to remain in that 'doghouse'."

Dog crate.

Basement.

Darkness.

Desperate to please the master who he knew would only hurt him.

The crank of the pocket watch.

Don't keep him waiting.

Whose voice was that?

"Don't keep him waiting," the mousey voice had come from the darkest corner of the basement.

Another child.

He wasn't alone.

There were so many children, so many mousy voices, so much muffled weeping, mouths twisting with anguish in the dark…

Don't keep him waiting…

Carter had pushed on the dog crate door—but who had unlatched it for him? Who had opened the lock, freeing him to go willingly, trembling but willingly, to meet the man?

It hadn't been the man. Not another kid. Not an accomplice.

There hadn't been a lock, he realized the moment Dr. Ling said his name. He had slipped away.

"Yeah?" he said, realizing the worst of it—maybe he could've fled at any time. Realizing that Ling was right. He had been a slave… and still was one.

But he had never known there had been others. His mind hadn't allowed him to remember. He recalled when the case and trial had culminated—Carter, a teenaged boy, having finally been rescued—that there was mention of other children down there.

But Carter hadn't *remembered*. He hadn't let the fact *touch him*. Hadn't let its meaning sink in.

And now Nahla…

Where was she right now?

The District Attorney, Sarah Hovey, had been concerned there could be others…

"Carter?" Dr. Ling asked again, calling him back into the room.

But he was being pulled under once again…

Other boys and girls in the basement. Other potential victims like Nahla now. The past blending seamlessly with the present.

But there was no way. He had been caught. Arrested. Put behind bars.

"Babe?" Kathy asked with genuine concern in her voice.

He hadn't felt her take hold of his hand, but he could feel her squeezing him now.

"I was a slave. I am," he murmured.

The slave becomes the master.

It was a radical notion, too radical to properly grasp.

Kathy was saying something kind, but he couldn't hear her.

His gaze fell, unseeingly, to the carpet.

The mastermind.

The controlling one.

The next thing he knew he was on his feet, and it wasn't until the crisp wind hit his damp forehead that he realized he was starting briskly up the avenue, duffel bag in hand, having abandoned his wife, Dr. Ling, and the very concept of remaining the 'slave' he had once been.

"YOU LOOK LIKE you've seen a ghost," said Danny, who had been waiting for him in the conference room with a thick stack of driver's license photos in a manila filing folder—all the perps from Crouse and Toliver's list that looked like Carter.

Dressed now in the flashy sweatpants ensemble Kathy had put together, a pair of mint-condition high tops on his feet, and two heavy gold chains around his thick neck, the ghetto-gold medallions of which rested on the firm wall of his chest, he took the folder, set it on the table, and began flipping through the faces.

"You okay?" asked Danny when he hadn't responded.

Were any of those kids, who were now adults, peppered within this stack? Would he recognize them if they were? If just one was? Was it wishful thinking to hope that someone from Raffi's circle—one of the men in this folder—had grown up with Carter in that basement?

"I'm fine," he said absently. "Just in a rush."

"How are you going to play this off?" she asked. "You're just going to show up with a bunch of

Xerox copies of people's drivers licenses, and Lacy Marcel's not going to wonder…?"

Should he tell her? He met her gaze, daunted by all the faces, by the fact no one had jumped out at him, and he had only torn through a fifth of the stack.

He searched her eyes, debating if sharing his mind-bending revelation with her was the right thing to do.

"You're acting *off*."

No, he thought. Not yet. He would keep this one to himself.

"Therapy," he said, writing his mood off with the only excuse that would make sense. Danny knew that's where he had disappeared during his lunch break anyway.

"I don't know how you do it," she agreed. "If anyone tried to crack my can of worms open, I don't see how I would make it out of bed the next day."

He laughed, slapped her shoulder good-naturedly with the folder, and thanked her, then made his way out of the 66th, Lacy Marcel and his strategy for getting a positive ID broiling at the forefront of his mind.

Whether it was plausible or not, the explanation he used with one very sexed up, dewy-skinned, and breathy Lacy Marcel—she had greeted him at the door wearing even skimpier yoga digs than she had the first time he had sauntered up to her door—was that a cop at the 66th was in his pocket, as dirty as an old penny.

Lacy didn't question him or glare at him sideways.

Instead, she pawed at him as if foreplay was on the agenda, flipped the Xerox copies one after the next, and bringing her plump lips to his neck, declared, "That guy I saw ain't in there."

He shoved her off, and she squealed, "Hey," falling to the couch, unharmed.

"Look again."

"Damn," she complained, taking the folder to do a better job this time.

As he stood over her, monitoring her efforts, his cell phone began vibrating in his pocket.

Damn, it was Kathy. She knew about his undercover stint; that he would be going in right after their session with Dr. Ling. She had packed the duffel bag for Christ's sake so was this call meant to sabotage him?

Or had he left so abruptly that she had been filled with genuine concern and needed to check in to know he was okay?

He killed the call and focused on Lacy.

"He looked like he could have been your cousin or something," she told him, frustrated not to find the guy in the stack. "Like y'all played on the same football team or something. You know what I'm saying?"

"Those are all of Raffi's acquaintances," he pushed.

"Then that guy I saw wasn't one of Raffi's boys," she shot back. "If he did Kayla and Andre, maybe he's from their circle?"

Or from Nahla's parents' circles? From Khan Rashad's or Sapphire's.

There were too many circles, too many characters to comb through.

Maybe Carter needed to look at his *own* circle, find the other kids, and work this thing from the dangerous inside out.

"God," he barked when Kathy called again.

He paced away from Lacy, staring at the screen of his cell.

There was no getting out of it so he told Lacy to keep her mouth shut—he knew how to play the thug, and she liked obeying as it turned out—and picked up.

"Carter, I know you don't have time," Kathy was quick to say, her voice calm and sweet—maybe Ling had gotten through to her in his absence. "I called the babysitter for the kids. I think we need time alone together."

"Okay," he stated, letting just enough emotion crack through, as he kept his sharp eyes on Lacy, warning her to keep her mouth shut.

"Not to try to work anything out," she assured him. "I don't want to fight."

He didn't either.

"We'll have the house to ourselves," she promised. "The kids will be out with the sitter by the time you get home."

He wanted to melt through the phone, collapse into her arms, and cry.

But instead, he uttered another emotionless, "Okay," stuffed his cell back into his pocket, and hoped like hell that what he was about to do wouldn't backfire like a bomb in his face.

"I'm a cop," he told Lacy, whose expression sprang with surprise. "I need you to come to the station with me."

"What?!"

"Now," he ordered, pulling her up from the couch by her arm. "I need to know exactly what the guy looks like and you're going to help me."

Chapter Thirteen

IT WAS TOO EARLY, but Danny woke with a chill in her bones that no amount of nuzzling against Tommy could fix.

She bundled up in sweatpants and a bulky sweater, and left him breathing heavily in favor of getting a pot of coffee going.

The kitchen was dark with promises of an overcast day.

She hadn't bothered turning on the lights.

Seated at the islet with her steaming mug of coffee, she looked out the window where there had never been much to see—brick apartment buildings across the way, their windows curtained, blinds drawn.

Few people were up at this hour, yet traffic growled along the avenue, headlights breaking the misting fog.

Nora had been on her mind.

Fear and longing.

Her mother, Nora, had gotten in the habit of sweeping and tidying her own stoop, like the first act of a melodramatic play that had no worthwhile, developing plotline. She had been making her presence known. She wouldn't be forgotten.

Danny had told Nora to stay away from her. It was the one condition that came with Danny not turning Nora in for the murder of her infant son. But more and more, Nora was crossing that line.

Nora was acting as though Danny didn't have it in her to make good on her threat. And Nora had also been acting as though she could wear her daughter down, and restore their relationship, and Danny would never have her arrested for infanticide.

She had to wonder now, was her mother right?

Or did she have the guts to take Jill's autopsy report on Gregory to her precinct, her department, and force the truth out into the open even if it made her scream and cry and lose all control of herself.

She wished she could do it...

If anyone had ever been a 'special victim,' it was her baby.

But she couldn't.

She wanted her mother to think that she was strong, that the decision she had made, sparing Nora from prison, was out of compassion, and not because she thought Nora didn't deserve punishment.

She deserved hell.

But the longer Nora was out there. On the stoop. Glancing over. Asserting her presence, and her *freedom*, the clearer it became to Danny that Nora might be functioning with the mistaken belief that she had done nothing wrong.

Maybe Nora had even slipped into some form of denial where she believed that her grandson really had died of S.I.D.S. and not by her murdering hands.

Confronting Nora again was an option, but Danny had little confidence it would be productive.

For the time being, all Danny could do was make sure her mother hadn't approached Tommy. Danny had been checking in with Tommy here and there to make sure her mother wasn't angling to tell Tommy what had really happened to Gregory, and what Danny *hadn't* done in response.

She couldn't think about this anymore, she told herself, as she tried concentrating on her coffee, its scent and taste, taking quick gulps.

The caffeine should launch her out of dark ruminations and it did, but minutes later, having poured a second cup and turned on the television—muted news—she found herself boomeranging.

Not back into thinking about her mother, but about Jill Andover, Damian Payne, and the tangled mess of their relationship.

Relationship?

Jill had called Danny, suspecting the man had drugged her.

Danny folded herself onto the living room couch, recalling the gut-clenching phone call that had implied rape. Yet by the time Danny had paid Payne a visit, Jill had again contacted him, eager for another date?

Heavy, twisted stuff.

At least Danny wasn't the only one whose personal life boggled the mind…

She wondered what skeletons Tommy might be hoarding in his figurative closet.

Maybe everyone had some unspeakable secret lurking right beneath the surface.

She remembered Carter's bold admission, how he had casually shocked a conference room full of detectives with it, herself included.

As she sat, drinking her coffee and resting her gaze on the muted television where a bubbly blonde joshed around with her retired-jock co-host, Danny mentally skimmed all the people in her life who could very well be hiding disturbing, perhaps unfathomable, secrets. Doing this helped her feel less messed up, less alone, and yet, she suddenly felt more worried for the state of the world. Wasn't every case she had ever worked the fatal result of someone's dark secret gone wrong?

This was no way to start her Friday, she concluded, so when her cell phone began vibrating on the islet, she wasted no time hopping off the couch to retrieve it.

"Franco?" she greeted, glancing at the clock above the stove. It was barely after seven.

"Carter's with me," he said. "You're on speaker."

"What, am I late?"

"Another photo arrived." That was Carter now.

She could hear the up-all-night in his haggard tone and recalled he had gone into the projects for the third time yesterday after she had supplied the file of potential suspects.

"I'll be right in," she told them, and just as she was about to hang up:

Carter asked, "Bring coffee?"

The distinct sounds of Franco pacing away and grumbling about his detective's complaints filled the background as Carter told her, "We're *out* in the break room, totally out of coffee, and since bright-eyed what's-her-name won't be in 'til nine—"

"Say no more," she said, the new receptionist's name having escaped her as well. "See ya soon."

As she turned for the bedroom hallway, Tommy rounded into the kitchen, his salt-and-pepper hair akimbo. He was wearing tight boxer-briefs, his sweatshirt barely pulled on.

"Smells good," he said, nearing her with heavy feet.

She accepted a quick kiss then told him, "I've got to head out. Coffee's fresh."

She was halfway up the hallway now, calling out, "I know your friend has that thing tonight at the bar, but…"

Her jeans weren't cooperating but once she wriggled them over her hips and secured her holstered gun around her waist, she finished her point.

"It might be a long one for me. I'll have to keep you posted."

"Hey, Danny?"

She knew his intonations by now and could tell he wanted to start a real conversation, but she honestly didn't have a second to spare. Another photo had arrived? She would've liked it a hell of a lot more if either Franco or Carter had told her that they believed Nahla was still alive.

"I'll talk to you later," she promised, grabbing her jacket at the door.

Tommy trailed after her.

"It's important."

She stared at him for a beat. Talking wasn't their thing, and she had never heard Tommy use the word 'important' in conjunction with it.

But just as she was about to ask, he ushered her out saying, "Go, go, we'll talk later. Let me know if you'll make it to the bar."

Grabbing a fistful of his sweatshirt, she pulled him in and kissed him hard in the doorway, then pushed him off and stared at him with her brow furrowed. "Don't scare me like that."

"Like what?"

Had Nora caught him off guard? Were her worst fears about to come true?

"Nothing," she said, eyeing him for a beat.

It wasn't until she had stepped into the elevator that she heard the click of her apartment door close, Tommy having watched her leave for as long as the hallway would allow.

She had every intention of hailing a cab, but Kensington wasn't known for its transportation conveniences like Manhattan or even other neighborhoods in Brooklyn.

She kept her eyes up, on the lookout for a cab just in case, as she walked briskly south, the chill in the air refusing to die even as the sun inched up the foggy sky. She walked all the way to the precinct.

Twelve minutes later, she arrived at the 66th sweaty and slightly out of breath, her jacket as well as her sweater draped over her forearm, not that any degree of stripping down had cooled her. She had three to-go cups of joe in a carrying tray in one hand, a bag of grounded dark roast in the other.

After swinging by the break room and checking Franco's office, she found the lieutenant and her partner in the conference room standing over an 8" x 11" glossy print that was lying on the table.

Jill and two squirrely members of her team were preparing to dust the photo for prints, presumably.

The District Attorney, Sarah Hovey, was also present, pacing the room the length of the spacious, kid-friendly room, her cell phone to her ear.

"That's what I'm talking about," Carter said, his gaze locked on the coffee in her hand, as he made a beeline for Danny.

She almost didn't recognize him. He looked like he belonged in a hip hop video.

She pointed to her own teeth and suggested, "Next time wear a grillz. It'll pull the whole look together."

"Ha. Ha," he said dryly. "I blew my cover anyway."

"On purpose?"

"Had to happen," he told her and was about to say more when Franco called her over to the photograph.

Staring down at the image, she breathed "What the—" as shock, confusion, and sharp clenches of dread roiled through her. "Who's the woman?"

She met Carter's gaze then Franco's, but neither had an answer for her.

Sarah was barking something about 'holding the press at bay' from where she was pacing near the vending machine.

Danny was fully focused on the photograph that had just changed everything.

In it, Nahla was dressed, as bright as a canary and twice as feathery, in a flamboyant headdress and skimpy bikini. She was on her knees, her hands folded in prayer, as she looked up, not at the camera lens, but at the woman who towered over her.

An adult woman.

Dressed identically.

Her back to the camera.

"Who the hell is that?" Danny demanded, but only to herself.

The others weren't holding out on her. They were equally stumped.

All Danny could surmise from the professional-quality print was that the woman was Caucasian. Even determining her height wasn't possible since there was nothing but Nahla on her knees in the frame for scale. Age would be a guess at best, anywhere from 18-50, who could tell? It could be a minor for all they knew.

"An accomplice?"

"Maybe," said Franco, but Carter had strong doubts.

"Come on, does that sound like our guy?"

To punctuate his point, he flipped the glossy print face down with a gloved hand, revealing another religious message that had been collaged on the back, one which Franco was obviously aware of.

Danny leaned in and read out loud, "You shall not bow down to them or serve them, for I, the Lord your God, am a jealous God."

It took a moment for the magnitude of the message to sink in, its resonance with the image of Nahla praying to, or perhaps begging with hands folded, an older version of herself—the false God, presumably.

You shall not bow down to them or serve them.

That's what the posed image portrayed—the mistake of worshiping a false God.

For I, the Lord your God, am a jealous God.

"Damn, Carter," she breathed, meeting her partner's gaze. "He thinks he's God."

Franco filled her in, "It's a quote from Exodus, the second book in the Bible. But he left the second part out. He intentionally perverted the message, which goes on to promise, pages later, that God is merciful and gracious, slow to anger, and will forgive transgressions and sins for those who seek forgiveness."

Surprised, she cocked her head at his recitation, and Franco mentioned with a shrug, "Sunday school."

She couldn't picture the lieutenant as a wet-behind-the-ears boy, all dressed up for Sunday school, but that was neither here nor there.

Jill neared them, and as Danny touched eyes with her, a fresh billow of tension blossomed between them.

Intuition told Danny that the M.E. knew of her little visit to Damian Payne's accounting firm, that Danny had gone even though Jill had called the whole thing off and hung up on her.

Jill probably knew that Danny knew—thanks to the financially-savvy date-rapist—that Jill had texted the man for another date *after* she had brought to the detective's attention the possibility of having been violated.

"Detective," Jill said curtly. "If I may."

She reached with gloved hands for the photo and brought it to her subordinates who had set up a little forensic table.

As forensics began sweeping a blue light over the photo and devising other methods to pull prints and Touch DNA, not that their killer-kidnapper would've been careless enough to leave any, Franco waved Sarah over despite the fact that her phone call had only grown more heated with showing no signs of concluding.

"I'll have to call you back," she told whoever was on the other end.

Danny guessed the Attorney General, but she couldn't be certain.

"I said I'll call you back!" Slapping her cell phone shut, she conceded without preamble, "We need to hold a press conference."

Carter looked more than validated, but Sarah was quick to burst his bubble.

"There's no way you're going on camera dressed like that."

"I'll change," he said, undeterred.

Sarah frowned, ran her manicured hand down her face, then sucked in a deep, fortifying breath. As if daunted, she warned, "We have to control the details of the case. These photos, the fact that they've been showing up anonymously, the fact that you people have no clue as to who's sending them…"

The insult landed heavily, but no one objected.

"I don't want any of it leaked. Especially not the God-complex, religious aspects, Jesus H. Christ." She widened her eyes as if haunted.

"We can announce an AMBER alert," Franco offered. "Use Nahla's school photo. Use the sketch of our suspect."

Danny shot a questioning look to Carter who filled her in, "My eye-witness from the projects, Lacy Marcel. I brought her in last night and it took 'til the sun came up, but we got a decent rendering of the guy she saw."

"*If—*" Sarah was quick to correct, "that's even the man who killed Samuels and Durant."

"Whether it is or isn't," Franco cut in. "Whether it's the man who took Nahla Rashad or not, we report as if it is, we leave out the triple murder, maybe that's 'getting it wrong' enough to provoke the guy out of hiding to correct us."

"Correct you people with more photos?" Sarah challenged, making no secret of the fact she had little faith in how they were handling things. Again, she ran her hands down her face, which was looking more and more dour by the second. "There's no way we'll get away with this."

"Talk to me," said Franco, not understanding.

Shaking her head now, the gears spinning at a blur inside her troubled mind, Sarah explained, "Kayla's parents, the Samuels? They have an audience. They're distinguished professors. Queenie and Raja '*give good photo*,' as they say, they're extremely intelligent and would give a shocking interview if given the chance. There's no way they're going to sit back and keep quiet if news reports are mentioning the abduction but not their daughter's murder."

"We could talk to them," Danny offered. "Get them to cooperate with our strategy."

"I already have," Sarah told them before frowning. "It didn't go well."

Danny wasn't surprised. Queenie and Raja hadn't struck her as the types to yield to 'white' orders. If Carter hadn't been with her when they had gone to the Samuels' home the second time, she would've been met with the same hard stares and brick walls she had the first time around when she had foolishly dared to show up alone.

"Now I've got Crouse and Toliver from Homicide," Sarah went on to complain, "going over my head and asking the Attorney General if they can report directly to the press."

Danny shot Carter a *no-surprise-there* look.

"I can't have that," she stated. "Homicide has no business reporting on a missing girl, and quite frankly, neither does SVU. It'll raise too many questions."

"You want someone in Missing Persons to run with it for the cameras?" Franco asked.

"Not especially." She doubled-down, conceding, "Nahla *is* a 'special victim'."

Danny understood her hesitation. No matter how they presented the details, the press was going to come up with their own stories. There would be no way of controlling it, not really.

This was about to be a serious mess, but that didn't mean it wouldn't solicit the response they wanted from their perp.

Sarah's cell began vibrating, and her whole body went tense, as she read the screen.

"I've got to take this. I'll schedule the press conference for nine," she informed them, as she paced off again to give the caller her full attention.

That gave them less than two hours.

And all they had were multiplying questions.

The woman in the photo. It didn't sit right with Danny.

She grabbed Carter's arm, as he turned to start for their desks and said, "Scopolamine."

Catching her point, "She was drugged?"

Danny lifted her eyebrows in response, "Wouldn't she have to be?"

"So, is she alive out there somewhere or dead?"

"Is she a captive like Nahla?" she spit-balled.

Who the hell was she?

Jill neared them, the photo sealed in an evidence bag in her gloved hand, and said, "Need any last looks, or can I take this?"

DANNY HAD TRIED Tommy twice. She had placed one call to his cell that went straight to voicemail, followed by an admittedly anxious sounding text message, which he also hadn't responded to. Probably for innocent enough reasons—he was showering, in a hurry to leave her apartment, or busy opening O'Toole's for the lunch crowd. Or maybe he had left his cell phone in the office while he rushed around.

It's important.

It worried her.

A thick fog had rolled in, the skies overhead balmy and overcast, as she stood staring unseeingly at the cell phone in her hand that wasn't ringing with Tommy's reply. She was acting crazy, letting her imagination get the best of her.

Reluctantly, she put her phone on silent mode and shoved it into the inner pocket of the black blazer she had thrown on for the press conference.

Beside her, Carter was putting her to shame in a crisp, tailored suit. They were standing outside of the Brooklyn courthouse where the D.A. had thought it the best location to assemble all the major news outlets.

Everything was set—the podium with its bouquet of microphones, the seating area filled with reporters, cameramen lining the back, everyone eager to get going before the skies made good on their threat to break open with rain.

Sarah clicked her high-heeled way over to the podium, tapped the microphones, and cleared her throat, then she glanced at Franco. He was ready, too, making a concerted effort to keep in front of Detectives Crouse and Toliver who were obnoxiously attempting to edge their way into what they probably thought was 'in frame.'

Without further ado, Sarah, with lights in her eyes and a stilted, unnatural tone in her voice, began reading, "On the evening of May 12th a six-year old girl by the name of Nahla Rashad was taken from her home…"

Chapter Fourteen

DAMIAN HATED PARTING ways with her, his little angel.

She hadn't been with him long, but he was starting to feel as though he couldn't remember his life without her.

What had his mornings been like before this daily routine had started?

He was now used to hearing the pitter-patter of her bare feet across the floor, as she snatched a book or DVD from the shelf, eager to begin her day.

What had his lunch breaks been like before Nahla, before this habit of driving home to the condo to make grilled cheese and tomato soup, then lying down with her for a short, sleepless nap?

What had his evenings been like before Nahla? Before their nightly ritual of dress-up and playtime with Jill whenever he had heavily drugged her and brought the stupid woman home?

Nahla had been taking more and more initiative in their playtime rituals. The girl loved picking out feather headdresses and belly dancing coin skirts for Jill to wear. Playing with Jill's heavily drugged body as if the blonde were her own personal puppet, Nahla never failed to smile. She often gave Damian ideas about how to frame each shot...

When he thought about it now, life without Nahla had been colorless drudgery.

Together, they were burning away the sins of her parents, of her godmother, of all who had worshiped a false god—dope and smack and crank.

Nahla was becoming more and more free, spiritually, and with that freedom within came freedom without. Locking her in the bedroom he had made for her, having converted his home office, was no longer necessary.

She was a willing slave; as willing as he used to be when he had been a child slave.

The circle of life was complete.

But Jill Andover was becoming a real problem.

He had chosen her carefully. It tickled him to have seduced the very medical examiner who had dissected and studied the three sinners whose lives he had justly ended.

She had seemed a wise choice.

In theory, he should easily have been able to pluck information about the investigations from her, but though she was consistently malleable when it came to him controlling her bodily movements and commanding her to obey his every order, he had struggled to get her to *talk* freely.

Call it a shortcoming of his mastery or a design flaw of the drug itself, but all Jill ever told him was 'yes.'

She had outworn her use.

She no longer amused him.

She was no longer proving very useful.

And she had gone and done the unthinkable.

She had remembered.

Just a hint.

Maybe it was only a suspicion.

But she had *told*.

And she had told a detective, no less.

She must be punished.

Severely.

It saddened him, as he thumbed the crisp edge of one of the glossy prints from his collection, seated as he was, in his office at the accounting firm. He had driven in early that morning to beat the traffic rush.

Jill's big, hollow eyes stared up at him from the photo. Glazed-over. Vacant. Zombie-like. As beautiful as she had ever been.

They all sinned eventually, didn't they?

To doubt God was a serious offense.

And Jill had doubted him in the most offensive way. She had gone behind his back and brought her concern to a detective.

Damian felt his jaw tighten, his hand clamped hard, the photo bending, as fury boiled through his veins.

He thought he would find some relief in the revenge of having mailed the photo of her and Nahla to that precinct, the one that should've known girls like Nahla—boys like he had been decades ago—were being tortured right under their privileged noses.

He had assumed the irony of Jill handling the photo, in complete ignorance that the woman in the photograph was herself, would've been enough to restore balance and quell his anger at her betrayal.

Thinking about it even now brought a satisfied grin to his face, but it wasn't enough.

Perhaps he would have her carve her own tongue out of her mouth. That punishment would certainly fit the crime.

Without warning a punch of emotion groaned out of him, and he slapped her photo face down on his expensive desk.

He didn't want to have to hurt her.

Yes, she had alerted that woman detective, but she had also, in her own small way, begged to be with him still. She had texted, called, and had proposed date ideas. She didn't want to believe her suspicions. And in so many ways, Damian wanted to fault himself. He should've administered higher and higher doses of Devil's Breath. He knew about the tolerance build up. Of course, there were risks to increasing the dosage, but it would have been better to accidentally kill her than to get sloppy and enable her to potentially remember…

To murder or not to murder her…

Some decisions were not so easy to make, and Nahla still very much delighted in their nightly play dates. Though Damian sensed she would be just as happy with any woman, it didn't have to be Jill, it wasn't lost on him that the girl had grown attached.

He didn't want to debate this anymore, it was making him sick.

Pulling out the lap drawer of his desk open after he had unlocked it with the small brass key, he briefly admired the photographs inside the drawer.

The photos were fanned out in an array of gorgeous images. He had been collecting them. Jill and his precious Nahla were posed artistically in each shot.

He placed the photo of Jill's face that he had been looking at onto the others in the drawer. Her doll-like expression of serenity stared up at him, though the glossy print was now bent.

He locked the drawer and grabbed two remote controls.

The first he used to power open the entertainment center that was handsomely disguised to look like a cabinet. The doors disappeared into the sides of the unit, revealing a flat screen TV, which Damian turned on with the second remote. The monitor and speakers came to life, and a little white noise played.

He checked his emails and tried not to think about killing Jill.

There came a knock at his closed door and before he could respond, the receptionist, Mindy, peeked her pudgy face in and exclaimed, "Oh! You *are* here."

"Yes, Mindy," he said dryly.

"I thought I heard someone in here," she mentioned, explaining her correct guess, as she offered him a thin stack of mail.

Damian didn't take the stack, so she set it on his desk

"What do you need?"

"Nothing," she said innocently.

He couldn't say he minded that she feared him, but her strategy of playing nicey-nice and lingering like some lonely child hungry for acceptance was highly irritating.

"Can I get you a coffee? I've mastered the espresso machine," she proudly stated, which reminded him of the bitter disaster she had nearly poisoned him with last month.

He was about to excuse her when a breaking news story stole his annoyed attention.

Eyes glued to the television, he held a single finger up to silence Mindy, and stared at the female detective who, only days ago, had dared to march through his accounting firm like she owned the place and had further dared to confront him.

Those big, sad eyes, and her slanted mouth that made her seem clever or perhaps wicked—she was standing off to the wayside from an older Latino man who dominated the podium, speaking slowly and clearly into a bouquet of microphones.

There were captions across the bottom edge of the screen reading:

'AMBER ALERT: Six-year old girl snatched from loving home.'

Horrified—*loving?*—Damian floated out of his chair and drifted towards the television, remote control in hand. He folded his arms and furrowed his brow, listening to their phenomenally inaccurate news report.

"So crazy," Mindy commented, coming up beside him. "I got the text message alert on my cell phone and started watching."

He was too intrigued by the lieutenant detailing the kidnapping event to pay attention to Mindy's idiotic opinion.

"I heard statistically that nine times out of ten, the kidnapper is always whatever parent that doesn't have full custody, you know? The parent gets fed up and takes their kid, that's what I heard. Like, it's not really an emergency. But this time, I mean, this is the real deal, you know? Like a stranger broke into their home and stole that little girl. There! That's her!"

Damian scowled at Mindy, but her attention was locked on the TV where Nahla's school portrait had appeared.

"Who are these sickos?" she wondered.

"Would you excuse me?" he snapped.

Taken aback, she stared at him, wide-eyed and largely confused for a fraction of a second. Then she murmured an apology and immediately retreated from his office, closing the door and leaving him to inch closer and closer towards the news report.

He would love to kill the female detective.

He suddenly could not take his eyes off of the mountainous African-American cop beside her.

The woman's partner? He had to be. There was a badge clipped to his belt, and the determined glint in his eye boasted the kind of NYPD arrogance that Damian had come to recognize in all officers of the law.

But it wasn't the man's attitude that had intrigued Damian. It was his actual face, the facial features, his stature, those lips, and the defiance in his dark eyes.

He was *familiar…*

The Latino lieutenant stepped back and the two detectives took his place just as the caption spanning the bottom edge of the screen changed to read, 'Det. Carter Dobbs and Det. Danielle Foster, 66th Precinct, Brooklyn'.

Carter.

Suddenly, he remembered.

Damian felt his eyes widening, as he drank in the sight of the Black man. The adult, who had once been the defiant black boy who Damian had come to know and trust and even love, all those years ago.

'They haven't been locking us in,' was Carter's optimistic revelation. 'We can make a run for it!'

'You'll never make it.' Damian hadn't wanted to deny the hope in his friend's heart. He had wanted to charge headlong and fearlessly into Carter's plan, but he had been

down in the basement longer than Carter. He had lived and learned. He hadn't had an ounce of hope left to try and break free a second time.

Days later, he held Carter in his arms, having slinked into the boy's dog crate, and cried with him. He hadn't said, I told you so, but he had been right. Carter had tried and failed, and been beaten so badly that his eyes were swollen shut.

A cop…?

Carter had become a cop…

A strange grin tugged at the corner of his mouth, as he realized the divine and wondrously accidental design that had been unfolding all along.

Damian took it as another example of how the ultimate creator had imbued him with Godliness for the highest reason. Sometimes he was more Godly than his human brain could comprehend—that's what mailing photos to the 66th Precinct had amounted to.

Divine inspiration.

He had been sending his messages to the lost one. His twin soul. The one he had never fully forgotten.

In the next breath, an alarmingly accurate sketch of his own face filled the screen, as the detectives verbalized the physical traits of their suspect—approximate height, weight, and age, all but Damian Payne's name.

The saving grace, if there was one, was that in the black and white sketch, Damian looked like a common street thug, absent of his horn-rimmed glasses and pleasant demeanor.

It filled him with thrill and terror.

And gave him so many fresh ideas…

Things just got very interesting.

Chapter Fifteen

OFTENTIMES, WORKING a case required exercising patience, a lot of it, and Danny was no stranger. But the ten hours that followed the press conference were brutal. Time passed at a crawl, as if the sand slipping through Danny's personal hourglass was dropping one grain at a time.

They had baited their perp as best they could without being obvious about it. Misrepresenting Nahla Rashad's home life as 'loving' ought to pique the killer-kidnapper's interest. They had omitted any mention of Kayla Samuels and Andre Durant's horrific murder and its connection to Raffael Sanzio's at the dump.

Danny and Carter had every reason to hope that their perp would crawl out of the woodwork to correct them, get sloppy about it, and reveal his identity.

The sketch wasn't enough.

Danny attempted to run the sketch through the system to see if there were any matches, while Carter sorted through hours of surveillance footage from the Kensington Projects courtyard. But there were two frustrating problems.

The first was that the department's facial recognition software had pinged over two hundred matches. It hadn't seemed especially accurate, and Danny wasn't one to accuse an algorithm of blatant racism, but the second problem made the first one a moot issue.

The majority of matches in the system—66%—were of currently incarcerated Black men. Since their perp obviously wasn't operating from behind bars, that left the results virtually useless.

Never-the-less, Danny spent her day slogging through mugshots and compiling a list of any match who was no longer in prison and who bore enough resemblance to the sketch to warrant an in-person interview.

If Danny's task was grueling, Carter's was no better and just as fruitless, though she sensed he would never admit it.

Somewhere out there a little girl was being held captive. And it was possible that an adult Vic was being held captive as well—the woman from the photo who had posed with Nahla in haunting mockery of a single Bible verse.

The detectives had absolutely no clue where the woman and child had been hidden.

Complicating matters were the Samuels' who were campaigning in the press for Nahla's safe return, as if the girl had been snatched from their home. Carter had chalked that up to a 'happy accident,' but it rubbed Danny the wrong way.

Pushing away from her desk, she rolled backwards and tried focusing her tired eyes on the other side of the bullpen to relax the muscles.

The hum of the room had softened, as the hours had crawled by, not that she had noticed until now.

Sunlight cut across the bullpen, stark orange and announcing that the day was now fading towards night.

"I told you about O'Toole's, right?" she asked Carter, as she stiffly rose from her desk and put on her jacket.

Carter had been squinting at his computer screen, closely examining the surveillance footage, but he took a break and looked up at her.

"It's a block from my place," she added.

"Yeah, I'll swing by," he told her.

When she mentioned, "Kathy can come, too," he shot her a *don't-push-it* glance. "Best beers in Brooklyn."

"Somehow I doubt that," he teased.

"Don't let Tommy catch you saying that," she humorously warned.

Danny had made a few calls, sent a few texts to invite others from the department to go. It wasn't that any of them would know Tommy's buddy, whose birthday bash it was. Danny barely knew the guy. But as a fine group of detectives, they hadn't gotten together outside of the precinct walls for a drink in longer than she could remember. Might as well take advantage of an open bar and a Friday night, she figured. Not to mention, when a day had been as long as this one, she had no chance of falling asleep. Overtiredness was a guarantee of insomnia, and for Danny, the antidote was alcohol.

"We'll get him, Carter," she tried to assure him when he sunk into what appeared to be a dark, ruminative mood. "We'll find the girl, we'll put the son of a bitch away. The promise you made to Queenie and Raja… It's going to work out."

Though his eyes locked with her's, he looked a million miles away.

"He's too smart," he disagreed, returning his focus to his computer screen.

"So are you," she countered. "Painting the wrong picture in the press this morning was a smart move. He's not going to be able to stand it. He's going to make a move."

"He's *been* making moves," he shot back hotly. "He's been drugging, killing, kidnapping, now he's got some woman involved. He's been throwing it in our faces every step of the way with those photos."

"He wants an audience," she reminded him. "He wants to be heard. *That's* his Achilles' heel, and sooner or later—"

"He wants control," he corrected her.

"Fine. But he wants to control what we *think* and what we *know*, and he's going to get more aggressive about it the more we show how 'wrong' we're getting it."

She studied his stubborn expression for a beat then reiterated, "It's a solid strategy, Carter, try to take a compliment, would ya?"

"I thought it was *your* strategy," he countered.

"Great minds think alike."

He mustered a smile, and Danny figured that was as good as it was going to get between them until she forced a little alcohol down his gullet.

She left him to it and trusted she would see him at the bar in a bit.

THE WOODEN SIGN for O'Toole's was swaying overhead in the evening wind, as Danny heaved the heavy entrance door aside.

Companionable, overlapping voices and raucous cheers spilled out, commingling with the hum of street traffic at her back as she entered.

She had never seen the bar so lively. It threw her for a second, as she waded through the crowd, angling her shoulders at times to squeeze through patrons and guests of the birthday boy, Tommy's friend, who definitely had a name. What was the guy's name? It completely escaped her.

She didn't see too many faces she recognized, which only made the prospect of Carter swinging by, or anyone from the department for that matter, all the more uplifting. Otherwise she might be doomed to cling to her boyfriend. She had never been that girl and she wasn't about to be.

After reaching the bar only to discover all three men behind it were not Tommy, she ordered an ice cold longneck beer—it was too warm in here with all the bodies—and set cash on the counter, which she should've known the bartender, having recognized her, would never accept.

He screwed his face up and told her that 'her money's no good here.'

"Tommy's in the back," he shouted over the music and din of voices when he returned with her beer.

He hadn't meant the storage room where they kept the bottles, but rather one of the large round tables that made up the majority of the far end of the room.

She worked her way through retired firefighters. Some wore glittery, cone hats and others were cheaply costumed in birthday bash regalia. There were clusters of single and ready to mingle ladies who had gotten in the habit of trolling O'Toole's for eligible men.

Danny found Tommy seated around a table with seven guys—*Lance!*

The birthday boy's name hit her as soon as she saw the robust, red-faced Irishman. The guy had once pulled Tommy out of a burning basement and saved his life.

The birthday cake in front of Lance had been mostly eaten. There was a mess of crumpled wrapping paper strewn across the table that made Danny wonder how late she was.

"Hey!" she said, upbeat and lifting her beer, as she locked eyes with Tommy. Rounding towards him, she said to Lance, "Happy birthday! Did you make a wish?"

Tommy stood and pulled her in for a fast, boozy kiss, then nudged the guys to make some room. This was as normal as it had ever been with them, and Danny loved it. As much as it scared her, she could get used to this.

There were a number of large screen TVs over the bar, and one of them was in her line of sight, which wouldn't have been a problem if it was playing a sporting event.

But as Lance went on to divulge what he had wished for, Danny caught sight of herself on the TV monitor. The local news broadcast was recapping the press conference from that morning. The news anchor summarized the case with promises of 'developments' that Danny knew for a fact they didn't have.

Tommy gave her shoulder a squeeze before wrapping his arm around her, but he barely realized her attention had been stolen. He was focused on the birthday boy.

It didn't matter that the TV volume was down, she knew every word that had been said at the press conference, and therefore she had absolutely no reason to watch. Yet she couldn't look away. It was sucking her in—the strange, ugly sight of herself.

The sadness that her eyes seemed to convey no matter what was actually going on in her life—was that how she really looked?

Unfortunate genetics. Sad eyes and a slanted mouth that led most people to believe she was smirking. Wickedly. As if she was deriving some kind of pleasure out of *every* situation.

Tommy was staring at her now, catching on to her distraction.

Leaning in, he told her, "You were great," then yelled to the table or perhaps the room at large, "wasn't she great? That's my girl on TV!"

She couldn't help but smile, as Tommy and the guys gave her kudos. It spoke to her inner teenager, if that uncool girl was still somewhere inside of her. But their accolades couldn't smooth over the sting of her greatest fear when it came to this case:

She didn't think they would find the girl.

The killer-kidnapper, whoever and wherever he was, could very well get away with it.

"Carter!" she called out the second she saw her partner working his slow way through the thick crowd.

She rose to her feet and waved, but the sea of people between them was too great.

"Give me a sec," she told Tommy and started off for her partner who she quickly observed wasn't alone.

Jill Andover was standing beside him. She looked around the bar as much as she could, considering the crowd.

Danny felt her heart kick out of rhythm.

She had invited Jill, yes, but she hadn't deluded herself into thinking Jill would actually show up. It was because she considered Jill a friend and not a hesitant Vic that she had greatly overstepped her bounds, disregarded Jill's wishes, and paid an intentionally intimidating visit to Damian Payne.

But that was no excuse, and though she had felt righteous about it at the time, she had since realized her error.

"Glad you could make it," she said warmly to both of them, while making a point to make eye contact with Jill, who looked dolled up and genuinely skeptical.

"We're the 'can't stay long' crowd," Carter explained good-naturedly.

"Oh, is that right?" she asked Jill since back at the precinct Carter had already built in his excuse for leaving the party early.

Jill seemed to shrink meekly. Her painted lips pressed into what appeared to be an affirmative smile, but came across a bit hostile.

Damian, thought Danny. She was still seeing the guy.

Vaguely, Jill said, "My Friday nights are usually booked."

"Well, I'm just glad you could stop in. Can I get you a drink?" she asked as she led her partner and the ME to the bar. "Just ignore the TVs," she suggested with a wink.

"And here I thought I would be able to get my mind off things," said Carter, staring up at the screen.

He seemed far less affected by the ongoing news report than she would've thought.

"I should really get the remote from Tommy," she said, "change the channel or something."

"What are you expecting will happen?" Jill asked, point blank.

She hadn't meant to come off as confrontational, Danny at least knew her that well, but the way she was looking expectantly at her and then at Carter made it hard to breathe steadily.

The detectives had had their doubts. Seeing doubt in the eyes of their associates didn't bode well.

As Carter humored her, providing an explanation without saying much—Jill might be the Chief Medical Examiner of all of Brooklyn, but it didn't make her automatically entitled to case developments—Danny took care of getting a glass of red wine for Jill and a cold one for her partner.

"Oh, you shouldn't have," said Jill, taking the glass Danny was offering.

"It's on the house," she said, brushing it off before clarifying. "My boyfriend owns the bar. You haven't met Tommy, have you? Neither of you have," she realized and quickly invited them to join her, as she started for Tommy's table.

She didn't get two steps before Carter stopped her.

"Another time," he declined. "Thanks for the beer, though," he said before knocking back a long haul. "Hits the spot."

Distracted, Jill suddenly wasn't sure what to do with her wine or where to set it.

"I thought I would have more time," she apologized, her gaze returning to the large picture windows.

She set the glass on the bar counter when a few patrons floated off their stools, unlit cigarettes dangling from their mouths, and apologized again, "Thanks for thinking of me. This was great."

She was backing away towards the exit now.

"Tell Tommy, happy birthday."

Danny didn't correct her.

Instead Danny excused herself from Carter, who was trying to get a look at Jill's mystery man on the other side of the window. She started quickly after her friend and offered, "I'll walk you out."

But Jill wasn't having it. She turned on her very high heel, stared up at Danny, her eyes a furious blue, and in a low tone asserted, "Please. I don't need you walking me anywhere."

Immediately, Danny's heart sank with remorse and she said, "I shouldn't have gone to talk to Damian."

Maybe it was the fact that she hadn't tried to defend herself, but Jill seemed taken aback with surprise, as if Danny's veiled apology had been enough to defuse the wall she had been preparing to throw up.

"I should've known better," said Danny when it was clear the window of this conversation was still open. "I listened, and in terms of what I heard you say, and *definitely* because I respect you as a personal friend, I went ahead as if it was my right to investigate—"

"It wasn't," Jill maintained even though there was zero fight in Danny.

"I know." She let that hang for a beat so that her friend would be more receptive to her explanation, which she anticipated wouldn't be quite as easy to hear if not swallow. "Sometimes a person in your position doesn't want to go with their gut—"

"Sometimes, Danny," she cut in, ready to argue all over again, "a person is wrong. Sometimes women get it wrong. They drink too much— And don't interrupt me, I know what you're going to say. That a person can't consent if they're inebriated."

Yup, she set her challenging eyes on the dramatic lips and smoky eyes of the other woman.

"But we both know," Jill sneered, "that little fact doesn't hold up anywhere. We both know how messy life is. Dating. Accidentally having a few too many. Bottom line," she asserted. "I know what happened, and I know what I'm doing. *You* must defer to *me*. Protect and serve, right? You should've listened when I told you 'never mind'."

Danny didn't hesitate to agree. She had apologized and agreed from 'go,' and she was glad that Jill was telling her off now. Anything to restore their relationship.

"You're right," she said again, this time feeling eyes on her. On the other side of the picture window, Damian was glaring at her through designer horn-rimmed glasses. "Have a good night," she said, using every shred of willpower not to tell Jill to 'be safe.'

"Thanks," she said on a breathy exhale, which Danny hoped indicated they had smoothed this snag over.

Jill started off towards the exit.

Danny watched her go. *We all have our secrets,* she thought. Still, there was something about the guy, Damian, that gave her the creeps.

Damian diverted his glare only when Jill stepped out into the breezy night.

As he greeted her with an awkwardly formal kiss on the cheek and began escorting her, his large hand on the small of her back, to a black town car that had been idling along the curb, Danny fought every urge to duck out onto the sidewalk, hail a cab, and follow the dark accountant and his—as far as Danny was concerned—unsuspecting date all the way back to wherever he was taking her…

To see if he would do it again. Slip her something. Take advantage. Leave her confused and blaming herself, and worst of all, ever hopeful that he was somehow not a monster or a rapist but the man of her dreams.

It turned Danny's stomach.

But just as she was about to look away from the street where the black town car had driven off, another monster caught her eye.

From the sidewalk, nearing the wooden door of O'Toole's, came Nora.

"Not on your life," Danny uttered under her breath, as she bolted for the door to cut her mother off at the pass.

Nora let out a little shocked gasp when Danny burst through the door. "What do you think you're doing?"

"You weren't at home—"

"You're not welcome here," Danny blurted. "What?" she cut herself off to ask. "You thought it would be okay for you to try me at home?" she asked, astounded.

"I need to tell you—"

"Stop playing games and just say it," she demanded, as a canoodling couple tipsy-walked around them to get into the bar, the joys of Friday night bustling all around them.

This was too surreal.

She needed to get back to Tommy where 'surreal' was at least divine.

"There's nothing you ever need to tell me. Ever," Danny fired off when her mother only continued to stare at her. "That's the whole point—"

"I can't do this anymore, Danielle!"

"Oh, you can't *do this* anymore?" she sarcastically challenged. She stepped in and threatened in a low tone, "Would you prefer to do *time in prison?*"

"I'm not well!"

That was blatantly obvious, thought Danny. Annoyed, she asked, "What do you mean, 'you're not well'?"

"I'm dying."

And just like that Danny Foster was out of gas.

❄

JILL HAD PROMISED herself she wouldn't drink. Not with Damian. Not at all. Clearly, she had been out of control. Throwing caution to the wind and acting like a college sophomore was not the way to show a man you were worth getting serious about. She was lucky he was still interested in seeing her.

She remained perplexed, as she carried on light dinner conversation from across a charming, candle-lit table at the little Italian restaurant she had suggested.

Accidentally drinking too much was simply out of character for her. She couldn't even remember the last time she had overdone it, and yet with Damian, other than the first few dates, she had gotten into the unconscious habit of sipping, sipping, sipping until, without warning, she was in the throes of a blackout.

Perhaps she had some kind of metabolic disorder... She should make an appointment with her general practitioner and have a few tests done... Until then, water with lemon would do.

Damian had enjoyed his veal and was thoughtfully swirling the single malt he had ordered. God, he was handsome. She had been taking mental snapshots of him all night in case this date turned out to be a courtesy in-person dumping.

She hadn't yet apologized to him for what Danny had done. She should've never made that phone call. The fact, or in her case, the *hunch* of the matter was that Damian hadn't taken advantage of her, violated her, nothing. She knew it in her bones. He wasn't like that. He would never do such a thing.

But more importantly, she had never discovered any of the telltale signs that anything foul had occurred.

As an M.E., she knew what to look for—inflammation, residue of either a condom or biological fluids, and bruising. She was certain she would have felt soreness, felt uncomfortable at the very least. All she had felt time and again, after having gone out on the town with Damian only to wind up at his place, was severely hungover and immensely embarrassed.

Then why had she, even momentarily, suspected him of one of the worst offenses?

"I was hoping," he began, lifting his dark, penetrating eyes from his amber liquor. Jill's breath hitched dreadfully in her throat, anticipating the beginning of a break-up speech. But he surprised her by suggesting, "we could take a little walk."

"I would love that," she said, as a warm gush of relief washed over her.

She remembered his satchel, however. He had come straight from the office, and it might be cumbersome to have to carry it along.

"The restaurant is open for another few hours. You could check your bag if you want?"

"That won't be necessary," he told her, as he got their waitress's attention gesturing for the check. "The park isn't far," he smiled. "It's a warm night."

"It is," she agreed, feeling slightly off balance emotionally.

It felt like she was waiting for the other shoe to drop.

She needed to clear the air between them, and so as they collected themselves from the little Italian restaurant, Damian having graciously declined her offer to pay for herself, she decided she would apologize for any stress her detective friend might have caused him.

She wasn't looking forward to this conversation, but she also wasn't looking forward to being on the receiving end of an 'it's not you, it's me' speech, no matter how beautiful Prospect Park was at night.

As they strolled along one of the many walking paths that meandered through the lush park, the romantic glow of vintage street lamps illuminating their winding way, Jill began working up the nerve.

They weren't the only two people outside enjoying the park, and perhaps it was an excuse to buy time, but she reasoned she could hold off on broaching the subject until they had reached a secluded area.

But Damian didn't afford her the luxury.

"I was surprised to hear from you," he mentioned as if it were a casual comment.

To Jill it felt like he had dropped a bomb.

Stupidly, she said, "Oh?"

Damian shrugged in his designer camel wool coat, touched eyes with her, then returned his contemplative gaze to his dress shoes, the outstretching path before them, the dark dome sky overhead, looking around.

"You thought I attacked you?"

God, she wanted to die. She felt her heart collapse, and she couldn't take another step.

"My friend, the detective," she stammered, sighed, and had no idea how to pick herself up from this. "She drew her own conclusions—"

"From what?" he challenged in the smoothest and least confrontational tone. It had her thrown, but his words, the question itself...

He blamed her.

She needed to get past this with him and desperation took hold.

"From the hangovers I've had," she told him bluntly, hoping the fib would stick. "I've never been one to drink, and Danny took notice of my state here and there."

"And she jumped to a wild conclusion?"

He was going easy on her, allowing her outlandish explanation to seem plausible.

"What she implied…" he trailed off, a look of astonishment coming over him. "Do you not remember the times we shared in my apartment?"

"I, uh…"

He furrowed his brow at her. Searched her eyes.

"We haven't slept together, Jill."

"I know," she said, the pitch of her voice so high she might as well have confessed that she honest to God couldn't remember a damn thing.

"*Do* you remember?" he asked, but the way he said it… What was he asking her?

"I might have a metabolic disorder," she blurted out, offering the only explanation that made sense to her at this point. "Maybe I reached a certain age and can't metabolize alcohol."

What happened next was so bizarre, so unexpected, it was impossible to process.

Damian's large hand came out of his coat pocket, he opened his fist, palm up, and blew white dust into Jill's face.

In an instant, she felt like a kid, sinking into a kind of euphoric fog. She couldn't make sense of the dust that had been blown in her face but was certain it must be a game. She remembered her childhood friends throwing snow at her.

She laughed and felt elated, but somewhere in her brain, some part of her mind was frantically struggling to make sense of it all.

Darkly, Damian's entire face dropped, and he complained dryly, "I wish you hadn't stopped drinking."

She was trapped in her mind, in her body, neither of which felt like it belonged to her anymore.

He added, "It's easier for me when you drink."

As he glanced around, presumably to be certain no one had seen what he had done, Jill willed her head to turn so that she could look for help, but it wouldn't move. She willed her voice to rise up from what felt like her belly, but it was stuck. *She* was stuck. And she had the strangest, happiest feeling, like she wanted him to think highly of her…

No, that wasn't it.

She wanted to *please* him.

"You should've invited me into the bar." He took rough hold of her upper arm and began walking her back in the direction they had come. "I would've liked to have met them. The detectives. Carter especially."

He was talking *at* her, not *with* her, but every cell in Jill's body was poised to receive whatever he had to say. She felt like a vessel that only Damian could fill.

You have to remember this, she ordered herself.

But when they reached the sidewalk, having found their way out of the park, the very notion of remembering had already escaped her. She only had a panicked sense that she had forgotten something extremely important. Her mind, her memory, was capable of storing two seconds at best.

"You know where he lives, correct?" he asked her. "That detective. Carter Dobbs?"

"Yes," she heard herself say.

"Do you know where you are?"

Her eyes barely worked.

"Tell me his address," he demanded, as she squinted hard in an attempt to spot a street sign. "Just tell me."

When she did, he pulled her against him and together they walked briskly, heading straight for Carter's house.

"There's something you're going to do for me," he told her, extracting an 8.5" x 11" manila envelope from his satchel. "If you mess this up, I'm going to kill you. Does that sound fair?"

She didn't want to say it, but the reply, "Yes," seeped past her lips.

Remember this, Jill! Remember this! she begged herself.

But when all was said and done, Jill Andover couldn't remember a goddamn thing.

Chapter Sixteen

CARTER ENDED UP having more than a few beers with Danny at the bar. It hadn't been his plan, but knocking drinks back with a bunch of strangers turned out to be just what he had needed.

He had also needed the long walk home to clear his head and sober up enough to face his wife.

He didn't expect an argument. He had texted Kathy after ordering his second drink at the bar so she wouldn't have to wait up wondering.

But it would've been wishful thinking to trust that she *wouldn't* question him the moment he got home.

When he reached his block, he slowed his brisk pace and really took in the setting.

Ordinarily, he rushed to and from his house. He often drove. Thoughts and theories weighing so heavily on his mind that he rarely *saw* it all. The charming row of detached one-family Victorians. All lit up with twinkling lights, the tree lined street picturesque, the truncated front yards of each home well-maintained.

It was as suburban as Brooklyn would allow. There was no substantial traffic. It was quiet, and at an hour like this, when the cooking smells of dinner had long since dissipated and fathers challenged their sons to quick games of one-on-one in their driveways, it was easy to remember that this was what it was all about, what Carter had fought so hard for, staying alive against all odds growing up. He might not have known it at the time—that this was the endgame, this beautiful life—but there was no mistaking it now.

He heard the rhythmic thuds of a basketball striking pavement as he neared his house and found his oldest son, Christopher, dribbling in front of the open garage where Kathy, wearing sweats, her hair knotted up in a messy bun, was standing with her fists on her hips.

He knew that look. Chris had defied her in some way and she wasn't having it.

"I'm open!" Carter called out good-naturedly to his son, who chucked the ball gracefully at him.

Kathy tensed up even worse.

"Play to twenty-one?" Christopher suggested, as he jogged up to Carter, who was now dribbling.

"No one's playing to anything," Kathy objected.

She was staring warning daggers at Carter as she neared them.

"Just one game, Mom!"

The exasperation in his son's voice told Carter that Kathy had been riding his ass all night, and judging the severe expression on her face, she wasn't about to loosen the reins just yet.

"Carter," she barked. "Would you please tell your son to go to his room?"

He stopped dribbling, and after failing to read his wife's expression, he told Christopher, "Hey, why don't you listen to your mother and go on inside?"

"Because she's flipping out for no reason?" he coolly offered. "Because it's barely past nine-thirty? Because all my homework is done? Because—"

"Alright," said Carter, silencing him. "Do me a favor?"

Obliging was the last thing the boy wanted to do, but Christopher sighed, slumped his broad shoulders in defeat, and reluctantly turned on his sneakered heel for the garage.

He dragged his feet the entire way, shuffling through the garage and disappearing inside the house, as Kathy looked on, white-faced and furious.

When Carter anticipated that she would accuse him of being late, staying out on purpose, or indulging in an affair—her greatest fear that they kept discussing in therapy—Kathy instead angled her worried blue eyes up at him.

Her voice suddenly trembled, as she said, "Someone slid something under the door."

"What?"

"Photos," she breathed.

It hit him like a ton of bricks. He wrapped his arms around her in an instant, but Kathy urged him back and stared up at him, this time with blame in her teary eyes.

"I don't want the kids outside," she asserted.

"Agreed. Show me the photos," he said, as he closed the garage door and ushered her into the house.

He felt his jaw tighten, and a deeply seeded ember of rage flared, hot as coal, in his gut, as he followed Kathy into their immaculate bedroom.

Carter's gut was already telling him who had slipped photos under the door.

The man who shared Carter's face.

Kathy opened a manila envelope that she had left on the edge of the bed, as she pressed her mouth tightly in a frown.

"I didn't want the children to see," she said, handing over a thin stack of what amounted to three photos. "They were taken today, Carter," she hissed, distressed, her voice so strained and shaky that he feared she would break down and hit him.

All three photos were black and white, and had an almost surveillance quality to them, as if they had been taken with a telephoto lens from very far away.

The first was an image of Kathy in the kitchen, doing the dishes, the late morning glare in her eyes. The photographer took the photo from the street outside.

Carter's breathing turned rapid and shallow looking at it, knowing that someone—a sick killer, a kidnapper, likely a pedophile—had been watching his wife, spying on his family, and clicking off shots as if he had the right.

He turned the photo over and sure enough, collaged in magazine-clippings of letters like all the rest, was a message. Carter narrowed his scrutinizing gaze on it.

"I didn't know what it meant," said Kathy, as she reached for the stack to indicate there were more messages on the other photos.

"He gave me fatty lamb," read Carter, confusedly racking his brain, but nothing jumped out or made sense.

"I mean, I know what it means," Kathy quickly corrected herself when Carter wouldn't allow her to get ahead of him by taking the other photos. "We're being threatened," she declared, trying to keep her voice down. "This is unacceptable, Carter."

"Stop," he barked, pacing away from her and flipping to the next photo, which was of

Christopher walking down the sidewalk in-between two of his athletic friends, each wearing backpacks and laughing—on their school lunch break.

Carter had told his kids a thousand times not to venture out to McDonald's. They were supposed to eat their packed lunches at the school cafeteria, but when had his kids ever listened?

He's targeting the kids.

Flipping the photo over, Carter read its message to himself—'He gave me not the best but the worst of his crops'.

Carter could feel Kathy's anxious eyes on him, but he hadn't formulated an explanation. There was nothing he could say to calm her or assure her that she and the kids would be safe.

His greatest fear was that they weren't safe, and realizing this caused his chest to clamp down and a wave of anger to surge up through his pumping veins.

"What will you sacrifice?" Kathy stated, which he soon realized was the message on the back of the third photo. Terrified, as if she already knew the grim answer, she demanded, "What does that mean, Carter?"

He was playing God.

But Carter didn't dare say that to his wife.

The man whose face he supposedly shared according to a yoga instructor in the projects; a man who had demonstrated his perverse power, the lengths he would go, the *rules* he had instilled and expected—*you shall not bow down and serve them for I, the Lord, am a jealous God, the sins of the fathers shall be visited upon the sons*—that very man knew who Carter was, knew all that Carter had, and wanted him to make a sacrifice…?

He stared at the third photo. The photo depicted the innocent and endearing image of his skinny son, Matty, waiting at the schoolyard, his nose pressed to a chain-link fence, thin fingers curled around metal like a lonely, caged animal.

The photo captured a certain sadness in the boy that Carter had never before noticed, though he was familiar with the routine. The chain-link fence was where Matty liked to wait to get picked up from school. Christopher, on the other hand, was perfectly happy playing basketball with his friends until Kathy or Carter showed up. But not Matty.

Kathy was pacing now, a wealth of nervous energy spilling out of her.

"Should we be happy there wasn't one of Amanda? Or will the next anonymous packet be all about her? What the hell is going on?"

"I need to make a phone call," he said distractedly, as he stuffed the photos back in the manila folder, realizing way too far after the fact that absolutely no one should've touched the packet.

He needed to get Jill over here and the whole forensic team—or did he?

"Carter!" she blurted, as he walked out of their bedroom, considering the options on the way to his office that he barely used anymore.

Kathy had turned the office into a makeshift exercise room.

Carter spilled past the dumb bells and exercise mats to get to his desk.

Jill and her team had dusted every photo and envelope that had arrived at the precinct for prints. But she hadn't found a trace of the guy on anything.

The perp had shifted his strategy of communication—his focus—from sending photos to the 66th to sending them to Carter directly.

If the images were any indication, things had gone from abstract to personal, not only in regards to Carter's investment in finding the guy, but in the guy's efforts as well.

The photo of Nahla and then of Nahla and the unknown woman had seemed almost allegorical. They had depicted a message, but weren't intended to be an actual threat in and of themselves, though a serious threat of course had hung in the air—how long would either be kept alive?

But these surveillance style photos of Carter's family…

Not only was it cutting far too close to home, but Carter knew with every quivering fiber of his enraged being that the man honing in on Carter's family had been the direct result of the press conference and the intentional misrepresentation of the crimes at hand.

The perp wasn't bothering to correct them, as Carter had hoped. He was punishing them. Telling them to get in line.

What will you sacrifice?

It was Biblical like all the other messages.

But he didn't have the education to understand the references—'fatty veal' and 'crops'—and if they pointed to a specific passage.

He had the lieutenant's cell phone number on speed dial, and once he was seated at his desk, he sent the call through and hoped it wouldn't be too late for Franco to pick up.

The lieutenant groaned something unintelligible through the line so Carter asked, "Sir?"

"Dobbs?" groaned Franco.

It wasn't *that* late.

"Yeah, it's Carter. I didn't wake you up, did I?"

"You did, but I needed it. I'm at the precinct, for God's sake. Don't ask. What do you need?"

"I had a thought," he said, wading cautiously and carefully into his point.

He wasn't about to jeopardize the safety of his wife and kids by inviting the department into this, not yet, not until he had absolute faith that his entire family would be better off with Franco or even Danny at the helm of this investigation.

If he got yanked off of it now, just because his kids had become a possible target, then this whole thing could spiral out of control.

"You woke me up from my desk nap because you had a 'thought'?"

Letting the jab roll off his back like water, Carter explained, "The guy's a religious fanatic, or he thinks he's God."

"I won't argue against that," he allowed.

"So, I was thinking…" Carter went on, coming up with alternative logic that would make sense. "With the whole 'I am a jealous God' stuff and 'Don't serve anyone but me,' and the image of Nahla praying to some adult version of herself…"

"You're sounding convoluted, Dobbs," he warned. "Cut to the chase."

"Right. What about 'sacrifices'?"

There was a beat of dead air on the line then Franco asked, "What about them?"

"Is God ever satisfied? Could you sacrifice properly and it would 'save your skin' so-to-speak?"

Carter hadn't realized the dark reference until the lieutenant snorted a grim laugh and said, "Kayla Samuels... couldn't save her own skin, literally."

"Jesus," Carter breathed.

"In terms of the perp," Franco went on. "I think we're dealing with a vengeful god, and in that case, I really don't know."

He sank, mulling the lieutenant's pessimism over, and stared unseeingly at his own puzzled reflection in the window.

"How would you serve God, then?" he asked.

"Where is this coming from, Carter?"

"It's coming from..." Thinking fast on his feet, he said, "Impatience. I thought the press conference this morning would provoke the guy—"

"Look, you have to give it more than a day. How did the surveillance footage from the projects go?"

"I'm more than halfway through—"

"Then focus on what's within your control. Get through the footage. You might find a match. There's always something to go on, Dobbs, you just have to find it."

Carter wasn't about to let this opportunity slip through his fingers. Franco was some kind of Sunday school expert. This was happening. Now.

"What about sacrificing fatty meat? Crops?"

"What, do you wanna slaughter a goat in the town square to get the psycho to hand the little girl over? Is that where you're going with this, Dobbs?"

"In terms of the Bible," he clarified. "You nailed that Exodus passage like it was written on the back of your hand or something."

"Yeah, well, they really drill that stuff in."

"What's an acceptable sacrifice?" he asked again, a bit too forcefully. All he could think was that if he didn't get this right, didn't figure the twisted logic out, and beat it, then he wouldn't have a choice and the 'sacrifice' would be made for him. "Abraham and Isaac come to mind, right? Like, be prepared to kill your son."

"But you asked about meat and crops," Franco countered, perking up now. "That's a reference to one of the first sacrifices in Genesis."

"What? Tell me."

"Adam and Eve had two sons. The older, Cain. The younger, Abel. When the boys were grown, God asked them each to make a sacrifice for him. Cain, who worked as a farmer, sacrificed a portion of his crops, and Abel, a shepherd, gave God the best of his meat as a sacrifice. The meat, which was fatty and therefore the best, pleased God. The crops, which the Bible does not explicitly say—people have interpreted it this way—were not the best of the bunch, probably overripe and 'from the ground.' It was as if Cain didn't want to give up his best crops but only those he thought he could live without. God made it known that he favored Abel's sacrifice of fatty *veal*, I believe. And so—"

"Cain killed Abel," he supplied, looking down at the three photos in his hands.

"God punished Cain for the murder," Franco offered.

But that was beside the point.

The original sacrifice.

The first murder.

All of it instigated by God.

"Thanks, Franco, I'll let you go."

"That's it?" he asked. "Aren't you going to clue me in?"

"If I'm being honest here, Sir, I'm not even sure I have a clue at this point."

"Patience," he reminded his newest detective. "There's no other way to play this."

Carter set the desk phone in its cradle and realized how poignant the lieutenant's last comment was.

He *was* 'playing,' or being *'played.'* This was a game. One he was certain he was meant to lose.

What did the photos mean? Why choose his kids? Did it mean that ultimately Christopher would kill Matty or vice versa?

Christ, just thinking about scopolamine and the perp's capabilities sent a shudder down Carter's spine.

Or were the photos meant to imply he would have to sacrifice one of them—Kathy, Christopher, or Matty?

Was he getting this all wrong? Was *Carter* supposed to choose who to be, Cain or Abel—sacrificing properly and getting killed for it, or sacrificing poorly and being driven to murder his own flesh and blood?

He was roused from disturbed thoughts when he heard the faint knock of a little fist on his office door.

Glancing over his shoulder, he found Matty creaking the door open, his sleepy eyes staring in.

"You should be in bed, kiddo. Come here."

Wearing long-john pajamas, the skinny boy pitter-pattered across the carpeted floor and hopped on Carter's lap.

As he held his son, perhaps tighter than he ever had, smelling the sweet scent of his clean hair, feeling the weight and delicacy of him in his arms, Kathy filled the doorway and met his gaze with the same look of grave concern.

He knew what she was thinking and hated that her stomach was in knots.

Softly so as not to rouse Matty who had dozed off in his strong embrace almost immediately, he said, "If the kids aren't in school, they're here. No play dates, no afterschool activities—"

"Christopher and Amanda are going to freak—"

"Too bad," he told her in the same tone he wanted her to use with the kids. "You'll take them all to school, drop each one off, I don't care how embarrassing it is for Amanda. They cannot go off school grounds for lunch. You'll pick them up at 3:25pm, you'll be early. They aren't to be out of our sight, not for one second, unless they're in a classroom."

She nodded. "And what will you do?"

He was going to find the other boys from the basement—the others who had grown up in the dark and lived by the tick of a psychopath's pocket watch.

He hoped like hell this case wouldn't destroy him.

Chapter Seventeen

IDEALLY, CARTER would've been the first one on the SVU floor at the 66th that morning, but he had wanted to see the kids off safely to school with Kathy.

It had been a long night, trying to get his wife to trust him about not involving the police. And it had been an even longer morning, waking Amanda, Christopher, and Matty a solid hour before their alarms were scheduled to blare, so that they could have a family meeting.

Carter and Kathy had instilled the grave importance that all three of them must abide by the new, strict rules. Neither parent told the kids the reason why they had new rules, or what was going on, despite their shrill objections and complaints.

Once Carter had dropped Kathy back off at the house, along with their shared car, and took a cab over to the precinct, the hour was creeping past eight.

The floor was buzzing with detectives working on open cases, including Danny who was back at it, looking slightly rough, as she hunted through the surveillance footage that Carter had been working on the day prior.

"How long did you end up staying?" he asked casually, having swung by the break room to grab a fresh cup of coffee.

As he set it on his desk, his heart lurching up his throat, he was so anxious to dive into his plan without her knowing, Danny gave her temples a little rub, brushed her side-swept bangs out of her eyes, and said, "Too long, but it was fun."

"Yeah," he agreed tensely. "Hey, you could've slept it off."

"A day after the press conference? When we have no more to go on than we did days ago?" she questioned. "I don't think so."

"If you need to take a few hours to lie down in the back," he suggested, referring to the cots in the back of the unisex locker room. "Or a half hour. It's better to have you sharp than struggling."

She considered it then, getting up from her desk, assured him, "Nah, coffee ought to do the trick."

As she made her way to the break room, Carter felt his face go long with agitation. If she saw his computer screen, she would ask questions, but at this point, time was of the essence.

He booted up his computer, gulping down coffee as he waited for the outdated machine to come alive, and tried to wrap his head around how many of them had been rescued from the basement.

He hated going back there. Mentally. There was a reason his psyche had essentially erased those memories. By the time he had been placed in foster care, he had effectively forgotten the worst of it, which hadn't boded well for the trial.

He reminded himself that he didn't have to remember the abuse, didn't have to open his mind to reveal to himself all that used to occur once the pocket watch had been cranked, wound up tight, and released to *tick, tick, tick*—counting down the seconds of how long the sexual torture would last.

Running his large hand down his face, he tried to recall how many kids had been down there with him, how many black boys to be precise. Three? Or had it been five? It had been dark almost at all times. There had been so much shame, each child tucked in his or her respective cage. It wasn't like they had gotten to know each other down there…

Some had died. Some had been sold as the years had passed. But everyone who had been there with him when the FBI swooped in to take down the entire sex trafficking ring had gone into the police reports, gone into foster care, and had been listed as witnesses to testify whether they ended up taking the stand—or their own life—before the case had gone to federal trial.

Carter had a concrete starting point, and it wouldn't require him to wrestle dark memories.

Walking gingerly to nurse what appeared to be a pounding headache, Danny returned with a steaming mug of coffee in her hand and eased carefully onto her chair.

"Franco might have a nip in his desk," Carter guessed, eyeing the lieutenant's office. The boss had yet to arrive. "Hair of the dog, as they say."

"What makes you think Franco stashes booze in his office?"

"He doesn't strike you as the type?"

Danny laughed then winced, holding her head, "Don't say anything funny or my skull will crack open."

"Christ, lie down. You're human, no one's going to blame you for it or think less of you."

Stubbornly, she refused and began silently combing through hours of footage, while Carter dove into his own quiet work of emailing the Victims' Advocacy Department of the Kings

County Courthouse to request the old list of witnesses from the federal case.

It was more than decades old, and he hoped like hell they hadn't archived the information onto some remote and unused database, collecting dust in a forgotten storage unit somewhere.

He would've much rather called, but he wouldn't be able to tolerate the questions that his partner would surely ask him. Hungover or not, she was smart as a whip. So, now he was doomed to wait.

In the meantime, he sent another email to the Boro of Brooklyn Foster Care Division, whose records he expected to be even worse, to see if he could track down the kids, using another angle, one which would hopefully provide last known addresses. If he had to contact each old foster family to get a line on where their now-grown foster kids were, it would be better than nothing.

From across their conjoined desks, Danny groaned, "This is brutal."

He couldn't tell her to lie down in the back a third time so he asked, "Coffee isn't helping?"

"No, I mean what we're doing right now…" She looked out the window to rest her eyes and said thoughtfully, "I can't believe we didn't get another packet of photos, a new message, something to prove how dumb we are, you know?"

Guilt hit him like a fist to his solar plexus, but he held himself back, stuffing down the strong urge to clue her in. His stomach twisted but he poured coffee on it. Taking nervous gulps, he attempted to commiserate.

"Something's off," she ruminated.

Carter's desk phone interrupted their moment, and he didn't hesitate to take the call.

"Dobbs."

"This is Sandra Murdock from the Kings County Courthouse," announced a husky sounding woman on the other end of the line.

Keeping his responses vague so as not to garner Danny's interest, he said, "An email response would have sufficed. This is a low priority."

"Since the case was Federal, I'll need your current investigation case number in order to get clearance to send the information you requested over."

Damn.

His jaw tightened, but he kept his tone as even and as cordial as possible, as he said, "I should've included that in my email."

"You can tell me now," she offered.

He really couldn't, not with his partner sitting two feet away.

"I'm already typing it now," he told Sandra and then sent the email through. "When can I expect to hear back?"

"I'll put the request in, and as soon as I hear back, I'll pass the witness list to you."

That wasn't good enough, but Carter resigned himself to the prospect of having no choice but to wait and bite his fist in the meantime.

He thanked her, returned his phone to its cradle, and shoved his proverbial fist into his mouth to tough it out.

The killer, the deranged man who was holding a little girl captive, who had taken photos of Carter's wife and kids, would be on that list. Carter could feel it in his bones. Whoever was behind this had come out on the wrong side of that basement. The abuse had shaped Carter into the man he was today. Moral. Just. Dedicating his life to stopping the kinds of criminals who had stolen his childhood.

Being treated worse than an animal for years had shaped the killer in a very different way.

But were they simply two sides of the same coin? Carter didn't want to let himself go there, as he hunkered down and began slogging through more surveillance footage that his gut told him would be fruitless.

Carter could have just as easily turned out rotten, perverted, and deranged… Wasn't that the typical result of having been brought up so horribly? The excuse every criminal wore on his sleeve? Why hadn't Carter sunk in that direction? Or more importantly, why hadn't the killer turned out to be *good* like Carter despite it all?

A sad realization struck him. The guy probably thought he *was* righteous and moral, but had taken it way too far, thinking he was God, the ultimate decider and destroyer, the one who deems sacrifices either acceptable or insulting.

The one who Carter was now expected to live his life according to, or else risk his family's safety.

It was a very long day before the email from Sandra popped into his Inbox, and when it did, he wasted no time opening the password protected PDF report.

He let out a defeated growl as he scrolled through the *twenty-eight* names, but quickly disguised his reaction with a cough.

"You okay?" Danny asked, once again rising from her desk to stretch her legs.

"Fine," he said without looking at her.

Eyeing the list more carefully, he counted sixteen female names, which could be ruled out thanks to Lacy Marcel's sketch of the perp, who was definitely male and definitely African-American.

Of the twelve males listed, a few had obviously Latino names, so crossing them off, he was left with ten suspects.

Were they all still alive? Still in New York City? Or had some of them chosen to move far, far away to forget the place that had stolen their innocence so cruelly?

The witnesses' addresses listed on the document were all the same—the orphanage that had taken in all the kids after the rescue. Which meant that he would have to get all contact information from the foster care division that he had also already reached out to via email.

But he wanted to get on this. He couldn't wait.

He plugged the number for the Boro of Brooklyn Foster Care Division into his cell phone, hit Print on the PDF, and like two ships passing in the night, Carter passed Danny.

She was returning to her desk with a fifth steaming mug of inky coffee, as Carter leapt up to catch his print job that was being spit out from the copy machine at the far side of the bullpen.

"Got something?" she called out, curious about his urgency.

"Hardly."

Quickly skimming the sheets to be sure he had them all, he ducked into the locker room where a few officers were joshing around and the receptionist was tucking a pack of cigarettes back into her purse.

He rounded into the next aisle of lockers where he could be alone and sent the call through to foster care.

By the time he emerged from the locker room, he had crawled through several yards of red tape, but managed to secure the last known addresses for all the non-Hispanic males who were alive. Not all of them lived in NYC, however, but that didn't mean they hadn't moved back to the city since the records were last updated.

There was a lot to go on, and it was daunting.

Hoping luck would be on his side, and the perp would be his first visit and not his last, Carter picked the first name on the list, as he grabbed his suit jacket from the back of his chair.

"You heading out?" asked Danny, her brow furrowed at the obvious streak of sunlight cutting through the bullpen that proved it was definitely not time to clock out.

"I'll be back," he said before lying in a discreet whisper, "therapy."

"Say no more," she told him. "I totally get it, but keep your phone on. I'll call you if there are any developments."

There was that knife-stab of guilt in his chest again, but all he said was, "Will do," and started through the bullpen.

He cabbed it into Manhattan, knowing the most efficient way to tackle this would be to knock on doors, talk to the former families, get a direct line on each suspect if possible. Carter wasn't sure how things would play out or go down when it came time to pay a suspect a visit. He would have to assume going in, erring on the side of caution, that each one was the perp.

The one who expected a sacrifice from Carter.

He would recognize Carter in an instant, but Carter was feeling pretty confident he would recognize the guy, too. The sketch rendering of the perp had been burned into the forefront of his memory.

Double-checking the address of a downtown pre-war building that looked as rundown as the weathered scaffolding braced against its face, he neared the call box then, certain this was the place, pressed the buzzer for Apartment 1L, as the loud hum of traffic grumbled along the avenue behind him.

"Who is it?" an elderly-sounding woman's voice cut through the static din of the call box.

"An old friend of—" Carter referenced the now-creased list of witness names he had been clutching with a death-grip the entire ride in. "Wallace Bronson."

"A friend?" the woman questioned.

"We grew up together," he admitted, the implication of which resonated heavily with the woman on the other side of the call box. "My name's Carter. I'd really like to—"

The blaring buzz of the entrance door unlocking interrupted his effort to explain further, and he started through the dimly lit, narrow lobby where the door of Apartment 1L was barely five feet inside.

The apartment door snapped open, constrained by its security chain lock, revealing a frail looking African-American woman, well past retirement age, with short gray hair and dressed in a warm-weather moo-moo of sorts.

"'Carter, is it?" she asked, staring up at him with skepticism in her remarkably blue eyes. "You know Wally from… from the *difficult* years?"

"Yeah," he said through the chain. "I know this must seem out of left field, but I guess after all these years I would just really like to know how he's doing."

"Well, come in," she said, but slammed the door shut.

The scraping sound of the chain lock coming undone followed, and when she opened the door again, she said, "I'm Milly, you come right on in, now."

As she led Carter into a homey and well-maintained living room that reminded him of the 1950s, she explained, "I'm sure Wally will be thrilled to see you."

"He's here?"

Stunned, Carter immediately felt ill-prepared to confront a man who could very well be his tormentor.

"He works odd hours, but he really ought to be up by now," she mentioned, as she ushered him to a couch that was covered in protective plastic.

She then hobbled down a hallway and disappeared.

The sounds of Milly faintly knocking came next. Murmuring. Carter presumed she was seeing if Wally was up.

Carter awkwardly debated whether to sit or remain standing.

When Milly emerged alone a moment later, he hadn't managed to get settled one bit.

"Please," she encouraged. "Have a seat. Wally will be right out. Would you like water? Something to drink?" He didn't respond right away but it wasn't because Milly gasped, "Oh!" her gaze having caught sight of the detective's badge clipped to his belt. "Oh, dear, Wally's not in trouble, is he?"

Gritting his teeth, the lie stuttered out. "No, not at all." To which he mentally added, *not necessarily.*

Milly shuffled off into the kitchen where she began bumbling around inside the refrigerator and cupboards, listing all the options—*orange juice and Pepsi cola and oh! Coca Cola, too, how 'bout that!*—as if she had completely forgotten he had declined.

As he picked one, not that he was thirsty, a lanky, dark-skinned man who appeared to be a good decade younger than Carter entered the living room.

The man wore sweats and socks on his feet. But it was the hollowed slouch he carried himself with that told Carter Wally had never recovered from what they had survived.

The roundness of the man's eyes, the sparkle of hope that to Carter seemed so sad, also indicated that old wounds had never healed properly.

But did the man's pathetic appearance indicate innocence?

"I'm glad to see you ended up in a loving home," said Carter, unsure of whether to shake Wally's hand or hug him.

He didn't want to do either, so he didn't.

"Yeah," he blushed, sliding his eyes to Milly with a stroke of embarrassment. There was nothing even remotely admirable about still living at home in your mid-thirties. "We take care of each other, you could say."

"Good," said Carter, as an awkward moment of silence swelled between them.

He was still standing like an idiot, so he finally had a seat, while Milly set a tray of orange juice down on the glass coffee table in front of him, and Wally continued to stare at him like he was seeing a ghost.

His voice trembling with sudden emotion, Wally told his foster mother, "Can we have the room?"

"Certainly," she smiled and shuffled her way up the hallway.

Soon the sounds of a television soap opera came faintly through the wall.

Wally's wide-eyed stare was putting Carter on edge, though the lanky man managed to slink into an armchair adjacent to the couch. Carter felt suddenly stuck.

"I remember you," he breathed. His eyes misted over with tears and soon his lower lip was quivering. "You were older." He was shaking his head now with impressed astonishment and looking Carter up and down. "You have a strength about you, I can see it. You're strong. I can tell you have a good life. Am I right?"

Choked up despite his greatest efforts not to be, he had to take a moment to swallow his emotions down. He remembered Wally, too. The kid had been just a baby when he had been brought in. By the time they were rescued, Carter was a teen and Wally had only been four or five. His young age had never exempted him from the abuse.

Carter felt his jaw tighten remembering that, and finally replied, "Yeah, my life is pretty good."

As he went on to mention Kathy, the story of how they met, and their three beautiful children, it became all too clear that Wally's physicality and actual demeanor didn't resemble Lacy's sketch, other than the shade of his complexion.

There was no way this was his guy unless Wally had a phenomenal alter ego...

That was Carter's conclusion until Wally said, "I've been keeping busy down at the Waste Management Plant. You know of it?"

"You work there?" he asked, suddenly suspicious.

Could Wally be the link that had enabled the killer to get inside the recycling plant and coax Raffael Sanzio to his gruesome death?

"Oh yeah. It's been a little over a decade now. I used to work the back of the trucks, you know, I was the garbage man who hopped off the rig, grabbed trash bags, and tossed them in. Then I drove for a while, but now I'm a manager at the facility."

"Really..." He leaned forward, studying the guy.

Wally must have read Carter's intrigue all wrong, because he went on to detail his responsibilities as if the detective was interested in changing careers. He then meekly boasted about all that he was doing for the environment.

After chugging down one of the orange juices, Wally said with a big smile on his face, "It's so amazing to see you, Carter. My God, we've all been wondering about how you were."

"I'm sorry? Did you say 'we've all,' as in…?"

"I attend a support group. It's not only for those of us who were at that particular location. All survivors of childhood sexual trauma are welcome. That being said, pretty much all of us are there… the men, I should say. It's a men's-only group."

"When does it meet?"

"Would you like to come?" he enthused, his round eyes misting over with tears once again. "Everyone would love to see you!"

"When and where," he asked, offering a terse smile. "I wouldn't miss it for the world."

IT WASN'T LONG before Carter found himself in the musty basement of a downtown church.

If he didn't know better, he would think he had stumbled into an AA meeting.

There was a circle of folding chairs in the center of the room. The table tucked against the near wall provided coffee and powdered creamers, black tea, a stack of paper cups, and an open box of doughnuts that had already been picked clean.

He had never seen Wally stand so tall as he was now. Carter watched the lanky man greet other survivors, as they entered and mingled here and there, checking in with as many as he could on a personal level and genuinely caring.

"I would introduce you," he said in a private murmur when he returned to Carter, who had been stirring heaps of sugar into his coffee. "But we take the 'anonymous' aspect of Survivors of Incest Abuse Anonymous very strictly. Once you introduce yourself at the circle, then light bulbs will start going off, and I'm sure everyone *we know* will want to catch up."

"I'm not sure I recognize anyone," he said, which was true, but only because he had been making a concerted effort *not* to place each face. Rather Carter had been trying to compare these adult men with what the sketch rendering of the perp had looked like.

"It could take time," said Wally, compassionately placing his hand on Carter's muscular shoulder.

"Tell me about Waste Management," he prodded, as more survivors filed into the room. The meeting would start soon, he could feel it. "Does anyone else here work there with you?"

Wally let out a little chortle. "I'm flattered you find it interesting."

He didn't, but Wally didn't need to know that.

"It's just me down at the plant," he answered though distractedly. His gaze was glued to the clock on the wall above the refreshment table. "Time to get things started," he smiled then left Carter in favor of the circle of chairs, some of which were already occupied with men nursing their coffees and doughnuts.

As the stragglers took their seats around the circle, and Wally pulled a black binder from the floppy knapsack he had been carrying over his shoulder, Carter made his hesitant way to one of the folding chairs.

It did not look comfortable. In fact, none of this did. And as soon as he sat down and glanced around from face to face, he discovered that a lot of these men 'looked like him' in the most basic sense—dark complexion, upwards of 6' tall, short or shaved hair.

Though some were slightly overweight with a paunch and others seemed far too old or young, too ratty and impoverished in their style of dress, or far too suited up like Carter, they all had that *look* about them.

The one that Wally, by contrast, did not possess.

Aggressive yet guarded. Jaw clenched. A distinct tension in the shoulders and hands, like they were in the habit of entering every room and situation with two fists in the air, ready to fight, not physically per se, but everything about their demeanor—their spirit, perhaps—was prepared to fiercely defend.

It had been vital in the basement, that on-guard, fight-or-flight constant adrenaline.

But it was no longer necessary.

Which only made seeing that attitude in these men—knowing he carried himself in the exact same way—heartbreaking in its own right.

Regardless, it wasn't lost on Carter that one of the men around this circle could have persuaded Wally to let him into the Waste Management plant the night of May 12th to lure Raffi in and murder him; One of these men could have proceeded to the second phase of his murderous plan, killing Kayla and Andre, abducting Nahla, and now tormenting Carter with photos of his own family...

As Wally read from the first laminated sheet in the binder that explained the rules of the meeting with an emphasis on 'no cross talk,' Carter stole more glances at the sixteen men around the circle.

The man directly across from him had the stature of a retired football player, not unlike Carter himself. His head was shaved, but the features of his face resembled the detective in absolutely no way. He had a long, narrow nose to match his oval face. Too young.

The next man beside him looked like a polished, bookish version of Carter, a sweater-donning J. Crew-esque look about him, horn-rimmed glasses, loafers, and a camel tweed coat draped neatly over the back of his chair.

Their eyes touched, but this was not the kind of environment where he could get away with a lingering gaze, so he quickly looked down at his hands, adopting the shy, introverted posture of most everyone else at the meeting.

"We have a new comer today," Wally went on after finishing whatever updates he had given the group. "A number of you may recognize him."

Carter wasn't paying attention.

The man with horn-rimmed glasses looked familiar, but after trying and failing to place him as one of the kids from the basement, he began racking his brain as to whether or not he had ever seen him around.

"Would you like to be the first to share?" Wally asked, jarring him out of tangled contemplation.

"Me?"

"It's fine if you don't want to," the thick man in sweatpants to his right kindly informed him.

"That's right," Wally agreed. He let the offer hang in the air for a beat then glanced around the room and asked, "Would anyone else like to start the meeting with a timed open share. It would be three minutes for each of us if everyone wants to—"

"I'll go," Carter decided, his heart already galloping in his chest.

He felt shaky all of a sudden at the thought of speaking, but if the killer was in this circle, then he would have to be shocked to see Carter—the detective from the news, the man who he had sent threatening photos to—which put Carter in an excellent position to bait him into revealing himself.

"Just give me a sec to collect my thoughts."

"Sure," Wally whispered. He had assigned the job of 'timekeeper' to one of the younger group members. Wally nodded to him now, and the guy tapped the screen of his cell phone to stop the clock, leaned forward, planted his elbows on his knees, and stared at the floor, as if all he needed was to hear Carter's voice and he would start the timer again.

Carter felt eyes on him and found Horn-Rimmed Glasses staring at him full on.

Where had he seen him before?

Had it been in the basement?

Why did it feel more recent than that?

Clearing his throat, he glanced down at his folded hands to gather his thoughts then proceeded to start truthfully with the aim of folding in the same sorts of lies and misinformation that might provoke his killer out into the open.

"My name's Carter," he began, keeping his eyes down, though he could feel the others around the circle staring. "Carter Dobbs, so when Wally said some of you might know me... well, you might. I know Wally from..." Why was this so hard? It was like his brain was constantly shuffling through what he could say and what he should omit. "From growing up, you could say.

"I've been in therapy, but…" Again, he trailed off, this time feeling his mouth tug into a little grin. "It was my wife's idea, not so much for me but for our marriage. I just can't get there in therapy," he told the group, now looking at the faces around the circle. Some kept their gazes down, others looked him in the eye, glimmers of empathy pouring out. "It doesn't really help, if I'm being honest here.

"Well, that's not true," Carter corrected himself, taking a thoughtful moment to recall one of his prior sessions.

It took him a long moment to mentally compose what he wanted to say.

"I was a slave. Never a child. A slave. I believe that. And in therapy, when I realized all of this, it was brought to my attention that I'm still a slave. I married a woman who…"

He didn't have the heart to paint Kathy in a bad light even if only anonymously to a room full of strangers.

"You could say our dynamic is master-slave, and I don't mean in the bedroom," he joked, a split-second later Kayla's secret lifestyle sprung to mind. Her whips and chains. Those dog collars. The BDSM photos. She had been a slave, as well. "Am I alone in this or do any of you feel the same?

"I know there's no 'cross talk'," he clarified, implying his question was either rhetorical or they could approach him with their responses after the meeting. "I just don't know how far I've really come if I've subconsciously kept myself in a position of oppression, if I still have a 'master.' I mean…" he trailed off, now coming full circle to the trap he had aimed to set. "I'm not a religious person, but I fear God. No one should worship a false god, some master you're a slave to, am I right?"

Horn-Rimmed Glasses was staring dead at him, but all of these men were guarded. He couldn't get a read on the guy.

"And yet, I do worship my wife. I've made so many *sacrifices*. Have I been sacrificing to the wrong master? What does the one true God want me to sacrifice?"

The timekeeper gave a little wave, indicating Carter's time was up, so he thanked the group, leaned back in his chair, and let out a rocky exhale of relief mixed with apprehension.

Horn-Rimmed Glasses was still staring at him even though Wally had turned the floor over to the next man who was now in the throes of sharing how his woeful week had gone.

Carter made a mental note to approach the guy at the first break, get his name, and see if he was on the witness list from decades prior.

Abruptly, he tuned back in when he heard the man who was sharing say, "I know there's no 'cross talk' as well, but I remember you, Carter, and the whole 'am I still a slave' dilemma is very real for me. Do I keep choosing people who abuse me? God," he cursed angrily. "I just wish he was dead." He cut his fiery eyes to Carter and told him, "I wish that son-of-a-bitch with his sick rules and his pocket watch would just drop dead already. How has no one murdered him in prison? I can't even look at a clock without my stomach turning to pure acid."

The man was still alive…? He was in prison…?

It was something Carter had never let himself fully acknowledge. He hadn't even allowed himself to learn his abuser's legal name.

"Talk about a 'God' you need to make sacrifices to just to save your skin," the man went on, referencing symbolism that cut to the core of the case.

But this particular man was too old and too overweight to be the perp.

"I would've done anything to stop the ticking pocket watch, and when he used to crank it," he shuddered at some dark memory taking hold. "At times, I was more afraid of the watch than of the man, like that brass timepiece was a more ruthless sadist than Jeremiah Daughtry himself."

Jeremiah Daughtry.

The name sounded so pious.

What a joke.

Carter's cell phone began vibrating from the inner pocket of his suit jacket, just loudly enough to be a disturbance.

He was about to silence it completely, when he saw Kathy's name flashing across the screen.

Immediately, he swiped his thumb across the LCD screen, accepting the call, as he sprang from his chair and ducked into the anteroom outside of the meeting.

"Tell me you're okay," he said.

"I'm fine, the kids are fine," she told him, though the trembling in her voice betrayed her. "More pictures arrived, Carter."

"How?"

"FedEx this time."

FedEx? He pondered. The guy would've had to have provided a return address, and Kathy, anticipating his question, was one step ahead of him, "The return address listed is the precinct."

"What?"

"He's obviously a very clever piece of work," she hissed. "Can you please come home? These photos…" Kathy's voice faltered. She was on the brink of tears. "Carter, they're of our daughter, and I'm very, very scared."

Chapter Eighteen

"HOW'S THE CASSEROLE?" Nora asked, cautiously optimistic that the silence they had eaten dinner in wasn't tense, but rather introspective, as if her daughter had been quietly appreciating their reunion.

That wasn't the case.

"It's good," she said, tense, as she glanced around her mother's cramped apartment in disbelief that she was even here.

She hadn't set foot in the place since confronting Nora about her infant son, Gregory's real cause of death, the day she had also warned her mother to stay the hell out of her life or else she would go to the police with what she knew.

Death changed everything, or so it seemed.

It had been the force that had driven Nora out of her life.

And, ironically, it was also the force that had sucked Danny right back to where she had started. Except this time she wasn't in denial about her mother's sickness. What was known could never be unknown.

The airless living room, where they were eating, seated at an old Formica table, was just as cluttered as it had been the day she had cast Nora out of her life—a hoarder's haven.

Glancing around, it was clear to Danny her mother might have never thrown a single thing out.

"Not too salty?" asked her mother, worriedly.

Danny had the feeling they weren't talking about Nora's cooking anymore, as if liking the meal equaled loving her mother. Sad logic. But logic none-the-less. There was a reason she had drunk way too much at Lance's birthday party, and it had everything to do with the bomb Nora had dropped on her.

That she was dying.

"What exactly are the next steps?" she asked, changing the subject from food to her mother's failing health.

Nora didn't look ill, per se, but Danny was wise enough to know that when it came to cancer, it was often the chemotherapy that ran a person ragged and not the tumors themselves.

"Did your doctor devise how to…" Her mind kept offering '*beat it*,' but no one survived pancreatic cancer, not in the long run. "What does he recommend?"

"Oh, all kinds of nonsense," she sighed, smoothing her boney hands over her blonde, wavy hair and giving her freshly dyed locks a little boost where they fell to her chin.

She had always maintained a manicured appearance no matter how dismal her babysitting wages, and though she was only fifty-nine, she carried herself with the innocent air of a grandmother.

Danny had learned the hard way not to trust that innocence.

"Radiation, chemotherapy, the whole nine yards," she explained. "But what's that going to do? Make me look and feel very sick, while only prolonging my life a handful of months at best."

"Is that what the doctor said? 'A handful'?"

"Oh, doctors don't know anything," she complained, as she took hold of the wine bottle she had been working on and topped off Danny's glass even though her daughter hadn't taken a single sip since she had sat down. As she generously refreshed her own glass, she said, "He talked it up like I could get as many as eighteen months out of it, but I doubt it. Besides, who wants to get strapped into a machine twice a day to have chemicals pumped through them?"

"People who want to live longer?" she offered.

"Quality of life is all that matters," Nora declared, "which is why it means the world to me that you're here. I don't know if it was the stress of missing you that weakened my immune system…"

Was she actually blaming Danny for inducing her pancreatic cancer?

Danny felt her gaze narrow into a glare, but she bit her tongue, unwilling to argue with the faulty reasoning of an old dying woman.

"But when you…" Her voice hitched in her throat and she became suddenly verklempt. "*Accused* me," she hissed, clutching her chest where her cardigan sweater hung unbuttoned, "of such a horrible thing…"

Why was Danny unable to speak up, confront her mother all over again if that's what it would take, and assert the facts? Danny hadn't been mistaken, Jill's autopsy had proved Gregory had been smothered, and only Nora had been in the apartment when it had happened.

Nora was now acting as though if she pretended Gregory had really died of S.I.D.S., then she could rewrite history and replace the truth with a fabrication. And yet, Danny was letting her.

"Well," Nora went on. "I'm sure the stress of it, and mind you I've been mourning my grandson's tragic death just like you have—"

Danny was gritting her teeth so hard she thought they would crack.

"The heartbreak of losing you, Danny. Knowing that you were so close yet so far away. Knowing that you *believed* me capable of such a heinous crime… When I received my diagnosis, I thought to myself, it made sense. I had been worried sick to the extent that I actually *became* sick."

Anger and guilt were at war inside of her. She wanted to reach across the table and throttle Nora for denying she had killed her grandson, and for blaming Danny for her declining health. And at the same time, she also wanted to curl into her mother's arms like she had when she was a little girl and sob her heart out that she was sorry.

This hold Nora had on her…

She was a slave to it, wasn't she?

"None of this is to say that I blame you," Nora assured her, even though that's exactly what she was doing. She offered her daughter a heartfelt smile, reached across the table, and squeezed her hand. "I'm just so happy you're here. I would like my final months to be a happy time. I don't want to leave this world with you hating me."

Tears had welled up in her mother's eyes, and Danny felt her own eyes misting over, her throat tightened with emotion. She didn't want Nora to leave this world with Danny hating her either. She couldn't stand that any of this was happening, but Nora had brought it upon herself.

And she had never explained why. Why had she taken Gregory's life that night?

It was sick.

Danny glanced away, blinking back tears in an attempt to hide them, and when she was certain her voice would sound steady, she said, "I think it's a good idea to box up a lot of this stuff. Donate some of it. Maybe have a sidewalk sale."

"Would you help with that?" Nora asked, ever hopeful to lock in more occasions to spend time with her daughter.

"I'm not sure how much time I have," she said honestly. "The case I'm working has been demanding and complicated."

"Maybe Tommy could help?" she suggested, much to Danny's surprise. Nora hated Tommy and had gone to great lengths to keep him out of Danny's life. "I know you think I sabotaged your relationship, but really, I just want to be one big happy family for the short amount of time I have left to live."

One big happy family?

Outraged, she blurted out, "Why did you kill my son?"

Chapter Nineteen

HIS WIFE HAD BEEN a mess for days after the FedEx package, which had been shipped from the 66th Precinct.

The envelope was thick with more black and white surveillance type photos, but their fourteen-year old daughter was the subject this time.

In one photo, Amanda stood in the bathroom, her hair dripping, as she clutched a towel around her. In another shot from the bathroom, Amanda was nude, her skin dewy with shower steam, she was stepping into her underwear. In the next photo, she was struggling to fasten the bra that was around her waist, and the images went on and on.

Their daughter's entire morning routine—putting on makeup, doing her hair, and barely eating breakfast.

It had disturbed Kathy.

Deeply.

And every time she cut her sharp blue eyes at Carter, the blame, torment, and distress that was written all over her face twisted his stomach with acidic knots.

It wasn't enough that they had been escorting the kids to and from school, not allowing them to participate in their afterschool activities, and watching all three of them like hypervigilant hawks.

When those photos had arrived, Kathy had gone from trusting Carter's judgment, and sitting tight while he handled things, to insisting again and again, either directly or with those cold blue eyes of hers, that he had to tell the police.

"I *am* the police," he barked.

"This is our daughter," she hissed, shoving the peeping-tom images in his face and whisper-shouting crassly after that. "She's naked! Look at them! That's our daughter! If she's not a 'special victim,' then I don't know who is!"

Nahla, Carter thought, as he wrangled the glossy prints out of her grasp and roughly slid them back into the FedEx sleeve they had come in. *That's who.*

When he left her this morning, Kathy was filling the doorway of their home, her arms folded, staring at him questioningly, he promised he would put an end to all of this. He just needed time.

Kathy objected as always, again insisting that 'putting an end to all of this' should very well involve the police.

But he knew—all the way down to the trembling marrow in his bones—that he didn't have the upper hand. He had a list. He was narrowing it down. But he didn't know who the killer was, where he was, or what the consequences would be if Carter didn't 'sacrifice correctly.'

The killer knew everything about him.

Everything.

Which meant that if Carter clued the 66th in on this, wherever the guy was, he would know.

He couldn't stomach to consider what might happen to his family if that were to occur, so he told Kathy in no uncertain terms to *trust him* and then he slid into the backseat of a cab to get to the precinct.

He didn't trust her to trust him.

She never had.

By the time he reached the break room of the SVU floor, eager to jumpstart his already shaky adrenals with a cup of hot coffee, he felt overwhelmed. It had been *days* since the press conference, *days* since the first envelope of photos had shown up, followed by *days and days* since the photos of Amanda had riveted both his wife and him to their cores.

All the while, Carter hadn't received further instructions from the killer in terms of how to make a proper sacrifice, what to sacrifice, or how to make it out of this unscathed.

The only clues he had were the disturbing messages that had been collaged across the backs of the photos of Amanda.

When Carter had arranged the photos in the chronological order of his daughter's morning routine, the collages on the backs of the photos had delivered one cohesive message:

Tick.
Tock.
Goes the clock.
Don't.
Keep me.
Waiting.

The back of the final photo read:

The sacrifice is nearing.

"Carter?"

He startled from perplexed uneasiness, the mug of coffee in his large hand having gone cold, to find Danny approaching him through the break room doorway.

"You okay?" she asked as if it hadn't been the first time.

"Just spacing." He cleared his throat, dumped the cold coffee in the sink, and as he poured himself a fresh mug, he asked, "Any next steps from Franco?"

She sidled around him, grabbed her own mug from the cabinets, and proceeded to pour herself a cup, as she complained, "Crouse and Toliver are trying to steal the entire case."

"How?"

As if the very threat had already exhausted her, she explained, "They're arguing that Kayla and Andre's murders weren't sexually motivated."

"Even though Kayla had been stripped of her shirt and bra and skinned?" he pointed out.

"She wasn't sexually violated," Danny shrugged. "And they're trying to get around the Nahla Rashad aspect, arguing there's no way of knowing that the girl was taken by the killer."

"Are you kidding me?"

"The evidence Jill pulled together from the dog crate proves the girl was there, but it can't prove she was taken by the *killer*."

"So, she just vanished from thin air?"

"No, Homicide is arguing that she was abducted by someone else and that the case belongs with Missing Persons, not SVU."

"That's horse crap."

"I doubt they'll be able to steal the case, Carter," she tried to assure him. "I'm just telling you what I heard. Nothing's official or Franco would've called us into his office."

"They're just gunning for it because it's a high profile case now, and they want the recognition," he balked a little too hotly.

"I agree," she assured him, and they stared at each other for a beat.

It was then that Carter noticed how rough she looked. Her eyes were puffy and she was wearing makeup, which wasn't typical. Her hair looked weird, too, like she had hair-sprayed her bangs to the side until they had turned into a stiff sheet of plastic.

She also looked pale and gaunt, like she hadn't been able to eat.

"Are *you* okay?" he asked, suddenly concerned.

Shrugging as a long sigh seeped out, she shook her head as if she wouldn't know where to start then gave him a pat reply, "My mother is… an actual nightmare."

He let out a hearty laugh. He had encountered Nora only once, but it wasn't hard to imagine the truth of Danny's statement. But then, reading her stoic expression, the way the light had darkened behind her eyes, he realized she hadn't meant to make a joke.

"Is something seriously wrong?" he asked.

"No, no," she was quick to assure him. "Just… family drama."

He was smart enough to know when his partner was lying to him, but this was one of those instances where he sensed prying would only be bad for both of them. Not to mention that time was of the essence. He had only stopped in the precinct to make an appearance. He had much bigger fish to fry, and he wouldn't be able to catch a single one here.

Realizing he had no use for his coffee, he again dumped the liquid in the sink, gave his mug a little rinse, and clanked it back into the overhead cabinet where it belonged.

"You going somewhere?" she asked.

"Yeah, I was going to do another undercover day at the projects."

She narrowed her skeptical gaze on him and questioned, "In your suit?"

"I've got sweats in my locker," he lied.

"I thought we exhausted the projects."

"The surveillance footage was useless," he agreed, but was quick to correct her, "that's why heading back in as C-Dog makes sense."

"C-Dog?"

He had added the 'Dog' part, but felt confident it sounded believable.

"Lacy Marcel is the only one who knows I'm a cop, and she hasn't let it slip to anyone."

"You know this for a fact?" she countered.

Not liking the confrontational nature of her particular brand of doubting him this morning, he planted his large fists on his hips and angled in on her, just one shallow step that brought with it a wealth of meaning—*back off.*

"You got a problem with how I'm moving on this?" he challenged.

Her guard didn't fly up.

Instead, she looked at him earnestly.

"I do, actually. I think you're keeping something from me, and I don't like it. We're partners," she reminded him, before stepping in and closing the gap between them to whisper, "I don't care who else in this department you cut out in order to have things your way. I've gone off on my own before, too. Sometimes you have to. But you don't exclude your partner. You want to go off alone? Fine. But I expect to be informed of what you're really doing."

Lightening up a touch, she argued, "How else am I going to craft a convincing lie to Franco if he asks me where you've run off to?"

"Re-canvassing the projects isn't convincing enough?" he shot back.

A sideways grin tugged at the corner of her asymmetrical mouth, giving off that 'wicked' smirk again, as she said, "Do I look convinced?"

Point taken.

"If you can't fool me, then you don't have a prayer of fooling Franco. You're not going to the projects. Am I right or am I right?" As he stared at her, jaw clenched and debating, she again reminded him, "I'm your partner."

There was so much to tell her.

He didn't even know where to begin, but he had to.

It was time.

So, he suggested, "Let's talk outside."

SETTLED BEHIND the steering wheel of the police issued Crown Victoria, Danny beside him on the passenger seat, he began rather clumsily:

"When we were with Crouse and Toliver—"

"And you mentioned your abusive upbringing," she smartly supplied, which gave him pause.

"I know you feel close to this case," she explained. "You're invested, and while everyone else is focusing on a 'killer,' you're the one who never forgets there's a little girl out there. A little girl who's in danger who needs to be rescued." She let that hang for a beat then asked, "So where are you running off to?"

"I'm closer to this thing than you realize," he told her, "so you need to slow your roll."

Her brow furrowed with keen interest.

Daunted—*how the hell was he supposed to begin?*—he decided that messily blurting out whatever came to mind was the only way to proceed since his thoughts were already being scrambled by nerves and anxiety.

Danny was smart. If she couldn't make sense of his ramblings, she would ask.

"The guy we're looking for… I know him."

"What?" she breathed in utter astonishment.

"I don't know his name. I just know that I know him, and he knows me. We grew up together."

"How do you know?" she asked with urgency in her sudden, cop tone.

"I just do," he insisted, unwilling to mention the photographs of his family, or how close to himself this thing really did cut. But he knew she wasn't about to let him get away with keeping anything from her, so he admitted, "It's a hunch. An angle I'm working. That's why I didn't tell you."

"What makes you think—"

"There were a lot of us being abused," he cut her off. "We were each abducted. We were kept in dog crates in a basement. It was a pedophile ring."

He couldn't look at her, but sensed she looked pained.

Instead, he studied the buildings across the parking lot, the way the early morning sunlight bounced off their glass windows. The treetops rustled, as a warm, spring wind breezed through.

"The crate they kept Kayla in," she said, articulating his logic.

But that wasn't the only component. "This thing is connected, and it's not just my gut telling me," he insisted. "One of the kids from the crates where I grew up, this guy Wallace Bronson, I paid him a visit."

"Okay," she said.

"There's no way he's our perp," he clarified to expel any suspicion she might have. "But he works at Waste Management, at the plant where Raffi was murdered."

Her eyes sprang wide as saucers, and she gaped, "He works at one of the crime scenes, and you've ruled him out? Why?"

"Look," he cut in, meeting her gaze before pulling out the list of witnesses from the County Clerk's office that he had been carrying around inside his suit jacket. "I obtained all the last known addresses of the kids who were abused with me."

He handed her the crumpled list, certain names had been crossed out in a ballpoint pen.

As she skimmed it, he went on, "It's a shorter, better list than the hundreds of ex-cons who match our sketch and probably had nothing to do with the killings. Wally hooked me up with a support group," he said excitedly. "Nearly all the local survivors from the basement attend. I went there."

"To one of the meetings?"

"I can't describe it, but I could *feel* him there."

"We should lean into Wally," she suggested, having shifted back into cop mode.

"You're not listening."

"I think I am, Carter. You've done excellent work, and hey, maybe this Wally character is innocent. He works at Waste Management, a site that is heavily locked and guarded at night. We know our perp got in there easily—"

"With the possible use of scopolamine," he pointed out.

"Fine, so the guy drugged Wally. Let's bring him in. Talk to him. See what he remembers in that regard."

"You're not bringing him anywhere," he said defensively. "I've already talked to him—"

"And?"

"And I'm working on it."

"That's where you're headed?" she guessed. "To another support group meeting?"

How could he tell her where he was going without telling her the whole story? He was absolutely certain that the killer-kidnapper was from his past. But he couldn't tell Danny everything and omit that the perp had taken photos of his children. He feared if Danny found out, his kids' lives would be at risk even worse than they already were.

No, telling her would be too risky.

She was already chomping at the bit to take the helm, and if she learned that Carter, or worse, his entire family had become a target, she would only work hard to convince him that he had to recuse himself from the case.

Failing that, she would move on to Franco. No cop was allowed to work a case where those close to him were Vics, whether dead or alive. It didn't matter that Kathy and the kids had only been spied on and photographed. They were still victims.

"Carter?" she demanded. "Is that where you're going?"

"No," he finally said, staring dead at her. "I'm going to Sing Sing."

"To the prison?" she asked, intrigued.

"To see the man who—" He felt his throat tighten and the words wouldn't come. "I'm going back to the start to finish this thing."

Chapter Twenty

THE MAN WHO HAD enslaved him. The monster who had ruled his moment to moment fate, who had selected or skipped him each soul-murdering night…

Children had shrieked and wailed, having been returned to their cages in the darkness…

Carter had fantasized about killing the man countless times, but his little, feeble hands would never have been capable…

This man, a monster, had filled Carter with more hate than a child's heart should ever have to bear.

Carter had remembered the man as a towering giant, so strong he could easily toss young Carter around like a worthless ragdoll. It hadn't mattered how much Carter had kicked and punched…

That man with the pocket watch had filled Carter with terror, as if the towering monster had been the devil himself, coming to steal his very soul.

And now, the same man was seated across from Carter in the Visitors Center of the Sing Sing Correctional Facility.

He looked frail and hunched, bird-boned, his face emaciated, his hands knotty and powerless.

Jeremiah Daughtry.

Carter couldn't believe that this puny disgrace of an old man, with watery eyes, a droopy mouth, and age spots on his sallow Caucasian skin, was the same man who had wielded the cruelest power over him for the worst ten years of his life.

He looked like your basic, run-of-the-mill gas station attendant from any given rural area. Old. Friendly. And sad.

The gray jumpsuit he wore hung off his brittle shoulders, the breast pockets as slack as his lower lip, his prison-issued loafers lace-less so he wouldn't hang himself.

Carter was twice, if not three times his size, and yet something inside him was wailing in terror—trembling so violently that it felt like his bones were aching.

In Jeremiah Daughtry's presence, he felt like the boy he used to be.

He felt scared.

And he also felt like reaching across the Visitors Center table and strangling the pedophile to death.

Worst of all, he had completely lost sight of why he had actually thought that confronting his abuser would result in figuring out the identity of the killer, the kidnapper, the brand-new tyrant in Carter's life.

Danny was waiting outside in the Crown Vic.

She had driven up with him, offering her silent and unwavering support.

He could bail on this insane endeavor at any time. Chalk it up to a failed strategy, get back to his list, the survivors' meetings, and beat the streets, maybe stage another press conference in an attempt to throw the guy off balance even further, not that their initial effort on the news had done them much good other than to jeopardize his family…

Then it struck him. Whether or not it benefited the investigation, he was here to face his past, face the greatest fear that had been lurking in the back of his mind and plaguing his soul, perhaps his entire life—those dark, forgotten memories that constantly threatened to surge up and destroy him.

Facing his greatest fear meant confronting the man who had caused it in the first place.

He stared dead at Jeremiah, the trembling in his chilled bones boiling into rage that gave his tone a formidable edge of strength.

"Do you know who I am?" he asked the prisoner.

The older man's voice sounded like wind over reeds.

"A Brooklyn detective?" he answered, his milky gaze turning curious, apologetic. "They told me your name, but I forgot."

The hollow timbre of his voice… It snapped Carter into a terrified tremble again, triggering some disturbing memory that he had to fight and push out of his mind. Sounds and smells. Touch.

Dr. Ling had warned him of the tactile triggers, how they were strung as tight as a bow to visceral memories, as if the body itself had the intelligence to store imprints of past traumatic events. But he hadn't paid her much mind since the phenomenon rarely, if ever, occurred.

When he uttered, "Dobbs," his voice had lost all kick. He swallowed hard, willed some weight back into his tone, and clarified, "Detective Carter Dobbs."

"I've been locked up a good, long while, Detective, so whatever you're here to ask me about, I can't say I'll be very helpful."

Jeremiah had no idea who Carter was. He didn't recognize him.

"You don't remember me?" he questioned.

Staring blankly, the older man seemed at a loss, then asked, "Should I?"

"You used to tell me not to *keep you waiting.*"

Jeremiah's tired eyes brightened with a gleam of recognition, not at Carter's face, but at the phrase.

A strange, perverse grin tugged at the dry corner of his mouth, as his gaze drifted off, unseeingly as if some fond reminder had taken hold.

"You kept me locked in a basement," he stated. Clenching his jaw and pressing his thick lips into a hard line, he felt his heart rate elevate to pounding heights. "You kept a lot of us down there."

"And I'm serving my time for it," he countered, as if the government providing him slop to eat and a roof over his head, at a prison where college kids came around to teach poetry for God's sake, was a punishment that could compare, in any way, shape, or form, to the crime.

Jeremiah cocked his head to the side and studied him. "I mean no offense, but I honest to God don't remember you."

Was that supposed to be an insult? Should Carter be offended that he had endured this monster's abuse in an 'unmemorable' way?

Once again, the urge to reach across the table and murder the bastard washed over him.

"What can I do for you?" the older man asked, still studying him, but sounding inconvenienced. "Have you come to solicit an apology? Or is this your big 'moment of confrontation'? Have you finally gotten yourself enough therapy," he began chuckling, "that you think it will help your 'healing'—" His tone was mocking now, and the monster he had once been was back, "—if you sit down face-to-face with the man who hurt you?"

It wouldn't have touched a raw nerve if the old man hadn't been right.

Carter refused to let on that the guy's intuition had been correct.

"It seems you have a copycat," he stated matter-of-factly. "A little girl has been abducted. The perp had to kill three people to get to her—"

"Ah," he mused as if the legwork, pre-abduction, was standard. "And how many people did I have to murder to get you?"

He was taunting Carter, rubbing in his face how he had massacred everything Carter had held dear as a four-year old boy.

"I don't remember life before the dog crate," he shot back.

"But you *know*," Jeremiah said. "My memory's a bit fuzzy on you, which is why I asked."

"As much as I would like to reminisce," he cut in sarcastically, though his tone was firm and emotionless at the reminder that the older man across the table had killed both of his parents in order to snatch young Carter from his childhood bed. "I'm here as part of an investigation. My unit believes—" he quickly lied, "you had something to do with this."

"How?" he demanded, suddenly incredulous.

"What appeared at first blush to be a copycat, we quickly realized, could more likely be your second stab at reinstating your pedophile ring."

He snorted a laugh. "Oh, come on. You think I would orchestrate something like that from behind bars? What would I get out of it?" he challenged then was sharp to remind the detective with a leering smirk, "I'm more of a *hands-on* type of guy."

"I think living vicariously through someone else's 'work' with the possibility of seeing a photo or two would be enough for you."

"So, I'm either a mastermind or a mentor," he surmised, unamused. "Is that what you think?"

"I think you tried your best to destroy all of us," he countered. "And the dangerous reality is that when a boy is abused in that manner, they can falsely assume that the only way not to be abused is to be like their abuser. They grow up and find themselves modeling their abuser's life, behavior, and *sexuality* in a desperate, scared, convoluted attempt to ensure they'll sit safely at the top of the food chain. Stay the most powerful."

"Is that what you've done, Carter?" he sneered. "Have you been raping little boys?"

It wasn't until Carter's fist connected hard against Jeremiah's jaw and he saw the smug bastard fly out of his chair that Carter realized he had thrown a bone-cracking blow.

He was heaving now, on his feet and staring down at the older man, who was laughing and writhing and nursing his bleeding mouth with both hands.

The guards were at Carter's heels, but he immediately put his hands up and promised, "No touching. I get it, no touching. I'm a cop."

One of the guards helped Jeremiah up while the other commented, "You didn't just touch him, my friend."

"I'm a cop," he repeated. "And I'm not done interviewing this inmate."

"Do you need medical attention?" the guard asked, as he helped Jeremiah to stand.

The older man cut his scathing eyes to Carter and answered, "No. I would like to help this detective's investigation in any way I can."

As Jeremiah settled back down on his seat, gingerly touching his swelling lower lip to check if he was still bleeding—he would live—the guards backed off and returned to their post at the other side of the room.

The other inmates and visitors went back to minding their own business, too.

Carter gave his punching hand a hard shake, sat down, and felt a silver lining of satisfaction.

"Have you reached out to any of us?" he asked curtly.

"How would I?"

"The witness list from the trial," he supplied, as he pulled the very list from the inner pocket of his jacket. "Your defense attorney would've had a copy therefore you would've had access to it."

"And you think I bided my time for decades then started making collect calls from Sing Sing?" he snorted.

"No, I think it's more likely that the perp I'm after sought you out. Who has visited you here?"

Jeremiah set his soulless eyes on Carter and stated, "The only one who's ever sought me out is you."

He studied the older man for a long beat, his gut telling him the monster wasn't lying, while his mind refused to give up. If he was telling the truth, then this truly had been a dead end.

He couldn't accept it.

Out of nowhere, he blurted, "Why the pocket watch?"

Melting all over again into a distant memory, a slimy grin creeped across Jeremiah's weathered face, and he admitted, "I just liked seeing you boys squirm." When his eyes met Carter's, he reached his bony hand into one of the droopy breast pockets of his jumpsuit and out came the shiny, brass pocket watch.

The older man set it on the table like some kind of offering.

"They let me keep it," he explained. "None of you kids mentioned it in your testimony against me, so it was never taken in as evidence. After some years of good behavior, I was allowed to receive it. My mom brought it to me. Oh, man," he remarked, leaning in and staring hard at Carter, that slimy grin on his face broadening into an amused sneer. "You should see your face. For a soot-black African you're white as a ghost."

Ignoring the man, Carter wrapped his fist around the pocket watch and felt its warmth, as its chain dangled down and clacked against the tabletop.

"I watch the news, Carter. I've kept up with the story, and I'll keep tuning in. You might think you're hunting some kidnapper, some killer, someone like me—like if you find that little girl, you're somehow really saving yourself; as if reaching back in time is possible. But you're in for a rude awakening, boy. Because the only person you're going to find on the other side of this thing will be yourself."

He let that hang for a long beat then warned, "If the man you're after is someone from the basement, someone you were in the thick of it with, crying and toughing it out together, just what in the hell do you really think you're going to be able to do once you find him?"

Jeremiah shook his head then advised, "Just let him be what he's become. I didn't go easy on all of them like I did for you."

He remembered him?

Carter glared at the guy then rose to his feet with the pocket watch clamped in his fist, to which he referred, "I'm keeping this."

That sly smirk was back on Jeremiah's face as he said, "I wouldn't have it any other way."

THE SCENT OF BLAND coffee filled the air, commingling with the musty smell of the church basement where Carter had arrived early to help Wally set up a circle of folding chairs for the Survivors of Incest Abuse meeting.

With every step he took, opening and placing each metal chair, he was acutely aware of the brass pocket watch, its hefty weight, in his slacks.

His gut had gotten him this far.

He knew that the perp he was after regularly attended this meeting. He had felt it last time. He just hoped this longshot plan, as off the cuff as it was, would pan out.

Once the chairs were set up, Carter joined Wally at the refreshment table and poured himself a cup of coffee, as Wally opened a box of doughnuts and selected a powdery, pink one to eat.

A few attendees began shuffling in. They veered towards the refreshments, so Carter and Wally drifted aside, making room.

In a hushed tone with respect to the somber, introspective atmosphere he had noticed these meetings required, Carter mentioned to Wally, "I would really like to share today."

"That's great, Carter," he enthused in a whisper. "There should be enough time for everyone."

"The sooner the better for me," he cut in, then provided an impromptu excuse, "I may have to duck out early. The wife."

"Of course, of course," said Wally thoughtfully, as he racked his brain, presumably giving a quick mental review to the agenda. "After opening remarks, you could share first," he offered.

"That would be really great."

He thanked him with an equally somber smile.

He was tempted to investigate the Waste Management Recycling Plant angle—if Wally worked there, it couldn't have been a coincidence that the killer had picked that site to lure Raffi into diving head-first into a trash compactor—Carter took a cautious sip of the bland coffee he had poured.

Wally seemed so innocent. There was something about him, the hopeful gleam in his eyes that seemed to constantly struggle against the defeated expression on his face. Carter's gut continued to tell him that there was no way this man had wittingly allowed a killer access to the Waste Management plant.

If he questioned him about it a second time—Carter was heavily wired with surveillance microphones and Danny was listening from an unmarked van across the street, recording his every interaction—it would only give her cause to alert the District Attorney, and of course Franco.

Yes, Wallace Bronson was how the killer had gotten into the plant with Raffi. And, yes, that alone made Wally look like he was potentially an accessory to murder.

But Carter didn't want Wally to have to go through an interrogation. If Wally accidentally implicated himself, not because he was guilty but because he had a tendency to phrase things clumsily, then Danny and Cruz would barge into the meeting, and Wally would be arrested on the spot.

Carter couldn't risk it.

He didn't want the lives of any of these men to be disrupted—not after what they had all been through—except for one.

The killer.

The group member who often kept the time floated in with two African-Americans, one tall, muscular, and athletic, in his mid-forties, though he carried himself with a bit of a depraved slouch. The other had a lighter complexion and was wearing sunglasses, though it was night.

Carter wanted names, but as per Wally's rules, the anonymity of this meeting prohibited him from approaching any of them in a formal manner.

So, he began memorizing faces with nicknames. The timekeeper wasn't a suspect based solely on his ethnicity—he was White not Black.

Carter mentally labeled the two men who had come in with the White timekeeper and were now stocking up on doughnuts and coffee at the refreshment table. They were Football Forty and Sunglasses At Night.

As others filtered in, Carter having taken a seat in the circle and working hard to push flashes of Jeremiah Daughtry—that chilling visit—from his mind, Carter continued to label each survivor with a nickname. His fist still smarted where he had nearly knocked Jeremiah's teeth out. A small price to pay.

Danny could hear him from her station in the surveillance van, he knew. She had solicited the help of only one police officer—Cruz—which rubbed Carter the wrong way to no end, though he didn't have a concrete reason to dislike the guy. He just wished he could play this all the way to the end without anyone in the department becoming the wiser.

It wasn't just about the safety of his family anymore.

It boiled down to privacy.

He was at this meeting. As a *survivor*. Not as a cop. And soon everyone at the Special Victims Unit, if not the whole of the 66th Precinct, would find out.

He was just glad that while Danny and Officer Cruz could hear him, he had no way of hearing them. The mics went only one way. It helped him concentrate on nicknaming.

Before long, the circle was full with sixteen men in attendance, Horn-Rimmed Glasses included.

The guy gave him the creeps.

Meekly clearing his throat then starting with a small voice, Wally began reading the opening remarks. Carter rested his gaze on his clasped hands. It would be inappropriate to continue to stare at the faces around the circle. But when he felt eyes on him coming from his left, he glanced up to find Horn-Rimmed Glasses staring dead at him.

Why?

He felt another set of eyes on him as well, this time it was Football Forty, the athletic guy who had first come in.

In a fraction of a second, he realized two things.

The first was that both men looked not only remarkably similar to one another, but they looked similar to Carter as well.

If Horn-Rimmed lost the glasses, he could pass for Carter's brother.

Football Forty ranked as more of a cousin, but the attitude behind his eyes reminded Carter of himself.

The second realization that slammed in, as fast as the first, was that Wally had been saying his name, inviting him to open the sharing hour.

"Yeah, ah, good evening," he stammered awkwardly, as he touched eyes with a few survivors before sliding his attention to Wally and apologizing.

"I spaced for a second there. It was an emotional couple of days."

Wally indicated for him to take his time, and once Carter had returned his gaze to his clasped hands, he took a deep breath, mentally composed himself, and said, "I, ah, I thought a lot about what—"

He scanned the faces around the circle until he found the thin man who had mentioned that Jeremiah Daughtry was still in prison, as opposed to dead, at the last meeting.

"*You* said last time. How here we all are, wrestling with raw wounds and tormenting memories while the man who did this to us lives his life out somewhat easily in prison."

The thin man, who Carter had nicknamed 'Slim,' nodded with massive understanding, his tight black eyes widening as much as they could.

"I sort of never let myself think about it," Carter went on, "the fact that my abuser is alive and well." He tried not to cringe knowing Cruz was listening in and learning way too much about him. "I went up to Sing Sing."

He was momentarily interrupted by the gasps and grunts of their collective surprise.

"I confronted him," he stated.

In the forefront of his mind, he knew his job was to provoke the perp, lure him into ultimately revealing himself once and for all.

But this felt real to him, opening up, sharing a major milestone in the journey of his personal healing.

Splitting the difference between wanting to be concise and needing to verbalize the warring emotions that had resulted from facing his abuser, Carter reached into his slacks, took hold of the warm brass chain, and pulled out the pocket watch.

The room fell quiet. If a pin dropped, he would've heard it clearly.

A number of survivors leaned in, eyeing the prop that had controlled them for so long, as it dangled from Carter's hand.

"He gave this to me, and at first I didn't know what to think of that," he went on, coiling the chain around his large hand until he had the brass face of the watch in his palm.

He studied it, as he admitted almost offhandedly, "It didn't go well. He was insulting and unapologetic, unremorseful. He had aged badly and looked small, and I hated that he had the power to strike a nerve with me. Maybe I hate that I didn't take this from him, or demand it," he ruminated, flipping the watch open and shut.

"He just *gave* it to me," he repeated, allowing the perplexity of it all to really sink in, acknowledging how confusing that was for him. "Gave it to me like it was nothing. Like it had no significance to him."

"Crank it," one of the men said, and when Carter lifted his gaze he found Horn-Rimmed Glasses staring dead at him like never before.

Wally reminded him that there's no 'cross talk,' but another man was already speaking over him, "That would be triggering. Wouldn't that be triggering? I can't afford to be triggered."

"Don't you want to remember?" Horn-Rimmed snapped. "Why are you all so scared of being triggered? Aren't you sick and tired of acting out in your own lives just because on some level you're itching to slip under the surface and finally remember what happened to you, every disgusting act, so you can actually move on?"

Suddenly, the room broke out in heated debate. No amount of Wally shouting reminders of the 'no cross talk' rule could quiet them.

Carter stood and yelled, "Enough!"

The men hushed and gradually resumed their seats.

When Carter had as well, he declared, "I'm not going to crank it."

Horn-Rimmed Glasses wasn't pleased, and while Carter tried to get a read on the guy—*was that his perp, or were those the emotions of a victim who had never become an aggressor?*—he carefully waded into the setup that he and Danny had devised.

"Last time, I talked about sacrifice."

Horn-Rimmed leaned in, his demeanor changing from anger to intrigue as Carter went on.

"I mentioned, or I should say, I admitted that maybe I'm a slave. Maybe I've always been one. But I want to break free of that…"

As he trailed off, he couldn't believe how true the statement was. He really did want freedom, not just from the pressure cooker of knowing that if he didn't get this right, there would be terrible, perhaps fatal consequences for him and his family; but also from the dog-house dynamic he had been trapped in with Kathy.

If he really could make a sacrifice and have all that vanish, he would do it in a heartbeat. But that wasn't what this was about.

"So, I've decided," he concluded, indicating the brass pocket watch, "that this will be my sacrifice. I'm going to leave it for God, and hope that it gets better."

He had them now. Each face around the circle was riddled with marked intrigue. But which of them was his man?

"Tonight, at midnight, I'm going to make my sacrifice. I'm going to leave it at the fountain in Prospect Park."

"In Brooklyn?" Wally asked, disregarding his own cross talk rules.

"That's where it happened, right?" Carter argued, knowing that since the meeting was in downtown Manhattan it might seem strange to do this across the river. "In Kensington. In the basement of a nice house. We were hidden in plain sight, weren't we? When we were brought upstairs, into that room," he reminded them, getting choked up. "What was the one thing we could see out the window?"

From across the circle, Horn-Rimmed breathed, "The park."

Carter nodded—*was that the killer?*

Carter went on, "It's symbolic, and I feel that if it means something to me… then maybe I can turn this around. Maybe I can free myself." He was looking straight into Horn-Rimmed's eyes now. "I don't want any more trouble or pain. I don't want to be indentured to anyone. I want to be free of all of this. And letting go of this watch… It has to be enough for God. It just has to."

"YOU DID GOOD, Carter," Danny told him when he reached the side of the van.

She was seated on a bench inside the back.

Cruz was in the front, behind the steering wheel.

As he carefully untaped the wire from his chest and pulled the battery box from its hidden spot at the waistband of his slacks, he felt pessimistic, "No one copped to anything."

"We didn't think they would," she reminded him. "Micing you was just a precaution to cover our bases in case we got lucky."

Cruz watched him straighten his suit jacket, a glint of envy in his eyes. It was no secret that Cruz didn't want to be a police officer forever. Who would?

Cruz updated them, "The lieutenant is getting the unit in place."

"Good," she told him before returning her attention to Carter, who was climbing into the back.

As he peered out into the busy downtown street, scanning for prying eyes of which there were none, she summarized, "The investigation might be going sideways, but it's going. Franco's on board. The D.A. doesn't care how we find Nahla, only that we do. This thing is way too high profile to play every hand by the book."

Carter slammed the van door shut then, once he had taken a seat beside his partner, Cruz fired up the engine and nosed his way into a steady stream of honking traffic.

"If one of them goes for the 'sacrifice'," he said, playing devil's advocate on Franco's behalf, "it's not exactly a confession."

"No, but it'll give us a reason to bring the guy into the station. Talk to him. He might not be the perp, but you know what? Having a reason to interrogate him gives us more to go on than we had yesterday."

Carter had shown her the photos. All of them. Franco was now also in the loop that Carter and his entire family had become targets.

"Knowing what you told me," she went on, "knowing what I read in those messages on the backs of the photos; He wants a sacrifice and you set it up perfectly. That was clear communication, I heard in there."

From the front, Cruz chimed in, agreeing, "Everything you said, Dobbs, spoke directly to the killer. I have a good feeling about this. No one but the perp is going to show up tonight. This Sting is going down in the history books."

Carter doubted it, but hoped Cruz was right. Hoped all this effort led to Nahla's rescue. Hoped his family could rest peacefully knowing the threat was no longer active. He hoped, above and beyond everything, as pie-in-the-sky and wishful as it might have been, that he could somehow really and truly be free.

Was it even possible?

It was a smooth ride over the Brooklyn Bridge, and minutes later they arrived at the southern corner of Prospect Park.

Cruz killed the lights and angled the van into a No Parking Zone that was already occupied with several other unmarked police vehicles.

Carter glanced down at the pocket watch in his hands—*the world of hell this thing had brought on*—and noted the time was nearly an hour before midnight.

"We've got eyes on the site," Danny reminded him. "But once you set the pocket watch down, we'll need you to hustle back here and watch the monitors. The last thing we need is for a total stranger to see you and just take the watch because they want to."

"I'll be able to tell you if it's a guy from the meeting or not," he assured her as he moved towards the van door and opened it.

"You've got a lot of time," she stopped him.

"I'm okay with that," he said. "I would like to get out there."

Danny must have clearly read the emotion behind his eyes—this wasn't just an investigation for him, it cut deep and saddened him that one of the survivors hadn't risen above what they had endured, but rather had sunk deeply into the muck and mire of mimicking their monstrous abuser—because she backed off, her expression turned empathetic.

"We'll be watching," she kindly whispered. "Carter?"

"Yeah?" he said, turning from the sidewalk outside the van.

"It'll all be over soon."

Nodding in optimistic agreement, he held her gaze, then started off into the darkened park.

When he reached the site—a grand stone fountain, dimly lit with flat, glass lights, its centerpiece an angel gazing serenely up at the heavens—he studied the statue's angelic face for a long beat.

He paced slowly around the fountain's circular shape, viewing it from all angles to pass the time.

When he had made a full revolution, he stared at the brass pocket watch in his hand.

Where should he place it?

Glancing up at the stone angel again, he considered her upturned hands. Were they level enough that he could actually set the watch right in the palm of her hand?

It was perfect.

All he had to do was wait. Let the time pass. Then set the brass pocket watch into the palm of an angel, a small sacrifice to make for eternal freedom.

But he couldn't just sit idly.

Crank it.

Horn-Rimmed Glasses' voice filled his ears, only to be shut down by another survivor's objection:

Wouldn't that be triggering? I can't afford to be triggered.

Neither could Carter.

Not at this critical juncture.

And yet, almost as if without his permission, his fingers found the turn-crank at the side of the watch.

He began twisting, winding the pocket watch, the gears faintly grinding, listening to the sound…

A sudden wave of dizziness swept through.

He clenched his jaw and kept cranking the watch, as far as it would go.

Don't keep him waiting.

Whose voice was that? Which boys? From what dark corner?

It hadn't been Jeremiah's. It hadn't been an adult. It had been one of them, one of the kids.

The sound of the watch clicking into its final, tightly-wound, position hit Carter's ears in such a familiar way that in an instant he forgot he was in the park.

He couldn't see the statue, he couldn't smell the crisp damp wind breezing through, he lost all sense of time and place.

He couldn't feel his fingers, which loosened on the turn-crank.

The hummingbird-fast metronome *ticking* of the pocket watch was all that existed.

It seemed to grow louder and louder.

And soon a flickering flash of something real—some dark memory that felt more real to him than the entire life he had built with Kathy—consumed him.

Don't keep him waiting.

"Who's there?" young Carter had asked.

"Damian."

"But I don't want to go," he whimpered.

The next thing he knew, warm arms were cradling him as he wept, Damian having snuck into his dog crate to hold him.

"I'll go," Damian had offered.

"What?"

"You don't have to," he told him. "That man probably can't tell the difference, anyway."

The child—an angel in that moment—had left him, walking fearlessly into a terrible fate meant for Carter.

But the back of the photos…

Carter thought, feeling his skin prick with beads of sweat, his heart racing.

It had said 'don't keep me waiting'.

Only the boy, Damian, had used those instructions with him down in the basement.

The boy who had *sacrificed himself to keep Carter safe.*

Could he have turned into a monster?

"No," Carter breathed, not wanting to believe it, his heart twisting and straining, nearly breaking, as the revelation took hold.

Time was running out.

It was nearly midnight, but though the memories of Damian refused to be ignored, Carter was suffering a full-on onslaught of flickers and flashes and images—Damian's young voice filling his ears.

But Carter had to do what he came here to do.

Stepping up onto the stone edge of the fountain, he tried to focus on the sounds of rushing water and not the incessant ticking of the pocket watch. Then, reaching over, he placed the brass relic of his tortured past into the palm of the stone angel.

By the time he stepped down, he felt drained.

It was a very long walk back to the surveillance van.

Not a moment after he sat beside Danny in the back, a grid of monitors in front of them, all showing a different angle of the fountain and surrounding areas, Carter spotted him.

"There!" he exclaimed, pointing to the middle monitor where Football Forty was lumbering towards the fountain.

Danny brought the walkie-talkie she had been grasping to her mouth, squeezed its side, and ordered, "Move in. All units move in on the African-American man in the red parka."

As Carter watched the monitor where the team of uniformed officers swept in and apprehended Football Forty just after the guy had taken hold of the pocket watch, he couldn't reconcile the fact that his gut had been wrong, but only slightly.

He had completely expected to see Horn-Rimmed Glasses show up.

"We did it," said Danny, relieved. "One step closer."

Carter let out a breathy laugh that didn't convey even a fraction of his partner's relief. With his gaze glued to the monitor where Football Forty was being handcuffed for what Franco would argue was petty theft—any reason to pull the suspect in for questioning—Carter told himself, *that's him, the brave child who sacrificed his innocence for me time and again, the man who had turned rotten and become the very monster they had hated as kids.*

But something about it didn't feel right.

Nevertheless, he had won.

The next day, on Franco's insistence that he take a personal day to be with his family while Danny proceeded to question Football Forty, Carter spent the bulk of the day with Kathy and the kids.

By nightfall, he decided to hire a babysitter to take Christopher, Amanda, and Matty out of the house—Carter wanting and needing nothing more than the freedom that came, if only momentarily, with burying himself in-between his wife's hot, inviting legs.

But…

He would forever look back on that decision as the biggest mistake of his life.

Chapter Twenty-One

"I'M OUT."

Damian didn't like the sound of that.

"What do you mean 'you're out'?"

"I need more," said Wally from the passenger seat, as he lowered the telephoto-lens camera from his forlorn face.

In response, the deranged accountant gripped the steering wheel with such force that his knuckles turned pale against his otherwise dark complexion.

Nahla was seated in the backseat, poised as perfectly as a porcelain doll and dressed the part.

They had been sitting in Damian's black Lexus. First, they had been parked outside of Carter's house until night had fallen and the kids had emerged with a pudgy, dimwitted girl whose every heavy-heeled stomp sent a jiggle up through her—the babysitter.

Then they had driven at a crawl, following and circling back on the kids and their babysitter, who looked barely older than Carter's beautiful daughter—though Damian reasoned she was most likely college-aged—as they had trekked north along Prospect Park Southwest to the only movie theater in Kensington.

When the sitter had held the door open for two very excited boys and a disgruntled-looking Amanda, shepherding her flock inside, Damian knew they were in for a two hour wait, at least.

It would be worth it.

Carter had greatly overstepped his bounds. More than once. And the punishment Damian had in store for him would be worse than what God had decreed to smite Cain; crueler than what God had asked of Abraham in order to teach the farmer the definition of the ultimate sacrifice; crueler because Damian wouldn't be so soft as to intervene. He would spare nothing.

"Did you make more?" Wally asked, as he returned the conspicuous camera to his eye, but Damian batted the long lens down, irritated.

"You'll draw attention to us."

"The lens is like binoculars. I'm just using it to see better."

"I know what you're doing," he snapped. "They'll be out when the movie ends. There's nothing to see."

Embarrassed, Wally capped the lens and twisted his mouth to the side, and the men sank back into pensive silence.

Damian contemplated the detective and his many brazen moves, from showing up at the survivors meeting to attempting to bait Damian with the pocket watch.

An uncontrollable grin tugged at the corner of his mouth. Carter wasn't the scared little boy from the basement anymore, was he?

It impressed him, but also made his blood boil.

How many times had he taken the worst of it, because Carter hadn't been able to man up? How many nights had Damian suffered torture meant for Carter? Damian had saved him time and again. Protected him.

He had given too much.

Looking at all that Carter had now—a badge, a career, a bombshell of a wife, three gorgeous children, and a picture-perfect home that practically had a white picket fence wrapped around it—felt like a slap in the face.

What did Damian have? What had he been left with for all those good deeds, all the times he had laid his own soul on the line so that Carter could have a moment's peace?

Rotten insides, that's what.

Perverted compulsions.

A desperate, driving need to puppeteer everyone around him, right wrongs using his own logic, and play God even though it never felt like he was winning.

"I know you're ignoring my question for a reason," Wally piped up from the passenger seat, interrupting him from sorting through the quagmire of irony that had, unfortunately, become his life. "But I thought you might have brought some?"

As payment, he surmised, finishing Wally's assumption in his mind. Hadn't Nahla been 'payment' enough? He had given his old friend time with the girl—she was close to being completely and thoroughly cleansed, but not quite. Damian had even let Wally take photos for his own personal pleasure.

"You're the only person I know who would do Devil's Breath recreationally," he complained, as he fished out a hard, plastic-encased ounce of the drug from his inner pocket.

"I cut it with cocaine," Wally reminded him, eagerly taking the white ball from Damian to inspect it. If Damian wasn't mistaken, he thought he saw Wally start salivating. "It keeps me going, relaxed and alert."

The ratios must be mostly coke if that was the case, but who knew. When it came to Wally, the guy might like zombie-ing out as a means to suspend himself from planet earth. He still lived with his foster mother for Christ's sake.

A fresh wave of anger was rising up in Damian's chest—*he wanted that pocket watch!*

Damian had sent Marcus into the park to retrieve it since the bulky man was a dead ringer for the sketch of himself that Damian had seen on the news.

He should've known that Carter had set the whole thing up. Marcus had been apprehended. Damian should've seen it coming, but he had been blinded by his own blood lust for that damned pocket watch.

Just as Damian felt the blood in his veins reach a boiling point, a stream of teenagers began filing out of the movie theater, Carter's kids among them.

"We'll do this on foot," he instructed, once again batting the massive telephoto lens down from Wally's excited face.

As his friend sheepishly tucked the state-of-the-art camera into the black, padded camera bag at his feet, Damian spied the freckled, bouncy babysitter, as she abruptly stopped to tie her laces. The larger, athletic boy was joshing around with his skinny brother, while their sister folded her toned arms against the night breeze and made coy eyes at a pack of exuberant teenage guys.

"Ready?"

Wally seemed to be. They both stepped out of the parked Lexus as the babysitter stood, placed her doughy hands on the little, skinny boy's shoulders, and steered him across the sidewalk, the older siblings having already reached the curb.

Damian walked straight for them, as Wally, having helped Nahla out of the backseat and taken her by the hand, arced to the far right, giving them a wide berth so he could wall them off from behind.

He had brought a sipping-straw, one he had clipped so that it was only two inches long. He had packed it with enough powdered Devil's Breath to subdue the sitter.

He was grasping the short straw tightly now in his closed fist, but if all went well—if Nahla was a good girl and did as she had been told—he wouldn't have to use it.

"Damian?"

He turned in the direction of the familiar woman's voice and found Jill Andover—dressed casually in jeans and a sweater, ballet flats, and a low-maintenance purse slung over her shoulder. She was crossing the curb on her way to the theater, presumably.

It took him a split second to cut his eyes at Wally, who looked thrown to the point of bewilderment at the unexpected wrench in their plans.

Damian gave his friend the slightest indication that Wally ought to back off. Wally steered Nahla over to the movie posters and pretended to find them interesting, as he waited for further instructions.

But the babysitter, along with Carter's kids, were already headed south along the edge of the park—the same route they had taken from the house earlier that night.

Damian made a mental note to murder Jill. He should've done it when the idea had first occurred to him.

Beaming a thousand-watt smile at her, he neared her and took both of her hands in his.

"Isn't this a nice surprise?"

"Were you about to see the latest Bourne movie?"

The entire franchise, along with Matt Damon's smug face, made him want to take an angry crap, but he guessed Jill didn't share his sentiment, so he lied, "I just watched it. You're heading in?"

"I was…" she lingered, making eyes up at him as if to suggest she would rather be spontaneous and spend time with him now.

The babysitter and Carter's kids were mere shadows in the distance. He should've told Wally to stalk them, but they hadn't worked out a hand signal for that.

Damn.

As he returned his attention to one very doe-eyed Jill—Christ she was pathetic, not the slightest clue in her supposedly brilliant mind that he had been drugging her, his latest foray into playtime with Nahla—he kept the flirtation going. He mentioned his hectic work schedule, since it was the 'end of the quarter' and all.

Damian was greatly pleased to discover Wally taking initiative. Holding Nahla's hand, Wally crossed the street, heading towards Prospect Park Southwest after the kids.

"I had some blood work done," she mentioned, her voice dropping into a serious tone.

"Oh?"

She gave him a little eye flutter then clarified, "I'm still waiting for the results, but…"

"Is something wrong with your health?" he asked, feigning absolutely no interest.

"Remember how I mentioned I thought something might be up with my metabolism?"

"You know, Jill," he interrupted after checking his naked wrist for the time that wasn't there. His eyes were glued to Wally and Nahla now, the mere specks that were Carter's kids in the darkened distance. "I have to be somewhere, and I wouldn't want you to miss the opening scene. It's… integral to the plot," he improvised. "Can we get together real soon, though?"

So I can kill you with my bare hands, you annoying waste of space, he thought so that a genuine smile would come over his otherwise irritated expression.

"Definitely," she said, disappointed, as she stepped in close, expecting a kiss.

He delivered a dry, chaste peck to her lips then gave her shoulders a little squeeze.

"Have a good night, Jill," he told her, as he backed away and forced himself to act as if he was drinking in the sight of her. "I'll see you soon."

"'Night," she breathed through a kittenish grin.

Once he had turned on his heel, he wasted no time.

After two speed-walking minutes, he reached Wally and spun Nahla around.

Stooping to look her in the eye—she seemed both stoic and tired, last night had been too demanding of her, but when had *Jeremiah* ever gone easy on *him?*—he instilled the fear of God in her with a few choice threats, then instructed, "There's a young boy up that way, a bit older than you. Do you see him?"

She swung around, her ragdoll arms lifting with centrifugal force to check, then swung back, so like the little girl she truly was that his heart strained with emotion.

"I want you to get him to play a quick game of tag with you," he explained. "Run up and tag him, then run off into the park."

"The dark park?" she questioned apprehensively.

"Oh, it's not that dark," he assured her, giving Wally a little wink.

Understanding perfectly, Wally started off into the park, getting into what would soon turn out to be the perfect position.

"Nahla, you wait here, and don't rush up and tag him until you see me talking to that blonde girl."

"The one who's walking with the boy you want me to tag?"

"That's right."

He gave her a pat on the head then without further ado—if the sitter reached the end of the park with Carter's kids, this wouldn't work —he started off on his brisk way to catch up.

Damian knew how to play the part of the hurried New Yorker, and as he came up behind the kids, the babysitter thought nothing of it.

Sensing him, she stepped aside and took hold of both the athletic boy and girl's shoulders, veering in-between them to steer both out of the rushing pedestrian's way.

"Thanks," he said, breezing past them, but then in a performed act of sudden confusion, turned on his heel, glanced confusedly at the lack of street signs across the avenue, and asked, "You wouldn't happen to know where Terrace Place is, would you?"

"Huh?" she responded, having stopped, the older kids still in her grasp. The skinny little boy stood awkwardly alone behind them. "I think you've got something mixed up," she began.

Nahla raced up to Carter's youngest son, the near-soundless pitter-patter of her ballerina feet drawing no one's attention. She tagged him, beamed a toothy grin when he met her gaze, and his eyes brightened. She then darted off into the park. The boy chased after her without hesitation.

Oblivious, the babysitter was listing off, "Windsor Place or Windsor Terrace are those two side streets, but there's definitely no 'Terrace Place'."

"Are you sure?" he asked, looking around to draw this out as long as possible, while Carter's teenagers began huffing and rolling their eyes impatiently.

A look of faint worry clouded over her face, as she glanced back at where the skinny boy had been.

"Um," she stammered, then asked the kids, "where's Matty?"

"You've got your hands full," Damian said, apologetically, fast to start back in the direction he had come. "Thanks anyway!"

He crossed the street so the sitter wouldn't ask for his help, as she went from slightly concerned to full-blown panicking in sixty seconds flat that she had lost one of the children she had been entrusted to watch.

As she began calling out, "Matty? Matty!" and the kids began scanning the dimly lit edge of the park, Damian picked up his pace and didn't stop until he reached his Lexus.

Behind the wheel, he pressed his cell phone to his ear and swung the car into the street.

The second he heard Wally's out of breath greeting, he said, "You have him?"

"Yeah."

The sounds of muffled screams and thuds—for a skinny kid, Matty must have been putting up one hell of a fight—came through the line.

"I'll bring him clear through to Atlantic Avenue," he told him, knowing that since the park was technically closed, there would be no witnesses through the vast acreage. Meet us there at the entrance in ten."

"Good boy, Wally."

As he hung up, driving around the perimeter of the park with a steady stream of traffic, he could almost see the smile on his old friend's face. It matched his own.

He couldn't wait to have the detective's son in his possession.

Then the game would really start.

But first things first.

Getting Matty Dobbs into the trunk of his Lexus might prove to be no easy task.

As it turned out, however, ten minutes later it went off without a single hitch.

JILL COULDN'T GET into this movie. Not only was she not enjoying it, she had completely lost the thread of the plot.

Damian was weighing heavily on her mind.

He had seemed off. Preoccupied. And not because of some prior commitment he had to rush off to. He had been staring at a middle-aged black man and his young daughter who had been dressed like a princess or a belly dancer, or something.

Why?

His gaze had followed those two all the way across the street, then he had rushed off in the same direction.

It was weird.

And her dates with him had gotten no better. She was still blacking out left and right, unable to keep herself from drinking. Was she a full-blown alcoholic? Just thinking about it made her head hurt with confusion so she tried and failed to understand why Matt Damon was flying down a fire escape chasing after what appeared to be a Russian mobster.

There was no use.

If she felt like doing anything that night, it wasn't watching the cookie-cutter plot of another Bourne movie nearly plagiarize its prequels.

She allowed herself a moment to space out in the cool, dark theater as flickering light from the silver screen flashed over her.

She wanted to call Danny. See what her friend was up to. Have a little girl talk if possible.

But there was no way to gab about Damian without the *detective* in her friend rearing her investigative head.

Maybe, this time, given Jill's blackouts and Damian's weird behavior just now, it wouldn't be such a bad thing to get a cop's take on the dark pattern. Afterall, she was starting to fear that a straightforward blood panel wouldn't be able to shed light on this one.

Had Damian been drugging her? Had her first gut instinct been right all along? Had she ignored red flags in favor of falling in love with a monster who had been masquerading as a successful man?

Just as it was beginning to feel like she was on the brink of an epiphany, the hard nose of reason muscled in and she decided…

…no, she wouldn't call Danny.

She would sit tight until her G.P. called her with the results of her metabolic blood work.

It was more likely she had mitochondrial disorder than that her boyfriend was some kind of rapist.

Right?

Chapter Twenty-Two

THE POLICE WERE at the house. Kathy was holding Christopher and Amanda, an arm wrapped protectively around each of her children where they all sat on the living room couch.

Seated on the armchair was one very remorseful babysitter. The girl was teary eyed and trembling, with a ball of soggy tissues in her hands.

Carter stood next to two police officers. His hands were planted on his hips, as he angled in on the girl, the intensity of his furious stare so penetrating that she cowered and avoided his gaze.

She glanced here and there at the other cops whenever she wasn't collapsing into another muffled sobbing episode.

Carter could feel his wife's terrified eyes on him, but he couldn't comfort her with a glance from across the room.

"You don't understand!" said Brittany, as she nervously picked apart the damp wad of tissues in her hands. "He was there one second and gone the next!"

"Why was he out of your sight?" Carter demanded.

At a bewildered loss for words, her mouth gaped open in distress, then she guessed, "Because I only have two hands?"

Blaming her had been getting him nowhere.

"I was helping someone with directions," she offered.

"Who?" he cut in, but one of the officer's jutted his hand up, insisting that Carter should let him handle it.

"I don't know—a man?" she told them.

The officer asked, "Can you describe him? Ethnicity, height, weight, build? What was he wearing?"

"Um," she stammered to jumpstart her memory. As she went on to list the man's characteristics, "Black, darker complexion black that is. Tall, way taller than me," the front door opened and Carter saw Danny entering his overcrowded home. Franco followed in after her.

What the hell was the lieutenant doing here?

"I think Matty ran off into the park," Brittany mentioned for the second time, interrupting herself from describing more physical characteristics of the man who had been looking for Terrace Place.

Carter had already told her there's no way his son would wander off into a dark park alone, not without a reason. Had Matty been forced against his will?

Carter couldn't bear the thought—so he held his tongue and joined his partner and the lieutenant where the tiled foyer met with the living room's plush carpet edge.

"We've got an AMBER alert out," Danny told him without hesitation.

"Franco," said Carter, greeting the lieutenant in a delayed reaction.

The lieutenant looked sickened with worry, as if it had been his own child who had gone missing—Carter had never seen the man's face so drawn, so pale despite his deep-olive complexion.

"Hey, yo', Lieutenant!" said the officer who had been coddling Brittany.

On the couch, Kathy perked up, perhaps sensing a critical development had surfaced.

"We gotta get a unit over to Prospect Park. Maybe the kid's still there."

"Do it," said Franco. He had never approved a longshot so fast in his life.

As the police officer pinched the two-way radio on his shoulder and relayed the order, Danny neared Carter, placed a comforting hand on his arm, and asked in a hushed tone, "You don't think this is related, do you?"

He cut his hard gaze to her and their eyes locked.

"Stevens is in custody," she said. "He looks good for all of it. Lacy Marcel IDed him in a lineup earlier today. He didn't have alibis for half the crimes, the others he offered up weren't verifiable."

Even though she had summarized all the reasons neither of them should worry that a deranged, drug-wielding psychopath with a God complex had abducted his youngest son, he could tell by her wavering tone, the glint of fear behind her big, brown eyes, that her uncertainty would put both of them on shaky ground.

Carter was already there.

He had been feeling off all day. Emotionally drained from the Sting the night prior. Spending quality time with his family without once having called in to the 66th for an update. And this was where his recovery had gotten him? He should've never let his guard down, but *hindsight* and all...

He asked a question he should've asked the second they had Football Forty in handcuffs upon his arrest in the park.

"What's Stevens' first name?"

"Marcus," she said, cutting her eyes to Franco, who was now offering a few reassuring words to Kathy and the kids in the living room. "Why?"

It came like a blow—iron-fist to his solar plexus. A cold sweat broke out across his chest. The man they had been hunting had to be named 'Damian.'

The name had only entered his mind through the flashback that had come over him when he had stood at the angel fountain. But Carter was positive. The brave child who had sacrificed his own skin time and again so that Carter could rest, if only for one more night, was named Damian.

Not Marcus.

Don't keep him waiting, young Damian had warned. That was before the kid had taken pity on him, before he had ever held him in his child arms, before he began saving him every chance he could.

Don't keep me *waiting*—the message on the back of the photo of his daughter had instructed.

In Carter's mind, it was all the proof he needed to know beyond a shadow of a doubt that the killer, the kidnapper, the brand-new monster in the dark, was 'Damian.'

But that wouldn't be enough of an argument to convince his partner, much less the lieutenant who was now joining them.

"Did Marcus Stevens cop to it?" he challenged, staring hard at Danny before sliding his skeptical gaze to Franco. "Did Stevens confess?"

"We're working on it," Franco assured him. "Foster has been leaning on him. He's weakening. We've got him for 72 before he'll get a real break from the interrogation and that break won't last long."

"So, where's the girl? Where's Nahla?"

Danny and Franco exchanged a heavy glance then his partner told him, "He hasn't given up the location yet."

"Did he have scopolamine on him?" he pressed, implying his skepticism that Stevens could possibly be their guy.

"Hey," said Franco, his voice kind, as he pulled Carter aside. "What did I advise when we spoke over the phone that night?"

Assuming the question was rhetorical, Carter only stared at him with an overt lack of appreciation on his face.

"Patience," he reminded him. "Now I need you to mentally and emotionally separate the case you've been working from Matty's disappearance. Separate them," he reiterated.

There was no way in hell he was going to do that, but maybe getting the lieutenant off his back and out of his living room, Danny as well, would free him up to do what needed to be done.

The cops weren't going to find his son in Prospect Park. A man named Damian had him—a man who had been sitting somewhere across from Carter in all those survivors' meetings…

For Christ's sake, he could've had him!

Carter had worked his whole life making sure his precious children would never have to experience even a fraction of the violating torture Carter had endured growing up. He had watched them like a hawk. Protected them. Double and triple checked every friend they had, vetting the families, making sure no pedophiles or registered sex offenders were lurking within those seemingly safe parents. He had never burdened his kids with harsh warnings about stranger-danger, never worried his wife either. Nevertheless, he had kept them safe from every dark form of abuse that existed in this cruel world.

Until now.

If anything happened to Matty, he thought, and his jaw clenched up tight.

"Can you do that for me, Carter?" asked Franco, anchoring him back to planet earth. "Can you separate the case from what's happening right now and trust our team to find your son for you?"

The lieutenant expected him to sit on his hands and wait for a different set of SVU detectives to find Matty? Was he out of his mind? It took everything Carter had left to muster an appeasing response.

"Yes, Sir, I can do that."

Franco gave him a companionable clap on the shoulder and promised, "We'll get through this. We will."

After a beat of bucking up demonstratively into a brave mode of operation, one which he would presumably like to see Carter take on, Franco began briefing him on where things with the case stood in terms of the District Attorney's agenda.

"There's a press conference scheduled for 8am tomorrow morning," he explained. "But if you can't handle it, Carter. If you need to be with Kathy and the kids, then Danny can make the statement. Lord knows Crouse and Toliver will be there to loop in the Raffael Sanzio connection. Sarah," he went on, using the D.A.'s first name, "wants to announce that this was, in fact, a triple homicide, that the killer is in custody, and that locating the girl is pending. Getting that out on the news should cause tips to come in. Someone should've seen something, which should help us find Nahla much faster."

Danny drifted over and stood beside Franco, actively nodding and touching eyes with Carter whenever he had it in him to meet her gaze—he couldn't concentrate on this, he needed to find his son!

"The Samuels are still dominating the story," she chimed in. "Queenie and Raja practically have their own timeslot on the Channel 9 news. Their new angle is that the 66th is unconcerned with Nahla's whereabouts because she's Black."

That got his attention.

"Christ," Carter breathed. "So, you really *do* need *me* up there," he surmised. The presence of a Black detective on the case would effectively combat any accusations Queenie and Raja made of racism-induced complacency.

"Again," said Franco, "only if you have it in you."

Brittany was full-on wailing now that the cops had finished with her.

She was standing alone, her red, damp face in her hands.

She wasn't his favorite person at the moment, but he still excused himself to offer her reassurances as well as a cab ride home. There was no way he would let her walk home in her current emotional state, not in the middle of the night.

"I'm so sorry, Mr. Dobbs," she squeaked. "I'll never forgive myself for this."

"Yes, you will," he told her. "You aren't to blame. Hey, look at me," he coaxed, garnering eye contact. She looked riddled with shame. "There's nothing you could've done. You gotta trust me on this. I work cases like this for a living, okay? When an abductor wants to take a certain kid, not much can stop them, and we're all really lucky that you didn't get hurt and that Chris and Amanda are safe."

"I don't know why Matty went into the park," she muttered, falling into a spell of utter confusion all over again. "And right when that man asked for help with finding Terrace Place. But the man with the glasses didn't take Matty. I would've seen it."

"What man with the glasses?"

"The man who needed help with directions," she clarified. "Not a different guy. I'm mentally fried, sorry."

"That's okay," he said, then quickly asked, "what kind of glasses?"

"I tried to describe them to the police officers," she said as if it had already been a struggle. "They were like that tortoise shell material, is that what it's called? But the thick part was only on top, like across the eyebrows, you know?"

Carter felt his stomach bottom out through the floor, and in the same instant, his heart lurched up his throat. "Horn-rimmed?" he asked.

"Is that what it's called?"

"Yeah, Brittany," he praised—*finally, he had him!* "That's what they're called."

Damian was Horn-Rimmed Glasses!

When the cab arrived, Carter tucked her onto the backseat and paid the fare, again insisting that she not blame herself for what had happened.

The majority of cops had filtered out of the house to join the unit at Prospect Park, and as Carter returned to the living room where his exhausted wife was cradling Amanda in her lap, Christopher having nodded off against her shoulder, Danny and Franco approached him.

"You could all use some sleep," Danny said at a hushed volume.

"If that's possible," Carter agreed.

Horn-Rimmed Glasses from the survivors' meeting.
Damian.
Was it enough to go on?
Could he track the son of a bitch down by himself?
Or should he bring his partner in on this?
Could he trust her?

His brain was clouding over from burnout as if the adrenaline that had spiked through his veins at Brittany's godsend description was plummeting and leaving him depleted. Drained. His tank was empty, burning nothing but fumes.

Franco assured him, "If the unit in the park finds anything, any clue about Matty, or if we get any leads, you'll be the first to know. Keep your cell on, but try to get some sleep."

With that, the lieutenant left them, closing the front door behind him on the way out.

"I know what you're thinking," Danny leveled with him.

"That me and my family received threatening photos and now my kid's missing?" he supplied, sarcasm thick in his furious tone. "But they're completely unrelated?"

"I know," she commiserated. "But sometimes coincidences really do happen."

"You don't believe that crap," he shot back.

"This time, I do," she maintained.

If he was debating whether or not he could trust her, he had just gotten his answer.

No way.

"I hope you're right," he told her, as he opened the front door, a biting wind whipped into the foyer and blew her long bangs sideways.

She stepped into the chilly night then turned to say, "Get some rest, okay?"

A small voice in the back of his mind urged him to clue her in, tell her they needed to look for a 'Damian,' and propose that they question the survivors.

She's always had his back, she could help!

But he couldn't risk it.

He needed to accomplish all of those steps on his own.

Alone.

He would have to.

Chapter Twenty-Three

SLEEP WAS AN EXERCISE in patience that Carter didn't have.

His wife was a nervous, shrill wreck, but at least after fighting to stay awake for hours, on guard that the criminal who had made good on his threat would come after her other children, Kathy—depleted and exhausted—had passed out in a heap on their bed, cradling Christopher and Amanda in her arms and leaving very little room for Carter.

It was just as well. They needed their rest, and Carter could use some peace and quiet to think and devise and strategize.

Sitting on his hands until the next scheduled Survivors of Incest Abuse meeting would induce heart-attack-level anxiety.

But the longer he sat in the cool glow of his laptop computer at the kitchen islet, the more apparent it became that the challenges he faced might just be insurmountable.

Like any 'anonymous-style' meeting—alcoholics anonymous, narcotics anonymous, and also the lesser known offshoot of the two, 'al-anon'—the names and identities of the members were completely concealed.

There was no information online. The national S.I.A. website, which Carter had taken note of during his first meeting, its URL having been clearly printed across the front of Wally's binder, had a directory of meetings by city and state, each linking to their own local websites. But no *names*.

He had gone down rabbit hole after rabbit hole. He felt compelled to hunt, yet he knew, perhaps only deep down, that he wasn't going to get anywhere.

And he didn't.

His ears were pricked and poised the whole time, on high alert to hear anything and everything on the other side of the front door, as if Damian might slide another packet of photos under the door.

At times, Carter rushed outside, certain he had heard footsteps or the faint scraping sound of a manila envelope plopping on the welcome mat.

But he was met only with stillness, the dimly lit street, and the stoop exactly how he had last left it. No further demands or immediate instructions from Damian, the man he had no way of finding. No chances to keep the game going in order to get his son back.

He had already lost.

His only shot was the meeting.

Why Damian would show up—anticipating Carter's participation, the detective's only means of coming face to face with him—was unclear to him. He would be lucky if Damian did show up ever again. Exceptionally lucky. The only ray of hope that shined in favor of the guy attending was that as far as Carter knew, Damian had no way of knowing that Carter was certain he was the killer.

But waiting three days?

He kept coming back to those insurmountable obstacles—time, patience, and the torture of enduring both—and insisted there had to be a better way.

And there was.

Wally Bronson.

It was the only name Carter had. The only *address*. The only connection to the rest of the survivors in the meeting.

Carter didn't know how long the meek and mild-mannered garbage man had been running the downtown Manhattan's S.I.A. group, but he felt confident Wally knew each member, by first name at least. And maybe he knew their addresses.

Damian certainly knew Wally, and as a matter of sheer logic, Wally had to know and trust the guy well enough to have let him into the Waste Management Recycling Plant the night of Raffael Sanzio's drug-addled so-called suicide.

The time on Carter's laptop read a quarter to five in the morning. The sun had yet to rise.

Calling Milly Bronson's apartment where her foster son had been living without reprieve would likely result in either one very confused elderly woman answering the phone in a panic, or his call ringing through to an answering machine.

By the time Carter revved up the family mini van, plumes of exhaust snorting out the tailpipe, the stark orange sun was piercing through buildings, as it crept up the hazy sky.

He knew he wasn't going to make the press conference in a few hours.

The slightest twinge of elation pinched his heart at the thought that by the time the District Attorney, Sarah Hovey, along with Franco and Danny, came on the morning news, Carter could have found his son.

He hadn't fired his police-issued Glock in months. It was resting under his left arm in a shoulder holster. Carter had already pushed the safety button out of its locked position.

He had no intention of hesitating. If the only thing that stood between him and his son was a man from his past, Carter was prepared to obliterate the son of a bitch.

Anything to safely rescue and return Matty to his mother.

The drive proceeded in a blur.

Carter was trapped in darting, tangled thoughts. Fears whipped through his mind. *Strategies* formed. How could he coax Wally into giving up all that he knew about Horn-Rimmed Glasses, AKA 'Damian'?

How was Carter going to proceed?

Haunting images came in flashes, interrupting him, pieces from the past.

Except that it wasn't Carter himself in those unsettling flickers, but his son.

Every time he forced one disturbing possibility down, another reared up in its place.

He gritted his teeth, demanding that he not go down that road.

Panicking over what Matty might be going through at this very moment—*enduring the same tortured hell Carter had grown up in?*—would only drive Carter insane.

Striking the steering wheel hard with the heel of his palm in a desperate effort to jar himself free of worrying his worst nightmare was already coming true, Carter unwittingly blared the horn, which set off a chorus of horn honking.

The driver in front of him retaliated and gave him the finger out of his open window. The vehicle behind him was lurching and bleating like an angry beast that didn't want to miss the light.

New York City traffic was a virtual battleground, and parking was synonymous to scouring for spoils.

Eventually, Carter found a spot and climbed out of his minivan.

As sunlight glared across the side street, he neared the address and had the fortunate timing to dart inside when a professionally dressed twenty-something breezed out, readying to light the cigarette she had clamped between her painted lips.

When he reached Milly Bronson's apartment door, he pounded.

Nothing.

It wasn't even six in the morning, so he didn't rush to any conclusions.

He pounded again, fist to steel, louder and harder and longer until he heard the confused shuffling of socked feet over hardwood floors inside.

Next came the sounds of light switches being flipped on and the alarmed murmurings of an elderly woman who was more concerned than angered.

"Who in the goodness gracious would be at the door—?"

Her voice was interrupted by her adult foster son's.

"I'll see. I'll handle it. Go back to bed, Mom."

"But who on earth—?"

"It's fine."

"Were you expecting someone?"

When Wally ignored Milly in favor of pressing his face to the peephole—Carter could tell by the shadows that flooded across the bottom edge of the steel door—the old woman demanded, "Wally, now, you answer me!"

"Yes, I was expecting someone!" he lied to appease her. "But he's early."

"Oh," she said softly, all panic having vanished from her tone. "Well, keep it down, please. It's very early."

Her voice was growing faint, and Carter pictured her trailing up the narrow hallway to her bedroom.

Wally wasn't the enemy. Wasn't a criminal. And Carter had to remind himself of that as soon as the door sprung open and the urgency of the situation clenched around his throat like two ice-cold hands.

"I need your help," he blurted out, as Wally's eyes widened with surprise and unshakable confusion to see Carter at his door.

He had tried with little success to figure out how much to tell Wally about the emergency he was in the midst of, versus how much to omit, but as he spilled into the willowy man's living room, his composure was gone.

"The man from the meeting," he began clumsily demanding, as he paced and turned on his heel, locking eyes with Wally. "He wears horn-rimmed glasses, and I think his name is Damian."

A peculiar look came over Wally. It wasn't just recognition, but something more, something Carter couldn't quite read.

The guy began tugging on the bottom hem of his sweatshirt, as he asked, "You seem really shaken up, Carter. Would you like to have a seat?"

"Is his name Damian?"

"What's this about?"

Wally's eyes were wide, but it wasn't with concern. More like intrigue. Did he find this amusing?

Carter nearly flew into a rage, and as he envisioned himself grabbing the guy by the collar and shaking the answers he needed to know out of him, Wally asked, "Has something happened?"

"I need his full name, his address, everything you know about him—"

"Is this about the—" his voice dropped to a hushed whisper, "*sacrifice* you made? The one you mentioned at the meeting? Carter, you seem highly triggered to me. It might've been too much trying to face Jeremiah Daughtry. Handling the pocket watch might've put you over the edge."

Carter angled in on Wally and looked him dead in the eye.

"Yeah, I'm triggered. And you're going to tell me what I want to know."

The intensity of his demand was enough to compel Wally to talk.

"Yes, his name is Damian. Damian Payne. It's an anonymous group, so I shouldn't be telling—"

"Where does he live?" he cut in.

"You seem really worked up, Carter."

"Tell me!"

"Has he broken the law?" asked Wally.

When Carter stalked even closer, breathing heavily, feeling his large hands knot into tight fists, Wally cowered and lifted his hands in surrender. He almost couldn't hold the detective's gaze.

"He's in Brooklyn. I've been to his condo once. I don't know the address, but I remember how to get there."

"Good," he rasped, taking rough hold of Wally's upper arm and jerking him towards the door. "He's not who you think he is, Wally. He didn't turn out like us."

"He didn't?"

It hadn't sounded like a genuine question, but as though Wally agreed.

Carter focused as fully as he could on the task of getting back into Brooklyn, with Wally on the passenger seat, as fast as he could.

When they reached the high-rise condominium that Wally insisted was the building he had visited Damian in months prior, Carter finally divulged the truth.

"He has my son."

"What—?"

"Stay here," he instructed before verbally confirming the exact condo suite number Wally had told him on the ride over.

"Should I call the police?" Wally asked, clutching his cell phone in his hands.

"I am the police."

"But—?"

"I'm going to take my time with him, Wally," he said darkly. "Jeremiah Daughtry shattered us. And Damian has taken up right where the old man left off. Thanks for getting me this far."

"What should *I* do?" he asked, bewildered in such a way that momentarily struck Carter as strangely disingenuous.

"Whatever you want. Take the train home. Sit here. I'll call for backup when the time is right."

"Whatever I want?" he questioned with a peculiar grin threatening to peel his lips back.

Strange guy, thought Carter, as he finally stepped out of the car, oblivious to the call that Wally was now placing, the warning he was about to issue, and the trap he was about to set.

Carter had played right into their plan.

But Carter didn't realize that until it was too late.

He pounded on Damian Payne's suite door with the butt of his Glock.

The sleek door drew open, and Carter was immediately met with a cloud of white powder flying into his face.

Damian kept blowing the fine substance off his open palm and into Carter's face.

In an instant, Carter's mind shut off in a terrified blink.

"Would you like to hand me your gun?" Damian asked coolly.

Carter screamed, but only in his mind.

He realized he wasn't himself.

A fog closed in.

Mentally screaming, as his body hardened to stone with a strange form of paralysis, Carter felt himself, his *free will*, shrinking smaller and smaller, while some other part of himself swelled—some elated, free-floating, joyous part of him that he never knew existed inside of him.

All he could say, all he *wanted* to tell Damian, was an obedient, "Yes."

"I thought so," Damian said, taking the gun easily. "I'm so glad you've arrived. Now the game can officially begin."

When they reached a backroom that had been stripped of all furniture, Carter found his son crouched on his knees inside a dog crate.

There was a second crate beside the one Matty was in. That dog crate was empty, its door wide open, as if to invite the subdued detective inside.

He couldn't hear his son cry, "Dad!"

All he could hear was the realest part of himself, trapped and mentally shrieking inside his foggy mind, telling him that this was the end.

Chapter Twenty-Four

IT HAD BEGUN to rain. Long, dreary drops. A dismal haze had settled over Brooklyn.

The courthouse where the District Attorney had arranged another press conference was glistening wet.

Danny had a bad feeling.

Carter was a no-show, which shouldn't have surprised her. His absence didn't pique any red flags for the lieutenant, but Danny had gotten to know her partner over the two months they had been working together far better than the lieutenant had.

He should've called. He would have. At least to inform her that he had taken Franco up on his offer to sit this one out and be with his family, while the unit searched for his missing son. But Carter hadn't confirmed with her one way or the other, and he had been unreachable all morning.

Something was up.

As rain ticked down, she watched the press conference from the sidelines—the stone overhang of the courthouse shielding her from getting wet.

At the podium, police officers angled large umbrellas over Franco's head, as he leaned in close to a bouquet of microphones, picking up where Sarah Hovey had left off, and setting the stage for Danny to state her portion of the case facts for the damp and miserable-looking reporters.

The anxious cluster of them were already shouting questions about Nahla Rashad. Had she been found? Was she alright?

Each time Franco held up his hand to insist they listen, they held their tongues, but it didn't last. Not with Queenie and Raja jutting out from under the stone overhang, egging the reporters on with demands of, "Where is she, huh? Give us our baby girl back!"

A confusing message resonated with the crowd, one which the D.A. Sarah couldn't reconcile, though she tried. She stepped in and thanked Franco, then she used a stern, grave tone to assure Brooklyn as a whole that Marcus Stevens would be prosecuted harshly for what was now revealed to be a merciless triple-homicide and abduction of an innocent girl.

Soon Danny was invited to the podium.

Bogged in unsettling thought—Nahla had yet to be found, there was no sugarcoating it—Danny tried not to bow her head too much to keep rain from her face, as she took Sarah's place.

There was also no denying that Carter's gut instinct was valid. She should've never offered him comforting words. She should have never backed Franco up that Matty's sudden disappearance had nothing to do with the case at hand.

Carter had been threatened, his family was a target.

And now Matty was gone.

What the hell was she doing here?

She recited the statement exactly how Sarah had prepped her. To her own ears, she sounded unconvincing, robotic, and monotone, but the crowd of reporters listened intently, and held their questions and comments.

Even Queenie and Raja, as eager to interrupt as they seemed, were absorbed in every word Danny spoke.

The elephant on the courthouse steps continued to be Nahla's unaddressed whereabouts, but there was patience in the gloomy air, as Danny went on to state how important it was for witnesses to come forward, which could help solidify this case. They had their man, but they wanted to build an iron tomb around him.

Detectives Crouse and Toliver were scowling from the sidelines, she noticed as she stepped aside so that Sarah could take questions now that the floor was open.

When she resumed her spot standing beneath the overhang, the homicide detectives glared at her, making her momentarily self-conscious. But she refused to glance their way and offer any degree of camaraderie. She certainly wasn't going to apologize with a look.

Then she felt kind eyes on her and found Tommy, shoulders hunched in the drizzle, at the back of the crowd of reporters.

She wondered what he was doing here, but when he offered her a proud grin, the complement of it warming her otherwise heavy heart, she knew exactly why he had given up sleeping in to be here. He, too, wanted an update on the case.

He loved her.

The press conference came to a close, and as reporters packed it in and police officers folded the oversized umbrellas they had been holding, everyone disbursing either into their vehicles or the courthouse, Danny descended the broad courthouse steps that led to the stone landing where Tommy was waiting. His twinkling eyes locked on her.

It wasn't until she reached him and the dwindling crowd scattered even more that she saw her mother beside him.

Her stomach dropped.

"That's my girl," Tommy praised as if there was nothing at all peculiar about his greatest antagonist pretending to be all buddy-buddy with him.

Nora must have attempted to smooth things over, but it didn't bode well with Danny.

She didn't want them alone together. Ever.

As Tommy planted a kiss on her cheek and gave her damp shoulders a squeeze, Danny felt her brow furrow at her mother and asked, "What are you doing here?"

"She caught me on the way out this morning," Tommy answered for Nora.

Of course she did, thought Danny. Nora had been basically stalking her, keeping a watchful eye on her comings and goings from the neighboring stoop of her own building.

Danny didn't like it.

Tommy shot her a private and very encouraging gleam, as if to assure her that he's okay with this and supports their reconnection.

Just because Danny had reconnected with her mother, didn't mean she wanted or needed Tommy and Nora to get to know one another, get along, or even be in the same place at the same time.

As Nora went on to comment on Danny's lack of poise up there, using a soft tone and careful wording to heavily veil the harshness of her criticism, Danny felt her stomach tighten.

Had her mother told Tommy about her cancer diagnosis? Had she dumped her diagnosis on the most important man in Danny's life without first consulting with Danny?

Had *that* been the impetus of Tommy's now serene ability to be around the woman who had consciously, actively, and downright cruelly done everything in her power to keep them apart?

Was he tolerating the dying woman out of compassion or pity, because Nora wouldn't be alive for long?

She got her answer as soon as Tommy offered to buy them coffees from a nearby curbside vendor, thumbing out some cash, which Nora readily accepted before shuffling off in the drizzle, the hood of her raincoat drooped over what Danny could only assume was a heavily sprayed hairdo.

"What did I tell you?" she said, not liking the emotional strain in her voice.

Tommy met her with a puzzled look, so she glanced anxiously at her mother who was over pronouncing her coffee order to the Indian inside the truck as if he had just arrived from the Punjab. "I want you to stay away from her."

"She has cancer," he said, reminding her. "Why didn't you tell me?"

"Because it—"

"This can't be easy on you," he interrupted, a pained look of empathy coming over his rugged features. "I know you went through a rocky patch there, and I also know what she means to you. Hey," he said, forcing some eye contact when she glanced away to conceal what she feared was a sickened grimace. "The past is water under the bridge. Let's get through this."

Nothing was water under the bridge.

And if so much as one word about the *real* past was uttered, bringing to light, to Tommy's attention, what had really happened the night of their son's sudden death—the secret she was harboring out of some perverse sense of love or loyalty or twisted rage towards her mother…

The very thought of it pierced Danny's chest with such burning fear that she felt the sudden twinge of a dark possibility.

Deranged as it was, her mind could barely grasp hold, could barely process the abrupt animal reaction that she now realized she would be capable of carrying out in order to guarantee that Tommy would never, ever find out…

"What's wrong?" he asked, reading her vacant expression.

She hardened her attention on him, locking eyes, and insisted, "Stay away from her. My mother is *my* business, not yours—"

"But—"

"You don't get to impose your compassion on me."

"What are you talking about?"

"Look," she snapped, taking a step back.

She didn't need him touching her. He had taken a gentle hold of her shoulders to force some kind of connection that she wouldn't be able to stand without crumbling.

"My relationship with my mother is complicated. My feelings about her diagnosis are complicated. It might not make sense to you, but you're putting way too much pressure on me by trying to insert yourself into the situation. Keep away from her," she warned.

Confused, taken aback, and staring at her as if she had just sprouted a second, monstrous head, Tommy let out a strange snort of a laugh.

"Fine," he said in a defeated tone, as he took a symbolic step backwards.

But he couldn't leave it at that.

He stepped in again, so close that she had to lean back, and accused, "I don't know who you are. You've been hiding yourself from day one. And if I have to suck it up and play nice with your crazy mother in order to crack open that hard shell you live in and learn a thing or two about you..."

His emotions got the best of him and he could only laugh sarcastically.

"Then that's what I'm willing to do."

"I don't hide myself from you," she said, knowing full well it was a boldfaced lie.

But what about *him*? Tommy hadn't exactly been an open book.

She had more to say, excuses were ready to fly from the tip of her tongue, but the lieutenant's barking voice stopped her.

"Foster!" he called from beneath the stone overhang where he had been huddled with the District Attorney and Detectives Crouse and Toliver.

Lingering, Danny held a warning stare on Tommy. Nora was already shuffling towards them, a cardboard tray of three to-go coffees in her boney hands.

But he held his ground. "You can't tell me to have nothing to do with her."

She felt as weak as she sounded, as she told him, "I wish you wouldn't."

"Foster!" Franco yelled again without a shred of patience.

Leaving Tommy with her mother was the last thing she wanted to do, but it was her only choice.

As she padded through the drizzling rain towards the courthouse, Nora calling after her something about taking one of the coffees, she knew deep down it was only a matter of time.

Her greatest fear would, sooner or later, come true.

And the deranged instinct that had cut through her mind moments ago made its second, sudden assault.

She didn't have to hear Nora comment offhandedly to Tommy about the 'family,' as rain ticked down all around them.

"It's just Danielle and me," Nora began explaining, "but nothing, and I mean nothing can tear us apart."

Christ.

Eventually, Nora would tell him what had really happened to his son. Danny could feel it in her bones. It was only a matter of time. Out of perverse revenge against Tommy for having dared to love Danny, or maybe because being cruel gave Nora a sick sense of pleasure, she would confess the reason why Gregory had died that night.

Not because Tommy deserved the truth.

But because there would be no better way to drive him out of Danny's life once and for all.

She should've never let her mother back in.

And somewhere in the pit of her soul, she knew that if she wanted to derail this nightmarish freight train before it crushed Tommy, there was only one way…

Waiting for cancer to kill her mother wouldn't be fast enough.

Chapter Twenty-Five

THE SINS OF the father, Damian thought to himself as he polished his horn-rimmed glasses with the hem of his shirt and stared down at the mountainous lump of his old friend, Carter, incapacitated behind bars, *shall be visited upon the son.*

The son who would not stop whimpering.

Matty had reached his spindly, long arm through the bendy bars of his own dog crate and into his father's. He was sort of petting him. It was sad.

Carter's eyes were open. A blank, vacant stare. A zombie with only the slightest hint of surprise lingering on his otherwise foggy expression. He was in there somewhere. Aware but not alert. Struggling perhaps. Mentally screaming at a body that would no longer work for him.

If only Damian could get the dosage exactly right. Enough to incapacitate, but not so much that all memories were certain to become whitewashed out.

For some reason, he wanted Carter to remember all of this.

Why?

A twinge of guilt—or was it hope?—hit his solar plexus.

He wanted the detective, his old friend, to live, didn't he? The sentiment twisted sharply like a knife.

If only he could get more skilled at approximating a victim's body weight—it was an effort to direct his full attention away from his emotions and onto the science of it all—Damian might be able to hone in on that fine line between allowing his victims to remember versus ensuring they would forget.

He wasn't much of a notetaker, but maybe he would start. Record dosages. Note his findings. He considered it a long-term goal, as he crouched in front of the dog crates and began studying his latest subjects.

They were perfect.

More symbolic to his message.

Better than Nahla and Jill, who had posed beautifully for him, but missed the mark in so many ways that were beyond their personal control, of course.

Jill wasn't Nahla's mother, and she had the wrong skin color, at least in terms of conveying the allegory of his message in photographic imagery.

If he was being honest with himself here—and he would *never regret* having saved Nahla from the extreme tortures her junky godmother had subjected her to in the name of scoring crank—Nahla hadn't been an 'ideal innocent' to rescue in the first place.

The lack of familial relation to Kayla. The fact she was female, her aggressor a woman. It just didn't fit the Biblical narrative.

Carter and Matty, on the other hand, were flawless.

Except for all the whining and whimpering, the damp cheeks and occasional shrieks for help.

Damian had made a promise to himself never to drug the children. A promise he was now seriously reconsidering.

"What has he done?" asked Damian, as he continued to study the skinny, little boy who refused to give up on his father. "What sins has your dad committed?" he whispered.

"Leave us alone!" Matty shrieked, a wild, desperate glint in his glassy eyes, as he glared at Damian. "Stop hurting my dad!"

"He's not hurt," he countered. "He's resting. Thinking about what he's done. Isn't that right, Carter?"

"He hasn't done anything."

"Oh, he's done *something*," he assured the boy, as he shifted his contemplative attention back to Carter, who seemed to be fighting to surface into full use of his body.

There was determination in his tight, black eyes.

"He's committed some kind of sin, surely," he cooed, searching Carter's vacant stare as if he would be able to find it. "And you're going to pay for it."

"What?" Matty trembled.

"I'm going to cleanse you of your father's sins," he explained, not that Matty would be able to fathom the concept. "But I need to know what he's done in order to do that."

Shrinking backwards, Matty coiled his boney arms around his legs and set his chin on his knees, then he stared daggers at Damian like a wounded animal, unwilling to speak.

"I grew up with your dad, you know."

Matty screwed his face up, refusing to believe it.

"It's true. Just like this," he divulged, indicating the dog crates that had the boy trapped beside his father.

Carter was growing stronger by the second, metabolizing the drug out of his system one painstaking gram at a time. Damian could see it in the twitch of the muscular cop's bulging muscles, but he was prepared.

"If he has sinned at all since then—and I know he has," he warned, insinuating Matty would find himself in even worse trouble if he kept it from him. "It was that he forgot. Or perhaps *ignored*. He turned his back on what happened. He moved on," he said mockingly, "as if such a thing were possible."

Air seeped out from between Carter's slack lips, and soon he was breathing the words, "Don't tell him."

Damian felt his eyebrows shoot up to his hairline, and he cut his gaze to Matty.

"See? Still determined to keep his back turned to the truth. He thinks he's protecting you, but I know what this is. I know why he found a wife and started a family. The ones in denial are the worst offenders. They're the monsters," he declared, his voice raw with sudden emotion. "Have you been doing to your son what Jeremiah used to do to us?"

Carter's limp hand stiffened, but Damian knew he was hours away from making a fist.

"Is that your sin?" he guessed. "A white picket fence on the outside. Hiding your compulsion, your perversion inside, behind closed doors?"

"Stop," Carter wheezed out.

He didn't sound desperate enough. Not to Damian's ears. There was no remorse.

"I've cleansed Nahla," he told the boy. "I'll do the same for you. But I want the whole world watching when I do it."

Without warning, Carter bucked forward, a hard grimace on his furious face, and flung himself like a sandbag against the bars. As they clanged, Matty cried, confused as to what was happening and distressed to see his father stripped of the power he usually exuded.

On his feet now, Damian looked down his nose at the detective and stated, "The sin of cowardice." He was nodding his head now, embracing how right he was. "That's what you were back then. A whimpering coward. And I pitied you, didn't I? I saved you."

"That wasn't your fault," Carter squeezed out then sucked in a heavy breath to push out his next point. "But this is."

"And I keep saving them," Damian asserted, as a hushed voice mocked him from the back of his mind.

Damian was certain that Carter had been touching his own son. Carter was no better than Damian. The blueprint of Carter's brain could've only built a demented foundation after surviving something like they had in the basement.

They were *all* demented, all the survivors that Carter had refused to acknowledge until now, until the coincidence of his case had intersected with Damian's plans.

Damian's plans had been born out of the divine ether!

That's how Damian knew Carter was no better.

Like all of them, he had built his life on rotten earth, on a crumbling foundation, on the lie that beneath it all nothing bad had ever happened.

The house might be pretty, but sooner or later, it would fall. Like a house of cards. Flimsy. And when it did, Carter would be left standing on the rotten truth.

That he was just like the rest of them.

Just like Jeremiah.

A victim turned perpetrator.

Having found the righteousness loophole—that cleansing the young of their father's sins could, and should, include exploring his taboo desires.

With that in mind, he flipped on a handheld television set—some relic he had picked up long ago—and set it on the ground in front of Carter's cage.

An updating news report came on, recapping a press conference.

Damian immediately recognized the detective's partner, as he tipped the screen and said, "A little something to keep you entertained."

"No," Carter barked, the strength in his tone catching Damian by surprise.

It wasn't enough to stop him from unlatching Matty's crate, gliding the wire door aside, and reaching in.

"Get away from me!" the kid shrieked again. He was quite the fighter. Nahla hadn't been nearly as obstinate.

As Damian dragged the skinny kid out by the back of his shirt, Carter pleaded, "Don't do this!"

The drug was wearing off.

But just as he reached into the front pocket of his slacks for the next plastic-wrapped gram of powder, his old friend caught him off guard with a question that instantly intrigued him.

"I was the first boy you saved, wasn't I? Maybe the only one back then, am I right?"

"You don't remember?"

"You helped me because I was weak. I couldn't take it. You're compassionate."

Damian knew when he was being baited, but didn't see the harm in a conversation.

As he kept firm hold of Matty's upper arm, the kid was whimpering and squirming from where they stood, he told Carter, "And you blocked my compassion out. Erased all of it from your mind."

Inching up the firm wire bars, some semblance of physical strength returned to the detective and, looking up, he locked eyes with Damian. "It's not your fault that you liked it."

The implication slowly worked its way through the twisted gutters of Damian's mind, and he breathed, "What the hell did you just say?"

"That's why you're doing this, why seeing a child in pain gives you an urge. The abuse you suffered is all tangled up in arousal, the concept of 'saving' them is, as well. You saved me, and your *reward* was Jeremiah's touch—"

"Stop it."

"And that thrill hasn't left you."

"Stop talking!"

"You're still rewarding yourself, aren't you?"

"Shut up!" he yelled, holding his ears, a critical error.

He had let go of Matty.

Matty bolted, sprinting through the room, and threw the door open.

But there was nowhere to go, not with the front door secured with locks, and Wally standing guard.

Damian didn't have to glance over his shoulder to know his accomplice had caught the kid.

Carter shouted, "This isn't about justice and saving children. It isn't about cleansing sins or clever quotes from the Bible. You aren't an artist. You aren't a genius, or God.

"You're a victim who blamed himself when his body responded to the abuse with sexual arousal. You embraced it, and now you allow that urge to rule over you. You like to play out what happened to you with every kid you so-call 'save.' The God complex is just smoke and mirrors. The crusade to 'save' is your delusional excuse to 'abduct.' You're a pedophile."

Damian felt drained. Tears were spilling down his cheeks, but it wasn't because Carter was right.

He wasn't planning on killing his old friend.

But now he had no choice.

"Who else have you 'saved'?" Carter pushed, on his knees now, his large hands wrapped around the wire bars that suddenly seemed not strong enough to hold him. "Nahla wasn't the first, was she?"

Hardening into emotional stone, he sneered down at the detective, "You're pathetic,"

"Maybe the others didn't need saving," he suggested, ignoring Damian's insult. "Maybe they fought, and you got wiser. Picked more carefully. Did more research, more digging. Is that how you discovered Nahla? When did you start using Devil's Breath? When did you start really playing God?"

"If you don't listen to the news report," he said calmly, as he turned up the volume, "you'll miss the breaking story."

Sharp as a whip, Carter slammed the crate door.

He was no idiot.

This was the part when Damian would excuse himself to *cleanse* the son.

But he was a little too riled up for Damian's taste so, carefully unfolding the plastic-wrapped powder he had pulled from his pocket, he said, "You're going to sit here, like you've always done, like a coward in a cage, while a stronger boy takes it—"

"I will kill you!" Carter rioted.

One blow and white dust flew from the plastic in Damian's palm into Carter's recoiling face.

"Watch the news," he suggested, rising to his feet. "If you're lucky, it'll drown out the cries."

Damian watched as Carter fought the heaviness of his limbs going limp and his mind liquifying into agreeable mush.

Then, when Damian was certain that the mountainous man wouldn't have the strength or mental wherewithal to break free, he shut and locked the door, and joined Wally, whose wide eyes told him they might have to change the plan.

"Jill called your cell," he said worriedly, as he held both of Matty's arms from behind. The kid had no fight left in him. "Three times."

Every day he promised himself he would kill that woman and every day he kept backburner-ing the task.

He sighed and scanned the call log of his cell, having grabbed it off the sleek, glass coffee table. Maybe he could work her into all of this one last time.

If not, he thought as he pushed the call through and pressed his cell phone to his ear, he would have Wally drug her and lure her into suicide, maybe at

Waste Management, maybe at the Brooklyn Bridge... He would come up with something.

"Jill!" he said warmly, letting the smile shine through his otherwise fake tone. "I was just thinking about you!"

"Were you?" she asked skeptically through the line.

He locked eyes with Wally then, mouth to cell phone, suggested, "How about you come to my place... right now?"

SHE FELT MOSTLY crazy—the five panel she had run on herself came up clean for the usual date rape drugs—and yet Jill couldn't shake the disturbing thought that Damian had been giving her something.

All of her metabolic blood work had come back, and she was healthy as a goddamn racehorse, so either it was a fluke that she was now prone to blacking out after a glass or two of wine, and suffering a brain-rattling hangover the next day, or...

She sincerely hoped the man of her dreams—one whom she had envisioned marrying and who she had fantasized would one day tenderly stroke her pregnant belly, dreaming out loud with her about what to name their first-born child—wasn't a calculating predator who had been drugging her in order to do god only knew what.

She feared to imagine, and wasn't about to let herself go there. Not definitively. Not yet.

Not until she had *hard evidence.*

As she neared Damian's suite door, drawing in a deep, fortifying breath and pressing the bell, she hoped like hell that the quarter cup of activated charcoal she had ingested would be dense and voluminous enough to absorb whatever drug he might slip her.

She had another quarter cup mixed with distilled water in an eight-ounce bottle in her purse.

If she became at all nervous, she would quickly excuse herself and guzzle down the gray sludge in the bathroom.

Hopefully, it wouldn't come to that. Hopefully, she would be able to somehow discreetly pour the wine—or whatever he offered her—into the second, smaller water bottle she had with her. Take it into the lab. Get it tested.

Then and only then would she allow herself to arrive at the dark conclusion that had been plaguing her almost as long as she had known Damian Payne.

The suite door swung inward, revealing one dapper looking African-American man.

Stick to the mission, she warned herself since the very sight of him lifted her entire being into a relaxed smile.

He had that effect on her. But this time she would have to fight her pheromones.

"It's unbelievable," he said in that smooth, deep voice of his that got her every time. "I was getting some work done, thinking of you, and when I took a break and found my cell, there you were," he flirtatiously summarized, as he pulled her in close and planted a remarkably passionate kiss on her eager lips. Her body responded against her brain's objection. "Missed calls and all. I missed you, too. Come in."

She edged cautiously into the foyer then told herself that if she wasn't as bold as ever, he might sense something was up, so she strode confidently into the living room area and announced, "I could use a drink."

With a coy smile she added, "Why does *your* wine taste better than any other I've ever had?"

Modestly, he frowned and said, "Could be the company that dazzles your palette…"

Her responding grin felt a little phony, but Damian was already heading into the kitchen where a grid of red wine bottles was waiting on a rack.

As Jill turned on her heel, taking in the living room, she got the eerie sense that they weren't alone. It wasn't a sound or the flicker of shadows. The living room was still and as immaculate as ever.

But the doors up the hallway were all closed.

It didn't look or feel right to her, like a recently paved road. With the bumps and dips—those imperfections—removed, it seemed strange and foreboding.

Her stomach gurgled loudly and holding it didn't muffle the sound. An embarrassed look of surprise came over her face.

The activated charcoal wasn't agreeing with her.

"Someone's hungry," Damian commented, as he neared her with two glasses of red wine in his hands.

She had kept her back to him long enough, she assured herself. He'd had ample time to slip something into her glass if he wanted to.

Good. Terrifying as it was, that's what she wanted.

He offered her the glass in his right hand so she intentionally reached for the one in his left.

"Ut-ah," he playfully muttered, insisting she take the glass he wanted. "You'll notice this one has a more generous pour."

Well, *there's* a red flag if she ever saw one.

As she took the wine that he clearly wanted her to drink, she reminded herself of the extra activated charcoal in her purse. She would not fall into oblivion this time. But she would have to *act like* she was.

Trying not to look apprehensive or downright terrified, she offered him another kittenish smile, clinked her wine glass against his, and gulped down three hearty sips.

Mentally panicking, she again reminded herself of how much charcoal was sitting in her stomach, it would absorb both the wine and whatever he had put in her drink. Once it worked its way out the other end, she could test it thoroughly for a wide array of drugs that went far beyond the five ones typically used to heavily inebriate a woman.

"I hope it doesn't hit you too hard," he commented, wrapping a strong arm around her lower back and pulling her in. "You're not drinking on an empty stomach, are you?"

"I should have a bite," she agreed. "Did you perhaps want to go out somewhere?" she nervously suggested. She felt lightheaded and it wasn't the alcohol.

Don't fall under, she mentally ordered herself. *You have to remember all of this. You have to make it out of here.*

"Where's the privacy in that?" he gently questioned, his dark eyes studying her—searching her big, blue ones—in a way he had never done before. "I asked, wouldn't you like to stay where it's private?" he said as if reiterating a point, even though he wasn't.

It was odd. Like an attorney posing a leading 'yes or no' question to trap a witness. There was only one right answer.

So, she told him, "Yes, privacy is preferable."

He narrowed his scrutinizing gaze on her and made some kind of decision she couldn't quite read. Then he lifted the bottom of her wine glass, helping her to take a few more sips.

There was no way to fake this. She had to swallow.

"Let's relax," he suggested as though it would explain his suddenly domineering mood. "Let's drink a little more wine," he went on, guiding her to the living room couch. "Does that sound good?"

Catching on, though her thinking was clouding over, she said only, "Yes."

"Good girl," he praised.

Good girl?

Had he always been so condescending?

Disregarding the insult, she focused on taking mental hold of her mission, but it felt as slippery as wet moss on a pebble.

She needed to ingest more charcoal. Whatever he had given her was far too strong, perhaps too fine. Some portion of it was being absorbed by her stomach, hitting her bloodstream, and crossing the blood-brain barrier.

Jill could almost see herself conducting an autopsy, verbalizing her findings into a recorder as she worked, the cadaver on the stainless-steel table none other than herself.

No, she mentally screamed at herself. *Her life would not end like that!*

She couldn't ask him anything, she told herself, as he stroked her blonde hair behind her ear.

The name of winning this game was using one-word responses, and she was pretty sure that word would have to be 'yes.'

But he wasn't talking, wasn't asking her anything, only raking his manicured fingers through her blonde hair and considering what to do with her next.

She had to get out of here, run tests, but she was fading, and fading fast.

"Jill?" he cooed in her ear.

Robotically, she replied, "Yes."

"What did you do today?"

He was testing her. He didn't want a coherent answer in the form of a sentence. He wanted a zombie who only knew how to parrot one agreeing word.

She remained silent, and it was enough to get him chuckling.

"That's my girl," he said, rising up from the couch. "I have an idea."

Taking hold of her upper arm, he urged her off the couch and escorted her into one of the rooms down the hallway—a room she couldn't remember ever having entered before.

It looked like a photography studio.

And as foggy as she had become, it wasn't enough to prevent the slightest gasp from popping out of her.

Photos of Jill were all over the walls.

Blown up.

Yellow feathers hanging off her every curve.

The little girl from the case—*Nahla!*—was featured in some of them.

Oh my God!

The realization hit her like a crowbar to the back of her neck, stunning her every synapse.

Her brain froze.

Paralysis of the most horrifying variety crept through her veins like cement.

It wasn't just the drug he had doused her with—*scopolamine! Devil's Breath! Just like Raffael Sanzio and Kayla Samuels and Andre Durant! Oh, God, was he going to kill her?*—but also the overwhelm of suddenly understanding she had been falling for the very criminal she had been investigating, the very monster Danny and Carter had been hunting.

It caused her mind to bend so sharply she feared it might break.

But she remained stiff and unmoving, keeping herself in a zombie stare that she assumed he wanted to see.

What now?

How was she supposed to get the hell out of there?

THUD!

Shrieking.

A boy?

"Damn," Damian hissed, as he angrily crossed the room and pounded his fist on the wall. "I said hold him!" he shouted to whoever was on the other side. "Don't touch him! Not before I do!"

But a tussle ensued, the scuffling sounds of which Damian couldn't ignore.

"For God's sake!"

He stomped over to Jill and commanded, "Stay!" then stalked furiously out of the room, slamming the door behind him.

She didn't hear him lock it.

The opportunity gave way to excited thinking.

But as soon as she realized she could make a run for it, the very notion escaped her foggy mind.

Something about help in her purse…? she thought confusedly, trying and failing not to slip under. *A mission in a bottle would help. Slippery pebbles…*

Charcoal! she remembered, mentally clawing her way out of the murky recesses of her drugged mind.

Scrambling, barely holding on, she found the activated charcoal mix in her purse and guzzled it. Three anxious seconds later, the fog lifted, but she knew her thoughts were still clouded.

Not so much that she couldn't creep as soundlessly as possible to the door and press her ear against it, though.

Murmuring voices were out there somewhere. On the other side of this door? Or in another room?

As soon as she considered the answer, she had forgotten the question.

Damnit! she panicked, chugging the dregs of the watery charcoal, as she tried to place where she was. Was this her apartment? It didn't look familiar. A random thought about making time to study for exams seeped up, and she suddenly realized she was losing all sense of time.

Another *THUD!*

A boy shrieking once again jarred her back to the present, and, determined not to lose the thread of reality, Jill threw the door open, locked her gaze on the end of the hallway, the scrap of living room beyond it, and made a clumsy break for it.

When she rounded into the living room, her eyes searching frantically for a way out—the thread of what she was doing was slipping through her limp fingers again!—she heard men behind her, voices, words, more scuffling.

Did they see her?

Her hands were on the door now—"Where the hell is Jill? Grab her!"

They were at her back, but she was already thrusting the door aside, spilling into the corridor.

She screamed for help, praying a neighbor would hear, as she raced towards the elevator, then realized the distress cry was only sounding in her mind.

By the time she dove into the elevator, Wally at her heels, the doors gliding protectively shut, she had no awareness she had dogged him.

When she reached the street, she ran like a madwoman into a night she no longer recognized, holding only one thought in her crumbling mind.

Danny!

Chapter Twenty-Six

"TELL ME IT'S not true."

The anguish she could see in Tommy's gray-blue eyes was painful enough, but taking him in as a whole—his pleading expression, the tension in his strong arms, his trembling hands whenever he held his head and paced away, unable to look at her—was so thoroughly heart-rending that Danny felt the blood rush out of her face, all sensation in her legs evaporating like ghosts in mist.

"Tell me your mother is a very sick woman who made up a very sick lie as a last-ditch effort to keep me away from you," he demanded. "Tell me that!"

But she couldn't.

As much as she wished she could, now that the truth had surfaced she didn't have it in her to cram it back down into the rotten earth and sit her pretty life on top of it all over again.

Nora had gone and done the unthinkable.

She had told Tommy.

Danny's worst fears were now raging up. And words would not come, not an explanation, not an excuse, not an apology.

Her throat felt tight, her mouth dry.

Tommy was staring at her so hard, she thought her skin might burn right off her bones.

Her living room felt airless. Only the end-table lamp near the couch was on, placing both of them in eerie shadows, as grotesque as the ugly emotions rising between them.

"You knew she smothered our son to death?" he accused, his voice low and filled with disgust. "And you did nothing?"

"I haven't known for long," she offered, hating her response, the flimsy excuse of it. She swallowed the raw lump in her throat. "I believed it was Sudden Infant Death Syndrome just like everyone else did. I didn't think to have an autopsy done until…" she trailed off.

The gleam of revulsion in his wide, horrified eyes was enough to shut her up.

"So, she confessed it to you like some kind of goddamn taunting maniac, and you shrugged your shoulders and thought to yourself 'maybe I shouldn't be so hard on Ma'?" he sarcastically questioned.

The laugh he let out, pure rage at the twisted surrealism of it all, propelled him into pacing another lap around the room.

As he raked all ten fingers through his hair, she meekly reminded him, "I stopped having anything to do with her."

"Seriously, Danny? Are you being serious right now?" he questioned. "In all your cop experience, does that punishment seriously fit the crime?"

"I was in shock!" she exploded. "To this day, I don't know if I comprehend what she did! It's too much!"

"Well, I comprehend it!" he shot back mercilessly, and for a dark flash of a second Danny envisioned putting her Glock in her mouth, the only surefire way to escape the nightmare that had become her life.

In an instant, she felt exhausted, her voice once again small. "I don't know how to fix this."

"I do," he challenged.

"You want me to send my dying mother to prison?" she fired back, and the look on Tommy's immediately offended face told her that going easy on Nora or defending her in any way would be a grave mistake.

"She's not dying," he said bluntly. "You know it, and I know it. That woman will live forever."

Then what did he want her to do? How did he expect her to fix this? There was something in his tone, some dark edge that sparked her most deranged fantasy back to life, the one she couldn't believe had entered her head, the one that, even if it let the fury out and gave her some semblance of relief, still wouldn't return Gregory to her arms.

"I can't send my mother away," she said, not because Nora didn't deserve it, but because the personal pain Danny would have to endure watching a process like that unfold, feeling the guilt that would surely come along with it, would kill her.

Yet she also knew the alternative risk could kill her just as easily.

And it did, as soon as Tommy said, "Then this, whatever this is between us, whatever it could be... it's over."

"No," she breathed.

"When you learned your mother killed our son, you turned a blind eye!" he yelled, closing in on her. "You went on screwing me, for Christ's sake, Danny! You sucked me into your life and made me love you, and the whole time you were protecting your mother! She killed our son! What is wrong with you?"

She didn't know.

"What the hell is wrong with you?" he demanded, but she had no answer.

All she knew was, "This can't be over, please."

He stared at her for a long beat, any shred of compassion he'd had for her was now drained from his face.

"Stay away from me," he warned, backing away towards the apartment door. After opening it, he looked at her one last time and said, "Tell your mother she won."

Danny stood unmoving in the dark.

The *click* of Tommy having shut the door on her, on them, on any possibility of a life together, echoed in her ears.

Soon his fading footsteps vanished down the corridor, the faint *thud* of the stairwell door sounded, and she knew he was really gone.

Less than a second after realizing that her hand was on her holstered gun—visions of ending it all rising up in her stormy thoughts—she keeled slowly over, overcome with emotion, and let out a silent sob.

She straightened up only at the thought of pouring herself a drink, and that's what she did, slapping the kitchen cabinet open, grabbing a bottle of whiskey and a shot glass, slamming both on the counter, pouring, and knocking back the sting of alcohol.

As it burned her stomach, she poured and shot another.

And another.

And another.

Each ounce pulling her one step further away from the edge.

If she had to drink herself into passing out in order to make the thoughts stop and her emotions settle, then that's what she would do. It sure beat eating the steel end of her gun.

She startled, a surge of hope rocketing through her, when she heard someone knock at her apartment door.

Tommy!

Racing to confirm he was there—that this wasn't over, it couldn't be, as broken as each of them were, they were still made for one another—Danny tripped but caught her balance, the effects of those shots kicking in and kicking in hard.

But when she threw the door open, it was the medical examiner, Jill Andover, waiting on the other side.

She seemed to be swaying.

"Danny!" she exclaimed, spilling into the apartment and clutching the detective's shoulders as they both stumbled in. "Danny, it wasn't Stevens."

"What?"

"It wasn't Stevens!" she urgently repeated. There was a cloudy glare in her eyes, and she was more than out of breath. It seemed her breathing was labored, like she had taken something. Or… like she had been *drugged?* "It was him all along!"

"Who? What are you talking about, Jill?"

As Jill gasped for air, in a desperate panic to will herself into making sense, Danny asked, "Stevens confessed so what are you saying—"

"No!" she protested, shaking her head in an almost childlike manner.

"Are you on something?"

"Damian!" she blurted.

It suddenly hit her, and she clarified, "You now know for a fact that Damian has been drugging you? We can go to the precinct right now—"

"No! I mean, yes! Danny!"

"What!"

Jill had taken firm hold of her shoulders again and was staring up at her so wildly that Danny thought the petite woman might jump up on her just to get her muddled point across.

"Damian is behind it all. Drugging me. Killing those men, and Kayla. I found the pictures! The photos of Nahla, of the adult woman with her!"

Danny's eyes widened with disturbed comprehension.

"That was you, Jill?"

"He's been drugging me," she confusedly explained. "I heard a little boy. Danny," she said with such severity that the detective's heart beat out of rhythm, "there was another man, I heard him, too. This thing is big. I barely escaped," she cried, collapsing into Danny's embrace.

Carter immediately entered her mind.

He had been unreachable.

AWOL perhaps.

His son had gone missing.

The perp, Carter had been convinced, was from his past.

"You heard a little boy?" she asked, urging Jill back so she could search her eyes.

She nodded, then she said, "I need medical attention."

Damn straight she did, but not before Danny learned the address of Damian Payne.

Chapter Twenty-Seven

IN THE HAZE OF his obedience, Carter tried with all his mental strength to recall the second man he had seen through the open doorway.

Had that been Wally?

Wally betrayed him?

Wally had chased after a woman who Carter had only heard through the walls.

Chased.

The woman from the photos?

Not an accomplice, but someone they had chased after to no immediate avail.

Wally had barreled into the corridor after her—*who was she?*—as Damian had trailed back into the room, fully trusting his minion to handle it.

Then Carter had blacked out, as his mind kept offering *Jill*—the specific pitch of her voice so familiar, *had it been Jill?*

The handheld television resting on the floor just outside his dog crate continued commenting on the collective relief felt in Kensington now that the killer and kidnapper had been caught, as dark dreams swarmed Carter.

Disturbing images of Matty, and also of himself as a young boy, had swirled and sank, surfaced and then snuffed out, as he had writhed unconscious in night sweats.

The response, "Yes," had been on his lips as he had woken, Damian's cold tone lingering in his ear, the command he had uttered, *'It's time for the real sacrifice'.*

He couldn't remember why it was so important to remember Wally's role, or the bizarre possibility that Jill had been sucked into all of this unwittingly.

His logic was tangled. It felt like he was operating outside of—and without—awareness of his body, which he now realized was dressed in Moses-like garb, a burgundy Biblical robe with a tasseled sash. The oversized sleeves pooled at his upper arms since his hands were being held high above his head.

Not *held*.

Raised.

Not tied or chained.

But free.

He felt a cold, heavy object in both his hands—a handle.

His vision came and went, blurring and focusing, and though his equilibrium was off, he managed to look up and see that a long, almost Medieval-looking dagger was in his hands.

It wasn't until he looked down and saw his innocent son strapped to what appeared to be a stone slab before him that he realized the gut-clenching nature of this sacrifice.

Matty's cheeks were stained with tears, streams of snot oozed from his nose and collected at a thick band of cloth stuffed in his whimpering mouth. He was dressed similarly, a burlap sack-like robe—like a young Friar Tuck.

But he wasn't meant to resemble a friar.

He was playing the role of Isaac to Carter's Abraham.

Every light in the photography studio was angled on them. Somewhere behind the glare was

Damian. A commanding voice from behind the light.

There was a faint rhythm in the air—a long hissing sound followed by a tight *pop*. It didn't take long before Carter realized his abductor was taking photographs of the Biblical representation.

It was worse than the *sins of the father.*

The scene he was depicting against his will was also far worse than the implied allegory of having worshiped a false god.

Those other photos might have been imagistic warnings, but they hadn't captured a crime in progress.

As soon as Damian ordered it, that's what this would become.

The ultimate sacrifice.

A father trusting so deeply in his one true God that he was willing to obey the order to slit the throat of his own son.

Except that Carter wasn't willing to obey.

He was trapped. His body was Damian's puppet.

His mind loosely scurried for a way out.

But it was as if the two had been severed, his brain disconnected from his body.

Damian *could* command him. Obeying the cruel god felt *right.* Yet the voice screaming inside his head—the realest part of him, his desperate soul perhaps—failed time and again to solicit even the slightest bodily response.

Charge at him!

But he couldn't.

Jab the knife into Damian's stomach!

But his large hands remained held high above his head, angling the deadly tip of the dagger straight downward at his son's tender neck, ready for the signal, for the command from Damian to make the ultimate sacrifice.

There's nothing stopping you!

But there was. A mental haze. A physical paralysis of sorts. But it wouldn't last forever. The drug had worn off once before. It would metabolize out of his system again.

He could only pray that he regained control before Damian voiced the fatal order from behind blindingly bright lights.

"Look here, Carter," he said from beyond the glaring wall of lights. "I want to capture the pain in your eyes."

Carter heard himself say, "Yes," as he squinted through the stinging brightness at where Damian's voice seemed to be coming from.

"Do you want to obey God?"

He hated himself for it, but replied, "Yes," and Matty immediately shrieked, but the cry was muffled by the gag in his mouth.

"Are you ready to sacrifice?"

He wanted to goad Damian into conversation, prolong what felt tragically inevitable, buy himself time for the Devil's Breath he had been doused with to burn out of his system; regain his strength and control, and strike when the bastard least expected it...

But he knew that if he uttered so much as one word beyond 'yes,' Damian would only blow another palmful of scopolamine powder in his face and the ticking clock would be reset all over again.

So, he finally replied, "Yes," and mentally willed his body to respect his own command, and *only* his own command.

He stared into Matty's terrified eyes, wide and glassy as they were, and tried to convey that everything was going to be alright.

His son squirmed on the stone slab, squealed into the thick gag, and shook his head in protest.

Damian's voice fired like a gunshot, "Now!"

But Carter didn't flinch, much less plunge the blade downward.

A flicker of hope swelled in his chest.

Angered, Damian stalked out from behind the wall of lights, lowering his camera and stepping onto the edge of the massive, white photography paper that effectively made up the seamless background. He studied Carter with a glint of fury in his eyes, as if the drugged detective had intentionally dared to defy him.

Was it wearing off?

Was this his chance?

Or had Damian's order lacked the specificity that Carter's drug-addled mind required?

"I said," he began repeating, "The sacrifice must—"

He stopped himself, presumably realizing that if he gave the order, he wouldn't be in the right position to document it with his camera.

Carter felt his fingers twitch around the knife's handle. Voluntarily? He tested it, mentally willing his fisted hand to squeeze around the handle.

His body was responding with a firmer and firmer grip.

That was him.

All him.

His breath quickened with excitement.

"At my say so," Damian stated as he turned his back on Carter, heading towards the blinding wall of lights. "You'll plunge the knife down and sink it into your son's throat."

Without thought, only a panicked sense that it was now or never, Carter lunged around his captive son, spilling more than running, his eyes locked on the back of Damian's head.

He sprang—clumsily, tripping, the knife clenched in his iron grip—and, wrapping his huge arms around the bastard's waist, tackled Damian like a linebacker out for blood.

On impact, Damian grunted once, then cried out when they slammed together against the ground.

The knife slid across the slick, wooden floor, but Carter didn't need it.

He was already flipping the son of a bitch onto his back so he could kneel over his chest and deliver blow after jaw-cracking blow to Damian's face.

"You didn't have to turn into this!" Carter wailed as he punched him again and again.

Damian did nothing but sneer up at him, egging him on, a creepy grin spreading across his bloody mouth, stained teeth bared and ghastly.

"We were the same! We could've turned out the same!"

"*You* could have!" he snarled just as Carter's fist made cracking contact with his jaw once again.

When Damian returned his hateful glare to him, Carter balled his shirt in his fists and just stared at him, both men heaving with rage.

"You could've been like us, one of us!" said Damian.

"You make me sick," he hissed.

"I loved you," he spat the admission through his teeth like an accusation. Furious that Carter couldn't make sense of Damian or his love.

But it wasn't as mind-scrambling as what Damian said next:

"Kill me."

He stared at Damian. Unmoving. Processing. The heaves of his hard breathing gradually calmed.

"Squeeze the life out of me, Carter," he suggested, a strange glimmer of peace brightening his otherwise hateful glare. "Become what you've always been."

When Carter didn't, Damian told him, "The real sacrifice isn't giving up your son, it's giving up yourself. Shedding this pathetic charade you call a life. Getting rid of the white picket fence, the perfect wife and kids, sacrificing the lie you've been living. A sacrifice is meant to empower, it's meant to uplift, it's meant to show you that you don't need—you've never needed—what God is asking you to live without. It's meant to help you arrive at being who you were always meant to be."

Carter's large hands had migrated to Damian's throat and wrapped around the man's neck. He was squeezing now. Gritting his teeth and failing to ignore how badly he wanted to do this.

"Be what you are, Carter. Let that animal out. And kill me."

Suddenly, Carter heard a man screaming in his ears, and as he felt his hands clamp tighter and tighter around Damian's neck, squeezing and trembling in a sweaty fit of confusion, he realized the screaming man was himself.

Despite being choked, "Good," seeped out of Damian to encourage Carter. "Kill me…"

"I'm not a slave," he told him as he gripped harder and tighter, choking the life out of the man who had saved Carter again and again as children. "You're not my god, you're not my master. You can't lord over me. I'm not your slave!"

Matty was sobbing now.

Carter didn't want his son to see this, but he couldn't stop himself.

Damian had been right all along—right and yet wrong. He couldn't fight it. This was one command—*kill him*—he wanted to obey.

"Carter!"

Danny's horrified voice cut through the insanity of his fogged brain.

Footfall followed, boots stomping and doors slamming open.

He glanced up and found his partner, gun drawn and backed by police officers, sweeping into the photography studio, the glare of lights not so overpowering as to obscure their rescuing infiltration.

"Carter, don't!" she yelled, rushing towards him.

"Don't," she repeated, her tone kind, as she urged him off the killer. "It's over."

They collapsed together beside Damian, who gasped for air, as two police officers swooped in and began roughly apprehending him.

"It's finally over," she repeated.

Though it might have seemed that way, it wouldn't be until Carter had returned Matty home.

When he did, his wife Kathy clobbered him with tearful kisses, overwhelmed with relief.

It was then that Carter realized the dark and unshakable truth…

It wasn't over.

It never would be.

His past would always be a part of him.

Damian as well.

Two sides of the same dirty coin.

Epilogue

THE BEAUTIFUL SPRING day felt like a mockery, as Danny stood stoically to the wayside.

Once again, she was outside of the courthouse while Lieutenant Franco addressed every major news outlet.

He had to lean into the bouquet of microphones. They had been positioned for the District Attorney's shorter height.

As he grasped the edges of the podium, at times sliding his attention to Sarah Hovey who was standing beside him, he continued to explain how an accountant by the name of Damian Payne had been trafficking both a new date rape drug called 'Devil's Breath'—a modification of scopolamine and other chemicals—and children.

The 'hub' of the latter crime operated out of—Franco cleared his throat and grimaced at the disturbing detail—a downtown Manhattan Survivors of Incest Abuse support group.

For the press, the irony was unfathomable.

As Sarah stepped in to answer questions regarding Marcus Steven's culpability—*was he an accomplice, or an unwitting member of the group who accidentally complicated matters?* She answered more questions about how she, as the district attorney, would proceed with the myriad characters associated with both Payne and the support group.

Watching, Danny felt herself sinking deeper and deeper into a blackhole of remorse.

She had lost Tommy all over again.

And this time, she wasn't going to be able to get him back.

"Nahla has been reunited with her family," Sarah went on proudly, and gestured to Queenie and Raja Samuels who were protectively clutching the sour-looking little girl from where they stood beneath the stone overhang.

They would likely make a statement to the press next.

Detectives Crouse and Toliver were also chomping at the bit to reveal to all of Brooklyn that their investigation of Raffael Sanzio's murder had tied into Payne's twisted game—their work had been integral.

Everyone would get their fifteen minutes of local fame, if they wanted it.

Danny didn't.

Neither did Jill, who, though present, had barely psychologically recovered from having realized the role Damian had made her play, against her will and even her knowledge.

Carter hadn't even shown up, that's how interested in notoriety he was.

Danny wished she had stayed home, as well, but if she had, the dark thoughts—the remorse eating away at her—would be all the more consuming.

Avoiding going home would amount to prolonging the inevitable.

It wasn't as though she could hang out at O'Toole's until she was sure it would be too late in the evening for her mother to linger out on her stoop, waiting to catch her.

O'Toole's would never again be an option. She wasn't sure how she would survive, having to pass

Tommy's bar every day if she wanted to get to the F train, or the more major avenues to catch a cab…

She returned her attention to the press conference when Franco began fielding questions about Detective Dobbs—alarming questions.

Somehow the reporters had gotten wind of Carter's childhood connection to Damian and, knowing that Carter's son, Matty, had also been abducted, they began shouting over one another, anxious not to allow the lieutenant to shuffle off before commenting.

"Did Payne's operation have any connection to Jeremiah Daughtry?"

"Prison visitor records indicate Detective Dobbs confronted Daughtry, was that in regard to this case, or Dobbs' upbringing?"

"A source tells me Dobbs nearly killed Payne after catching him, is this true?"

Franco barked, "No comment," into the microphones then, after touching eyes with Sarah as if to suggest this press conference was going sideways, he stated, "Any further questions can be addressed to District Attorney Hovey. The 66th Precinct has officially closed this case."

As he walked off, once again giving Sarah the podium, Danny used the interim to excuse herself.

When she reached the street, Jill caught up to her.

"I don't know what to say, Danny." Her eyes were purely apologetic, and it pained Danny. Jill was as much a victim in all of this as anyone. "If I had trusted my gut in the first place and let you pursue Payne—"

"Don't blame yourself," she cut her off, but Jill was already voicing her conviction.

"No, I ignored the red flags. I didn't want to believe it."

Danny didn't interrupt her a second time, and because of it, Jill seemed unsure of what else to say.

The women stared solemnly at one another, as traffic rushed along the avenue beside them. Familiar gritty sounds underscoring all that couldn't be said.

"All's well that ends well," Danny offered and it was enough. It had to be.

"Did it end well for Carter?"

Danny twisted her mouth to the side, wondering.

"I hope so," she said finally and gave her friend a heavy smile and a little hug.

She should stop by Carter's. Even if unannounced.

But she didn't.

After parting ways with Jill and taking the long way home, zigzagging her way up sunny streets and across warm, breezy avenues on foot, she came upon O'Toole's.

But she kept her head down and her legs moving until she reached her apartment building.

She didn't pad towards the entrance and duck inside, however.

A sudden swell of anger had stopped her.

Her eyes were locked on the stoop of Nora's building, those stupid potted plants. An old woman who wasn't her mother was struggling to open the door.

Danny didn't know why she did it, but she quickly jogged up the steps and grabbed the heavy door so it wouldn't slam into the elderly woman who was shuffling bags of groceries across the threshold.

After helping the woman with her bags—she had a ground floor apartment—Danny felt the instant magnitude of what it meant to be standing inside her mother's building.

That dark feeling she had been wrestling with reared up again.

"Why did you kill my son?" Danny had demanded. *"Why did you have to do that?"*

As Danny stood there in the polished lobby, a starburst of rage flaring in her chest, she recalled Nora's flat, unemotional response.

"I thought you wanted me to."

The next thing Danny knew, she was taking the stairs two at a time.

When she reached the landing of her mother's floor, the blame in that response of Nora's—the implied accusation, as if Nora, a caring mother, willing to do anything for her daughter, had had no choice but to read into Danny's deepest, darkest desires and do what her daughter couldn't…kill a baby—had bounced around her skull so many times, she couldn't think straight.

But Danny didn't want to kill her baby!

She pounded on the door, acutely aware she was losing control of herself.

She didn't care.

"I thought you wanted me to."

"Why the hell would you think that?"

Nora had immediately countered with, "Why the hell are you here, Danny? Because you can't live without me. I can't live without you. Everything else, everyone else, is expendable. Tommy doesn't matter. Gregory never mattered. All that matters is you and me."

You and me.

Danny didn't know where she ended and her mother began, and realizing that felt like a smothering sandbag on her chest.

She pounded harder, and when her mother answered the door, those aged eyes of hers brightening at the pleasant surprise of her daughter's unexpected arrival, Danny spilled into the apartment, a murderous rage flowing through her boiling veins, and took Nora by the throat.

"Tommy doesn't matter. Gregory never mattered..."

No! she screamed back, but only in her mind, as she towered over Nora, her shaking hands squeezing the woman's throat, cutting off her air supply, pushing Nora's frail body backwards against a stack of boxes—hoarder that she was—that was straining not to topple over.

"All that matters is you and me."

You and me...

This woman had cost her everything.

Danny had nothing now.

Nothing.

And still Nora continued to invade her.

It was never going to end! she told herself, as her hands tightened more and more around the woman's neck.

Nora's body was losing strength, though she clawed at Danny's face in an ugly struggle.

Never going to end!

Unless…

Unless Nora was dead.

Danny no longer recognized herself.

It was as if she had slipped out of her body and was watching herself from the sidelines—the quaking rage flowing through her, the murderous intensity in her eyes, the animal bloodthirst seething out of her—as she squeezed the life out of her mother.

Watching herself… but not recognizing herself… *that couldn't be her.*

It couldn't.

But it was.

She had turned into a maniac.

And just as the light was dimming behind Nora's eyes, Danny knew that if she didn't stop, she would be a killer…

THE END

Please take a moment now and leave a review if you enjoyed this novel!

ALSO BY MIRA GIBSON

Thomas from the Sea

Who Killed Leeanne?

The Kensington Killers: The Complete Series
Lunatic (The Kensington Killers, Book One)
Crank (The Kensington Killers, Book Two)
Maniac (The Kensington Killers, Book Three)

The New Hampshire Mysteries: The Complete Series
Daddy Soda (A New Hampshire Mystery, Book One)
Rock Spider (A New Hampshire Mystery, Book Two)
Tar Heart (A New Hampshire Mystery, Book Three)

ABOUT THE AUTHOR

I write mystery novels, detective novels, sleuth mysteries, and psychological literary fiction! You can find me most days working on my computer in the sunshine of beautiful Long Beach, NY where I dream up small town characters and write dark mysteries that are filled with unsuspecting tenderness.

Find me on Facebook! **/MiraGibsonAuthor**

Visit MysteryRoyalty.com to learn more.

Copyright © 2016
Published by: Mira Gibson

For questions and comments about this book, please contact www.mysteryroyalty.com